MW00967262

ALSO BY BRUCE BOSTON

FICTION

Jackbird
She Comes When You're Leaving
Skin Trades
After Magic
Hypertales & Metafictions
Short Circuits
Houses & Other Stories
Night Eyes

POETRY

All the Clocks Are Melting
Alchemical Texts
Nuclear Futures
The Nightmare Collector
Cybertexts
Chronicles of the Mutant Rain Forest
(with Robert Frazier)

OMNIBUS

The Bruce Boston Omnibus

Stained Glass Rain

Bruce Boston

Portions of *Stained Glass Rain,* often in different form, have appeared in *The Barrelhouse, Berkeley Poets Cooperative, Gusto, Mean Lizards, New Worlds, The Open Cell,* and *Sequitur.*

FIRST EDITION

This novel is a work of fiction.
Any resemblance to persons living or dead is coincidental.

Library of Congress Cataloging-in-Publication Data

Boston, Bruce, 1943–
Stained glass rain / Bruce Boston.
p. cm.
ISBN 0-938075-30-6 (trade paper ed.). — ISBN 0-938075-29-2 (signed ltd. ed.)
I. Title.
PS3552.0777S73 1993
813'.54—dc20 93-5326
CIP

Trade paper edition ISBN 0-938075-30-6
Signed limited edition ISBN 0-938075-29-2

OCEAN VIEW BOOKS
Box 102650
Denver, Colorado 80250

With special thanks
to Maureen McMullen,
t. winter-damon, Don Webb,
Larry Whitney and Lee Ballentine
for their advice and encouragement.

Stained Glass Rain

PART ONE

"...any life expands and flowers only through division and contradiction. What are reason and sobriety without the knowledge of intoxication? What is sensuality without death standing behind it? What is love without the eternal mortal enmity of the sexes?"

Herman Hesse
Narcissus and Goldmund

1

CHRISTINE Leslie was New England wealth. Christine Leslie was so pale that one could trace the fine blue veins of her throat, a delicate river map with estuaries, tributaries and shoals. In the proper light the blue could change to silver-blue metallic threads, intricate networks of detailed electronic circuitry. Christine believed in those veins. She trusted her blue-veined throat. She believed in her mirrors more than money or graceful poems or salamanders that changed color in sunlight.

As a little girl in church she would inspect the rococo ceiling, throw her head back so her ribbon-thatched hair, blue on blond, would tumble over her ears and into the pew behind. She would ignore the priests and the swinging censors and the mumbling ritual. Amidst the heavy and liquid music she would bare her throat to the vaulted baroque, hoping those veins might catch a sacred imprint, rearrange themselves in some blessed stigmata of sanctity.

At nineteen, as a Radcliffe sophomore, she abandoned the confessional for a black lover. It wasn't college that changed her so much as the trips to Greenwich Village with her Jewish roommate, Liz, who introduced her to Raymond, whom she quickly knew as "Ray." Raymond wasn't her first but he was the first that mattered. He bore her on weekend cruises through brass and iron bedsteads. He called her "Tina, Baby," and at times it seemed the twining sheets had joined their jagged dance.

Christine saw her black man as a necessary adventure, a tool to add to her ritual handbag *in nomine Patris et Filii et Spiritus Sancti* that would later impress some dewy radical riding the high stirrups at Harvard Law, or a New England country squire with perishable eyes and a runny nose. For Raymond, her youth was a barrier. She was almost too young, too callow. Her lineless face and blank, beautiful eyes bore no history. Yet she was a fine showpiece. Like his gold chains, his pearl and onyx rings, she made his blackness shine. He explored the rivers and estuaries with his pink tongue. Her eyes, catching his reflection, adopted a darker mien. And the fresh soil of her body trapped his falling seed and gave it firm root.

She left him. She fled home and confessed to her mother with candied tears. She beat her fists clenched white against quilted bedspreads. She threw tantrums of absolution: "I didn't know it would happen! I didn't know it would be like this!" She dried her eyes only so that she could begin to cry again.

Fortunately, her timing proved right for a European summer. The nimble knives of a Swiss abortionist emptied her eggshell belly and she fell back to the New England net of her family bosom, now sporting the beauty of a woman, blue-veined throat intact and pulsing. Yet for three months she had fucked her way through France, Italy, and Spain, a summertime whore who would not return. Perhaps in a prolonged fit of masochism she was once again trying to become pregnant. Perhaps she was trying to accumulate the necessary experience to add distance to the past.

Back home, her parents had prepared the proper retribution to expiate her betrayal of their heritage. They brought her collegiate career to a premature conclusion with a business-rich husband whom she could not trust. His chin was lost in his collar and he made love like a salamander. He made love like those graceful poems that change color in sunlight and in the morning there was black bristle on his throat. His name was Leonard and he called her "Darling." When he was annoyed he called her "Christine," a hard edginess slaking his voice. He bought her a rustic shingle house on the Cape, weighted with the dusty vintage of early Americana. In seven years she gave him three children, and in each baby's throat could be found quiet veins just below the surface, holding the patient promise of full bloom with the passing years. For seven white Decembers she waited alone in her woodpanel bedroom while he tended his business, a Christmas profession, somewhere in the great Midwest.

After seven years she could take it no longer. The ritual of domestic ennui was sucking away her beauty like some great scabrous insect. Leonard still sought out her bed twice a week with tedious regularity. She was full to her throat and choking, her veins about to cross circuit and short out in blue electric suicide.

The year before, in a Boston hotel room, her father had succumbed to a massive coronary. The woman abed with him at the time was more than young enough to be his daughter. Less than a year before, her mother had embarked upon a massive nervous breakdown. Claiming her family's wealth as her own, quartering her mother in an exclusive Vermont sanatorium, leaving her husband to his Xmas toys and her children to their plump and well-paid nanny, Christine fled to New York City.

She rented a huge beam-ceilinged loft in the West Village. She took to wearing turquoise rings and sunglasses indoors at night. Leonard came to see her just once. He stood by the high east windows, installed for a painter's light, turning his hat in small red hands. Although it was the middle of summer, he wore his perpetual business suit and tie. They talked and talked, but like all of their conversations it ended as it began, a casebook study in noncommunication. Leonard frowned and pursed his lips. He said she could have the divorce and left with a short nod of his chinless head.

Christine thought about going back to school.

She read existential novels.

She had a brief and violent affair with an abstract sculptor. It took nearly a year and two court orders before he would leave her alone.

She thought about trying lesbianism. Without desire it remained only a thought.

She began a tepid affair with a second-rate jazz drummer who taught her how to smoke pot.

She started to paint and joined an encounter group.

Every Tu and Thur 7-10, she shared her confusions and vented her frustrations with an obese British M.D., two Jewish girls from Queens—one rich with a nose job, the other poor with a hook—an alcoholic cabby who beat his wife or kids or both every Saturday night, and an adenoidal window dresser who aspired to the gay life without guilt. The leader of the group was a twenty-five year old psychology student at NYU named Bill Benson. Benson wore wide ties, narrow lapels, and a mask of beneficent confidence. He had quit smoking by chewing his nails to the quick, and saved his nails by eating cough drops. He called himself a neo-Freudian gradualist and was sure he knew where it was at...or at least the proper direction. After watching Christine cross and uncross her legs for nearly half a year, he invited himself to her loft one afternoon "to give your questions on theory the attention they deserve." While they were sitting on the couch, drinking coffee, Christine noticed him leering at her. "You have the sexiest feet I've ever seen," Benson announced without preamble. He made a grab for one and Christine pushed him away. "Get out of here!" she shouted. "You stink of cough drops. Just get out!" After that, she never went back to the group.

Her life had moved from innocence to experience, through tedium and horror to absurdity. Finally, all else having failed, she took to writing poetry.

2

THE NIGHT sky rains loosely scattered droplets. They gather on the shoulders of David Jacobi's gray leather jacket and spill over to flow in tiny rivers down its folds. Jacobi watches the highway, arm outstretched with thumb curving out and upward, dark eyes squinting and lips compressed. The frustration of standing rideless through sun, wind and rain has begun to wear thin the acid afterglow with which he'd left Berkeley.

He is four days out, somewhere in the Ozarks and headed for Greenwich Village. Traffic is light and mostly tourist. Family-packed station wagons with bouncing kids and jumbled luggage. Aging dry mother-wives with pinched white faces telling their wheelhunched husbands they should have stopped at the last motel or hamburger restaurant. Jacobi seldom got rides from tourists. His heavy mop of almost-black hair and dark Zapata mustache scared them off. Some would stare incredulously, slightly angered because he was blocking their view of the hills. Other would sweep by oblivious, seeing just another billboard or crooked telephone pole. Sometimes an adolescent girl would give him a shy fleeting smile and Jacobi would grin back and wiggle his thumb at her.

The rain has soaked his hair through to the scalp and the night air is cool with a dampness that reaches the bones. Jacobi hops from one foot to the other and beats long arms against the leather to keep his circulation going. His waterlogged canvas shoes squeak softly as they clap against the wet pavement. Out of the distance and rising fast, bobbing up and down over the low hills, he spots a pair of high head lamps. As they come closer he makes out the multiple running lights of a diesel truck. Jacobi hoists his thumb into the air again.

The diesel roars upon him and lunges past, throwing a heavy blast of wind and water against his bent body that nearly bowls him over.

"Damn trucks!"

He catches his balance in a half spin, then hears the gears descending and the squealing of the air breaks. A few hundred yards up the road the truck is slowing. Jacobi tosses his duffel bag over his shoulder and breaks into a careful run on the slippery asphalt.

The driver doesn't speak until he has wound the gears back into high and they are once again swallowing the night at a steady mile a minute. "Pretty wet out there, huh? You want a smoke, bub? They're not filters. I can't stand that damn cotton!" He laughs, a hoarse and loud laugh breaking in the middle.

"Damn right, man, me neither," Jacobi yells back, falling into the driver's jargon like a lost brother of the open road. He sucks greedily on the cigarette, feeling the nicotine lift grow through his body. He leans back in the seat, closing his eyes, letting his clothes dry in the warm bouncing cab.

The driver has short-cropped thinning brown hair and a dark sagging and pocked face with sad pouches under the eyes. He holds the wheel tightly, wide hands with crooked once-broken fingers. He talks baseball and dirty jokes and trucking stories and how next year or the year after he will have his own truck and "no more of these fuckin' company runs damn right I will." Jacobi listens, the duffel bag resting securely between his legs. Nestled near the bottom of the bag, in a powdery oversized aspirin bottle, lie the seeds to a money tree—two hundred capsules of LSD-25. He will sell them in New York City. It is 1965 and acid is about to make headlines. Sometimes, especially when he is high enough, Jacobi thinks they may be the seeds to a revolution.

In Berkeley he'd taken a cap with his friend Mulligan and like all of Mulligan's drugs it was fine, the finest acid Jacobi had ever taken. They went to the hills above the city, to Lake Anza and up the stream that fed it. The drug came on strong and fast, knocking through the long time layers of Jacobi's hard agnostic shell. Mulligan rolled in the grass with fits of cosmic laughter. The forest around them pulsed with shadings of green uncountable and what had been dirt beneath their feet changed to soil in their hands. Each handful teeming with formerly unseen microscopic wonder.

Jacobi watched the stream flow over its rough course and flowed with the stream and fed the lake and became the lake all in one and gliding the lacquered walls of the lake in broken and reverse ellipses he saw fishes of velvet and metal scale iridescent in the slow liquid green while his mind slipped lower amid the silt and mud his ego died a watery death and there was only sight smell sound touch taste and the kinesthesia of his body all one sense and beating in coital waves like the tides of the final flood and fire until his sentience was reborn in circling bits and snatches a flashcard tom-tom movie of phylogeny reconstructed from the blind mute unconscious up—amoeba amphibian mammal quadruped biped eros thanatos the oedipus revealed the incarnation of the mythic patricide relived the hidden associations that had always set the boundaries of his everyday life bobbing to the surface in a floating crystal chain.

Later that night at Mulligan's place Jacobi decided to leave Berkeley for the remainder of the summer. He was through with the stale routine of middle-class kid working his way through college. He was through with books for awhile, too. He wanted to replace the vicarious with the actual, to realize a score of fantasies or outlive them in the attempt. Like acid, he would kick out the jambs, break the pattern of his existence and open the doors to new experience rushing in pall-mall. He would hitchhike to New York. He would wheel and deal like Mulligan. He would have women like popcorn.

They were mostly down until they began smoking some of Mulligan's grass, then they started peaking again. The walls melted and ran with color. Jacobi's hand transformed to a grinning lizard head. Mulligan kept taking his sunglasses off and putting them back on, chuckling to himself, a fat and happy satyr. They'd been without food all day and the grass brought on their hunger. Jacobi checked out Mulligan's refrigerator. All he found was half a carton of coke and an archaic bowl of rubbery lime jello peppered with black and mushy banana slices. This set Mulligan off in a throwback to his afteroon laughing fit. Jacobi finally steered him down to Mel's where they ordered cherry pie and coffee. They were feeling so good even the ill-tempered stringy hen of a waitress couldn't bring them down. And the cherries in the pie looked so intensely real that at first Jacobi was afraid to eat them.

Jacobi and Mulligan spent that night wandering the campus and the deserted Berkeley streets. The cop cars cruised by them as if they were transparent. And their minds seemed transparent to one another, for although they didn't speak, they still managed to communicate on some subtle level more ancient than language. Or perhaps they only thought they were communicating. By that time it didn't make any difference.

The driver stops the truck at a hilltop cafe and buys Jacobi a hamburger and a bubbly golden bottle of Miller's. The beer warms Jacobi's veins. Back on the road he lets the inverted pendulum swinging of the windshield wipers carry him into a hypnotic dream-rich sleep.

He awakens suddenly. The truck is parked on a siding and the driver's hands are moving over his legs. Jacobi yells out incoherently, pushing him off. The man strikes back, shoving him hard against the door of the cab. Jacobi grabs his bag, fumbles the door open and leaps quickly to the ground. The driver slides across the seat and swings his legs over the side to stand on the running board of the cab. Jacobi can just make out the bullet silhouette of his head, dark against the lighter darkness of the night sky.

"I can take you all the way to Chicago, kid."

Jacobi begins walking away from the truck.

"You stupid punk, damn lousy punk!" the man cries out after him, then dives back into the truck. The diesel coughs solidly into action and lumbers back onto the road with a splattering of mud and water.

The rain is still falling, now sifted to fine mist.

"Damn trucks," Jacobi repeats, pulling up the collar of his jacket, the mist a soft static behind his voice.

A rank and wet organic odor spills from the blackness of the surrounding hills. The dampened wood of the telephone poles, dark and spongy, gives off the smell of creosote. He climbs onto the highway and begins walking backward, facing the oncoming traffic, thumb out, watching the mist move in the lances of the headlight beams.

New York and acid revolve in his sleepy head, a choreography in a hall of mirrors, reflections multiplied to the vanishing point.

3

SHE awakens too early, lying on her back in the wide and empty loft, waiting for the black edge of night to succumb to a gray city dawn. The smooth wooden beams of the ceiling are still undiscernible in the darkness. On a bedside table the electric clock hums faintly, only sound in the room, luminous green hands reaching for five a.m. Her jazz man has been touring for the last three weeks and she has confined her sleeping to half the double bed. The remainder lies neatly made.

5:30 Right hand between her legs she indulges in a pale masturbation, hoping it will tire her enough to return to sleep. Mouth barely open, thin rose lips, thin sighs seeping from her throat, face framed by a net of tawny hair, a few strands stretched damply across one cheek and darkened by her sweating in the moisture-heavy air.

When she has finished she goes to the window to flip on the air conditioning. Its noisy drone submerges the humming of the clock.

6:00 A blue bead curtain hangs across the threshold to the kitchen. She crosses without parting its strands and a few lines of beads cling to her nightgown, trail over her shoulders, then fall back to their brothers with a jangled clicking. She makes coffee, two cubes of sugar, cream heavy, the top sprinkled with cinnamon. She drinks it sitting by the kitchen table, smoking a menthol cigarette. Next to the spice cabinet hangs a dated seaside photograph of her three children. Thus she confines her shades of early domesticity to the kitchen's enamel and stainless steel pocket.

7:00 She has showered and dressed and painted her face with long-acquired skill to soften the lines of aging real and imagined that her mirrors give back to her. Her eyes are now alive with make-up. Sitting on the bed she pulls her stockings up the length of slim white legs, brushing the flesh with her fingertips to confirm its smoothness. Above mid-thigh she hooks the stockings to the clasps of a white silk garter belt. She stands and the skirt falls back to her knees.

On her desk there is a metal ring memorandum book, each dated page slotted by the hour. She turns the page to the new day and the hours are empty up to one entry in the evening.

8:00 *Poetry Reading—St. Marks*

Will she read or not? Christine runs a mental finger along the list of her latest work, testing each poem's soundness, separating the vocal poems from the paper poems. The decision can be postponed until later.

She shuts off the air conditioning to allow the sounds of cars and voices rising from the street below to enter the solitude of her hermitage.

4

IF you fly into New York like a high gliding bird the city rises to meet you, a relief map in action with the sparkle of glass and steel catching the sun's movement in its own. Gray-blue ribbons of river slice the city. Central Park looms, a giant green eye patch on the face of Manhattan. And Manhattan floats solidly, forty billion tons of concrete and steel buoyed by the Hudson and East Rivers.

Jacobi didn't fly.

He came up the Jersey Turnpike with a bow-tied fat-jowled salesman puffing and cursing behind the wheel of a fender-bashed '63 Lincoln.

Stereotypes so true, thought Jacobi.

He came up the Jersey Turnpike and it was as bad as he remembered and worse. The air noxious with burnt diesel. The land a blackened slag heap of industrial waste. Factory upon factory lining the highway: Monsanto, Clorox, Shell, Esso, Quinton-Merck. Kingpins of the exchange and no bowler to match them. Smokestacks like black rubber tubing blown full and rigid against the horizon by the volumes of their belching poisons. So many trucks vying for the road that at times they would surround the car with a dark roaring wall and throw their smoke running across the open sky above.

Five days after leaving Berkeley he came up the Jersey Turnpike past the garbage pits of Newark and through the damp echoing Lincoln Tunnel to stand in Time Square wearing faded blue jeans, dirty tennis shoes, white t-shirt, duffel bag perched on one shoulder and gray leather jacket over the other.

The limpid dog days of summer have already begun their slow procession into fall. Jacobi stuffs his coat into the duffel bag, watching the hot city watch him, city of angles and changes and hostilities, the city with pockets of difference from one block to the next. He feels dwarfed by the city's size and indifference, yet strangely exhilarated by the variety it has to offer. He remembers those first grass highs two years earlier when he and Michael, still novices in the world that drugs opened, would walk and talk the city streets for hours, taking it all in, laughing like maniacs, echoing their ideas off the buildings, the night sky and one another. That summer they had burned with raucous and blind confidence. They had spun scintillate webs of logic, lattice works of insight and condemnation that seemingly overshadowed the buildings of the city like silver nets enclosing a cargo of helpless gray fish. It had seemed as if their very shouts couched political inevitabilities that could bring the system crashing down around them. Now the specifics of those conversations had fogged like forgotten dreams, individual contributions lost drifting into the leveling blur of memory. Here and there a word or phrase continued to ring clear. Yet the themes had been superseded and undercut by the distance of two changing years and eight growing seasons.

Jacobi begins walking to get the city back into his blood, to move through the pockets of difference and see how they have changed. His cross-country momentum carries him in wandering circles squared by the city blocks. He celebrates his arrival with three cooling Italian ices. He finds the West Village predictably completing its decline into monopoly capitalism. The Inferno, a basement and alley coffee hole where he had worked two summers earlier, is now a chic boutique and bootery with plate glass shining. Where before above the door in scrawled yellow paint on bare brick a sign had proclaimed: "YE WHO ENTER HERE ABANDON ALL HOPE," now an overhead black light is mounted, strobing rapidly in the filtered daylight of the alley. Jacobi watches the breasts of a ruffle-bloused mannequin go incandescent several times in the semi-darkness.

In Washington Square he surveys the houses on the north end of the park, momentarily attempting to remember in which one Henry James had lived. His eyes pass over the checker players, old ladies, alcoholic bums, two interracial couples perched on the edge of the dry and scummy fountain, black on white and white on black. After wandering back uptown he grows weary of his haphazard strolling and decides to head for Michael's pad on the lower Eastside. On the subway the women's eyes avoid him, staring straight and glassy or mole burrowing into paperbacks, newspapers, slick cover women's magazines, until Jacobi knows for sure he is back in New York City. He finds Michael's address, a faded brownstone next to a parking lot, the windowless wall facing the lot tattered weatherworn with illegible poster remnants. Jacobi climbs a dingy stairwell three flights to #27, a blackened brass number plate and below in a neat white paper rectangle:

MICHAEL C. SHAWTRY Poet & Poetaster

Jacobi knocks, quietly at first, then louder. There is no answer so he trudges back down and across the street to a Jewish deli where he blows ninety cents on a submarine sandwich and a coke, food of the city. Back on the sidewalk he surveys his swollen belly and licks the grease off his teeth. The sky is now dark and a cool breeze is fluttering in off the East River, relief from the mugginess of the day. Jacobi sees a light where he guesses Michael's room to be, so back up the stairs dragging the duffel bag behind.

The guess proves itself. From a wide crack under the door light spills yellow into the dim hall.

Once more, Jacobi knocks.

On the day that David Jacobi reached New York, Michael Shawtry was in seclusion: fasting, meditating and writing. He hadn't answered his door or been out of his apartment for two days and he was attempting to complete the longest and most ambitious poem he had yet written.

His room is as barren as a Trappist cell. Hairy tan burlap curtains shroud the doors to closet, bathroom and cubby-hole kitchen. Walls flake paint that has long since faded to a dirty drab. The furniture consists of a scarred mahogany bureau, two crumbling concrete bricks serving in place of a broken and discarded front leg, and an equally scarred chair and table. On the table are scattered papers, a notebook and a rickety black L. C. Smith typewriter that Michael had picked up for ten bucks and repaired himself. In the corner by the window a thin mattress lies on the floor, lone gray sheet only partially covering its narrow pin stripe. Ouspensky's *In Search of the Miraculous* tops a short pile of hardcover books stacked near the bed.

The room is illuminated by a single overhead bulb, hanging bare on a rusted chain.

Hardly the setting for inspiration, but Michael is so far inside his head that it doesn't matter. It is unlikely that Jacobi's first series of knocks even pierced his consciousness. He walks the room slowly, barefooted and bare to the waist, wearing baggy white beach trousers. His pale and already thin body now reveals its ribs. His hair is shabby blond and the flesh of his chin and cheeks shows in narrow patches through a curly soft and pubescent light brown beard. A natural widow's peak in the center of his forehead plus his blue-violet eyes lend a touch of sensuality to his face that is otherwise absent. When he turns too quickly in his pacing his uncut toenails scrape against the bare wood floor.

The poem lies unfinished and growing slowly, in the typewriter, scattered over the desk, in his notebook, circling in his head. He has been without sleep and every three or four hours he repeats the same ritual. Crossing to the bureau he opens the top drawer and extracts a small lump of Arabic hash and a black plastic pipe with Japanese lettering on one side of the bowl. He lays a sheet of the poem on the floor. Sitting cross-legged in front of it he shaves a few curling slivers off the hash with a double edge razor blade taped on one side. Cupped across the bowl of the pipe and over the edge is a rough patch of tin foil dotted with an irregular pattern of pin pricks and darkened in the center. With the flat side of the razor blade Michael carefully scoops the shredded hash off the poem and onto the foil. Drawing a wooden kitchen match from his pocket he strikes it on the floor, lights the pipe and pulls deeply on the single drag. He watches the match flame descend the wood, holding his breath. When it's halfway down he shakes the match out, rises and goes into the bathroom. He flips the still glowing match stick into the open toilet and listens for the split-second sizzle. Then he exhales.

Hash makes it harder not to eat, harder not to sleep. In this way Michael Shawtry pushes himself to the point of collapse so that he might test the compulsion of his discipline and have the vision he thinks necessary to turn his language into poetry.

Jacobi closes his hand to a tight fist and begins pounding with the side of his palm.

"Shawtry, open up! It's me, Jacobi," he yells to the rattling door and at last breaks through the spell the poet has cast about himself. The lock snaps and the door edges open a few uncertain inches. Michael stares out, his eyelids clicking a notch wider and his eyes bugging into the dark hallway.

"Jacobi?"

It is the first thing he has said in two days and it comes out as a croaking whisper. He peers over Jacobi's shoulder and into the shadows as if he were expecting someone else.

"Right! I wired from Omaha. Didn't you get it?"

There is a moment of silence as Michael blinks and begins peeling the clouds of concentration from his mind, bringing himself back down to the world he has escaped. Finally, he swings the door open and hesitantly accepts his friend's proffered hand. Once inside Jacobi drops the duffel bag. He shakes Michael's hand vigorously and begins pounding him across the back. "Wake up, man," he yells, "I can't be that unrecognizable after only two years." Suddenly letting go of Michael's hand he turns to appraise the apartment. "Jesus, with your money, why are you living in this hole?"

Michael stares about his own abode uncomprehendingly. Jacobi repeats the question.

"Oh, my old man cut me off when I dropped out of school," Michael replies mechanically.

"You mean you've been reduced to gainful employment?"

"No, my mother still slips me a little now and then, enough to get by on."

"Well, at least you're *looking* more the part of the starving artist."

"Playing the part more, too," Michael adds. His brain is still coming up from its two-day dive into the unconscious. The walls of the room, the spare furnishings, and Jacobi rise into his senses as a fresh and simple reality. Yet throughout their conversation he has trouble concentrating. Lines from the poem he has been working on throw transitory images into his mind with slowing recurrence. And now that he has been taken from the poem, the hash high begins to take over his mind, adding thoughts and images of its own.

They talk for several hours, Jacobi lying on the mattress with his head propped against the wall, Michael with his legs on the desk, chair balanced on its hind legs and rocking with his weight. They talk old times and new, knowledge and nonsense. Jacobi chain-smokes, using the open window and city night sky as a bottomless ashtray.

As their talk progresses, Jacobi begins to sense that it is a new Michael that he is confronting. Older, naturally. Even his present would-be beard would have been impossible two years ago. And the two years have drained the baby fat and baby glow out of the skin of his face. It is now paler and more set in its adult cast. But the difference comes through in his actions as well as in his physical appearance: the expressions in his eyes, more self-assured; the movement of his hands while talking, dipping and cutting in sharp angles and hooks, building boxes in the air rather than climbing and descending low rolling hills in lazy arcs as they once had; the carriage of the body more erect, the looseness of the joints pulled together and tightened as if by alum. The Michael he now confronts seems less of a sounding board for Jacobi's ideas and more his own man, and consequently there is the reserve that follows from being his own man.

Thus their conversation becomes both a renewal of friendship and a jostling for position, a game of exploratory repartee. There is no doubt the old friendship is still there, less certain for now, with many other hours, days and experiences laid over it, but still there.

Eventually the talk circles around to the acid and Jacobi's plans to deal. When Michael first hears of it he feels a slight breeze of paranoia slip through his head and through the apartment. He flashes instantaneously on the mental picture of Jacobi in a checkered cap dodging down the length of a dark wet alley with blue-suited police in frantic pursuit. He rejects the image and reconsiders his friend, who is straining with one long arm enveloped shoulder deep in his still-longer duffel bag.

Jacobi's hand closes on the grainy glass of the aspirin bottle. He tugs it out and tosses it across the room into Michael's lap. Michael unscrews the top and shakes several capsules into his open palm. They are transparent red gelatin packed solidly with what appears to be a whitish powder. He holds one cap up toward the light, balanced between thumb and forefinger. "So this is it, huh. The religious vision in a nutshell. How about a cap free as a *bon voyage* present?"

"Are you going somewhere?"

"I don't know. Where can it take me?" Michael asks, dumping the loose capsules back into the bottle. They fall back to their brothers with a soft tapping, like tiny teeth, barely audible in the room.

"I can only give you words and examples," answers Jacobi, "and none of them captures the experience. It's basically nonverbal. I could talk for hours and not tell you a thing."

Michael keeps playing with the bottle, tossing it awkwardly into the air, tipping his balanced chair back and forth to catch it. "Any experience is basically nonverbal when you are trying to describe it to someone who hasn't had the experience," he lectures back, "but still we're sitting here talking, communicating something to each other. So give me the words and I'll see what I can make of them."

Now, in spite of Jacobi's protest, the pent up words come tumbling out of him as if they had been awaiting the proper cue, like rain waiting for the first crash of thunder, slow and fast with frequent pauses in between like the scattered off and on rains of the Midwest Jacobi has just crossed. "Each time I've taken it it's been different, not all of it, some of it stays the same, like the externals, the way it heightens my senses, the hallucinations, the intense awareness of the body, but in here," Jacobi taps the side of his skull with a forefinger, "it's been different nearly every time." He is up and walking the small room now, and as he talks and paces and his hands shape patterns in the air, Michael watches his friend's dark eyes burning with the fervor and energy of a new love.

"The last time was the strongest and the first time it really hit me metaphysically. It was the whole Blake trip, the mystic vision of the body, the mind and the world as one. I couldn't see things in terms of dualities anymore, everything connected, everything made sense, not in any literal way but in a subjective way that was all the more powerful and complete because it was subjective.

"I tried to tune my guitar. I'd get it tuned, start to play a song, then discover it was still out of tune. Finally I realized that each tuning, every combination of notes, sounded harmonic to me."

Jacobi pauses, thinking out his words. He is standing by the room's lone window, one foot up on the sill. He catches the falling ash from his cigarette and rubs it into his jeans until its grayness merges with and is lost in the cloth's blue ground. "But that was the last trip. At other times it's been pure insanity, paranoia, megalomania, schizophrenia, you name it. Instead of spreading my awareness throughout the world it's left me circling incessantly within my own head, more confused than I've ever been and trying to figure out the same things over and over again without getting anywhere."

Once more Jacobi pauses. While he has been speaking the urge has grown upon Michael, steadily and spontaneously, the impulse to take a capsule of the acid there and then, to put an end to the explanation, to catch up with his friend's experience and capture and share in its essence immediately.

Our compulsions are to live out, Michael thinks. Why suppress them? A bottle must be uncorked to flow, a bird uncaged to know the sky. Or so claims his latest poem.

"But even the bad trips have seemed worthwhile afterward," Jacobi continues, as Michael once more unscrews the bottle, slips one cap into his palm, rolls it between thumb and forefinger until it is sticky with the dampness of his hands. "Each time I've come back a little different, a little more aware, almost...," Jacobi stops short as he catches from the periphery of his vision the quick red arc as the capsule jumps from palm to mouth. "Christ," he stammers, clapping a hand to one side of his head, "at least you could have let me finish."

"Go ahead," says Michael calmly, "it won't come on for some time yet."

"No," Jacobi shakes his head, "you don't need any more words now. But I've just come three thousand miles. If I'm going to guide you, let me at least take a shower before you take off."

"First burlap on your right," Michael nods toward the bathroom door.

As Jacobi begins undressing, Michael bums a cigarette from his nearly empty pack. Stretching out on the bed he looks up at Jacobi, catching his friend's eyes with a contagious and slightly maniacal grin. Jacobi helplessly grins back and tosses his wadded and dirty shirt at him as he exits to the bathroom.

The shower cleansed the dirt of six days on the road from his body. The steamy air cleansed his smoke-filled lungs. And it felt as if the heat were cleansing his mind and soul. His cross country trek had been a real downer after the acid, confirmation that the two coasts were probably the only places in the country that were livable. What was it that Mulligan had called the rest of America? "A vast Sahara of cultural aridity." Cultural aridity, neon and billboards, Jacobi thought. A road often no more interesting than the double red line scrambling through map yellow that described it, hours spent in single-lane eternity behind twenty-mile-per-hour trucks, mountains holding a distant purple promise that upon approach lost its purple, but kept its distance with barb wire and corporation cowboys. There had been another America, in his head and only there. A painted desert and Buffalo Bill America imprinted from too many years at the parallel bars of officious learning. Now Jacobi knew that the buffalo were dead and the desert was painted only with beer cans.

After he finished washing, Jacobi sat down in the tub and let the shower beat a hot tattoo on his back, and he didn't leave until the water had turned lukewarm. Back in the other room he found Michael stretched upon the mattress, on his back with eyes closed, arms placed carefully over his chest and crossed at the wrists, as if he were awaiting a visitation. As if he were expecting to float ten feet in the air and pass a ring around himself, a Persian magician's trick with no strings attached.

5

TONY Bosano is a second-rate aging drummer, but still a drummer. His ears cannot avoid the noisy rhythms of the track-clicking train as it pulls north along the eastern seaboard. Their beat spells a labored monotony and lulls him into a sleepy trance. Tony needs the sleep for he is tired of traveling. He is tired of one-night stands in bars playing straightened jazz for the locals. Tired of requests for "Stormy Weather" and "Melancholy Baby." Tired of old hotels with bowed lump mattresses and brown stain cockroach walls, of not making it while seeing black men pass him by on their way to the top of the jazz world. Tony is tired of cheap suits and much of the time he is tired of Christine.

But now he needs her.

When the train stops in Philly he calls long distance.

"Hello, hello, Tina…Tony!…The tours over, baby, I'll be home in a few hours…That's wonderful. I'll have dinner for us…It's good to hear your voice, baby…You too, Tony. How did it go?… Ah, same as usual. Once you get into the South they still think Dixieland is where…" They fill their three minutes with assorted loose ends and familiar endearments.

After the call, Tony buys a pint of Jim Beam, pulling the necessary money from a loose conglomeration of coins, keys, bills, and broken cigarettes in his catchall coat pockets. Back on the moving train he puffs the stub of a cigarette to ignition with the flame from his scratched but still flashy silver lighter, uncorks the whiskey bottle and begins to sip slowly. The scenery he has seen before passes in front of his tired eyes like a painted paper roll repeating itself in endless circles just a few inches from the train's window. As the night comes on he sees the lines of his own face, also too familiar, reflected in the glass of the window, laid in double exposure over the darkening landscape.

He takes another swallow of the whiskey. The burning alcohol warmth spreads through the width of his chest and he listens for a clever turn in the train's clicking rhythm so he will know when he is high.

Christine lowers the dead phone gently into its cradle and begins to generate the necessary enthusiasm for her man's homecoming. She will not attend the reading tonight, the choice has been made for her. When Tony called she had been working on a poem. Gathering the papers from her desk she squares them to a neat stack and files them in the second drawer, alphabetically by title. She checks her kitchen cupboards and with a bluegreen fountain pen makes a list for the store.

chianti
veal
consomme
mushrooms
broccoli
French bread
parmesan

After a quick trip to the corner grocery, Christine ties a bright sunflower apron to her waist and begins preparing the meal. Sometimes in the ritual of meal-making she could concentrate on the precise movements of her narrow hands and achieve the security of a kind of mindlessness. At other times, extraneous thoughts would not leave her alone. No matter how she tried to repress she would free-associate a host of unwanted memorabilia. Today, the work on the poem has already keyed her mind to tightness, and now that the poem has been pulled from beneath her, it must unwind of its own accord.

Three wooden chopping boards of increasing size hang in diagonal on brass hooks over the kitchen sink. Christine selects the middle *moderation in all things my child* board. Placing the board on the counter and the cutlets on the board, she slices away skin and bone with sharp turns of a stainless steel knife. She cuts the veal in slender strips and sprinkles each lightly with flour, begins to brown them in a large blackened *as the spade ace that's what he was his black cock his black thighs the lamp moving highlights on his back* skillet, its bottom slaked with a fine coating of olive oil *and summer in Italy and the dark boys with clever hands and silver bracelets riding their smooth wrists.* She washes the mushrooms *poison toadstools in the woods little girl you're such a pretty little girl* one by one, breaks off the stems, quarters the heads. With long fingernails she peels the outer skin from a clove of garlic, shreds its insides on a small metal grater. She chops one half of a large onion to fine fragments, nascent tears gathering at the corners of her eyes *crying how long no more only little girls cry time to be a big girl now.* Blinks twice, wiping them away with the backs of her wrists and slightly smudging her make-up. She turns the meat with a three pronged *one two three the Trinity the genitalia good things in threes bad things in threes happening* cooking fork, places the mushrooms, onion and garlic into the pan and from her spice cabinet adds a pinch of marjoram and half a teaspoon of oregano. She bends to light the oven, setting its white and black *and white and black and white could have had a black baby blue veins hidden for good then in its brown neck* indicator at three hundred degrees.

At the sink she washes the fresh broccoli, cuts away the tough stems and tears off the bitter *I'm not bitter darling I only think you should have considered the children before yourself* flower leaves. She gathers the loose stalks and ties them with a short length of white cotton string *Mommy Mommy do the cat's cradle* so they will stand upright and cook evenly throughout. She slices and butters the French bread *Rimbaud Villon the spongy heavy leg Impressionist women on the Louvre walls and so unlike me,* covers each slice with cheese spread and minced garlic, reshapes the slices to a loaf and wraps them tightly in foil. The kitchen clock reads 6:15. Tony is due by seven. Christine pours half a cup of dry cooking sherry *voulez-vous couchez avec moi, cheri,* a can of tomato paste and the consomme over the lightly browned veal and mushrooms. She covers the skillet with a glass lid and places it in the heated oven.

In the living room she arranges her dining table: cloth and napkins of Irish linen, slender azure candles in silver holders. Dutch *dikes lesbians put his finger in the hole and held back the sea her dyke fingers after my hole* china, narrow-stemmed wineglasses, silver setting for two *just two now, just one or two.* She washes and remakes her face to satisfaction *and still I'm beautiful and still I'm beautiful after all* in the bathroom mirror. Kneeling on the couch by the window she lights a cigarette and relaxes for a moment. Then up again to put a Bach concerto *you can hear the organ for blocks from the church listen to the organ Tina they brought it all the way from Germany can you hear it Tina yes Mommy yes where is Germany* on the stereo at just audible volume, then back to the couch, watching the city light up for the night. When side one of Bach *they took it apart in Germany and brought it on a boat across the sea* has finished it is nearly seven. Christine checks the meat and turns the oven to low, goes back to the window to wait for Tony *will he hold me tonight or collapse to sleep from too much food and drink.*

7:15 Christine lights another cigarette and turns Bach *and put it back together and you can hear it for blocks it is such a grand organ listen can you hear it Tina oh yes Mommy yes* to the other side. The veal is slightly overdone and she shuts the oven off, sliding the French bread onto the lower rack so it will warm and melt the cheese.

7:30 She telephones Tony's apartment and there is no answer. She begins pacing, living room to kitchen and back again. It is not the first time he has stood her up, not the first time and by now she has lost count.

8:00 Bach *and now they have stopped playing and the priest will speak to us listen to the priest Tina his voice is as beautiful as the organ* has concluded side two with a mathematically precise crescendo and Christine has decided to dine by herself. Taking the chianti from the refrigerator she opens it with a bone handle corkscrew and pours half a glass. She forks several pieces of meat and mushroom onto a small kitchen plate and adds a slice of bread. She eats standing by the kitchen counter. Adding a sip *moderation moderation* of wine to each careful mouthful *moderation my children the Lord awaits our sins as we await his forgiveness abandon and gluttony are the devices of the Devil are you listening Tina yes Mommy.* When she has finished she washes the dishes and makes coffee, two lumps of sugar, cream heavy, the top sprinkled with cinnamon.

8:30 She undresses, dresses for bed, selects a bilingual edition of Lorca from the bookshelf. She stretches her body in the bed, a quilt lined with giant flowers pulled over her legs, nightdress open and the book riding on her small breasts. She reads the English half aloud and silently stumbles through the Spanish. She secretly tests the poems against her own. *Yes Mommy yes.*

11:00 Christine hears a tromping on the stairs followed by a soft rhythmic thumping on her door. She closes Lorca on the bedside table, ties her open nightgown closed and hooks the door chain before answering. Tony stands outside, shoulders hunched, beating drum rolls on the door with rigid forefingers. In the harsh hallway light the bags under his eyes stand out and his suit looks more rumpled than usual. His face, once puppy-dog pathetic, now seems only pathetic. Christine unhooks the chain and Tony slides past her and into the apartment.

"Sorry, I'm a little late, baby," he mumbles, tottering toward her with an attempted kiss. His lips slide along her cheek as Christine pulls back. She shoves him away with one hand, the other rubbing the side of her face.

"You're four hours late, you need a shave and you're drunk." She speaks with level loudness and eyes straight into him, generating her displeasure as earlier she had generated her enthusiasm.

"I'm drunk, I'm drunk," Tony mimics. "Aw, just had a few for the boys in the band." He reaches for her with awkward hands. She pushes him back a second time. Tony attempts a bashful smile, but it collapses into a cough and he bends to the side, rolled hand rising to his mouth.

"Stop your blubbering, Tony, and I'll heat up some coffee." Speaking in the same even tone, two controlled notches below anger. She crosses to the kitchen with straight rapid steps, slippers clapping against her heels, nightgown furling behind her in the breath of her movement.

"Yeah, baby, sure, you do that." He stands rocking unevenly by the doorway, rubs his sagging rough and liquor-numb cheeks. His eyes circle the room, moving in and out of focus, the white and candled table, her unmade bed, the shelves carefully crowded with records, books and art pottery. He loses focus completely on the design of the oriental rug, blinks several times almost losing his balance, then remembers Christine. He follows her to the kitchen, tangling himself in the bead curtain. "Damn fuckin' beads, lousy beads."

Christine stands at the end of the narrow room, next to the stove. Her arms are folded in front of her, legs straight and slightly spread, hands in tight fists next to the rib cage. She eyes Tony coldly as he unwinds himself. He meets her stare for several seconds, then gives up with a rasping simian chuckle. "Fuckin' beads," he repeats.

Tony yanks the refrigerator open, nearly falling forward and into it as the door swings back. He spots the nearly full chianti bottle and pulls it out.

"Get your hands off of that, Tony."

He ignores her, grabbing a glass down from the cupboard, nearly dropping it. Christine advances a step toward him, eyes widening.

"Get your hands off of it, Tony! It's five dollars a bottle and I didn't' buy it to keep your high going." Voice slipping a notch higher.

"You can afford it, bitch," Tony answers, sloshing the wine into the glass, loose droplets running over his hand and dripping to the tile counter. He throws his head back to drink and his Adam's apple bobs twice as he finishes the glass in two swallows. "Rich bitch, rich bitch," he chants.

Christine draws a full breath into her lungs. "I'm not going to fight with you, Tony. Just get out of here." Pointing. "You can take the wine, but get out."

"Won't fight with me cause she's a rich bitch and a fuckin' phony." He raises the bottle, shaking it over his head. The booze has given him back his balls. "How many you been diddlin' since I was gone, rich bitch? You're supposed to be horny when I come home. How many jigs you been diddlin'? That was your first one, wasn't it, a fuckin' jig?"

Christine is overcome by a blast of pain and outrage shooting up from the depths of her being. Her arms spin away from her body, palms snapping open and back, a tightness in the wrists. "Get out, get out!" she screams, tendons of her neck taut, staccato pulse tripping the blue vein throat.

Tony sweeps his arm along the wine-splattered counter and his empty glass flies off to spin by Christine's shrieking and break crashing against the stove. She feels a shredded rain of fragments splash against her bare legs. Tony staggers back through the beads and the beads click against the wine bottle. They click against each other like stunted wind chimes. The apartment door slams shut. There is a crash from the stairs.

Several seconds pass. Christine has brought her breathing under control, but a lessening tension still clings to her body. She snaps the flame off under the bubbling coffee pot and it dies with a muffled popping. She goes to the hall and looks down the stairwell. Halfway to the second landing lie the broken and scattered remains of the chianti bottle. A dark puddle stain has spread over the carpeted stairs. It momentarily freezes her attention like an oversized inkblot, but she is unable to tack an identity upon its shapelessness.

Christine moves into action methodically, almost rehearsed. From a cupboard under the kitchen sink she takes a plastic bucket, a stained yellow sponge and a sheaf of old newspapers. She fills the bucket with cold water and the sponge dances in the aerated faucet stream and then bobs to the surface. She carries the newspapers and bucket to the stairs. As she is setting them down the door on the second landing clicks open and Christine's downstairs' neighbor peers out. A fleshy thinness clings to his soft and pallid face. His balding blond head offers a blurred reflection of the overhead light.

"Everything all right up there?" he asks, a practiced lisp tagged to the corners of his words.

"Everything's fine, Mr. Mekas," Christine answers unevenly. His intrusion has broken into the mechanism of her actions. The past tension returns doubling through her chest and throat. She is squatting on the stairs, knees bent and bare, the nightdress tucked around her thighs, the newspapers spread before her. With thumb and forefinger she carefully lifts the larger pieces of glass onto the printed page.

Mr. Mekas steps into the hall. He is wearing a red satin kimono with white pattern stitching and belled sleeves, tight and high mandarin collar hiding the lines of his neck. The kimono falls to his knees, flanged widely, leaving his stick bone legs protruding. Maroon Turkish lounging slippers cover his feet.

"Oh, what a mess!" he exclaims as he sees the stairs "Is there anything I can do?"

"No, Mr. Mekas, everything is all right," Christine repeats with irritation, rolling the glass-filled newspaper sheets into a bumpy package.

"Are you sure? I was almost asleep and then I heard all this noise and shouting and thought there might be some trouble." He speaks rapidly, voice rising and dipping in a scratchy contralto.

Christine doesn't answer. She tries to ignore him and concentrate on her cleaning, splashing water over the carpet with the dripping sponge. Mekas advances up the stairs, gathering the kimono about his waist like an ill-fitting dress. He stops a few steps below Christine, standing over her bent form. She is about to look up until she feels a flush rising to her cheeks and neck. As she scrubs the wine stain, Mekas' curling slippers and bare calves, thickly covered with short blond bristle, invade the line of her vision. She lowers her eyelids, squinting to block them out. A hodgepodge of extraneous images reels through her head like some amateur filmmaker's confused attempt at surrealism—the veal dinner, the bubbling coffee pot, her ex-husband's sad-dog eyes, Tony's beard-rough and drunken kiss scraping along her cheek, the standing hair on Mekas' calves *moderation moderation!* The glass fragments embedded in her ankles have begun an itching pain that turns to sharpness when she lowers her weight against them. Mekas' voice comes down to her from a different reality, its overtones warped by the distance.

"It really is a mess and wine stains are so hard to get out," he rattles on in non-sequitur fashion. "Personal relationships can be so sticky. You're usually so quiet upstairs, almost like a ghost. Half the time I don't even know you're there. I'm afraid that I'm the one that causes most of the commotion in the building with the parties and all. I've been meaning to ask if the noise ever bothers you."

"Only the squealing," Christine manages, a strained huskiness clamping the volume of her voice.

"Some of the boys do get a bit carried away at times," Mekas beams, lightly exploding with a broken chain of laughter. He raises one leg a step further, leaning forward and lowering his voice to a confidential whisper. "But you can't have a good party without a little nonsense, hmmn?"

Christine shies back, gripping the bannister, her scrubbing unfinished. Hastily she grabs the wadded newspaper and the handle of the bucket. Turning her back to Mekas, she rises and nearly runs the half flight to her apartment.

"Oh well, better wine than blood," he calls after her retreating figure, barking another short laugh as exclamatory punctuation.

Back in the familiar refuge of her room, Christine leans her back against the door, the bucket hanging weight in her right hand, the glass-filled paper almost weightless in her left. There is a muscle twitching somewhere in her body and its spasms lessen slowly and irregularly as she regains her composure. She places the bundle in a wastebasket by her desk and carries the bucket to the bathroom where she empties it into the toilet. The water has picked up a rusty brown tint, the wine coupled with the dirt of the carpet.

Sitting sideways on the blue fluff bathroom rug she searches the flesh of her legs, extracting the minute grains of glass with a steel tweezers and depositing each on an open rectangle of yellow tissue. When she has finished the tissue is speckled with tiny red dots.

The clock by the bed reads 11:33. Christine unties her dressing gown and picks up Lorca from the night table. Pulling the covers over her legs she finds the poem where she had left off reading. She lies with body stretched out, head propped by a pillow, the book held with one hand and riding on her small breasts, edging up and down with the movements of her breathing. With free hand Christine feels her belly, her hips, the tops of her thighs.

She remembers the broken wine glass still lying scattered across the kitchen floor.

6

FOR whatever memory is worth Michael remembered it afterwards in parts scattered, nonsequential and intensely visual. For the first two hours he kept going up and up inside his head. He didn't know how high, but higher than he had ever been before and still higher with the world dropping away from him like the tail view from an accelerating rocket. Some time after that his flight leveled off, but by then he was no longer Michael.

He was a great blond and blue-eyed bird skimming over the city. The city was a turning gray plate afloat in a sea of liquid mercury. The city's buildings were dull gray spikes revolving on the plate. The people of the city were small, minutely small, not ants but beads, mechanical beads caught in an endlessly cycling bead game, trapped in the clockwork movement which the city had become, their individual random movements, hopes and desires seen in the overview as immutable pattern. Michael had the overview. He had stepped off the board, flown off the board. He was watching the players from miles above. He was a bird watching Michael Shawtry from above and Michael Shawtry was lost-insignificant among the sheer mass and volume of players. He was a great blond bird beating its wings in the air to hold stock still at the null point of objectivity. He was power and vision and death and a new model of god and somewhere along the line of the past he'd known and sensed it all before.

He hovered over the city and listened to the million voices and understood each one and understood them all. He circled and wheeled and dived. He jackknifed through layered sheets of ice-white clouds. He cried a god-bird call into the wind and the wind cried back to him. He hovered over the city and time passed on the wind.

The bird hovered and time passed again and he was no longer the bird and he was falling.

Spiraling back into the city.

Macrocosm to microcosm.

Free falling weightless like an astronaut.

Metamorphosed, trying on gills for lungs, fins for wings, scales like shiny armor in place of plaited feathers. Sailing through the city beyond and beneath, Michael moved down dark tubes and tunnels floating, some sixth radar sense maintaining his equilibrium, always keeping him equidistant from the walls, always telling him which turns and passages he should take to escape his enemies.

The liquid through which he moved was of the consistency of embryonic fluid, or at least how he'd always imagined embryonic fluid: warm, viscous, peppered with soft clotty constantly-moving particles. He remembered why he was swimming. He remembered his enemies coming after him down the tunnels. He could feel their giant wing-fins throwing waves that carried through the liquid and swept against his back, upsetting his radar equilibrium. They were dark undulating shapes that had coagulated and spawned in the silt and mud recesses of stagnant pools and blocked drainage holes where the current did not carry. They had grown gargantuan in their own filth, nurtured and sustained by the consumption of poisons fed back upon themselves. They were the repressed demons of his unconscious, unleashed and hungry for their rabid field day.

Suddenly one of the beasts was diving down upon him jaws snapping and it was a cartoon monster and it was a yellow dinosaur chasing him down the beach and it was an inflatable rubber beach toy and he was about to laugh but those dripping jaws looked real enough and he was about to cry scream laugh scream if only he could think straight scream laugh he opened his eyes.

He opened his eyes.

He was in his room, lying on the bed.

Jacobi was sitting by the table, puffing his usual cigarette.

Michael could hear the noises from the street below coming through the open window.

Everything seemed normal until the movement began.

It came with a slow pulsing that grew faster and faster, vibrating through all of his senses. When it reach peak intensity it did not collapse. It kept weaving and pounding steadily. The drab walls of the apartment flowed with movement. Their scaling paint patterns were no longer seen as accidental but contrived, created by the hand of a subtle master artist anonymous of course anonymous thank God since his name would burn the brain. The brain. The brain. His brain had been involuted, reversed, yanked back and forth through the eye of the needle of birth. He could now feel the blood flowing through his veins and arteries. He could sense the air currents in the room. The surface of his skin felt hypersensitive, totally alive. A shifting multicolored film lay across his field of vision as if he were perceiving the fluid on the surfaces of his eyes, only the colors moved in a patterned geometric dance. He remembered the photographs he'd seen of molecular structures, crystals, the cycling dance of electrons mating, a distant image of the yellow and blue charts in high school chemistry.

There were thousands of thoughts and images caroming with the impact of billiards through the neural corridors and connections of his brain, too fast to catalog or remember. He was thinking in multiple combinations simultaneously, perceiving entire chains of logic not step by awkward step like some plodding crustacean, but with all of the links within reach at once. Inductive or deductive, the chain was circular and he could look at the circle from the outside.

Michael saw language for what it was, concentric symbols overlapping and built layered around a kernel that was symbol, too. He saw the yo-yo going around the world, the corpses that fertilize the plants that feed the bodies that grow to corpsehood.

"How are you feeling?"

Jacobi had said something, but it registered merely as naked sound, strumming syllable chords that matched his vision and touch in perfect tune and became part of the cantata of movement rather than coming together to form man-meanings in his head.

"How are you feeling?"

The question came again. Michael couldn't answer. Speech was beyond yet below his capabilities. He laughed, a high pitched donkey braying. He sat up in bed and the room rocked as if he had just become prime mover and had yet to master his new found powers. He looked at his hands. He discovered that by concentrating he could eliminate the moving colored film at will. His fingers grew from his hands, jumping, their tips recreating themselves in projection until they swept the boundaries of the walls. He could control this also, and when he censored out the hallucinatory effects he found textures and shadings in the objects around him that he had never noticed before. The flesh of his palms was not one flesh color, it was dappled with no less than a hundred variations. To his telescopically heightened vision the ridges of the rough floor boards loomed like the ragged mountains of a moonscape.

Michael looked toward Jacobi, who was staring at him smiling, half a burning cigarette dangling from his lips, its thin stream of bluish smoke mushrooming to gray billows as it rose toward the ceiling. Michael smiled back. Jacobi was beautiful. He was so completely inimitable Jacobi that he was beautiful—the dark almost sinister eyes, the tousled mop of black hair and broad curling mustache, the long lean body, the way he held his head slightly to one side. Michael had to laugh again, rolling back onto the bed, a bellyborn laughter that brought tears to the corners of his eyes.

When the laughter subsided, Michael stood up. As he moved he felt the shift in muscular tension throughout his thin frame. He was aware of all of the parts of his body at the same time. He walked toward the bathroom so he could look at his face in the mirror. At the doorway he became distracted by the heavy weave of the burlap curtain. Each strand as it turned and tunneled its complex way through the other turning strands looked ultimately solid, ultimately precious, Arabian silk rather than worn burlap. Michael realized that time had taken on the same quality. Each instant seemed precious, each moment recreated the following moment, each bit of time-stranded consciousness extended to interweave with a thousand others. Time was a flowing umbilical and in every minute the possibilities of all future minutes were tacitly obvious, the flower in the calyx, the seed within the cup of the petal, the cotyledon tucked within the seed.

In the bathroom mirror Michael looked at his face like an amnesiac seeing himself for the first time. The face he saw was young, but not without character. There was a willful cut to the eyes and mouth. The jaw beneath the beard was small boned but square and rigid. Already there were shallow furrows of concentration plowed across the flatland of the brow. Small straight wrinkles radiated from the corners of the eyes like pin wire spokes.

As Michael watched his face, one characteristic after another became accentuated—the soft skin, the pale eyelashes, the scrubby beard. Next all of the features began to change, one at a time like the slide projections employed in police identifications, changing eyes, nose, mouth, ears, hairline until the proper combination for a mock-up of the killer's face was obtained. Michael's face in transfiguration became a killer's face and more. The features thickened, the hair turned dark and coarse, the eyes became limpid, the nostrils flared, the lips curled drooping. He had become the sensualist absolute. The features thinned again, the hair grew blond, spare and plastered back, the cheekbones heightened, the complexion paled. He was the ascetic saint. The rate of change accelerated. Within the space of what seemed a few seconds he became bulging forehead intellectual, crooked toothed hunchback, sly Jew, aquiline Roman, inscrutable Oriental. The changes became increasingly erratic. The features of his face passed into inhuman and subhuman categories—dull-eyed Neanderthal, grinning ape, furry faced monster with protruding canine fangs where his eye teeth had once dwelt. Just as Michael felt a scream of horror bubbling to his lips, the changing circled back again through human to suprahuman, nearly angelic. He confronted the face of some future descendant of mankind, evolved beyond sin or error. Then back to monster again. Michael watched the cycle fascinated until he grew accustomed to its curious rhythms.

Back in the other room he found Jacobi still smoking his cigarette. Or was it another cigarette? It might have been an hour or only a few minutes that he'd spent before the mirror. Time as duration had become totally subjective. The battered alarm clock by his bed showed nearly midnight, four hours since he had taken the acid.

Michael crossed to the window and stared out over the tenement roofs, through the leafless forest of telephone poles and antennas. The air outside was cooler. His view of the city was marked by a pleasant wavering insubstantiality. He lowered his gaze to the street. The passing cars and flashing neon signs merged to a beautifully volatile light show, a flickering neuron dance cast against the backdrop of the darkness below. He remembered his earlier god-bird view of the city, and in that remembering he realized that he must be coming down, reclaiming the consciousness of his identity and losing the spontaneous state of non-reflection that the drug had produced. The sensations throughout his body were abating somewhat. He closed his eyes. The blackness was still heavily laced with a shifting symmetry of colored patterns, but their intensity had lessened.

He spoke to Jacobi for the first time. "I think I've peaked already, I'm coming down." His voice echoed through his head with an enhanced timbre, the vowels richer and fuller than he had ever heard them before.

"Do you want to go outside?" Jacobi asked.

"Sure, why not?" Michael answered after a moment's hesitation. Into the street, he thought, the reality of the street.

And for whatever another memory is worth, Jacobi remembered the first few hours of Michael's trip as uneventful. He tried to stay awake so as not to leave his friend alone on the acid. It wasn't easy. Jacobi was exhausted, both from hitching cross-country and from walking around the city. He sat by the table with his chin on his hand, nodding off, the weight of his eyelids pulling his head forward and once almost pitching him onto the floor before he caught himself.

For the first few hours Michael remained on the bed, nearly motionless. He might have been sleeping, except that occasionally his lips would part slightly and his body would quiver throughout, as if with internal laughter so far inside it couldn't get out, didn't even know there was a way out.

Jacobi could just as well have not been there. He smoked cigarettes. He read Michael's poetry and notes scattered across the desk. He examined the stack of books by the bed—Ouspensky, Gurdjieff, Suzuki, Spengler, Ehret—pausing to puzzle over the esoteric complexity of Gurdjieff's diagrams. A few paragraphs held his interest momentarily, but shortly his weary mind began to wander and he give up reading.

Coffee, he thought, that will keep me awake. He searched the kitchen cupboards. They yielded rice, walnuts, raisins, apples, orange tea, mint tea, sassafras tea, rose hip tea, but not a mote of coffee. When he returned from the kitchen he noticed a change in Michael, a tautness in his prone posture that had previously not been present, as if a string twined through the vertebrae of his backbone had been turned tightening. It seemed to Jacobi that if he touched Michael or spoke to him the latter might snap broken like an overdrawn rubber band. As the next hour passed the tautness was gradually replaced by a profound agitation which took complete control of Michael's body. He lay upon the bed, curling and uncurling his toes, clenching and unclenching his fists, clutching at the rumpled sheet, twisting his head and neck this way and that with contorted grimaces of overwhelming ecstasy or horror. Jacobi couldn't be sure which. He had never seen a trip so totally withdrawn before.

Michael's bare chest and face were soon drenched with sweat. The veins on his temples stood out. The cords of his neck became constantly pulsing columns that glistened with moisture. He ground his teeth together as if he were trying to masticate the flesh of some sinewy animal. Just when it seemed that the tension had reached a breaking point and his friend's body would collapse clicking like a broken machine into the convulsive spasms of an epileptic fit, Michael opened his eyes. He expelled his breath sharply from between parted teeth. Immediately, his straining movement ceased. The musculature and posture of his body altered rapidly, as if the baleful incubus that had been wracking his limbs had now fled defeated in fright with that sharp puff of breath.

Still, Michael remained upon the bed, motionless again but for his eyes which now circled and recircled the ceiling and walls of the room with widening amazement.

"How are you feeling?" Jacobi asked.

There was no answer. He waited a short while and then repeated the question. Still no response, momentarily, then Michael exploded with laughter, a high-pitched donkey braying. He sat up in the bed and began staring at the palms of his hands. Jacobi noticed that his eyes were fantastically dilated, the tumid black bug of the cornea nearly eclipsing the blue iris. He was still breathing heavily from his previous straining, and his cheeks and forehead were darkly and unevenly flushed like the sloppy rouge job of a children's dramatic production.

When Michael looked up, Jacobi smiled at him. Jacobi didn't like the smile with which Michael answered. It was beneficent, patronizing, and slightly insane, the mask of infinite forgiving wisdom that one displays to a wayward child. The acid glow that Jacobi had seen so often in other faces was now diffused throughout Michael's, yet it was lacking much of the warmth he was accustomed to in others. Jacobi found that he could remain removed from it. There was no contact high. There were no vibrations of extended joy, none of the scurrilous sainthood that Mulligan projected, but rather the withdrawn sainthood of a Christian martyr. Even now that Michael had come out of his trance he was still internalizing the drug, taking it into his own realm like a special prescription from his private doctor.

Jacobi's tiredness was beginning to pass away from him. He was feeling that second wind that comes beyond the resisted and overcome desire to sleep. His mind was more alert. He watched Michael with renewed interest as the latter broke into laughter for a second time, rolling back onto the bed. Jacobi felt he should speak to him, make contact in some way, but he couldn't think of what to say.

Eventually Michael's laughter subsided and he stood up, rocking unevenly on his new footing. He walked toward the bathroom slowly, arms extended for balance, placing each step with exaggerated care. He paused by the burlap curtain that covered the doorway, running his fingers over the rough fabric and examining it with the scrutiny of a textile merchant. Finally, he pushed it to one side and entered. Jacobi could see his outline through the loose weave of the curtain, bobbing back and forth and up and down in front of the mirror. Jacobi knew that trip well enough, the thousand and one changing faces: ancestors, descendants, friends, lovers, all the facets of humankind reflected back through the self.

After several minutes Michael emerged and crossed to the window, walking with more assurance now. Looking out into the street he spoke for the first time. "I think I've already peaked. I'm coming down."

"Do you want to go outside? " Jacobi asked.

"Sure, why not? " Michael answered. He nodded his head and once again gave his strange smile.

True, Michael was coming down, but it wasn't until he got into the street that he realized how high he still was.

Back down into the street, back into the other reality, the night town street.

Adrift. Cut adrift. Treading light through a neon sea. Bobbing like a cork, up, down, moving with the crowd. Easy. Easy now. So many faces, alive. The neon rippling across their faces like colored water. Their pores in magnification, each pock mark. Chartreuse. Mauve. Cerise. Gamboge. Ugly pored skin. Ugly faces, frightened.

No, not frightening, not to me, thought Michael, insisted Michael, never really frightening when you see what you expect to see. Of course they're ugly. Human, frightened, ugly. Can't soar over the city like a great blond bird. Not the many, only the few, the other breed, the outsiders with all the insight. Like me adrift in this neon sea. Jacobi in tow, down and sleepy, watching me and waiting for a freak-out. No, not now, warm and sensual now, can handle anything he can handle, more, maybe more, yes, more.

Thus Michael came down silently through the city night, self-satisfied, turning within his own thoughts, walking and looking, walking and looking, mainly circling through the environs of the East and West Villages. Jacobi followed, supposedly guiding him. His exhaustion came on again, passed, and came on still again before morning. For him it was like any other night walking the city streets. He realized that he hadn't even been in New York for a day and already he was feeling overexposed to the city, already it was losing what little charm it held for him. It smelled like the city and tasted like the city—sweat, disease, garbage, poverty, decay, alcohol, ennui, sewage, semen, money and speed. It left its city dirt gathering grime along the inside of his collar. It tightened his shoulder blades and forced him to don an extra coat or two of psychic armor.

Their walking that night was not like their walks of two years earlier. The cockiness with which Michael had taken the cap of acid was now replaced by his peculiar quietude. Throughout the night he remained singularly uncommunicative. Jacobi did most of what little talking there was, far apart and disconnected comments that Michael refused to pick up on. Their whole night's conversation could not have covered half a reel of tape.

From Jacobi's vantage the only significant event occurred near morning, when the sky changing for day had just tried on that nameless colorless shade not black or gray but just short of either. Michael paused in front of a small commercial art gallery near the outskirts of the West Village. He looked toward Jacobi slowly and then nodded to the window with exaggerated drama. Jacobi's exhaustion had now passed into the stage of a clear and empty-headed intoxication. The window display struck him with memorable intensity in distinct disproportion to the hazy remainder of the night.

Three large canvases were mounted upon wooden easels. At the bottom front center of the window, a trio of spotlights shone upward to lay its three-fingered hand of illumination upon the paintings, one digit to each, with the fingers splayed by the spreading of the beams yet splayed too late to cover the oblong of each canvas in its entirety, so that all the pictures remained part light, part shadow, truncated and inverted cones of brightness with two small dark hypotenuse-drooping right triangles ringing their lower corners.

The painting on the left was a multicolored *pointillist* abstract, with the layers of oil applied to such a degree of thickness that the composition had taken on the sculptured depth effect of a bas-relief. Showing through at points of transparency in its crater-strewn and volcano-pocked surface there was a shiny enamel red that belied the rough patina of the landscape and hinted at a molten core, a surfeit of lava straining ripe for escape through the first veins of weakness. A small card tacked to the vertical wooden beam of the easel that protruded above the painting proclaimed the title: "Cosmos II." Jacobi idly wondered if in "Cosmos III" the volcanoes blew their lids and splattered the canvas red like spouting lava geysers.

The painting to the right was a dim gray black blue and white acrylic seascape, the kind one finds by the score in Sausalito tourist shuck shops, with a tortured swath of clouds and a mangled tree silhouette reaching out from the rocks and about to topple into the water. The branches of the tree were etched with such artificial and parallel perspicacity that it looked as if they had gained a complete agreement with the wind, the same wind that churned the ocean to an irregular battalion of whitecaps that charged the beach and inevitable destruction with the collapse of each wave. The title read "Seascape."

And the painting in the middle, the centerpiece of the secular triptych, the *pièce de résistance*, the sole reason for

Michael's weighted nod, of course, thought Jacobi, but of course, of course, of course, enough to top volcanoes, whitecaps, tempests and teapots, a painting of Michael himself!

He stands in the middle of his room, or rather a distortion of his room, too narrow and long and blurred and slanting intentionally out of perspective so that the eye is bewildered by a plenitude of vanishing points that divide and multiply like malicious amoebas, so that one wonders if a spot of epoxy is keeping the lumpy pen from rolling off the inclined plane of the desk, one wonders why the chair still stands erect despite its misshapen legs, one wonders what contortions of a concert virtuoso's hands, fingers and thumbs were required to pound a lettered tune upon the crooked keyboard of that melting humpbacked typewriter. The view angled down upon Michael from above, as if the artist had worked from a suspended scaffolding. Michael's image stared up out of the canvas from the veering ill-focused quagmire of his room, head thrown back and unsmiling, hands in his pockets in the same slouching posture he held before the window as he stood next to Jacobi at that very moment, attired in the identical outfit he now wore, his day-in-day-out baggy black sweater and white beach pants. In the painting his forehead was splotched festering with a nascent case of the hives and his head swollen out of all proportion to his body, as if he were leaning into a funhouse mirror. Yet he was depicted with such a greater devotion to mirror detail than his surroundings—the folds of his rumpled clothing, the individual hairs at his temples, the very shadings of his eyes—that he dominated the painted room and the viewer's attention completely, looming confident like some mad Latin papa-dictator in elevator shoes and full military dress regalia on the steps of the Imperial Palace he has just seized from his predecessor with a bloody sabre-wielding *coup d'etat.* This effect was further heightened by the colors of the painting, all off-color browns, blacks, and whites like a tinted fading daguerreotype, except for Michael's burning blue eyes which, through some technique of the artist's gimmickry, faced the viewer from no matter what direction you approached the canvas and seemed to follow you in semicircle when you walked from one side of it to the other. The small white card fittingly proclaimed the painting's title: "The Recluse."

"An infamous immortality, huh?" said Michael, breaking into Jacobi's reverie. He paused. "She told me those oils could last without fading for hundreds of years."

"She?"

"Yeah, Linda. She painted it from a photograph."

"You don't mean...?" Jacobi recoiled as his first abortive love affair of two years earlier encroached upon his memory.

"That's right, your Linda, the very same," said Michael. "She's still around, living over in Brooklyn Heights. She split the Village as soon as she started making it."

"Is she still as fucked up as before?"

Michael laughed and laughed again before answering. "Hey, man, who ever told you it was going to get any better? Everybody is still as fucked up as before."

7

THE ACID had moved David Jacobi on his pilgrimage to New York in order to break the pattern of his existence. His last trip with Mulligan demanded some definitive action. The psychedelic didn't tell him what kind, but it did reveal his previous actions as primarily those of a somnambulist, a sleepwalker whose dream world consisted of an intellectual grid of rigid delineations imposed upon and obliterating the fluid reality beneath. That grid had distorted his perceptions and blocked his senses. But the acid had shattered this old world view to the bedrock, and all the way across country and now in New York, a reformation process was taking place. Jacobi was still digesting and assimilating the experience, coming down and at the same time waking up to the possibilities of how his life might be transformed.

There was no certitude with regard to what he was seeking. He knew that it wasn't "enlightenment." That term implied mountaintop contemplation and the removed state of visionary wisdom touted by the literature of the East. If he were to exist in an enlightened state, Jacobi wanted it coincident with immersion in the world, not only of the senses, but the world of give and take humanity that surrounded him.

An erotic sense of awareness, the ability to master any environment, to react spontaneously in any situation, a level of maturity advanced far beyond what is normally meant by adulthood—these were all extensions of the state of consciousness, or unconsciousness, that Jacobi was after, and he felt sure that the first step was to abolish not only the false dualities in his perceptions of the external world, but those within himself. If he could get his mind and his senses together in the right place, time and way, maybe with acid and maybe without, the rest would follow like the numbers going round a clock.

If New York City were to be the place where he would achieve his vision, it gave no portent, except perhaps for the dream.

When they returned to the apartment they both collapsed, Michael on the bed, Jacobi lying naked upon Michael's' open sleeping bag thrown across the bare wood of the floor. They slept through the sweltering day and into the sweltering night, and somewhere along the track of that sweaty dazed sleeping, Jacobi dreamt the lines of a poem. Perhaps it was because of the notes, the diminished after tones, that Michael's poetry had left sounding in his head. But later, after he discovered the coincidence, Jacobi often thought that Christine's restless soul had left its body that night and wandered through the streets of the city until it had sought out his own, transmigrating, whispering words in his ear like an echo from the future that had been derailed onto the wrong time track, caught an express when it had been ticketed for a local and somehow arrived before it was scheduled to depart.

In his dream he found himself in a deserted city, a planned and automated city that was cleaner and colder than New York, a city where concrete had won its final victory over flesh and soil and soul. Block after barren block slid by him until gradually he passed into the city's outskirts. Here the coldness, the immaculate buildings and wide windy esplanades, were replaced by heat, dirt, rickety wooden hovels, and narrow winding up and down alleys. The walks were filled with crowds, and each street was an open marketplace of hawking vendors and wary buyers prattling to one another in the endless tongues of commerce. Hirsute beggars squatted along the sidewalks, clanking tin cups against the cobbles. From the passing doorways barefoot whores called out to him. Their cheap perfumes mingled with the odors of the market stalls. It all seemed real enough, but it existed apart from him. It held its distance, the ephemeral distance of a dream, and his own body remained insubstantial, not flesh and touch and bone but an amorphous veil trailing behind him.

Eventually he passed up a flight of stairs and into a room. A faceless yet beautiful woman was lying upon a bed. Now his body took on form and he was suddenly lying beside her. They were both naked and he pressed himself against the long-limbed warmth of her flesh. Their forms were indistinct, their pores merged, their outlines overlapped. She spoke to him in a foreign tongue and he did not know the words, but still he knew their meaning. She was an artist. The room was covered with her work, fantastic creations doomed to transience because she could not afford the proper materials. Intricate drawings on assorted scraps of old wrapping paper were tacked to the walls. Small human statues that could have shamed Rodin were fashioned from bars of soap.

He was standing by the window, looking down into the throng that pulsed and spilled through the narrow alley below. She came up behind him silently, encircling his waist with her long arms. Somewhere the sun was setting, casting the rough rooftops in the lacquered shades of twilight. She spoke again, this time a poem, repeated and repeated until it took on the hypnotic rhythms of a mantra that carried him into other dreams he would never remember consciously.

Jacobi was the first to awaken—Michael still slept—and in awakening he almost lost the poem dipping back into his unconscious. Though it was through no volition of his own, it did not vanish. It remained, like a lone fruit on a nearly barren tree at the desolate borders of awareness. Ripe for the picking, it clung in his head like a promise that carried through his drowsiness.

He stumbled to the open window for a breath of air. No luck. The tepid air within the apartment continued into the street. It was late evening already, but there was no breeze to dry the sweat from his pores. In the kitchen he turned on the tap with numb hands and splashed cold water over his face and head, bending sideways to gulp several mouthfuls. He looked out of the kitchen window, down into the narrow alley on which it fronted. The narrow alley.

The narrow alley.

The rhythm of the poem circling in his head brought him fully awake. He hurried back to the other room, and with the water still running droplets down his forehead he began to scribble on a scrap of paper he'd picked up from Michael's desk. The words flowed onto the page line by line, automatically, as if he'd tapped the core of some formerly unknown reservoir within himself.

> charcoal drawings on orange wrapping
> paper running in the dampness of
>
> our room the silver steam pipes
> dripping and sounds that rise
>
> from the narrow alley scaling the
> bare brick walls like purposeful
>
> insects the city is a kind of swamp
> tonight a mud gray swamp a sweaty bog
>
> praying for a stained glass rain

Michael was standing in front of the bathroom mirror, snipping away at his beard with a rust-spotted scissors.

"I read some of your poetry," Jacobi told him, "while you were up on the acid."

"Oh yeah, what did you think?" Most of the time the scissor clicked on empty air. When it did connect and a severed curl plummeted into the sink, Michael would jerk his head back as if his hair had nerve endings. He would then carefully survey the stage of his trimming before continuing.

Jacobi stood in the doorway to the bathroom. "Some of the images are great," he said.

Michael gave up with an exasperated shrug. "This is ridiculous," he said. He tossed the pair of scissors clanking back into the medicine cabinet and slammed the mirror-door shut after it. He gave the beard one final hapless glance. Jacobi stepped back as Michael walked past him out of the bathroom.

"Some of the images are great," he repeated, "but you need more continuity."

"That's always the problem," Michael stated, "to tie the intense images into a continuum, to exist at the top of perception all the time." He scratched his chin. "If I could do that I'd be more than a good poet, I'd be a fucking visionary. That's what acid is all about."

"You think so?" Jacobi asked.

"Sure," Michael answered. "I know so." He stood in the center of the studio, hands on his hips, small head jutting forward, legs slightly spread, braced against an oncoming wind that Jacobi couldn't feel. "Whether I've always been aware of it or not, yesterday is what I've been after for a long time. I just never had the right tool to get me there before. Yesterday, I got answers to questions I hadn't even thought of asking yet." He nodded toward the desk. "Writing has put my head in some pretty fine places, but never anything like that. It was like being on the very top of existence, my senses turned on all the way. You can call it whatever you want—the mystic vision, subjective truth, the third eye—I don't care about the words. All I know is that if I could feel that way all the time, I wouldn't give a damn about writing anymore. There'd be no need to."

The direct and deadpan way in which Michael spoke made it hard for Jacob to take the speech seriously. If it's such a revelation, he thought, how can he discuss it so calmly, with such cold assurance.

"But I know I'm going to lose its essence," Michael continued. "My brain's classifying system is already in the process of getting it all neatly figured out, fucking up the memory with labels, just like any other memory. Shit, I'm talking about it, that alone is killing it whether I like it or not." Then he added, half-jokingly, "Maybe I should take another cap today."

"You can't stay high on acid all the time," Jacobi told him. "It's just like anything else. After a while you build up a tolerance and have to keep increasing the dosage to get the same effects."

Michael shrugged his narrow shoulders. "That's too bad, it might be worth trying."

Acid's not that simple or easy, Jacobi thought as he watched Michael stretching out on the bed and bumming another one of his smokes. I've taken it a score of times and it's still a mystery to me. Even Mulligan's not that definite about it, and he's taken so much it must be second nature to him by now. Michael's still halfway high. This last time I had flashbacks for nearly a week afterwards.

Then Jacobi second-guessed himself.

Or maybe I'm not high enough anymore, too logical to grasp what Michael's saying, maybe it's time *I* took another cap.

He remembered the poem he'd written earlier and realized that its tone was closer to existential despair than it was to the vision he'd experienced on his last acid trip. After a moments hesitation, he decided to show it to Michael. He took the crumpled piece of paper from his pocket. "Here, I did this while you were asleep."

Michael sat up in bed to take the poem. Then rising, he spread it out on the table directly beneath the bare overhead bulb. He ran his hands over the paper several times to smooth out the creases.

"You have lousy handwriting," he said, squinting his eyes. "That means you're a good abstract thinker, but poor at learning languages."

"Thanks," Jacobi laughed. "Skip the graphology. What about a literary analysis?"

After Michael read the poem once, Jacobi watched his eyes circle back to the top of the page. When he finished the second time he spoke. "Not bad, it carries a mood across, but the last line has already been done."

"What?"

Michael crossed the room and hunched into the dark cluttered recess of the closet. He began burrowing like a gopher. Old socks, shoes, shirts, books, papers came sliding onto the floor. "Take a look at this." He was holding a slim hard-cover volume with a tattered paper jacket. Leafing quickly through the book he found the page he wanted, then handed it to Jacobi, his pointing finger designating the appropriate line.

"I pressed my forehead against the pane…and began to pray for a stained glass rain," Jacobi read half-aloud. He looked at the cover of the book. The title was in white script on a sky-blue ground.

"Well, it can't be that bad a line if it was published," Jacobi said.

"Are you kidding?" answered Michael. "All kinds of crap gets published. Anyway, that chick's got money up the spleen. She had it printed herself."

"You bought a copy."

Michael shook his head. "Wrong again. She gave them away free at the publication party, autographed no less. If she ever really makes it, it might be worth something."

Jacobi opened the book and there, in a feminine script nearly as regular as the print on the cover, the name was repeated. The dots over the "i's" were tiny perfect circles. The "t" stood rigid and upright, like a clean cross awaiting the body of a crucifixion. He turned the book over. On the back of the jacket was a dust-covered photograph. Jacobi wiped the dust away with one hand, then wiped his dusty hand on his jeans. The picture that emerged was of a young round-faced girl swinging in a field of sunflowers: wide eyes, the swing at one peak of its turning arc, her breath about to go out between square white teeth, long legs stretched forth and held closely together, dress blown back to her thighs.

"Maybe we were meant to be soul mates," Jacobi speculated.

Michael chuckled sarcastically. "I'd say bed mates is what you have in mind."

"The two aren't mutually exclusive," Jacobi informed him.

"Forget it." Michael was crouched on the floor, pushing the accumulated pile of debris back into the closet. "You'd have to bridge the generation gap. That picture is ancient. She's too old for you."

"How old?" Jacobi asked. He began to leaf through the book, scanning a line here or there.

"Oh, in her thirties," Michael guessed with a final shove. "But then again, you know what Ben Franklin said about older women?"

"What?"

"They do it well, they don't tell, and they're grateful as hell."

Jacobi looked up. "Did Ben Franklin really say that?"

"Not exactly in those words," Michael admitted.

Three nights after the scene with Tony, Christine drank herself into a vodka and orange juice stupor. Their relationship had been a sinecure against her waves of despair, another line holding her wayward ship to the dock of sanity. Now that he was gone, she began to drift, the routine of her life collapsing around her. The drinking experience was both alien and frightening. Next morning she was hung over dreadfully and the flesh of her face looked heavy and dead in the mirror. Her thoughts went to her father and his yellowed skin and rotting liver and how toward the end he drank even more to kill the pain. Her thoughts went to Tony drunk and she felt sick with him and sick with herself.

She took a hot shower and put on a new dress. While applying her make-up over a greenish pallor it suddenly occurred to her that she had nowhere to go. On Tuesdays and Thursdays she would walk down MacDougal Street to Washington Square and her class in Renaissance literature at NYU. Today was Saturday.

She tried to work on her poetry. The pages stared back at her, dead as specimens in their glass museum cases, cold as the rows of steel bars lining the fire escape outside her window. She thought about writing letters. There was nothing to say that she was able to say. There was no one to say it to.

She cleansed her face with a cold sticky cream, took two prescription sleeping pills, and went back to bed.

Still...she could not sleep.

Her mind wandered beyond her control and she thought of a girlfriend from college who had attempted to kill herself with her father's revolver. The girl had failed in her suicide attempt, but managed to perform a partial lobotomy on herself instead. When Christine visited her in the hospital, she was slow and happy, and it seemed you could look down into her eyes forever without seeing a thing. Her eyes were hollow, echoless caves.

8

JACOBI had arrived at Michael's on a Wednesday. After Michael's stunt with the acid they both slept on and off through Friday afternoon. Michael was recuperating from his two-day sleepless fast, Jacobi from six days on the road. On Friday evening Michael took him to a small macrobiotic restaurant near Tompkins Square. Jacobi devoured the meager meal quickly and lit a cigarette. The surrounding diners, frail and bony types mostly as pale as Michael, shied away from the smoke as if it were mustard gas. Jacobi stubbed the cigarette out on the edge of the tile table—there were no ashtrays—and watched Michael finish his food. His friend ate slowly and deliberately, using chopsticks and placing small morsels between his soft pink lips with dramatic care. Throughout the meal he talked about his parents—"My father's the original phantom capitalist, scarcer than eel bones. Even I have to make three appointments before I get to see him."—and when the check arrived it was Jacobi who wound up paying most of it——"Look, man, I'm a little low on cash until I see my mother again, and you know that scene. I'm just not up to a third-degree right now."

It occurred to Jacobi that Michael was undergoing a self-imposed sentence of abstinence and poverty to counterbalance the moneyed years of his childhood.

Saturday morning. Michael begged another cap of acid from him. Supposedly he would pay for both caps as soon as he had the money. He wanted the two of them to drop together, but Jacobi said that he didn't "feel right for it." In truth, the idea of taking acid amid the hostile walls of the city with laconic Michael as his sole companion didn't appeal to him. Michael took the capsule about noon and repeated his performance of the previous Wednesday, four hours of near catatonia followed by a stroll around the city. This time he strolled by himself. Jacobi was trying to make connections to deal the rest of the acid. Michael had been no help there. Jacobi remembered the painting—"The Recluse" is right, he thought. Michael no doubt knew a score of likely customers after all the time he'd lived in the city, but it was impossible to get him to go see any of them.

Michael's only suggestion had been to unload the acid in quantity to Billie Raintree, the same dealer who had first turned them on two years before and who was still operating in the East Village. That meant selling at cost or close to it, and Jacobi wasn't ready for that.

There were eight million plus people in New York City, two million in Manhattan alone, probably close to half a million in the Village. More than a few probably wanted to take acid and would buy Jacobi's acid, but he was at a loss as to how to contact them so that business could begin. Initially, he had planned to use The Inferno as his base operations, but The Inferno was gone. He checked out a few nearby coffeehouses, hoping to spot a familiar face among the crowds. He sat by himself, drinking cappuccinos one after another, soaking up the cafe life as it underwent its typical Saturday night explosion all around him. The scraping chairs, the noisy clatter of loose conversation and clinking glasses, the bobbing cadres of cigarettes, the faces ravaged by too much dope or too many bad affairs, the facile laughter, the foot games under the tables and the hand games above—all combined to create and perpetuate the illusion that something was actually happening here...and perhaps it was. As the evening progressed in such confined and airless rooms the smoke seemed to condense to a bitter oil through which all must wade: hustlers, artists, watchers and actors, mad poets, women like wolves and women like snakes, women as fragile as butterflies, bearded student politicos, outspoken philosophers of every persuasion and would-be dope dealers. It tinted their flesh gray and dulled the colors of their clothes. It made the unreality of their games, pastimes and passions seem even more unreal.

The tableau was almost identical to the one Jacobi had worked in night after night two years earlier. The unending repetition of the play still held his interest. All of the parts he remembered were present and cast, but in the space of two years the players had changed. He went home that night alone and with the acid still bouncing in his pocket.

Sunday. He awoke to the racket of Michael's rattling typewriter. His head and mouth felt fuzzy from the night's excess of caffeine and nicotine. Michael was still half-gone on the acid and typing furiously. As he beat away on the noisy machine, Jacobi could see the bones moving through the thin flesh of his bare back. He was redoing the poem he'd been working on when Jacobi arrived, his latest "epic," now altered through the insights that the acid had given him. In the latter part of his second trip he had envisioned the poem as a potential organic entity, still imperfect and inert, like a vat of amino acid in which certain elusive changes were required to fire the spark of life. Now he understood what changes were necessary, and he had to transcribe them to paper before they fled from his mind.

Jacobi, still sleepy, sat on the edge of the bed watching him. He felt the heat and humidity of the summer city as a palpable burden that bound his limbs and enveloped him a net of lethargy. Michael remained seemingly unaffected. Sweat covered his body, but nevertheless he bristled with activity, almost as if he were feeding off the energy of his visions. Jacobi was beginning to realize that Michael's current life was composed of periods of relentless activity coupled with intervals of total exhaustion. He wasn't interested in or capable of becoming a participant in such a compulsive cycle.

As he sat that day watching Michael, while his body remained bound by the heat, Jacobi's mind traveled freely. He began to realize a few other things—that the fantasy he had projected from Berkeley was now confronting the objective reality of New York and dissolving before it, that he had yet to culture the proper identity to become a dealer or the spontaneity to become the man he wanted to be, that he was still too self-aware, too much inside his own head. He should have singled out new faces in the cafe crowds to deal the acid to rather than searching in vain for the faces of two summers past. He remembered what Mulligan had said to him about dealing before he left Berkeley: "Getting busted isn't the problem, Davy. If you're careful enough, and smart enough, whether or not you get busted breaks down to a question of luck...no, the real problem is more subtle than that. It's the old capitalist trip...alienation. Marx was right you know, people become objects. You start to think of them in terms of how much dope you can sell them or how much dope you can buy from them, what kind of profit you can turn. Each new person you meet becomes first of all a potential customer, an object. That's the real thing about dealing you have to watch out for and control." Well, here he was in New York and he couldn't even find the customers to turn into objects. He wondered what Mulligan would have to say about that.

Jacobi didn't fight the lethargy he felt enveloping him. He flowed with it. It was the path of least resistance, probably the most spontaneous thing he'd done since arriving in the city.

That night he went to the cafes again, not with any hopes of dealing but merely as an observer. He watched the ceaseless flowing from table to table. He watched the women. And there were women there who watched him, and perhaps he could have had one—particularly one amber-eyed girl who looked Spanish—but none triggered the proper urge in him to respond. He was still too much in limbo. He had withdrawn from one course of action without choosing another.

The next morning he awoke early and left the apartment. Michael still slept, so soundly that he hardly seemed to be breathing, and his eyes hung partly open, staring like those of a dead man. Jacobi's malaise had left him, replaced by a peculiar sense of anticipation, of waiting, for what—the end of his money,

Judgment Day, the fall of Carthage?—he couldn't say. He took the subway uptown and spent the day in Central Park, poor man's haven from the city within the city. He wandered the pathways, and bare to the waist lay baking in the sun. The bottle of acid was still riding in his hip pocket, but he had forgotten it, or at least pushed its existence to some level of his mind from which it did not surface. He bought himself a small notebook and began writing. He didn't know if it was the poem he'd dreamt or Michael's poetry that had given him the impetus, or perhaps the urge to further order his ideas by recording them in black and white. It wasn't really poetry that he wanted to write. He had more in mind a rambling novel that would relate his sexual exploits and spiritual awakenings. But he discovered that he could only put down scattered images and phrases, bits and pieces that failed to coalesce and were as fragmented as his vision of the world. It was then that he saw acid in a new light, as pure energy, blind Dionysian energy that had catapulted him out of his old existence. He understood that the trip to New York, ostensibly spontaneous, something wild to do, was in fact an attempt on the part of his intellect to bind and channel that energy, an enforced "spontaneity" that merely served to dampen the impetus for change the acid had given him. That impetus needed direction and order, but it had to be an intuitive order that sprang from a deeper part of his being than the conscious mind.

"To remain lucid in ecstasy."—he didn't know where he'd heard the phrase, probably from Mulligan, but now it rang through his head again and again, clear as a meditation bell. That was the goal, experience clear and pure as polished crystal, the ecstasy of the acid high and the natural lucidity of the uncluttered self operating at levels apart from the artificial constructs of logic. More words? Labels to distort the experience? That was what Michael would say, but Jacobi was beginning to believe that words could serve him well as long as he remembered they were only words...symbols...approximations.

When he returned to the apartment that evening he found Michael still sleeping. He had remained unconscious throughout the entire day.

Waiting and waiting—that was Tuesday. Jacobi tried to lose himself in the mindlessness of becoming a tourist on his declining funds, the whole plastic trip: Rockefeller Plaza, the Empire State, the Staten Island Ferry. It was hopeless. Throughout the day his sense of anticipation increased in intensity, dogging his path like an albatross, gaining on him slowly but with assurance. Waiting for that stained glass rain. Waiting for the seasons to change. Waiting for the Pope to dance naked across the Vatican Dome. Waiting for an MGM spring with bluebells, daffodils and fresh frozen sunshine. Waiting for sex, love, wealth, power, madness, earthquakes, plagues, death, cosmic rebirth and the final revolution.

He came back to Michael's tourist-tired to sleep late into the following day. That evening they were to attend a poetry reading together. Michael spent the day putting the finishing touches on some of his work. Late in the afternoon he prepared his usual meal of cooked rice and vegetables, and shared it with Jacobi. Afterward, Jacobi, his hunger barely nicked, went across the street to buy a meatball submarine and a beer. He brought them back to the apartment to eat. Michael, sitting by the typewriter, eyed the sandwich as if it contained the haunches of Satan rather than cheap breaded-down beef.

Michael saw Jacobi as a messenger who had brought him the acid...but now that the acid was here, and he saw how it could complete his existence, carry him to heights he had never imagined, he was beginning to view the continued presence of the messenger as a complication. It wasn't anything his friend actually did that disturbed him, but the vibrations he gave off, of restlessness and purposelessness. There had been a time when he'd admired Jacobi—his intellect and ideas, his tendency to look convention in the teeth and give it a swift kick—but Michael had long since concluded that a desultory existence was the worst sort.

"Look, man, you can't stay here any longer. The formula is simple. I've got to write, and I can't write unless I'm alone." He swung his feet off the desk and the front legs of his chair fell back to the floor with a solid clump, period to his last sentence.

So it had come to that, Jacobi thought. He was surprised, but only mildly. Michael had changed. Perhaps it was his commitment to writing, which he'd talked about before but never acted upon. Or merely his self-imposed seclusion. Perhaps the two were one and the same.

"If you kick me out, who's going to feed you acid and cigarettes?" Jacobi asked, turning away and rolling onto his side in the bed.

Michael ignored the question. "But I do know where you *can* stay."

Jacobi thought for a moment, his eyes unconsciously tracing and retracing the borders of symmetrical water stain on the wall. Suddenly he spun around and shot upright. "Oh no, not Linda's," he exclaimed. "Not a chance!"

Michael enumerated the advantages, ticking them off on his fingers. "She'll be glad to see you. She'll sell half your acid for you. And you'll get to lay her on top of it."

"No, I couldn't take it." Jacobi was on his feet. "I'm through with the Jewish-mother trip. Once was enough." His hand made a solid swipe from left to right.

"She's crazy about you, man," Michael answered unperturbed.

Jacobi stood in fount of him, leaning forward. "Yeah, crazy to get her claws into me again."

"So tame her," Michael laughed.

"Man, I've been that route and it's not worth the scars. Find her some other masochist, not me. She painted your picture, not mine. If you think she's so great why don't you take her on?"

The poet spread his palms in mock supplication. "Look, I can't write with a horny sculptress hanging round my neck. All you want to do is deal acid."

Stand off. Jacobi went to the window. He lit a cigarette and leaned his forearm against the glass, looking out at nothing in particular. He pulled on his mustache and smoked. Michael put his feet back up on the desk and started rocking in the chair again, his perpetual balancing act. He picked up a pen from the cluttered desk and on the shiny ink-filled cover of his notebook he scrawled new doodles over the old. Jacobi finished his cigarette before speaking.

"All right, let's go to Billie's. I'll sell the acid there. If I'm going to split I'll need some money first."

"But the reading is tonight," Michael protested.

"Well, come on then, let's go. We've still got time to make them both!"

Jacobi felt that he'd at last shifted out of neutral and into gear. The light was green. The brakes were off. There was a road ahead. He couldn't tell what was on it, but at least it was a road.

9

BILLIE'S was a commune, crash pad and illicit drug outlet all rolled into one confused, frenetic combination.

It was a dark dirty basement apartment, even dirtier than Michael's, even darker in the daytime since the shades were pulled. In the summer heat its bare brick and plaster walls oozed moisture like some dark fecundating womb. A scratchy stereo blasted constantly—Beatles, Byrds, The Blues Project...

It was a mossy twilight zone and in the uniform shadow of its filtered daylight, vision, sound and even touch seemed less distinct, nearly tenuous.

A mousy girl with curly brown hair, most likely Billie's current paramour and the latest meth addict he was trying to cure, answered the door and subsequently disappeared into the shadows. Billie was out so Michael and Jacobi sat down on the dusty carpet, backs against the wall, to wait. The large room was packed with a ragged assortment of people, mostly young, mostly asleep or stoned and staring into space. A barefoot youth lay stretched on his belly, the stereo speakers booming a few feet from either ear, his open palms and his body thumping the floor in a spastic beat that bore no recognizable connection to the rhythms of the music. On a broken down hassock in one corner hunched a dark heavy-set man with one sleeve rolled up. He stared at the floor and methodically picked his teeth with a matchbook cover. Every few seconds he would glance up and around the room and run the hand with the turned-up sleeve through his thinning hair.

There were two separate speed conversations going on at the same time, overlapping and interweaving, with much pacing, gesticulating and shouting to overcome the music. Their content was a ceaseless barrage of the hippest drug jargon peppered with obscenities for exclamation marks. Their content was confusion and a lack of communication that was all the more pitiful since the participants remained totally unaware, each buzzing on solo into the elaborate realms of personal fantasy.

Near the center of the floor, a tall and heavy blond girl sat cross-legged, nearly in a yoga posture, playing aimlessly with a tattered deck of cards. Her ankle-length gypsy skirt was pulled up around her hips, leaving her long thick legs bare. She would lay the cards out and then shift them with her fingertips into different patterns as her lips moved soundlessly. Then she would scoop them up, shuffle and begin again.

She had taken no apparent notice of the newcomer's arrival, but presently she slid across the floor without rising until she was next to Jacobi. She had a full face with high cheekbones, but her mouth gaped black from missing teeth and her eyes gaped with premature aging. She placed one hand on Jacobi's leg, just above the knee.

"I'll tell your fortune, lover," she said with a slightly demented smile, a smile she repeated at odd intervals, without apparent cause or purpose, throughout their conversation. Afterward, long after he had forgotten the fortune she told him, Jacobi was to remember the strange juxtapositions of her face. For when she wasn't smiling, the demented look disappeared from her eyes to be replaced by an ineffable calm. As she spoke to him, her expression changed from one moment to the next, like the countryside on a day when the sun passes in and out of the clouds, from light to a thick umbra of shadow, from lucidity to madness.

Jacobi took the girl's hand in his and nodded his head in agreement.

"Me, too!" That from Michael, scooting around Jacobi and slipping into the same cross-legged posture as the girl.

"Together," she answered, once more smiling crookedly and crazily, holding up her free hand with the palm outward and the first two fingers pressed against one another in a Boy Scout salute. The incongruity of the act made Jacobi laugh.

With the same hand she took the deck from between her legs and began to slowly lay out the cards one at a time. The back of each card depicted two packs of Chesterfields, regular and king, overlapping on a black ground. Jacobi succumbed to the suggestion. He pulled a cigarette from his pack, but couldn't light it without letting go of the girl's hand. He nodded to

Michael, who took a cigarette for himself and lit both, nearly burning his fingers on the match flame before shaking it out.

The girl dealt twelve cards in three parallel rows and then began to turn them over one at a time. Her lips moved soundlessly again in some private incantation. The remainder of the deck balanced on the inside of her right thigh. The fifth card that she turned over was the joker. "Some leave the joker out," she said, looking up, "but it counts, too. Sometimes it's the most important card of all." The smile again, passing like a shadow.

When all of the cards had been turned over she paused for several seconds to study the array. Then freeing her hand from Jacobi's, she began the fortune, pointing to individual cards as she spoke. Jacobi noticed that the skin on the backs of her hands was dry, her nails unevenly chewed or broken away. Her voice had suddenly reduced itself to an affected sing-song, pausing on the off-beat syllables. Jacobi had to lean forward, straining to hear her. Still, much of what she said was lost in the music blasting from the stereo.

"You are the jack of spades," she began, designating that card on the bottom row. "...surrounded by all the suits and the joker...in a house of changes...no time...the salt of the earth and the salt of the sky...nothing the same...without family...the lightning journey...the joker is laughing and the queen of diamonds is love...the joker is a kind of madness you are drawn to and the queen is...the oppositions are many...a time for travel when the dark rains ring...a break with the past...movement beyond the self...the continent unravels..."

Michael broke in, shifting closer to the two of them. "Am I the joker?" he asked.

The girl's finger slid immediately to the top of the array, to the ace of diamonds, as if Michael's question had been anticipated. "Diamonds are wealth and the ace holds all." Michael frowned. "The ace...one...the single path for you alone..." her hand moving back to Jacobi's card, "...you touch each other from distance only...in conflict you move apart..."

then back to Michael's, "...there is bright hunger...forbidden taste...there is..." then hesitating and falling away from the cards and into her lap like empty puppets.

Just as she was about to speak again the stereo clicked to a halt and as if on cue, the door to the basement swung open banging against the wall, throwing a shaft of dusty daylight across the cards and over her bare thighs. For one frozen moment, as all eyes in the room swiveled toward him, Billie Raintree stood in dark silhouette against the brightness beyond, his features indistinguishable, legs and one arm akimbo like the stick limbs of an undersized scarecrow, beneath his other arm a bumpy package clutched tightly to his side. Then the door swung shut, the daylight retreated, and the moment ended as the scene in the apartment broke into an erratic flowing.

Billie's arrival was like the coming of a beggar king to his underground court. People moved. Some aimlessly, some tentatively approaching him, others retreating, still others entering from hidden alcoves and adjacent rooms. It was as if a score of orphan satellites had found their mother planet and were jostling into position for the proper orbits. Only the kid stretched on the floor by the speakers remained oblivious. His body kept thumping as if the music had never stopped, as if he were trying to fuck the threads out of the carpet.

Billie Raintree paused before his encroaching court of followers. In spite of his Indian surname, he looked about as much like an Indian as an alligator. Somewhere along the line he'd had a Sioux ancestor whose patronymic had held sway even though his bloodline had been lost, diluted by the interbreeding of an Anglo-Saxon deluge. Billie was short and scrawny with the skin of a sickly child, showing gray in the smoky gloom of the apartment and white with splotches of yellow in the daylight. He wore black boots, tight blue jeans, a shapeless and shedding brown sweater, and sunglasses to hide the bags under his eyes. His nose ran constantly, whether from an allergy, a perpetual cold, or an unending series of addictions and withdrawals, was unclear. A frail chain of wooden beads and a well-chewed toothpick, which Billie often shifted from one side of his mouth to the other with a quick movement of his tongue, completed his image.

Billie was both con man and patriarch, a breed as old as the hills yet now operating in the peculiar context of dealer and urban tribal chief. Being on the make, being the center of attention, was his way of life. He would never get rich because with enough money there was no longer a need to be on the make. He would never quit dealing because that was what gave him his power. His strange moral code or lack of one led him to be overly generous at times and totally untrustworthy at others.

The group gathered in his immediate vicinity melted back as Billie's gaze swept by them. His glance settled on Jacobi and Michael as the only newcomers. He lifted his sunglasses onto his forehead and shifted his toothpick, in perfect mimicry of a racetrack tout, to peer at them.

"Ah, satisfied customers returning once again," he announced to the room at large, "the sign of a fair and honest dealer." He was apparently unaware of Jacobi's two-year absence, or didn't consider it worth mentioning. His voice was loud and reedy. The circle around him undulated slightly, but nobody bothered to contradict him. "Step right this way, gentlemen, right this way," he chanted, bobbing past them and down the hall.

Leaving the girl to her cards, Michael and Jacobi rose to follow. The dark man with the turned-up sleeve hesitantly tailed the trio to Billie's doorway, but Billie, once inside the room, shut the door in the man's face.

"Leeches!" he declared. "I have to keep some of those bastards out of here or they'd steal me blind. They come here to score and then forget they ever had another home, and most of the time they don't have the money anyway. I'm the one who has to do all the hustling. I pay the rent. I buy the food. One of these days I'm going to kick the lot of them out. I've done it before and I can do it again." Billie's periodic "house cleanings" were notorious and temporary. Without his entourage he was lost.

Cushions and low tables. India-print bedspreads draping the walls. Candles and incense holders. This was the king's inviolate chamber. The girl with the curly brown hair lay stretched across the bed, idly puffing a joint. Billie slapped her on the thigh. She smiled wanly as he sat down beside her and dropped his package onto the table before him. "Shit, I've been working my ass off all day just to score one fuckin' kilo," he said, pulling off his boots and tossing them roughly into a corner.

He ripped the paper from the package to reveal a large greenish-brown brick. As he broke it in half there was a cracking of stems. A minor hail of seeds popped loose to roll crookedly across the floor. The stale air of the room was suddenly permeated with the fragrance of fresh sugar-cured grass. Michael inhaled loudly and smiled. Billie sniffed several times, wiped his nose on the back of his sweater arm, and went into his spiel.

"Well, there it is, gentlemen...fresh from the farm at twelve bucks a lid and they're all full ounces. I'll weigh it out right in front of you." As he talked he was busily and expertly breaking the key into smaller chunks. "I know twelve is a little steep but this stuff is pure dynamite, more colors than you can handle. Besides, when things get scarce, the price goes up, it's a simple law of supply and demand. Even at twelve it's cutting into my usual profit. Hey wait, tell you what, one for twelve or three for thirty. Would you believe that? Got to keep the market moving or everyone loses. Come on, Louise, baby," he gave the girl another whack, "roll the gentlemen a few samples so they can see what they're buying."

Jacobi watched the performance silently, aware that Billie's spontaneous palaver, the hype of the dealer, was beyond his capability. He was also aware that the very force of Billie's talk somehow extended his presence throughout the room and placed him in a superior position with regard to any transaction that was about to take place. Jacobi was wishing the acid were already sold, that he had Mulligan sitting by his side rather than Michael. He didn't have the inclination or the stamina for the game of haggling that was going to be necessary to extract the maximum price.

"We didn't come today to buy. We came to sell," Jacobi said, making it plural, putting Michael on his side with the hopes of gaining some leverage.

Billie's enthusiasm melted away immediately to be succeeded by a mask of cool reserve. He arched his narrow brows. "Ah, you've changed roles since I last saw you. Congratulations. Welcome to the profession." He offered each of them a loose handshake and smiled fulsomely. "What have you got to show me?"

"Acid," Jacobi answered. "A hundred caps at 350 micrograms a piece." Before leaving Michael's he had transferred a hundred caps of the acid to a new bottle—that still left him almost a hundred to deal on his own at a higher price than he could hope to extract from Billie. He hauled the bottle out and handed it across the table. Meanwhile the girl, oblivious to what was transpiring, had finished rolling the two joints. She laid them down next to the open key and stretched out in the bed behind Billie, who was examining the acid.

"You can get at least five dollars a piece for them," Jacobi said. "Give me three a piece and you can have the lot." He thought it was a fair offer that would save both time and hassle, but he wasn't about to get off that easily.

Billie chuckled, rolled his toothpick, wiped his nose, and the haggling began. Up and down. Round and around.

"I can't get five a cap for these unless I sell them one at a time."

"Well you can still make plenty selling in small quantities, batches of five or ten."

"But how can I be sure this is even acid."

"Take one. In an hour you'll not only be giving me my price but half your operation."

"I've dealt acid before, but none of it looked like this."

"It's from California. It's Owsley acid and if you don't know who Owsley is you shouldn't be dealing in the first place."

Up and down. Round and around. Billie talked away from the acid and circled back to it again. The telephone rang several times and he interrupted their dealing for short muffled conversations about other deals. So it went. Billie thriving on it. Jacobi bored and loathing it, but wanting as much money as he could get. The girl, Louise, stoned dull and drifting to sleep behind Billie on the bed. And sly Michael, mad poet and hunger artist, while the battle raged, silently proving his sleight of hand by pocketing the two sample joints she had rolled.

Jacobi understood that the quality of the acid had little to do with what was going on—nor would it when Billie sold it in turn. No matter how much he put it down now, once he were the dealer he would praise it like manna straight from heaven, prime nectar from the cups of the psychedelic gods. Put down, that's what the game was about, not only of the acid but of each other. That's what so many conversations were about, Jacobi thought, only here it was more blatant and there was something concrete at stake, the money and the dope. Whoever could win the game of putdown would win the deal. And in the end it had to be Billie Raintree. For verbal adroitness Jacobi could match and top him. He could stone him with words that he didn't know, put him down when he didn't even know he was being put down. But as far as endurance went, as far as the sheer weight and volume of bullshit one was willing to spew out, it was no contest, for Billie not only cared about the money and the dope, over and beyond that he cared about the game itself. He cared even more about the game. That's why he was a hustler and nothing else.

Eventually he beat Jacobi's price down to two hundred dollars for the lot. That was that. It was the same price Jacobi had paid Mulligan for the acid. He had traveled three thousand miles to sell half the seeds to his money tree at cost.

Billie unlocked a battered steamer trunk, bolted to the floor in one corner of the room. He extracted a rumpled wad of bills and counted out the two hundred in tens and twenties. Once the exchange was complete, he was all enthusiasm once again. He ushered Jacobi and Michael back through the gloom of the apartment.

"Come back, come back," he said, as he was closing the door behind them. "I'll have some fantastic Thai stick in a week or two." He wiped his nose and spat his toothpick into the street. Without its usual fixture, his face broke into an awkward and toothy grin. "If we keep going, maybe we'll turn the whole world on yet."

Bullshit, Jacobi screamed fiercely within his head, bullshit, bullshit!

Outside the sun was down and so was he. His stomach was turning slow flip-flops. It occurred to him that if acid were really a sacrament, as some claimed, he'd just been a party to blasphemy of the highest order.

10

THE READING at St. Marks was rigid and uptight and a travesty of what Jacobi expected a poetry reading to be. It was held in a side room on the ground floor of the church, an off-white windowless room with empty niches on its walls and its rear corners crowded with religious leftovers. A powdery plaster statue of the Virgin and the baby Christ, which had not been turned to the wall, observed the proceedings indifferently. Folding chairs had been arranged in slightly curving rows with space left for a center aisle. They were the same kind of chairs used in bridge tournaments. Jacobi concluded later that the atmosphere was not far removed from that of a bridge tournament, or perhaps an encounter group with all of the encounter covert rather than overt, but still with each member taking a turn at stage center, a single folding chair that faced the assemblage. There was no lectern or table for the poet, who was forced to stand or sit, poems in hand, with no barrier as a shield from the spectators. The lights were too bright and the room was hot and stuffy.

Jacobi and Michael arrived late, but the place was barely half full. A number of people stared at them as if they were disturbing a wake. Michael strolled in casually, coughing several times, clattering his chair around, bumming a cigarette from Jacobi and lighting it. A chorus of irate whispers circled the room before the poet who was reading continued. Michael joined the chorus by whispering, "The show is usually better than the poetry."

Although Michael often attended the readings at St. Marks, it was only because they were one of the few outlets he could find for his work. He viewed both readings and the people at them with the same disdain that flavored the rest of his views of the world. He remained a nebulous figure on the outskirts of the New York poetry scene, in part due to his asocial stance, in part because he couldn't stomach the pretension and hypocrisy involved in making it, i.e., getting published in a prestigious journal. In some circles he had gained the reputation of a talented young eccentric whose criticism was frank to the point of insult. In most circles, he had no reputation at all.

Michael was right about the show, Jacobi thought, it wasn't bad. At least there was variety, a veritable city circus, a collection of misfits, freaks and borderlines. What else could one expect the medium of poetry to attract in America in the nineteen-sixties?

Why this strange menagerie of all ages, shapes and sizes had come together on this particular night, in this particular place, drawn from the sweaty morass of summer flesh known as Manhattan, was unclear, but Jacobi was pretty sure it didn't have much to do with literary appreciation. Most of the participants seemed primarily interested in reading their own work, and a number left as soon as they had accomplished this. Polite though generous applause followed each performance, but there was no discussion of the poems. It was as if no one could be drawn away from the universe of their personal creations long enough to seriously consider anyone else's.

Michael was right about the show, Jacobi thought, but he seriously doubted if Michael realized that he was as much a part of the show as any of the rest, that they watched him as he watched them and were perhaps even more unkind in their judgments. For although there was no discussion, Jacobi felt as he observed the faces of those around him, that by the time each poet had completed his or her turn as the center of attention, said poet had been mentally dissected—clothes, face, flesh, bearing, intonation, style—by the other participants. A slip of the tongue or mispronunciation, a clumsy movement, a poorly chosen bit of apparel, and the appropriate number of points were lopped off one's running status total within the group. This was most apparent by the reception of nods and glances that greeted certain readers who served as objects of universal, though tacit, ridicule for the rest. All in all, the name of the game was poetry, but the game was something else again.

As for the poets: a plump and rubicund young man with a turned up mustache, baring is oh-so-existential despair in a pregnant monotone with a careful inch of silence between each word so his tumbling adjectives would not crowd one another; an old lesbian and her slightly younger mate, alternately chanting an apocalyptic sex epic to stoke the fires in their loins; a post-adolescent, the scourge of acne still fresh upon his face, trying to howl like Ginsberg; a dark "Michael" mumbling cryptic pronunciamentos into his beard while his eyes strayed up and back in a reverent gaze as if an angel were hovering over his shoulder; and of course, Michael himself, pacing back and forth in front of the room, never glancing up but only at the page in his hand, reading his cynical-mystical poetry as if it were a racing form of wisdom with the results wire-photoed. And so it went, reader upon reader, each strange in some particular way, and few that could pass down a street of Middletown, America without causing a few eyebrows to arch and the local constables to take note.

As Jacobi listened, various sensations percolated through his untuned ear. He became more convinced that if he wanted to write, it wasn't poetry. His mind wandered. It occurred to him that there had been more real poetry in the fortune the crazy girl at Billie Raintree's had told him. Maybe, though he hated to admit it, even more poetry in Billie.

Michael nudged his arm. "There's your soul mate," he whispered.

Jacobi looked up. The next moment he was aware of her and she filled his consciousness. She wore heels and a summery flower-print dress. As she approached the front of the room she walked close to the wall, almost shrinking into it. She moved gracefully, yet in every step she took he could detect a split second hesitation that had blended into her movement, causing the toes of each foot to turn slightly outward just before it was placed. In the midst of each stride she seemed to be questioning the direction that stride was taking her, and even further, to question the reason for all of the steps that had carried her to this one and the future steps that would inevitably propel her down an uncertain path that had somehow been triggered by the puzzle of the past. Then she came closer moving along the wall and he could see the wide blue of her eyes, the white flesh of her arms and the sheen of her blond hair swinging just below the neck, and all at once she had become a woman he wanted.

She was beautiful, no doubt of that, though hardly recognizable as the girl in the swing. It was difficult to say whether the years between the snapping of that picture and the picture Jacobi now saw had been kind or not. In terms of physical aging they had been, she could still pass for under thirty, but she was thinner and a certain hardening had taken place, a coat of sleekness and sophistication applied and polished year after year, coat after coat, until its very thickness, the nature of the materials composing it, and the drying process itself, had created a sparkling though brittle veneer through which she seemed to view a world gone slightly out of focus.

Jacobi sensed immediately that the proper blow—emotional, sexual, spiritual—could shatter that sleek mirror surface that reflected back the values and forms of the reality through which she moved, and then, once the broken fragments had been cleared away, reveal something more. The girl of the swing? Feminine warmth and maturity? A composite of his own anima figures? A mud gray swamp of confusion and despair? He didn't know but he wanted to find out. He wanted her body, her face and the touch of her long pale hands. He could imagine the cool flow of those hands as they moved across his flesh.

As he watched her sitting down in front of the room, rattling the sheets of poetry she held, crossing her legs and uncrossing them again in her nervousness, he felt his growing erection bent by and trying to grow through the cloth of his jeans.

Not a woman since Berkeley, he thought, not a woman since Berkeley and then some. Now would it be this woman? They had both written the same line of poetry. Or rather she had written it and he had dreamt it. Now that he had seen her, he couldn't get that out of his head. There was a connection between them, a point in space-time where their minds had dwelt together. Although she was unaware of his existence, already they were intimate in a sense.

She read a mixture of poems similar to her book, lyrical odes to the American spirit, the city and the country, the visions of Crane and Whitman fused by a feminine hand. She read, but he hardly listened. He was eyes rather than ears. So were the other males in the room if he'd bothered to notice, eyes like his own that ignored her words and turned inward to project their own images upon the image she presented to them. She read, making excuses for certain poems beforehand, reading in such a way as to play them down, self-criticism to deflect the criticism of others. Jacobi failed to notice. His sexual longing had become a prism through which his perceptions were funneled, distorted and magnified. He was thinking of the woman in his dream. Christine was that woman, the same whiteness, the same long limbs. Although a thousand women could have been that woman, he had decided then and there it was Christine Leslie and no other.

By the time Jacobi's awareness returned to center on the content of what Christine was reading, she was nearly through. She ended the last poem on a high note, her voice breaking slightly, so it was unclear whether or not she had actually finished. A moment of strained silence followed before she gathered her poems together and rose. Then she received the same applause as the others. Jacobi watched her walk hurriedly back to her seat, trying to catch her eyes. But she only looked downward at the floor, her gaze refusing to stray from the path ahead of her.

As the reading had progressed the air in the room had grown increasingly stuffy. Now the lack of oxygen coupled with the bright lights and heat had created a heavy headache atmosphere. When Michael nudged Jacobi again and tilted his head questioningly toward the door, Jacobi quickly nodded his agreement. Christine seemed out of reach for the moment and he'd already heard enough poetry to hold him until the rains came.

Even the New York air smelled fresh to them after the stuffy room and the poetry. Overhead the sky was a tenuous black, only a handful of stars showing, the rest banished by the city lights.

"Come on," Michael said, "let's get stoned. That scene was too heavy for me." He walked into the thick shrubbery in the shadow of St. Marks and Jacobi followed. Michael fumbled in his shirt pocket and brought out one of the joints he had lifted at Billie's.

"Hey, where did that come from?" Jacobi asked.

"Compliments of friend Billie," Michael replied.

Jacobi laughed with satisfaction. Michael handed him the joint and then struck a wooden match against the rough brick wall of the church. Jacobi leaned forward, cupping his hands around the flame. He lit the joint and pulled deeply.

They smoked in silence, passing the burning weed back and forth, their fingers touching in the dark so as not to drop it. The grass was harsh with a slightly oily aftertaste, almost like hash. When they had finished, Michael snubbed the roach out with thumb and forefinger and popped it into his mouth.

"How are you feeling?" he asked.

"I'm really blasted."

"Yeah, me too," Michael chuckled.

They walked out onto the East Village streets. The neighborhood was in the process of making the transition from tenement to bohemian tenement, in another few years the press would label it "hippie." As they walked, Jacobi experienced the sensation of a cool blast of air pressing against his forehead, blowing the thick overgrown hair back from his temples. He felt as if the air were passing through his skull, sweeping the accumulated cobwebs out of his brain. His body felt loose and natural. Suddenly he realized that he was grinning from ear to ear. He looked toward Michael and saw the same grin.

"Wow," Jacobi laughed, "what do you think this stuff was cured with? Opium?"

"No, man, it's just good boo," Michael answered.

"Boo, boo," said Jacobi.

"Boo, boo," laughed Michael.

"Good boo, good boo," Jacobi chanted, bouncing down the street in a rolling gait on the balls of his feet, beating his palms against his thighs in a syncopated rhythm that overcame the droning sing-song the reading had left sounding in his head. Michael quickened his steps to keep pace. They walked almost running, both of their faces fixed in wide smiles. The streets and buildings of the East Village rushed by and through their senses. Michael was thinking about taking acid again. Jacobi was thinking about Christine's body.

"You were wrong," he told Michael. "She's not too old. In fact, she really turns me on."

"Oh, yeah," Michael answered, so stoned on the night, the grass, the infinite reaches of time and possibility, he wasn't even listening.

11

BILLIE'S joint was either the strongest and strangest grass Jacobi had ever smoked, or it contained something more than just grass. His span of consciousness was reduced to the breadth and width of a flyspeck. His head was enveloped in a bubble that somehow muffled and distanced the impact of his sense impressions without reducing their clarity.

On top of this, their path was devious. They wandered in and out of and backtracked through assorted bookstores and newsstand cul-de-sacs in vain search for a paperback on Tantric yoga that Michael wanted to buy. Jacobi wondered how and from where Michael planned to materialize the money for the book if they did find it, and stoned as he was, he mentally noted that it wasn't going to be from his wallet. He found the idea somewhat unnerving that he was helping to support the errant heir, though still heir, to a banking fortune certainly in the neighborhood of several hundred thousand if not the magical million. If Michael wanted to be cast in the role of starving artist, he needed to find another patron to supply his needs, meager as they might be.

At one point in their circling, after the quest for the book had been abandoned or momentarily forgotten, Jacobi came down enough so that his faculty of memory was once again operative. They were in Washington Square. The night pulsed under the warm oppression of a typical New York City summer and the park was crowded with people, their faces anonymous in the dark above the shifting blotches of white shirts and pale pastel dresses. Michael was stretched on a bench trying to demonstrate a yoga exercise, while Jacobi was leaning against a nearby tree with his arms wrapped around the trunk, his hands moving slowly back and forth across the grainy damp bark. At the same time they were for some reason involved in a discussion about women and the seduction of women and Michael's supposedly voluntary celibacy.

"You can seduce a lot of women with just enough bravado and persistence," Jacobi was telling him.

Michael was lying on his back and had just swung his legs rigidly into the air until they were perpendicular to his body. "Bravado, bullshit!" he said. "You never got past Hemingway. It's simpler than that. What it amounts to is that you have to put up with a lot of crap and listen to their nonsense until three in the morning and then maybe, just maybe, if they're in the right mood, they'll let you slip it in." Michael's arms were still at his sides and his palms flat on the bench, but his legs had rotated another ninety degrees until his shinbones were around his nose and his toes touching the bench above his head. "This is great for the lower back," he announced from between his legs. "You should hold this for the count of ten and the knees have to be kept locked."

Jacobi let go of the tree and stared at the gymnastic curiosity. It had also attracted the momentary attention of several passersby. "Horny intellectuals always hate women," he stated in response to Michael's last comment, "unless they happen to be women themselves. Then they hate men."

In one fluid movement Michael poured himself out of the posture and was once again sitting upright on the bench. "Look, man, the way I see it is that most of what we call sex is no more than a superstructure built upon the reproductive urge…an extrapolation…much ado about nothing. It's not that I hate women. I just don't have any use for them."

Jacobi thought for a moment and decided that his friend could be right on both counts. Most women failed to interest Michael as people because of their inability to grasp the prime urgency of a metaphysical solution to life, a foundational *raison d'être* upon which to construct one's sand castles. At the same time, Michael seemed to have found enough workable sublimations for whatever sex drive he did feel. And as for himself, he was probably too caught up in what Michael thought of as a superstructure, too obsessed with the conquest and the chase.

"Now let's try hyperventilation. If you do this right, it's just like getting a hit."

Hyperventilation, from what Jacobi could make of it, consisted of breathing deeply and rhythmically until one got an overdose of oxygen. Nevertheless, it seemed to do the trick. The next thing he knew they were buzzing back down Fourth Street and into the East Village, higher than ever. Once more their path became devious. Eventually they ended up at the party that served as a sequel to the reading they had attended earlier—apparently Wednesday night was a double header for New York poetry aficionados—but not without incident. When Michael suggested returning to his apartment, Jacobi aptly responded: "That place is only going to bring us down. This is Manhattan. There must be something worth doing at night."

Michael's initial expression of offense at the comment faded to blankness before his eyes brightened and he thought of the party. There was always a party after the readings. "It has to be in one of three places," he stated with a forefinger raised next to his temple. He took off with Jacobi trailing after his billowing and straggly blond locks.

Strike One—A bare hallway which, though seemingly immaculate, was haunted by the faint reek of garbage and decaying fecal matter, and a blank door that echoed hollowly to their knocking.

Strike Two—The door swung open the three inches that the silver chain allowed and an aged Italian woman with cantaloupe skin looked out at them. "Go away," she said. "Go away. Go away." It sounded like the only English she knew. The frayed irises of her eyes looked like well-chewed olive pits.

Michael stepped back from the plate and scratched his head. "It's been a long time since I've been to one of the parties," he explained, "and the population of Manhattan is indeed a transient one. However, we've got one more chance. Let's take another swing through the West Village."

Home Run—They were not only out of the ballpark, they were in a different ballpark altogether. It was the party all right, and everything from the doorknob to the canapes spelled money, money gone slightly bohemian. Michael beamed and helped himself to a cracker topped with boiled egg and caviar.

It was a wide sunshine room—since it was night the sunshine was fluorescent and multicolored—with bay windows, skylights and a deep pile grass-green carpet. Shiny aluminum air conditioners hummed thoughtfully at several windows, banning the heat and humidity. Elaborate mobiles revolved in the shifting air currents. The paintings on the walls were actual paintings and the furniture consisted of various permutations and combinations of struts, slats, polished or roughhewn planks, and flamboyant swaths of cloth strung across twisted wire frames. At first glance, several of the chairs seemed to be either in the process of devouring their occupants or about to launch them into orbit. The party was already in full swing, but full swing for this crew consisted of a slow chug. The pale drinks bubbled their alcoholic fitness. All of the smoke was tobacco smoke and the talk was cocktail talk, with an occasional glissando of drunken laughter. With a few exceptions and additions, the assemblage comprised most of the older people who had been at the reading. One could tell, if not from their appearance—beards, berets, patterned stockings, cigarette holders, corduroy and sandals—then from their conversation—alienation, the bomb, Sartre, socialism, Communism, Cage, Pollock, Artaud—they were all trying on the label "bohemian" for one reason or another, some probably because it was in the family, others because nothing else seemed to fit. They were scattered around the room shifting like loose droplets of water, singly, in pairs, and even a few puddles.

At the center of a central mill pond, the largest cohesion, a rawboned dykish woman with a cropped mane of iron gray hair sat astride her lily pad, a green barstool, croakingly extolling the virtues of T.S. Eliot over Ezra Pound—"Pound's a fascist and you can see it in nearly everything he wrote!"—to an attentive tadpole audience. In spite of the air conditioning she was perspiring fiercely, and in spite of the perspiration and the fact that she was indoors she wore a pair of elbow-length dove gray gloves. Given the rather worn tenure of her diatribe, Jacobi couldn't understand the volume and avidity of her listeners until he later discovered that she was one of the major patrons for the group's publications.

By this time the high from Billie's supergrass was finally wearing thin. It had down shifted into a hunger phase, an unnatural hunger, a mad infant in the belly crying choruses and litanies of black gibberish hunger. Michael had joined the flow of the room, wandering about, drinking rapidly—to get high again—nibbling on whatever he considered edible—which seemed to vary with his mood; Jacobi even caught him downing a piece of German chocolate cake that night—and listening for a likely conversation to which he could adhere. Jacobi mustered as many hors d'oeuvres as he could upon the white square of a napkin—it was a question of placement and spread of the palm—and with a scotch and water in the other hand, settled back testily into one of the less voracious-looking chairs. Its mandibles closed around him and he felt it try a few tentative nips at the base of his spine before it decided to let him be.

Once his hunger and thirst had been satisfied, he began to look around the room, to observe "the show." It was what he did at most parties until he became stoned enough or drunk enough to join in the general inanity. After only a moment he spotted her, but not all at once: first the moving flowers of her dress, then her crossed legs, one hand with a cigarette, the other with a drink, finally her upturned face, thrown into level planes of lightness and shadow by the lighting of the room—clips and spots of her, like a paper doll, seen through the revolving bars of the cage of arms, legs and bodies winding back and forth between them. She was seated on a divan by the long window at the other end of the room, at the rim of a tepid puddle of four or five lanky, bespectacled and balding intellectuals, would-be Arthur Millers or prototypes for an aging Philip Roth. All of the group were standing except her and she didn't seem to be doing much talking, but still she maintained the appearance of rapt involvement in whatever was being said, listening and smoking intently. Periodically, she gave away her indifference with restless glances that trailed around the room, actually too rapid to really see anything—like Jacobi—and then fell back to snag on the lengthening ash of her cigarette or the dying bubbles in her drink. She looked as if she were waiting for some marauding bandit-knight to seize her and take her away from it all. Yet each time one of the speakers glanced down at her she would smile, cock her cigarette away from her face, and her eyes would fill with interest.

Michael, who was by now on his third or fourth predatory circle of the room and whose jaws were laboring joyfully upon whatever delicacy he had just billeted into his mouth, coasted to a stop next to the group and listened for several seconds. Then he started talking, so loudly that Jacobi could almost hear him from across the room. It was something about "stale collaborations" and "male combinations." Several of the Arthurs leaned away and looked at him askance, but Christine blipped with a muffled laugh, bending her head forward with one hand raised to her mouth so that a lock of blond hair, nearly lank, nearly boyish it was cut so short, fell across her face. As the Arthurs regrouped for their weighty parley, locking shoulders to exclude Michael—who was on his way to the bar for another drink in any case—she recovered her poise, shaking her hair back so the milky column of her throat, catching the light and revealed like a soft underbelly, flashed across the room. Uncrossing her legs and lifting them sideways onto the couch, she slid one palm up and down her stockinged calf. As Jacobi was to tell her later, at that instant he found her "infinitely desirable."

Michael dipped in his walk as he glided back past Jacobi. "Turn on the bravado, Papa Ernest," he nodded, then convulsed with merriment in appreciation of his own wit.

Bravado, thought Jacobi, persistence and bravado. Persistence was no problem—an ox could be persistent, a plodding turtle could make it up the Andes—but he evaluated his current bravado at a pretty low ebb, perhaps an all-time low, somewhere in the neighborhood of two hundred dollars. But it didn't really matter. He'd already decided that he was going to have her, if not this night then another. It was as plain as Pound's fascism, as clear as the water in his scotch. His dream had told him and the sixth sense below his belt was telling him, if not so esoterically, more immediately. The brain and the body, he thought, together as one.

He watched her, searching for points of vulnerability, trying to type her, trying to figure out how to come on. She was older than any woman he'd been with. She was the first woman; the others had been girls. He asked himself, "How do you come on to a woman over thirty?" and the answer came back, "Just like any other woman." To have her he would play the necessary game. If it was to be as Michael saw it, nonsense until three a.m. and then slip it in, he'd travel the turns and tedium of that route. Like Mulligan, he would try on the appropriate role, whatever fit the moment. Then once their bodies had come together he could reveal himself inch by inch, like slowly pulling back the covers from a bed to show that the sheets are only part satin and there are always a few pernicious crumbs from past cracker feasts that one can never sweep away.

The food that Jacobi consumed should have completed his descent from the grass. He should have been yawning and stretching, ready to curl into a dreamless sleep. But now the scotch coupled with his sexual excitation had caught and lifted the tail end of his high. And the more he drank...and the more he thought about Christine...the steadier and surer he seemed to become. Someone had dimmed the lights but what was happening around him only became clearer. He had sprouted antennae that now reached into every conversation. His vision was without periphery, the full three hundred and sixty degrees. He was giving himself delusions of grandeur so he would have the confidence to seduce her.

Despite the liquid and liquor composition of the party, despite the constant motion, the scene was not one of any real flux. The normal observer could have exhausted its variety in fifteen minutes, just in time for a commercial break. In contrast, Jacobi's alcoholic-erotic-hallucinogenic awareness was perceiving more all the time, additional aspects with every moment, stripping away layer after layer to the bare stagehand reality beneath. Words sprayed him like an hail, interspersed with the tepid cocktail lounge jazz vine-creeping from concealed speakers.

"...well, how do they put the silicon in anyway?...and afterwards she started to sing "Just Wild About Harry." Now that's what I call a sense of humor...we actually spent most of the time in Venice and Rome. Myself, I wanted to get out into the countryside, see the real Italy...I wouldn't let them stick a needle like that into me, not on your life...take Negroes, for instance, they don't have any existential worries...so what if the "cat" poems are trivial, they're still delightful, a nice touch of lightness to make up for dreary *Prufrock*...nobody ever told me that she was a lesbian...there's a lot we don't tell you darling...(pickled laughter)...who says it causes cancer?...gin and tonic...rum and coke...Stan Getz...you put the lentils in first...even Mailer would make a better president..."

The mobiles tinkled. The stereo, unnoticed or ignored, repeated the last record. Two escaped olives and a maraschino cherry convened a stolid tête-à-tête-à-tête beneath a blue glass coffeeless coffee table. The woman with the gray gloves kept playing with the pearls strung doubly around her neck. She was drinking as fervidly as she was talking and the more she drank the more she sweated, yet still she refused to take off her gloves. By the bar an overripe redhead had given up on drinking herself into stuporous oblivion and was settling for suspended animation. A man with a pear-shaped head and a shoeblack mustache, equally bilious, was cooing omnivorously at the back of her head. Michael remained the most incongruous element in attendance. He continued his erratic circling of the room, involving himself in quixotic sorties with this group or that individual and drinking at a pace that outdid Jacobi.

But all of this was irrelevant, incidental seasonings in the potpourri. Christine was the main ingredient and that was where

Jacobi's attention remained, expanding on her gestures and mannerisms, drawing clues from which he could create cerebral journeys of foregone conclusion until he had her pegged, pared, trisected by a glossy centerfold and all but supine. The spot next to her on the couch stayed vacant. Still, he kept expecting it to be filled by some lean and square-jawed leading man, though properly cultured—a Mel Ferrer type—who would pop out of the background to supersede the glib, bookish coterie that surrounded her, who would provide a temporary obstacle that would tantalizingly postpone Jacobi's inevitable possession. But her lover, if there was one, had to be marked absent. Each time she finished her drink, she had to wait for one of the attendant and more attentive Arthurs to politely trot to the bar and back, ice cubes jiggling.

She smoked too much and she didn't drink enough—not for Jacobi's purposes. As for himself, after the second scotch he switched to bourbon and then started alternating. He lost track of the count first and the alternations second. The whiskey started singing in his blood. The blood began singing in his ears—Handel's *Hallelujah Chorus* on the left channel and *The Bacchanal* from *Samson and Delilah* on the right, with John Handy's *Spanish Lady* phasing in and out between, though that may have been on the stereo—drowning out the fourteenth round of the Pound-Eliot marathon, increasingly bellicose but as bloodless as ever. His vision was Leica-clear and steady as a tripod, with certain images so intense that they lodged a dull violet pastille of pain at the bridge of his nose that faded to lavender-gray as it dissolved through his forehead and down cross his temples. Suddenly he noticed that the room was less crowded. Three of Christine's group had disappeared—or perhaps had merely been refracted into another lens—and all that remained of the fourth was a reduced wavering shadow upon the rug that could have been mistaken for a poorly cleansed wine stain. Christine was left stranded, a wilting wallflower who couldn't leave now because there was no one to whom she could announce her departure or blow a parting kiss.

Jacobi realized that if he were going to jump, now was the time to do it. He decided to jump. He jumped.

Almost too far.

Past the slowly twirling mobiles and the iron-gray dowager with Christine and the couch, slightly atilt, rising toward him along with the picture window and its speckled twinkling view of the city's lights, star light star bright, spread out behind her—he hadn't realized they were so high, so far—and thinking momentarily that he would just keep sailing, past leggy Christine, osmosis through the glass and out over the city, a biped balloon treading the thick night air, a blot of humankind shrinking smaller and smaller in the distance of his mind's eye.

Somehow, in time, he rediscovered gravity and traction in the grassy pile of the carpet.

"Hullo," he articulated.

"Hello."

"*Bonsoir,*" he added.

Looking up at him she drew back her shoulders, inclined her head in the opposite direction to the pitch of the room. Her nose was slightly retroussé, the cheekbones high, the blue eye shadow no bluer than her eyes. Two halves of a smile playing at the corners of her mouth met in the curl of her upper lip. "*Bonsoir.*"

"*Buenos dias.*"

"*Buenos dias.*"

"*Kali spera.*" That one stopped her. The lean leading man pounced-toppled into the vacancy on the couch. "You're looking beautiful, tonight," he said. "Have you got an extra cigarette?"

After that it was easy, almost too easy. Once they started talking their sentences fit together like puzzle pieces, an end-to-end puzzle that stretched winding to her bedroom like a verbal yellow brick road. The momentum of their conversation wove a wall around them that turned the rest of the party into pure backdrop.

"You have a contagious grin," she told him, grinning.

"I know," he answered, cupping a hand across his mouth. "I caught it from a friend."

With the proper degree (acute) of ceremony he told her about the coincidence in their line of poetry. Borrowing her blue-green fountain pen he wrote the line out on a party napkin. When she handed him the pen he saw that her wrists were as slender as those of the first girl he'd taken out in high school, as delicate as those of a child. In the crisscross fibered texture of the napkin the ink ran and the lines of the individual letters began to form tiny rivers: it wasn't just the misperception of his drunken vision. Christine responded to the coincidence with the appropriate degree (oblique) of interest, leaning forward to read the lines aloud with a soft expletive of delight.

He told her: "I liked your book."

"Really, I'm flattered," she answered, looking flattered, even flushing a little along the ledge of the cheekbones. God, Jacobi thought, if only the party retreated a little farther, over the hill or across the river and into the trees, he could take her there and then, right on the couch.

He lit *her* cigarettes, both for her and for himself. He got her a fresh drink, and another, and a third. Break down the barriers, he thought, loosen both mouths at once.

She began talking poetry to him. Duncan, Ginsberg, Spicer, Lamantia. Sonnets and sestinas. She was serious about the stuff, no doubt of that. He nodded agreement, bluffing, drawing her out, lost in a lyrical forest of arcana, but still managing to keep time to the iambic pentameter of her swinging leg and the trochee of her pulsing throat.

After that it was almost too easy, but still he might not have made it if it hadn't been for the joint.

"It's getting late," she said, attempting to summon a yawn that remained comfortably encamped at the back of her jaw. "I have to be getting home." She faked it, arching her back, long fingers tapping her lips.

Might he accompany her? An element of protection? Not safe at this late hour—whatever hour it was—for lovely ladies on the Manhattan streets. Rapers and robbers and muggers and things that go bump in the night.

"But of course," she accepted—Was her smile mischievous, naive, or merely drunken?—but first she had to get her wrap. He had to say good-bye to a friend. All right? All right. High road and low road and meet you at the door.

Jacobi ferreted out Michael in the hallway on his way back from the bathroom. "Hey, man," he said quickly, "let me have that other joint."

"What joint?" Michael inquired, eyes widening. He was very drunk and very pleased with himself. In the course of the evening he'd managed to put on, exasperate, and alienate at least half of the people there. A few brother souls as aberrant as himself had found him amusing and even joined in his gaming.

"You know what joint," Jacobi whisper-shouted. "That chick at Billie's rolled two."

Michael blinked in the spray. "And I'm the one who copped both of them," he stated, affecting a slight upper-caste British accent.

Just then, accompanied by the gurgling of water, the bathroom door swung open. Michael's face was spotlighted by the illumination that coursed into the dark hallway—red-rimmed eyes, damp nostrils, the colorless flesh through the transparency of his beard, pink ears and lips. Jacobi looked down, repulsed, into the countenance of a small, nearly hairless rodent.

With a forearm he pushed Michael flat against the wall as a pair of dove gray gloves swung smartly past them. "And you've got a gram of hash back at your place and two caps of my acid on account," he said, reaching to extract the joint from Michael's shirt pocket and transfer it to his own. "Catch you later, man."

Jacobi rushed to the door in time to meet Christine, while Michael remained behind, more than a bit bemused, his weight still resting against the wall where Jacobi had placed it.

It *was* late and the streets were for the most part deserted and silent. Traffic lights blinked an indifferent yellow and reality, daytime reality, played possum until dawn in the shadows. In front of a shuttered cafe a fat man in a grease-spattered apron was washing down the sidewalk. The hose he was using coiled and glistened like a black snake, and the wetted pavement was still warm enough to erect a turret of gauzy steam upon the city cement. The falling droplets were cool against their flushed faces and the backs of their necks.

They walked hand in hand, or with his arm around her waist. He knew it was corny, but it was right. Her in the flower-print dress, him in his jeans and blue work shirt. He was the youngest son of a rich wheat farmer and she was the beautiful daughter of the publisher of the hometown gazette. All they needed were front lawns, elm trees and slamming screen doors to complete the portrait of middle America. Even the incongruity of the joint seemed right when he pulled it out.

A touch of the inevitable future, Jacobi thought.

He lit up and offered it to Christine. Her perfect forehead wrinkled in puzzlement before it registered upon her what it was, then she shook her head. But when he put his arm back around her and they kept walking and he tried her again a block later she accepted, almost absentmindedly, as if she had forgotten her initial refusal. After riding in Michael's pocket all evening the joint wasn't as full as it had been, but it seemed just as potent. In the few puffs that it offered each of them their senses were radically altered. The silent city came back to life for them in a hundred subtle ways. Their bodies leaned more closely together. If they had been an inch more stoned, even a millimeter, instead of supporting one another they would have been staggering together, hauled in as a public nuisance by some cruising bored cop.

Jacobi had passed through such a gamut of emotions and sensations that evening since leaving Michael's—the dealing at Billie's, the reading, the crazy circle-walking with Michael, the false parties, the real party and Christine, the joint the scotch the bourbon and now the other joint—he was now passively accepting whatever trip his consciousness laid upon him. He was no longer trying to sift the real from the unreal, and that very distinction had grown increasingly vague in his mind. After the second joint, his walk with Christine reminded him of his last walk with Mulligan, their acid walk together, when with each sidewalk square the two of them became inseparably locked for all of time in intense moments of mute rapport. Only with a woman the connection was in some ways more complete. For not only did their expressions and gestures speak to one another, their bodies moving against one another spoke, their softly groping hands upon one another's sides—for now Christine's arm was around his waist too—traced tactile codes of decipherable intent.

They walked down store-lined streets, deserted and brightly lit, past files of mannequins who eyed one another silently from window to window, who here or there had been dismembered of an arm or leg but whose spotless clothes remained in place, guarding a neuter and plaster of Paris sexuality. They walked down darker residential streets where there were only the street lamps, the lights of passing cars, the occasional beacon of an illuminated window shade or drapery behind which voices mumbled unintelligibly or a radio cried, keeping back the night.

As they moved from the circular domain of one streetlight to the next, they watched their shadows, the ones growing taller in front of them, and then looking over their shoulders to the ones shrinking smaller behind. Each time their passage was momentary and ever lasting, and by the time they'd traversed it the nature of light itself seemed to have changed in character. Thus Jacobi assigned each street lamp an individual identity. One was an orchid of phosphorescent yellow, one an Impressionistic dab and swirl of Van Gogh yellow, one a golden bread crust yellow—and all were the yellow bricks in the road that led to Christine's building, up her front steps, to her door.

She turned to face him, falling back against the wall of dark stone that made up the archway. The grass had surrounded her in a sweet and vapid haze. She had fallen through a hole in time, and then another. She was back in front of the shuttered restaurant, a princess entrapped in the turret of mist. She was in Paris, barely twenty, slightly mad, slightly in love.

Jacobi leaned toward her, one hand upon the wall. With her heels on she was taller than Michael. He kissed her and her mouth tasted of scotch, not stale scotch leftover from the party, but as if she had just taken a drink and it was still burning upon her lips. The effect upon him was more immediately intoxicating than any alcohol. The flush came back to his face, flooded down in a wave of warmth across his chest, belly and thighs. He wanted her with a physical ache that extended beyond the borders of sexuality. His lips moved across her cheek, the fragrance of almonds and sugar, flashback to a childhood memory, a trip to the corner store, his fist filled with more pennies than he could count. His tongue brushed the down at her temple, dampened a soft strand of hair next to her ear. He bent lower, reaching for the vulnerable throat.

"I have to be going in," she said, "to bed," half-whisper, her palms pressing him back, one on each side of his chest.

"I know," he answered.

She managed to find her keys and get the door open with her back to him, his arms around her waist, his nose burrowing in the straight falling hair and rubbing the nape of her neck. With one leg reaching into the hall, her hip holding the weight of the door, "No," she said, "I can't," sighing, head back, face turned up for a final kiss, the lips, the blue eyelids, almonds and sugar, her throat now unshielded and yielding.

On the way up the stairs he held her tightly. They locked again briefly on the second landing and longer outside the door to her apartment, her tongue now answering his sporadically until they were both feverish. "*Mon cheri,*" she manufactured out of her past. "*Mon petite cheri, mon cheri.*" After one futile attempt she gave him her keys and he opened the door. Symbolic of the final surrender, Jacobi thought. Once inside she weaved past him and turned, slightly off balance. The room was still dark except for the light from the hall. "Would you like some coffee?" she asked, at this last moment reverting to the pretense that he was a platonic caller, a friend of the non-existent family, that they were going to have a chat about poetry or politics or encyclopedias, that they were about something other than what they were really about.

"No, just you," he told her as simply as he could, closing the door in time to catch her as her balance did go off and she toppled forward into his arms.

Jacobi reached behind Christine's legs and lifted her against his chest. Her hands curled about his neck, twining in his hair. As his eyes adjusted to the faint illumination cast by the city lights through the high windows, Jacobi could make out the bed at the far end of the room. He carried her the length of the studio, her breath warm upon his throat, her weight within his arms. He laid her across the bed and began to undress her. The wrap unwrapped. The dress unzipped. The shoes sliding off and falling to the floor. The blue stockings unclipped and rolled down the length of her legs, his lips impatient and already upon her thighs.

Christine didn't resist. She was far less aware of what was happening than Jacobi realized. What his ego took for the passivity of her surrender was merely helplessness. The tingling with which Billie's grass had invaded her walking and vertical body had changed to numbness, withdrawal, nearly anesthesia, now that she was horizontal and relaxed. Jacobi was a male form moving above her. He was whomever she thought he was. One minute Leonard, the next Tony, in another instant her black man or the cleft-chinned obstetrician who had assisted in the delivery of her third child. Christine couldn't move even if she'd wanted to. Her limbs were strapped to the bed, encased in bindings of surgical cotton. She was as dismembered as the store-window dummies. Decapitated, too! Broken in half. There was a body on the bed and there were strange hands moving over it, while her head had flown away to perch on the edge of the bookshelf, a curious, but removed and sleepy, barn owl. She knew that body, but she couldn't quite make the connection as to whose body it was. It was impossible to tell in the dark. Was it her mother? Her daughter? Her roommate from college? Was it the celebrated body of some famous movie actress. Was she watching an erotic underground film or had the laws of censorship finally blown away like dry leaves?

Once Christine was naked, Jacobi quickly undressed himself and turned back the covers. She lay motionless beneath his touch, white on white against the sheet, a perfectly preserved alabaster frieze uncovered at the third level of the Assyrian excavations. He had no doubt that she was the woman of his dream. *They were both naked and he pressed himself against the long-limbed warmth of her body. Their separate forms were indistinct, their pores merged, their outlines overlapped. She spoke to him in a foreign tongue and he did not know the words, but still he knew their meaning.* But no, there was only silence. There was only the chill and immobility of marble in her flesh. The long pale hands which he now kissed and pressed between his own were cooler than he could have ever imagined.

For a reason he didn't bother to fathom, Jacobi was repulsed and yet excited all the more. In any case, he hadn't brought her this far to succumb to such a very literal frigidity.

After that it wasn't easy, it wasn't easy at all.

He went to work on her with all that he knew, everything he had—hands, fingers, lips, teeth, tongue. He tried on the role that fit the moment, no longer seducer but sorcerer. Flesh became time and touch became its flow. Hours transpired in the space of minutes. Movement was the sign of the coming resurrection, the end of history. He forced open her pliant but motionless lips with his own and his tongue worked like a soft spade, pressing on the ridge behind her teeth, across the roof of her mouth, pushing against her tongue until she had to push back just to breath. A cold wind blew through the apartment, down from the mountains, to confront a hot sirocco sweeping in off the plains. His hands were upon her slack breasts, thumbs and fingers pinching the nipples until they were as solid and erect as he was. The room became windless, the air as still and sticky as that of forest before a storm. Jacobi bit her stomach, the taut flesh at her hip bone, his tongue and teeth moved into the dark shading that gave the humanity of the frieze away, then back to her mouth to impregnate her with her own juices. A ruffled bird, rudely called back from approaching slumber, watched the one-way fury upon the bed with wide unblinking eyes from the safety of its perch among the books. And somewhere, somewhen, from one chill moment to the next, as his fingers spread the lips of her cunt or his tongue, unwittingly in the dark, rushed downstream along the icy rivers at her throat, her body began to respond. Her legs moved, knees rising upward in the bed, coming together, her thighs closed and rubbed upon his moving hand. Her body gave voice to her throat, vaporous sighs lacking the identity of consciousness. Her hands, circulation magically restored, slide across his shoulders, around his neck, pulling his head down to a tongue which suddenly sought his own. Her body began to offer up its long-limbed warmth, while unnoticed by Jacobi a frantic bird with blazing wings circled above the bed, fled back to the bookcase, then to the bed, back and forth, back and forth, a feathered and flailing yo-yo. And her body was coming almost before he was inside her, and then he was, deep within, the deepest in years except for foreign objects of surreptitious self-excitation, driving at ground zero, so deep that it hurt, like his teeth biting at her neck and shoulders, and her body was coming, he could feel her thighs tighten, the acceleration of the spasms closing upon his cock, and in the midst of it, between the pleasure and the pain, the frantic bird could flee no longer and her voice, Christine's voice, broke crying from her throat, and her eyes were open and she recognized him, not Leonard or Tony or any other phantom from the past annals of her personal history, but for who he was, a man in the present, a man she wanted and was giving herself to, and she came back to him fully awake and aware, beyond the alcohol, beyond the dope, beyond her own pretension that she could not be picked up by a stranger at a party and taken home and to bed.

Then she was moving beneath him consciously, fucking for the sheer joy of it, no longer a sophisticated New York divorcee, no longer the brittle veneer, but an awareness broken down to pure excitation, an animal hungry to mate, making love with the full energy of her being in a way she'd forgotten was possible.

And now that she had let go, Jacobi could too. Before he had been fucking her with his ego. Now he gave himself to the act. She became the driving force in their coupling and he was the one along for the ride, stunned by the force of her passion, surrendering his body to hers. As they rocked together she bruised her lips on his cheeks and forehead. Her teeth found his flesh again and again. Her cheeks were rubbed raw by the stubble of his beard. Her ivory fingers raked the dark, muscled earth of his back, her thighs were a bracelet of white silver sliding across his hips. She spoke his name over and over, "David...David ...David!" somehow stressing a different syllable each time although there were only two. And oh God, she was coming again, so soon, crying out again, incoherently...

One floor below and thirty-odd feet away, the highest pitch of her screaming nearly woke Daniel Mekas, who had fallen asleep in bed while watching a late movie. The movie was over and the station had signed off for the night. The blank tv screen had lost its horizontal hold and was casting the otherwise lightless room in a slow strobe. As Mekas turned in his sleep, gently massaging the remote control unit, the rate of the strobing increased imperceptibly. Several miles to the north in uptown Manhattan, a pair of wrinkled and age-spotted hands, at last minus their dove gray gloves, kneaded the docile and well-recompensed flesh of a nineteen-year-old girl-boy. About the same distance south, on Atlantic street in Brooklyn Heights, Linda Bernstein, painter and at least for the moment not-so-horny sculptor, slept soundly and with satisfaction, her arms around a not dissimilar though considerably more virile youth. Farther to the east, at his apartment in Queens, Tony Bosano had passed out alone but for the company of an empty bottle. If the neighborhood bar had been open, he might have still been drinking. Tony's binges were few and far between, but they were long ones. Swinging back to the Village, just a few blocks from our lovers, Billie Raintree was on top of dull Louise and fucking in silent monotony with a rhythm that did not change. It didn't really matter since she was for the most part asleep. In the next room, still abundantly crowded, a vacant-eyed blond girl kept laying out a deck of cards again and again, searching for the fortuitous combination that would predict her ascension to the role of royal lady of the court. Stretching far to the north, over two hundred miles to the relative coolness of a Cape Cod summer night, three rich children, each with a room of their own, turned fitfully and simultaneously in their sleep. Their father was away on a business trip. Their mother had left them some time ago. And falling again to Manhattan, once more uptown but this time on the rim of Harlem, an amber-eyed girl, younger than Jacobi, who looked Spanish but was actually Filipino, slept as alone as she could in her family's three-room, eight-occupant tenement apartment. And reaching across the width of the continent, three thousand miles to the pioneer West, to the college city-town of Berkeley,

California, where, although it was several hours earlier, Dennis Patrick Mulligan, a faint smile clinging to his lips, was already fast asleep after coming into his fleshy palm amidst a series of well-wrought Amazonian fantasies.

And one last time to the east, to the depths of the East Village, to Michael Shawtry—altered by his grandfather from the German "Von Shauter"—who walked toward the East River with his sandals slapping next-to-noiselessly on the cement. Michael chose the most dimly lit streets for his passage, and from a distance, because of his black sweater, he appeared as a bodiless form, white pants and bare blond head. When he reached the river he saw that the lights on the farther shore were invisible. A summer fog had gathered over the water, creeping in on little cat's feet. All over the city people cared less and less about poetry. And back in the West Village, just off MacDougal Street and three floors up, David Jacobi, figuratively speaking, released nearly a month's worth of celibacy into Christine Leslie's sated eggshell belly.

12

MORNING after the make. Still early. The partially open curtain drops a bar of sunlight slantwise across the shadow covering their bodies, along his chest and over her belly and touching the fingertips of her open palm before it is cut off by the bulk of the bed shadow to reappear running along the carpet and up the wall where it catches the burnished edge of a heater grill and cuts a Braque print in half, still another plane amidst the cascading cubes. The bar of light shifts with the rising sun, its angle slipping a few degrees to the acute, alive with twirling dust motes. It warms first her right nipple, then her left, sparkles to spun gold the blond hair on her forearms, bends around his chin and over his high cheekbones, carries through the translucency of his eyelids to the slumbering cornea to illuminate the landscape of his dreams. His eyes click open, blank with the vacancy of sleep. He closes them again, rolls onto his belly, his cock flopping upward, pressed between belly and bed by the weight of his body, a slow erection growing. His hand slides along her side, one, two, three, over the ribs. She dreams she is being tickled by a plumed bird, brilliant colors, red, yellow, green, a jungle parrot prancing across her stomach, nibbling at her cunt, its tail feathers brushing along her ribs. She laughs in her sleep, mumbles a blurred chuckle to the room, and smiles with lips compressed and eyes still closed.

Jacobi free-falls back into the dream that the moving sun has disrupted. *He is in the park, not any particular park but a park of rolling tree-scattered vistas and neatly tended lawns. Slender summer girls in white net dresses stroll in groups, smiling, talking in low voices, laughing with one another. Christine is among them, first with one group, then another, always slimmer and more beautiful than any of the rest, always beyond his reach. As she comes closer he can see that her long fingers are playing with a string of pearls around her neck, twirling, moving with the speed and complexity of a stitching machine, too fast for his eyes to follow. Her face radiates the heat of the sun. At her temples the blond hairs shimmer. Her tongue licks beaded perspiration from her upper lip, wide eyes flash in every direction, blindly, through him as if he were not there. "You're looking beautiful, today." "Thank you." You're looking lovely, today." Thank you." You're looking beautiful today." "Thank you."*

"Good morning."

"Hmmnn."

"Good morning, sleepy," she says, sliding her body against his.

"Morning," Jacobi grunts, rolling to face her. He encircles her waist and brings their bodies together, lips touching her shoulder. Thus they lie momentarily as he drifts back into sleep.

Melange of desert sun, burning rocks and desert sand. And white sand and flat French beaches. Hot sand. Fitzgerald in white pants and Zelda the emasculator. Stiletto heels and well-shaped calves. She sips martinis very dry and laughs at the pilgarlic. Proper parties. Proper teases. Quite untouchable. Sleek bare arms screaming: "Touch me!"

He opens his eyes again as he feels her hands on his cock pulling him to wakefulness. He pushes her back in the bed and leans over her, running his hands across her breasts, slowly up and down the length of her body. She is thin and the bones are too prominent, but her skin is smooth and fresh as that of a young girl. His lips begin moving down her side, over hips and thighs, pressing into the smooth flesh. His tongue tastes her skin. He inhales her fragrance. There is a small quarter-moon scar on the inside of her right thigh, just above the knee. She has Roman feet, toes straight and narrow with the second longer than the first. The wiry forest of her pubic hair thins to fine down several inches below the navel.

He plants kisses up and down her body until she is restless with excitement and squirming beneath his touch.

"I want you," she whispers wetly.

Jacobi rises and crosses to the window. He pulls the drapes open so that her body is now completely immersed in sunlight. She closes her eyes against the brightness, stretching her limbs in the sudden blanket of warmth. He stands at the foot of the bed, his eyes full with her whiteness.

"Come here," Christine tells him, "I want you!" Her voice from deep within her throat, her arms reaching out.

He laughs, coming down on top of her and into her arms, his cock falling sideways across her hip bone, then moving dead center, its head nestling in the hairs of her cunt. His palms press against her back, pressing them together. He kisses her shoulders and arms. He licks the column of her neck and becomes conscious of the blue veins for the first time. Christine laughs with unconstrained delight, reaching down and pulling him into her. Already she is wet and warm, ready to take all of him. She gasps once as he enters, then expels her breath in short explosive sighs as he begins moving within her. He enters at different angles, but maintains a steady beat of fucking. *He explores all the corners, charts the reefs and shoals. With astrolabe and compass he maps out the China and South Seas of her cunt, computes a set of tables on the local tides. He stations troops in the Lower Sudan, sets up trade routes to Nairobi, sends a sampling of spices to the Duchess of Vichy, constructs a hydroelectric dam across the Ganges and illuminates the Black Hole of Calcutta.* With the speed of his movement he builds her toward climax, then moving slowly, with conscious intent, he brings her back down, and finally up again, faster and faster until she begins to cry out YES DAMN IT YES with her arms flung back on the sheets OH YES her thighs locking about his hips YES her body twisting ten directions at once as his motion suddenly halts poised deep within her and he comes and pulses and comes nearly matching her cries with his own...and falls forward against her shaking chest...letting his cock shrink slowly smaller within the closing walls of her cunt...before rolling off and onto his back...and onto his side and away from her.

Afterwards, as always, Jacobi feels like being alone. All of the women he'd been with were just the opposite. He vaguely remembers Christine holding him last night as he drifted off to sleep, and he expects the same from her now. He hears the bedsprings creaking with her movement. He expects her arms to envelope him any second. Her lips brush against his shoulder. And then she is up and disappearing into the bathroom.

Jacobi exhales a sigh of relief. He is lying with eyes closed, shoulders hunched, knees drawn up and chin tucked, nearly a fetal ball. He is drifting off again…or at least trying to. An older woman, he thinks, an independent woman. Watch out, he dream-thinks, she'll come back and drop *me into her womb. Close and lock the zipper so I can't escape. Complete blackness inside. Floating as in space. Coordinates unknown since there are no stars to mark them by. A scarred quarter moon rises in the east, though it could just as easily be north, south or west. Not a silver moon, or even yellow, but a chunky pomegranate slice pocked with craters from edge to glowing edge. By its light he sails through banks of steamy clouds, above a dream landscape both familiar and dream strange. Beneath him the countryside unravels, a patchwork of savannas and tropical forests, a rugged crosshatch of rivers and winding roads, a land of cities illuminated by the lights of dusk. The cities do not lie in circular clumpings but spiral out at random across the hills and forest like the arms of mutated starfish. The roads do not connect to one another or to the cities but dead end in the middle of the country or turn back to curl upon themselves.* Christine comes out of the bathroom, but makes no attempt to drop him into her womb. He hears her bare feet padding across the floor—wood, carpet, wood—the clicking of wooden beads. *He is stranded on a dark jungle highway, thumb hitched in an oppressive jungle wind. Beyond the gravel borders of the road he can hear animals moving through the brush, large animals. And beyond that, beyond his reach, the rush and rumble of a river. The moon slips higher, cycling through its phases as it rises—from half to gibbous to whole, and back to new to begin again. Even in its fullest phase it remains a faceless and indecipherable moon. He stands upon the deserted highway, bathed over and again in the changing fractions of its bloody light. His arm grows tired and numb. The night continues to reign.* Again he hears the clicking of beads. *The moon continues to cycle. Nine months go by before he hitches a ride with a gnarled and noxious little man, full of chewing gum and dirty rhymes. He is a licensed plumber with a brand new Continental. They ride out in style, headlights on high, air conditioner blasting, the stereo crooning crescendo love songs, left front whitewall edging the broken yellow line.* He feels her weight upon the bed. *The attending physician fills the tanks, checks the oil, cleans the windows, yanks Jacobi out by the collar and tosses him aside as if he were a clot of placental smudge. It is his fourteenth straight still birth. He prescribes stimulants, depressants, hallucinogens, every kind of sex, and breast feeding by all means.*

Jacobi opens his eyes. Christine is sitting beside him, sipping a glass of orange juice and holding another one out for him. A blue satin robe covers her body. As he rolls onto his back and reaches for the juice he becomes conscious of his nakedness and pulls the covers up about his waist. He gulps thankfully, realizing he is dehydrated, thus his dreams of the heat. Amazingly enough, he feels no trace of a hangover. The exertions of their sex have purged the night's poisons from his system.

When he has finished drinking he sets the glass on the nightstand. "Thanks," he says, not looking up, not knowing what else to say, the awkwardness of the morning after beginning to set in.

Yet when he does look up to meet Christine's eyes, the feeling vanishes. She is watching him with an expression he has not seen from her before. He meets her gaze and they stare at one another for a full half minute with awakening curiosity. Neither can turn away and neither wants to. It is a moment both childlike and brutal in its candor. They are overnight lovers really looking at one another for the first time. A full half minute of unabashed curiosity and exposure until the blood colors Christine's cheeks, and with eyes suddenly downcast from his still staring, she retreats. She assumes a expression more appropriate to the conceits of her life, cool and demure, an expression Jacobi can no longer read.

Yet the floodgates to her unconscious still swing freely. Her mind is drenched with unfamiliar thoughts, rushing forward of their own accord. *My body, he knows my body, he's after more, or just thinking of a way to leave, no, he's not that crude, not like Tony, more sensitive, young, I gave him my body, coming, he's still a boy, what is he doing here, probably expects to talk now, what to say to a boy, young, not a line on his face, still staring with those eyes but I won't look up, I like his dark eyes, our bodies together coming, the best in years, staring like a boy, curious, I won't look because he's after something...me, thinks he needs an older woman...who does he think he is anyway?*

"Who are you, David Jacobi?"

Why did I say that, so stupid, all business like Leonard, he'll think I'm hard, I am hard next to him...yes, he'll know it, a real bitch...that's what he'll think.

Jacobi recoils from the question before he realizes it's the same thing he's been asking himself since California. He sorts through a host of possible answers—a marauding knight, a track star who blew his athletic scholarships on nicotine and his academic ones on cannabis, a quiet acid fanatic who thinks he has nirvana by the tail, a dope dealer who has failed miserably at his chosen profession, former friend of poet-recluse Michael Shawtry and about to be booted from said poet's domicile and left homeless.

"Don't you know me?" he finally answers. "I'm the Junior Senator from Montana."

It makes her laugh. "Tell me more," she says.

"How much would you like to know?"

"Everything!"

She falls forward on top of him, burrowing her head into his belly, turning it into a joke as he has, with his arms moving beneath the robe to help her slide it off, her flesh seemingly softer each time he touches it, they retreat away from their identities and back into one another's sexuality, her mouth upon his chest, the sun still pouring through the window, they are about to make it number three.

The phone rings. Too loud, almost like an alarm at the far end of the loft. Christine is up and moving quickly across the room to answer it. Jacobi is left alone in the bed, watching his erection go down.

"Hello, hello…hello, Leonard…no, stop, I can't hear you…the connection is bad…I said the connection…What?…no, no, stop…yes, yes…" Her face blanches and she suddenly looks her full thirty years and more. Jacobi is shocked. She pivots away from him, crouching and lowering her voice, speaking directly into the receiver so he can barely hear her.

He turns to sit up on the opposite side of the bed. Taking one of her cigarettes from the pack on the nightstand, he bites the filter as he lights up, trying not to listen. He has nearly finished smoking by the time he hears her muffled good-bye and the headpiece clicks into its cradle. When he turns to look at her, Christine is standing with arms at her sides and palms out. The sun is shining on the upper half of her body and her face and shoulders look as white and inert as the notepaper on her desk. The sun is shining through the windows but all at once it is a cold sun.

"My mother died yesterday," she tells him without looking up.

It sounds strangely like an apology.

13

AFTER the death of Christine's father, her mother had slipped swiftly and open-eyed into a vacuous insanity—wearing the same dress day after day, forgetting to comb her hair, wandering into the street barefoot, "an embarrassment, my God, an embarrassment!"

With Leonard's help, Christine had her promptly committed and promptly forgot about her. For the next six years the old woman received the finest of care, wheeled and drugged and washed and fed, sitting in the sun and watching television. The first satellites went up to orbit the Earth and she gurgled. Kennedy edged his way into the Presidency and although she had been a staunch Republican all of her life, she smiled blandly. That same Kennedy was struck down by an assassin's' bullet and she didn't bat an eyelash. Newsreels of the growing war were so many John Wayne movies to her...only why was it taking so long for the two-fisted hero to arrive?

One day a particularly observant nurse observed that the deterioration of the old woman's body had surpassed that of her mind and she was dying. The staff, with emergency bells ringing, got her into an operating room and onto the table and went through the appropriate motions with the knife, but already it was too late. She was a case for a priest rather than a surgeon.

By the time Christine arrived for the funeral, Leonard had made all the necessary arrangements—the body flown down from Vermont so it could be placed in the family plot, a hotel reservation in Boston for Christine, a four-star Catholic ceremony with all the trimmings, even the headstone had already been cut. A decrepit mad woman doesn't have much of an entourage and the church was for the most part empty. A few relatives and old friends who had come out of courtesy or curiosity. Leonard and Christine. Their eldest daughter, Melissa—the two younger children remained at The Cape—trying to put on a somber expression for a grandmother she had never really known. Several professional retainers, unalterable elements in the American way of death. And one small nut-brown old man, perhaps a former lover unknown to the family, perhaps merely a funeral lover.

The coffin was open, but as Christine filed past with the rest the wrinkled and powdered face topped with its ball of fluffy gray-white hair was nearly unrecognizable to her. It was a creation of the cosmeticians of Thanatos that forced itself upon her unwilling eyes, not an image of the mother she held in memory. She looked away quickly, afraid that the dead painted eyes might unhinge themselves and fall open, still full with insanity, or worse yet, with the accusation of neglect.

Outside the church, the weather demanded a picnic in place of a funeral. The day was bright and summery. A playful breeze tried to kick Christine's hair loose from the black band of mourning that bound it. The brightness, after the dim candle-lit interior of the church, brought spots to her eyes and made her momentarily dizzy. She faltered on the steps and Leonard grabbed her arm to help support her. His touch was irritating. Just as their daughter had turned looking up to discover the reason for the delay, Christine pushed him away.

The drive to the cemetery seemed interminable. As they inched past Boston Common, Christine had the urge to leap from the limousine, shed the shoes that were pinching her toes, and run barefoot through the grass until she could find the enclosed sanctuary shade of a leafy tree or a circular hedge of privets. The traffic jam in which the procession became entangled didn't help matters. The interior of the car was sweltering, and Leonard, typically tactless, tried to pump her for information about what she had been doing—Are you still seeing that musician fellow?"—"Is your writing enough to keep you busy?"—"Are you getting any closer to a degree or just taking classes?" It was the usual nonsense. Christine, with polite agility, managed to dodge or deflect most of his questions and steered the conversation back to their children, the only topic about which they still, or ever, had anything in common. Leonard Jr. was losing weight. Sophie loved sailing and was learning to play the guitar. She could see for herself what a young lady Melissa was becoming.

"Of course, they miss you very much," Leonard assured her.

When they finally reached their destination on the outskirts of Boston, more than half the company had somehow been left behind. The wreaths and bouquets clustered around the grave site far outnumbered the small circle of mourners. Christine's thoughts wandered back to dwell upon and resurrect the grief she had felt after her father's death and funeral. She turned the sequence of events over and over in her head, trying to recapture the cleverest details, the scroll work on the coffin or the color of the pastor's eyes. Before she knew it, the shovels were tapping the earth tight upon the mound of her Mother's grave and it was thankfully over.

She stayed in Boston an extra day to spend some time with Melissa. They had a fancy lunch together, went to a band concert at the Common and afterwards, shopping. Christine bought her daughter a new outfit. It was red with white piping like a fiery sailor's suit.

"My mother died yesterday," she'd said, and although it had sounded like an apology, Jacobi could see the shock upon her face. He'd come quickly to her side, draping the robe about her shoulders, putting his arm around her and leading her back to the bed. Her body no longer seemed erotic to him, but small and vulnerable. The sense of concern that welled up in him, the need to protect her from harm, took him by surprise, but there was no time to assess his feelings. Over the next few hours not only did he attempt with some success to calm and comfort her, he helped her to prepare for the trip north, booking the reservation for the flight, calling the taxi, even making sure she had packed everything she would need. Their intense sexual rapport had shifted swiftly to an intense emotional one. It only seemed natural that he should accompany her to the airport, and more natural still in the course of their conversation in the taxi, when his imminent expulsion from Michael's surfaced, that she should hand him her keys and say, "Wait for me. I'm not promising anything. But wait. Please," and that he should take the keys from between her long fingers without question, and as she was about to leave the cab, frame her face with his hands and kiss her gently upon the cheek and not so gently upon the mouth. Spontaneity was what he had wanted. There was no telling where it would lead him, but at least for the moment, spontaneity seemed to be his.

After Christine's departure, Jacobi had gone back to Michael's to pick up his things. The scene there was awkward, but a partial rapprochement occurred when Michael produced ten dollars for the two caps of acid he'd taken, and Jacobi apologized for his actions at the party. "You know, man, I had an awful lot to drink. I guess I got a little out of control." Michael nodded, though whether it was because he understood or merely agreed was unclear. They shook hands, still a bit awkwardly, but it was apparent that their friendship, at least in some form, had survived.

Jacobi then proceeded to move into Christine's apartment and try it on for size. He ate the food in her refrigerator. He read her book of poetry line for line and actually did like it. He explored the rooms and the objects in them, the inanimate extensions of her self, searching for some clue to betray her identity. The place was too perfect, almost like a movie set. The bookshelf was properly literate, weighted with the emphases on poetry and contemporary novels, but with a decent smattering of non-fiction—political science, philosophy, history and art history—exhibiting no particular bent. Her records were classical or late jazz, the prints upon the walls were all accepted works of Impressionism, Expressionism, Surrealism, most of which he had seen before. The closets were stuffed with expensive clothes, the drawers with silky underwear, in black or red or cool pastels. But if the particulars of her individuality were hidden somewhere beneath the stock trappings of her apartment, the limits of his search failed to uncover them.

In the kitchen he puzzled over the unfamiliar names that crowded her spice cabinet. He discovered the photograph of her children. It revealed two little girls who looked like they might mature into less attractive versions of Christine. In their child faces the chiseled beauty of her features had been blunted by a duller strain. The little boy in the photograph was fat, too fat for a child, implying an outrageous appetite or a glandular condition. In his swollen face the dull quality had proven victorious without conflict.

On the second evening of his stay, Jacobi found himself bored and wondering what to do. Sitting by Christine's desk, which his search and his conscience had stopped short of rifling. he unfolded the money from his wallet and counted it...twice. There was just over two hundred dollars both times. He could make it back to California, hitching again, maybe with a few days in Cambridge first. Or he could await Christine's return and see what was in the offing. Whatever they had begun was still unfinished, but whether or not it was worth finishing he wasn't sure. Coming together with Christine was the first real thing that had happened to him since his last acid trip, and now she seemed to be occupying his mind equally. The idea of taking acid with her, of making love to her on acid, appealed to him. But that was part of the problem. Every time he started to think about her, he started to think about taking her to bed, about her slender body twisting beneath him and her nails digging into his shoulders and the muscles of her cunt tightening around him as he moved within her. Any attempt at objectivity with regard to whether he should go or stay was lost in a rush of sexual imagery so vivid that he felt like hopping a flight to Boston there and then just to have her again. Perhaps he'd catch up with her browsing at the undertaker's and they could dive into a cushioned coffin for a quick one. Or if it was at the cemetery, an open grave might do. The contradictory combination of passivity and passion that he had discovered in her so far was intriguing at the very least and irresistible once his appetite was whetted. He'd decided already that it was worth staying if it meant sleeping with her again. But she might not return for another week, and when she did, what if she were still grief-stricken, oblivious to whatever she had promised—nothing, really—and outraged at his horny presence?

As he mentally toyed with the idea of her body for the hundredth time—thighs, breasts, belly, back—the telephone rang, again so loud in the one-room apartment that it startled him. He let it sound several times before deciding to answer, thinking it could be Christine checking on his presence, or Michael, in search of more acid or maybe even some company. When he did answer, the other end of the line was alive but silent. After several seconds it clicked dead. A moment later the phone rang again and the routine repeated itself. Jacobi hung up a second time, concluding that someone else had just discovered his occupation of Christine's apartment.

About twenty minutes later he had sunk back into the pronged depths of his sticky reverie—New York, Cambridge or California, Christine or no-Christine, yin or yang, roll over and start again, action or inaction, one hesitant thumb edging toward the red button, another toward the black, and two more twiddling in his lap—when his thoughts were disturbed by a solid rapping that had been rattling the apartment door for some time. Jacobi answered it to look down into the eyes of a hawk-faced man whose shock of dark hair twisted into more curls than he cared to count. The man's suit was expensive but rumpled, his jaw muscles tensed.

"Where the hell is Tina?" Tony Bosano demanded loudly. "Tina. Tina!" he shouted, trying to see into the interior of the apartment around Jacobi, who stood blocking the doorway.

Jacobi's response was immediate and automatic. He later felt immensely pleased with himself because it was exactly the sort of thing Mulligan would have come up with.

"Oh, you must be looking for Miss Leslie," he answered amiably, summoning a boyish grin. "She vacated yesterday afternoon, moved to the East Village. I'm the landlord's nephew and I'm helping to get the place cleaned up."

Tony paused, thrown off balance. His brow crinkled, flattened, and crinkled again. He was frantic enough in his confusion to fall for it.

"I have a copy of the forwarding address if you'd like it," Jacobi continued, taking a folded slip of paper from his wallet. "You know something? My uncle has been losing all of his tenants lately to the East Village. I can't say that I blame them though. It sure is a hell of a lot cheaper. And a lot more ethnic. It's just getting too damn commercial around here."

Tony had taken the paper and was holding it in front of him like a distress flag. "Yeah, sure...uh, thanks," he mumbled, turning back toward the stairs.

"No problem," Jacobi added. "Maybe you could tell her she left some stuff in the basement that we're going to have to get rid of if she doesn't come by and pick it up."

He got the door closed just in time, then collapsed against the wall, doubling with silent convulsions of laughter at the parting expression on the man's face. So there was someone else in the background after all, he thought, wiping the tears from his eyes. Then he started laughing all over again. The address he had just given the man was Michael's. Assuming he didn't realize he'd been duped, that the man actually trudged up Michael's dingy stairwell in the hopes of finding Christine, Jacobi wondered how "The Recluse" would deal with an irate suitor.

14

SHE came back from Boston still wearing black like a good mourner should, black dress and shoes and black band pulling the hair straight back from her wide clear forehead, fashionable black worn to advantage against her ash blond hair and the milkiness of her complexion and her straight measured movements, but no one could deny it was black all the same. The return trip she barely remembered. There were the usual doors opening before here and closing behind. The taxis. The hands opening for her money and closing upon it. The plane barreling its way through drifts of clouds closer than clouds should ever be, even blurred by their closeness. Christine remained oblivious, internal, drawn within a self-contemplative fog and questioning the solvency of her own emotions, still slightly appalled that the reality of her mother's death, beyond the initial shock, had meant so little to her.

Without knowing exactly how, she found herself again climbing the stairs to her apartment. Past the first two landings. The familiar carpet wearing thinner. The stubborn wine stain, hallmark of her last disaster with Tony. She slid the key into its lock and opened the door.

She stopped stone still without entering.

The curtains had been drawn against the afternoon sun and the room was for the most part in shadow, but even before her eyes grew accustomed to the light and she saw him, she sensed his presence by the male smell that now overlaid the customary feminine odors of her room. He was asleep in the bed, his body molded by the whiteness of the sheets. It could have been any man sleeping there. The shadows of the room were deep and his head partially turned away toward the curtained window. But as Christine stood motionless in the doorway, the details of his face, the expressions of his eyes and mouth, came rushing upon her like a shot that left her trembling. She had never allowed herself the hope—and the fear—that he would still be there.

Christine glanced down. The brass knob on the door had swung inward, just out of reach. Without stepping into the apartment she could still lean forward and grab it, close the door as quietly as she had opened it, go back downstairs and across the street. She could call from the pay phone at the corner grocery, her hand cupped across the mouthpiece, tell him that she was just leaving Boston and wanted him out by the time she arrived back. She could write her poetry. She could find someone closer to her own age, closer to her own kind. She could reconcile with Tony. She could write an epic poem. She could buy another outfit, do the apartment over, add this to the long list and that to the short list. The knob shone like a hard golden egg sunk in the nest of dull wood that surrounded it. Jacobi turned in his sleep and the sheet fell away from his body. With two breathless steps she was inside and closing the door behind her.

Christine put down her bag and crossed the room silently. She watched him as she undressed. He looked more like a mature boy to her than a man, out of the pages of Whitman or the "boy" in Pound's *Second Canto*, with the soft skin of his cheeks and the jagged mustache, his face calm as a child's in sleep. Shoes off and dress off. Bra, stockings and panties. She stood over him naked. There was no time to hang up her clothes so she left them in a pile at the foot of the bed.

Then she was beside him, flesh to bare flesh, and he rolled over without waking and stretched his arm encircling her, hugging her to him as if he'd known she were there all along.

They embarked on a three-day fucking bout interspersed with wine, dope, and food, a two-party orgy with Jacobi on top of her and inside and going for the gold medal. It was sex like they'd never known before and they gave themselves to it completely. Jacobi knew that he'd be headed back to the West Coast by fall or sooner. Christine had already convinced herself that she couldn't hold a man his age for any length of time. After three days they emerged like two sated monsters coming out of the deep. They looked at each other and the world about them and each other again. They held hands and sat together talking and Jacobi out of cigarettes again smoked Christine's Salems, breaking off the filters and lighting the other end with loose shreds of tobacco escaping to mix among the twisted mountains and valleys of their lovers' bed. They talked through the night opening their lives to one another, the decade and more between them lost in the merging of their bodies. And both of them realized together that whatever was happening to them and between them this was only the beginning. And rightly or wrongly, Christine gave it a label.

"I love you," she said.

Over the next few weeks their infatuation with one another extended to the worlds of illusion they could create together, sexual games that would link them like two figures carved from the same block of stone. Jacobi had been back to Billie's and picked up a lid of the supergrass. Coupled with their rampant desire, it served both as a means to break down their inhibitions and as a source of inspiration. Their sexual theatrics did not come as shields to the self. They seemed to know each other already in a way that transcended facts and figures and the petty habits and idiosyncrasies that would later surface to wear threadbare their body love and nick at their infatuation with boredom and bother. Rather they came as extensions of the self, for each role they assumed was capable of revealing how much of the character of the role was inherent in their respective identities. These early games were precursors of more serious ones to follow, later endeavors that were to be played for keeps and become inextricably entwined with the fabric of their everyday reality. Often the sexual aspects of the drama they were enacting took a backseat to the play itself, and Christine would rise to the reality of a particular role with more fervor and thespian fortitude than Jacobi had ever anticipated.

Once he had her assume the role of a lower class French whore, à la Henry Miller, make-up and apparel to boot. They negotiated a deal in which she hassled him up to fifty dollars before an agreement was reached. Then in the cheap hotel where they went, she was totally uncooperative—"*Non-baisez la bouche... non-baisez la bouche!*" He practically had to rape her, and that wasn't easy. The strength in her slender white limbs surprised him. It ended with a dry uncompromising fuck after which Christine immediately went to sleep. Jacobi arose, stealthily dressed, pinned five dollars to the crotch of her panties, and left her there. Christine awoke and returned to her own apartment an hour later ready to tear him to pieces. She found him sitting in bed grinning, smoking a joint and leafing through one of her cook books. Her anger collapsed bubbling into laughter and there was nothing to do but join him.

After those first few weeks they became less frantic in the pace of their explorations. It was not because they were sated, that seemed impossible, but because they began to realize that they had time, that their desire was not abating, their affair was not an "overnighter" or even a "fortnighter." They were becoming sexual connoisseurs, vicarious observers of their past private orgies, reflecting upon them and judging them almost as if they had happened to someone else. At times it seemed a host of individuals had been involved in their couplings, a cast of extras from some Fellini film that had yet to surface in the States.

Also, after those first few weeks, Christine's old defenses began to reappear. Her blue blood began to reassert itself. Jacobi had released too much of the woman in her, unleashed to many hidden desires. Her head with its hardened ethic of existence and survival couldn't assimilate all that was happening. In consequence there was a gradual retreat on her part, almost like a repentance for too much pleasure. It began when she awoke alone in that bare hotel room, alone as she knew Jacobi must eventually leave her. It was the classic abandonment scene—the still-damp sheets, the torn window shade, the grease-speckled walls, the crooked light fixture hanging dismally overhead. Its parody value was lost on Christine. For her life had changed too rapidly, so rapidly that it had taken her a full two weeks just to catch her breath. By the time she got around to asking herself whether or not she wanted to be involved, involvement was a reality. She felt as if Jacobi had run blindly off a cliff holding a rope tied to her ankle, and only now had the speed of their falling slackened enough so that she could look around and take stock of just where they were falling to. She had stopped writing and attending the readings. Her class at NYU was forgotten, as dated as the literature with which it dealt. Tony with his scenes and his pathetic needs, except for a few unpleasant phone calls, seemed out of another era. There were no more empty hours, no evenings of solitary self-castigation, they were full with David Jacobi—his drugs, his voice, his ideas, their shared fantasies, his rising cock rising to her call and up and into her as if it had been tailored for her cunt. Yet tinging it all was the fear of commitment to a man so much younger than herself.

Christine began to watch her mirrors more carefully. She saw or imagined changes in her face with vague premonitions of what they might portend, and she liked them and she didn't like them and she didn't know whether she liked them or not. Oh yes, her aging was there. She was no longer twenty-one or twenty-five or even thirty. A real affair, not like the sham with Tony, would probably make her age faster. But the question remained—Did David Jacobi offer her an easy aging or a hard aging? For now, she only knew it wasn't a dry aging, and there was always his face and eyes and his hands with their sculptured veins and muscles calling her back to bed and the long circle of his arms enclosing her.

Jacobi was going through changes of his own, just as rapidly as Christine, only he welcomed them without question. He'd been riding a wave of confidence ever since he'd seduced her. It was a compensation for his failure as a dealer. If his trip to New York were a ritual of manhood, then Christine had become his first real woman. And she responded to him like a woman, more open than anyone he'd been with, sharing her desires, giving pleasure for pleasure, breaking into tears because "it's so good, David!"

Jacobi had stopped asking himself what he wanted or what he was doing. His day by day existence with Christine was full and intense enough so that he could live day by day, so that he could postpone the tedium of psychological and philosophical speculation to an ever-receding future. Even though his existence lacked the clarity he sought, there was certainly ecstasy, and a kind of spontaneity. And at some level he understood that the complex of emotions he was feeling was too involved to analyze, too multifaceted to "understand" in so many words.

Of course they were hiding things from one another.

At first with Christine, before he really tried to uncover her, they were only the typical womanly secrets. With exasperating femininity she never would tell him her exact age or weight. On Jacobi's part there was the fact that the sum of his "writing career" consisted of the poem he had shown her plus two short stories he'd done for a class. His fiasco as a dealer. His plans to return to California in the fall. Despite such salient omissions, he was the one who did most of the talking when they were together. Later, once Christine began to trust him, once she felt sure that he was locked in her arms as securely as she was locked in his, this would change. But for now their conversations—after dinner, after making it, after a joint smoked on the open-air coolness of the fire escape, usually abed, a bed perpetually unmade since his arrival—dwelt in the realms of his obsessions, its boundaries set by the limits of his values, and Christine found herself warily treading the earth of a strange and sometimes frightening land—dope, dealing, grass, acid, Mulligan, acid, the political and spiritual bankruptcy of America, social protest, heightened consciousness, sexual freedom, mysticism, acid. His were the concerns of a younger generation that she had to strain looking over her thirty-year-old shoulder to see, that she often felt herself turning vainly to reach with a crick in her neck and arms suddenly too short. And in the course of relating them, the portrait Jacobi painted of himself was far more the vagabond and free thinker than he had ever been. Still mistakenly involved in the game of seduction long after she was his, he selected and expanded upon the data from his past to create a biography he thought she would find appealing. And as Christine consumed this creation, his own self-image began to change. He began to see himself as he wanted her to see him, as a young hustler and myth maker, a Kerouac on the make, a prophet of the revolution to be.

Jacobi sensed the restraint that had come over Christine as she began to take an inventory and appraisal of their lives together. The clues weren't hard to spot: the way her limbs sometimes drew back willfully from his in their love making, the looks that further paled her pale features, the ambivalent stares he would catch in her eyes before they spun away from his or her hand rose to slide across her face, to push back a stray lock of hair and change her expression to the ungiving blankness of an empty slate. He didn't understand her retreat, but he didn't press. Pressure was a businessman's game, and from the particulars of her past that she had already revealed, he knew she'd had enough of that. Instead, Jacobi rode with her withdrawal, just as he was riding with life in general, turning freely on the crest of a wave but oblivious to the beach upon which it might strand him, sun-drenched Tahiti or the bitter chill of an Aleutian Island. All that he was certain of was that sooner or later he would leave her, that she might be his first real woman but she wasn't going to be his last, that he would return to Berkeley and the draft-free security of college, if not for the fall semester then the winter. Of course, Christine wasn't making it any easier with her "I love you"s, albeit unanswered, with the limbs he couldn't get enough of, with her conjugal sighs and her hands that tenderly rumpled his hair. But through it all his return to the West still hung in the future at some unmentioned date, the break to end an idyllic interlude once it had gone stale.

Meanwhile, there were the barriers that Christine had hastily and belatedly thrown up to stay their further sexual and emotional involvement. Jacobi ignored or sidestepped them. There were other interactions operating in their relationship with which he could become absorbed besides the sexual and emotional ones. He felt that Christine, unknowingly and on a pragmatic level, was helping to complete in him what the acid had begun, the reawakening of his senses to an erotic level of awareness. He began living with his senses immersed in the everyday objects and perceptions that surrounded him. The variety of the fragrances that she wore introduced him to the textures of smell. The slightly bitter taste of her flesh after a bath, the salt of her sweating, he juxtaposed to the meals she prepared or the dry sauternes that she loved and often consumed too readily. The blond, white and rose of her naked body made him a student of shadow, color and form. He was becoming sensually aware of the world around him, the world beyond his thoughts, and simultaneously, one aspect of Christine's retreat involved a reentry into the external world—so they could spend less time alone together, so she could again try on a few of the roles she had played prior to Jacobi: New Yorker, sophisticate, literati, woman about town. Only Christine discovered as they began moving into that outside world that the osmosis which had occurred between them during their brief but intense hibernation had already made of them a couple. It was now David Jacobi and Christine Leslie against the world, appraising and judging it together with the snobbery of the self-sufficient, speaking in lovers' whispers, exchanging glances, knowing nods and coded smiles only they could understand.

They dined in fine restaurants and amidst the gliding waiters and muffled conversations and white table cloths and soft merciful candlelight they were *both* twenty-one and in love for the first time. One waiter, either remarkably astute or unastute, made the fortuitous *faux pas* of asking Christine for her I.D. before serving the wine and was tipped more handsomely than usual. She exposed Jacobi's naive taste buds to the cuisine of the world, nudging him beneath the table when he fastened on the incorrect utensil. There were times when he couldn't decide whether she was a greater treat to his palate or his prick. He had been raised on the crude quantity of American food—meat and potatoes, second helpings, Sunday afternoon roasts with the relatives in for the day, mealy hamburgers on white bread at the local drive-in, pizzas and coke. He'd never had anything to say about it. It was the same thing everyone else was eating, except for the occasional health-food freak like Michael. Now there was suddenly veal marengo, *cioppino*, cornish game hens stuffed with raisins and wild rice, asparagus with chestnuts, beef *teriyaki*, sauteed frog legs, lamb curry, *coq au vin*. Jacobi had never realized that there were so many ways to prepare food, that to the seasoned gourmet a cut of beef or a leg of chicken could take on all the subtleties of a Kantian discourse.

They toured the art galleries, modern and traditional, public and private. Jacobi rediscovered the masters through Christine's eyes. The geometry of della Francesca, the rounded plasticity of Poussin's toy figures, the lambent brush strokes of

Matisse. For a few years she had pursued painting as seriously as she now did poetry, but had destroyed all of her canvases in a fit of despair. They attended concerts and plays and even a few parties for which her blood blue lineage was the magical ticket of admittance. Jacobi absorbed all of it and enjoyed it all—except for the time one of Christine's posh friends, actually only an acquaintance, eyed her with malign envy and Jacobi as if he were a well-groomed pet hound.

For many of their excursions, his duffel-bag wardrobe proved insufficient. Thus there were the buying sprees. Clothes were one of Christine's more blatant and long-standing fetishes. She loved the feel of expensive fabrics next to her skin. Every new outfit for Jacobi she matched with one for herself. Before he knew it he had three suits, which was one more than he'd left in California, and as far as he was concerned, two more than he needed. Of course Christine was picking up the tab, just as she was for everything else. She responded to a protest Jacobi had yet to voice. "Don't worry," she told him from the background as he posed stiffly in triple mirror reflection, "it's my charitable contribution to college youth, American higher education. It's redistribution of the national wealth, and you're in favor of that, aren't you? Anyway," stepping to his side, "you look wonderfully sexy in that jacket." Jacobi shrugged his shoulders and the jacket rippled across his frame like a second skin, and what could he do but agree?

Oddly enough, Michael began to seek out their company and join them much of the time. It began one evening when he turned up at Christine's apartment to ask Jacobi for ten—ten!—more caps of acid on credit. "Now that I've proven my good intentions and ability to pay," Michael beamed, "there shouldn't be any problem. Besides, I didn't notice any raft of cash customers beating down your door." he added, smirking gaily. Jacobi complied with the request, handing over the acid somewhat reluctantly, and ever gracious Christine, since evening was coming on, invited Michael to stay for dinner. "Only the salad and vegetables," he assured her. Nevertheless, by dessert the conversation had been reduced to poetry and not much else. Jacobi sat back sipping wine and watching Michael and Christine roll the ball back and forth. Michael became so involved that he even forgot to bum a cigarette. Once he realized that Christine had some brains lodged beneath her sleek blond locks and that she could throw a few recondite tidbits his way, he began to treat her with less deference and eventually as a relative equal, a rare exception in his behavior toward women.

From that night on they began to see more and more of Michael. Sometimes Jacobi felt that Christine the woman had more to do with Michael's conversion than Christine the poet. Judging from his friend's intense stares, Michael was infatuated with Christine and enjoying her vicariously and ethereally through Jacobi's possession of her. At other times, it seemed to Jacobi that Michael was merely seeking approval and acceptance, and that he and Christine were serving as parental substitutes. To Christine, Michael was no more than "young, a little crazy, and a little sad." In any case the three of them, walking and talking, with Christine usually between and her arm around Jacobi's waist, soon became a familiar trio on the Village streets.

As the days of summer, 1965, drew to a close, Jacobi's and Christine's lives merged in a comfortable pattern with Michael on the periphery. In spite of her retreat, the two of them hadn't deadlocked. They were still going through changes. Each time their bodies or their minds met they were giving to one another and taking from one another. But also, as the days of summer drew to a close, Jacobi's planned departure grew imminent, "the break to end an idyllic interlude once it had gone stale."

Only the interlude was far from stale.

Jacobi had already half-decided that he would spend the fall with Christine and not return to school until the winter semester. He could outwit the lumbering bureaucracy of the Selective Service System with specious letters and address transfers for that long. Mulligan had been at the game for over a year now. But the problem of his ultimate leaving was still there. It would rise uncomfortably into his head at odd hours, invading the unthinking sensuality of his existence, to then be dismissed like a bad vapor, only to rise again, a stubborn page that would not stay folded. When he did leave, would he be able to tell her outright? Or would he merely go out for a loaf of bread or a newspaper one morning and never come back? The more he mulled the problem the clearer it became that he was not the carefree vagabond of his self-portrayal.

Ultimately, such speculations proved weighty but irrelevant. One Friday, late in August, a very different sort of break to end their idyll and alter the unfolding pattern of their lives was already moving upon them.

The day had been exceptionally warm. They slept late and dined early, a light supper of cold cuts, salad, crackers and pinot blanc. Then they went back to bed. The fuck was sweet and funky and fine, with Christine on top of him and leaning forward so he could nibble her breasts or she could push her tongue into his mouth or they could just stare into each other's eyes as their rhythm built toward climax. Just before he came, Jacobi rolled her body to the side and then beneath him while they remained locked.

They relaxed side by side, sweaty and euphoric. After a few minutes, Jacobi lit the proverbial cigarettes, one for her and one for himself. She was lying with her back to him, and after he reached across her body to give her one, he nestled more closely to her, gently cupping a breast with his free hand.

"You have four birthmarks on your back," he told her.

"No, six," she exhaled.

"I know. I was just seeing if you did."

She laughed softly. "Caught in my vanity again, eh?"

Silence. His hand stroking her breast and their legs beginning to move against one another's.

"I have a friend who claims every birthmark is the sign of a reincarnation." he said.

"What does he say about freckles?" she asked, turning her slightly sun-speckled nose toward him. They had been to the park the day before.

"He says they're ugly."

"You bastard!" she cried in mock outrage, pulling out of his embrace and turning quickly to bite him on the neck.

"Ow!" Jacobi yelled, pushing her away. "That hurt."

"It was supposed to," Christine told him. She was up and headed for the kitchen. "Wine! That's what we need. More wine." A knock on the door sent her scurrying back beneath the sheets.

Jacobi slipped on his pants. "It's the devil come to tryst with you," he whispered.

"No, it's probably Mekas coming to make sure you're free for the evening," she taunted back with an evil grin. "I told him you were...but very expensive."

It was neither. It was Michael Shawtry. He strolled into the apartment aimlessly, blinking as if he'd just forgotten something.

"I smoked some hash," he told them.

"So what's new?" Jacobi asked.

Michael looked toward Christine who had pulled the sheet up around her shoulders. He gave her one of his all-knowing smiles and nodded slowly. Then his expression cracked as he remembered why he was there. "Oh!" he said, somewhat blankly.

"Oh?" Jacobi repeated, altering the inflection.

Michael took a crumpled yellow envelope from his pocket. "It came for you this morning."

Jacobi took the envelope. It had been opened and there was nothing inside. "Great," he said to Michael. "where's the telegram?"

Michael dug into his other pocket and pulled it out. He watched over Jacobi's shoulder as he unfolded the sheet and read:

ARRIVING LA GUARDIA STOP TEN P M STOP
BOTTICELLI

"Who's Botticelli?" Michael asked.

"Botticelli is a fifteenth century Italian Renaissance painter," Christine recited expertly from the bed, "perhaps best known for his *Birth of Venus.*"

"Botticelli is Mulligan," Jacobi told them.

PART TWO

What is the practical value of a clock that runs faster and faster?

A long enough and strong enough lever attached to one of its hands could conceivably travel at such a speed as to carry us into another dimension.

15

SOME projected sensualism or evil onto the fleshy immobility of Mulligan's reposing face. Others noted merely an incurable indolence. In action his face flowed to facile mobility. He became jackanapes and poser of foolery, rubicund court jester buoyant with nonsense parables, crude mimic, affable grifter.

Most of all Mulligan loved drugs, sex, food, sleep, people—in what order he could never decide, but he took them in whatever order they came. In the process he became many things to just as many people. A former girlfriend, faded with time in his memory, had dubbed him Botticelli because he reminded her of one of that painter's angels. Although the nickname stuck, the girl must have been blind, actually or with infatuation. Mulligan was fat. All the Mulligans were fat, with pig or pug noses, blue eyes, and a loose scattering of freckles riding over their noses from one cheek to the other, as if they'd been garnished with a few shakes of cayenne as a finishing afterthought.

16

MULLIGAN could be a good logician when he wanted to be. On occasion he would rap with Jacobi the way Jacobi was used to rapping, directive and analytical. Most of the time he was totally non-directive, hopping from one subject to another, never following any argument to its conclusion in a single conversation. He often seemed to contradict himself in terms of literal expression, perhaps never in terms of actual content. But there were other contradictions: his actions in opposition to his words, the expression in his eyes conflicting with his actions.

After listening to Mulligan for hours one could sort out sense from much of the nonsense, a distillation of meaning. The only trouble with Mulligan's philosophy was that it was like bathtub booze. Everyone distilled it differently.

17

MULLIGAN remembered south of Santa Monica a yellowed cottage motel a stale cheeseslice sandwiched between the beach and the asphaltbacked band of one-oh-one—don't cross the road Denny you have to play on this side of the road—it was fourlanes wide miles wide seemed wider even than it was long he paced back and forth on its beachside a roundfaced lonely only child staring inland to other motels in the distance vision segmented by the paintshiny color flashes of speeding cars going up down the coast seldom stopping business was bad he played in the anthills by the roadside came home stubby limbs bitedappled and swollen—that boy is a masochist this from his uncle inveterate sponger of cottage number one soaking up cheap wine with due regard for that appellation—but changed their minds two years later when they found him dissecting a dead cat with a screwdriver the dissembled parts neatly deposited in seashell dishes—you monster! you monster! his mother screaming to his childish wonder and afraid to really look at him ever since—Mulligan remembered warm nights afterdarkness moving from cottageback to cottageback peering on tiptoe into the lighted windows each offering a tridimensional technicolor scenario like his toy viewmaster only real and in motion with the carswoosh and waveroar in the background taking turns at drowning each other out Mulligan remembered his first intro to the world of sex he remembered like a photograph a black whore with too much make-up and a white sailor who left the lights on her breasts like chocolate Easter eggs and wondering if they were bittersweet or milk he remembered one day playmates that he exhausted in one day because he knew that was all they had and usually only an afternoon Stevie from cottage three the boy with the red shirt whose father drove a red car Patsy with blond hair and a burn along her temple come to the beach with me Patsy no no mommy and daddy say I have to play in the courtyard oh run to the beach with me naked my little burnt beauty.

Mulligan remembered all of this until he was eleven and his old man made it on the commodities market finally and they sold the motel and moved to Beverly Hills and then he remembered Jews jewelry furcoats swimmingpools the world of Southern California high school where football was what mattered and he couldn't play football because the sharp bones of his adolescent brothers dug bruises in his soft flesh or any of the other sports since he was all thumbs and fat thumbs at that he remembered being Irish among Jews hopelessly posing as a false Jew and eventually sinking into books and the anonymity of a fat A student with black plastic glasses and a zippered binder who got excuses from phys ed on account of a trick knee which wasn't much to remember.

Mulligan chose a large university to retain that anonymity and also because he was still under his father's thumb and Berkeley was close enough to be allowed yet far enough to stay away. Once at college he discovered that his intellect could carry him socially the way it never had in high school. He grew expansive. The books he had been reading, the books he had been compiling in his head, came tumbling out in rampant coffeehouse conversations. Exactly because he had been so lacking in a social exterior before, Mulligan now found that he could try on exteriors like different coats: fur, leather, tweed, sackcloth or silk. With some friends he became the rational intellectual sewing up his arguments with pinpoint stitching, with others the rabid idealist divorced from reality, with still others the pragmatic politico or angel-eyed fanatic.

After a year and a half at school he finally crossed that highway too the other side and blew his first joint. Within a month he was dealing part-time. By his junior year his awakening mind had stripped away enough conditioning to see his classes for what they were, a deadening routine of rote memorization and regurgitation. The things he was burning to do, all that seemed relevant to his changing awareness, had to be cast aside for bonehead psychology experiments or French vocabulary quizzes. It became increasingly clear that he was learning more from the states of consciousness produced by his drugs than from the courses he was taking. He dropped out, started dealing full-time and kept learning, if not from the drugs themselves from the life they led him to, the people he met, the scenes that transpired, the manipulation of money, dope and people with a profit at the end.

That summer he moved to an apartment in San Francisco. That summer he grew by leaps and bounds. Using the aura and prestige of the dealer as his springboard, he slept with his first woman and his eighth. He learned life in the city inside out until it left its foul taste in his mouth and mind. He started shooting amphetamines. In the space of months he became the meth megalomaniac *par excellence*—he would synthesize protein and feed the world, he would buy a coal black Harley and cruise the Pan American Highway tip to toe, he would become an astronaut, first foot on the moon. His late-found penchant for talk blossomed to passionate obsession, rapping through the nights night after sleepless night with ex-cons, heroin addicts, prodigal playboys, homosexuals, would-be artists, expiring beatniks. He played black games with his friends and lovers. He burnt other dealers and was burnt in turn. Faster and faster, a fast stick in the veins, flash-talk-crash, flash-talk-talk-crash. Eating only rarely. Downing molasses by the cupful in a losing battle to fuel his blood sugar. His weight fell off, the flesh of his fleshy face sagged, dark circle wreaths hung round his eyes blotting out a score of freckles. He nearly crucified himself on that amphetamine spike. He toyed with addiction as if it were an awkward kitten he could out jump at the last instant. Almost too late, on the verge of burning his brain out, on the verge of becoming thin and losing his Mulliganness, he discovered it was a sleekly muscled tom with killer fangs.

He came back to Berkeley in the fall and slowed down the hard way. Three times a week. Twice a week. Once a week. Back into the soft drugs. Back into books and lesser addictions: coffee, cigarettes, alcohol, tranquilizers. Making the transition from active to passive. He was living three blocks from campus. He'd wake up about noon, stroll over to The Terrace for some food, watch the Bay and the girlflesh, soak up the sun and read. Some days he'd wander through the library watching other people read. Or he'd just lie in the sun.

In the early evenings he became a regular in the Telegraph Avenue scene, up and down the street looking for connections, in and out of the coffeehouses. Then in the late evenings he'd hit the bars on San Pablo—The Blind Lemon, The Albatross, The Steppenwolf—talking and drinking and listening, playing darts or chess and trying to pick up girls.

It was a pale and desultory existence, and at times he would find himself dripping a cold sweat, craving the drug that could break his round of lethargy and send him arcing back with bright dynamo energy, buzzing through daylight and night lights. Yet by January he had left all of his addictions behind him. If we survive we sometimes learn. At the age of one and twenty Mulligan had savored and exorcised the need for ritual self-destruction.

He got back into school part-time to get back on his father's payroll, but by summer he was out again and into Mexico. He stayed in Guadalajara with an ex-bistro-owner from Greenwich Village who expounded his theories on drugs, women, America, and "dropping out for good" through the tequilaheated afternoons. He disappeared into the Sierra Nevadas for three weeks and came back with eighteen dollars in pan-mined gold. In the fall, speaking Spanish like a native, his hair shaggy and a spare reddish mustache draping his soft mouth, he tramped and hitched further south through the banana republics of Central America, through strings of tiny villages, each riddled by the sameness of the poverty of exploitation, through tile and stucco cities whose dark inhabitants lounged like droplets of liquid copper against their pastel walls.

At the turn of the year, after a Latin Xmas and with a tropical winter tan covering his freckles, Mulligan started north again. He made it to Mexico before his Irish luck ran dry. One of the multifarious native maladies, which he had thus far been able to dodge, had finally caught up with him. Or it may have been the shellfish he'd caught and roasted on an open fire and eaten the night before. He awoke with a dryness in his throat that after a few swallows turned to pain. All at once it had spread to his stomach and head and chest. He vomited and the began coughing short bullets of white phlegm into the sand. Fever heightened by the heat of the day swept over him in waves like the ocean rolling in.

The heat was suddenly excruciating. The sun was touching the sand. The heat was a coat of shifting needles.

At his back the rain forest was stretching onto the beach, growing all around him, over him. The roots of living plants curled between his fingers and toes. Vines laced his heaving chest. With each white chunk of phlegm he coughed up he was expelling part of his whiteness. Cough and there went the Protestant ethic, cough cough, the rest of Christianity thrown in, cough, The Dark Ages, cough, The Renaissance, cough, Karl Marx with a clown's hat and China saucers for eyes, cough, the Industrial Revolution played backwards, cough, the Great Depression, cough, ahem, cough, Sigmund Freud down the drain. If he kept coughing enough he would die or his blood would lose the sum of its whiteness and he'd be transformed into a native. Not a Mexican, but a real native, an Aztec or Navaho.

In his Levi watch pocket there was a battered cap of acid he'd carried throughout his travels. It was the only pill he had and in his delirium and misery, he decided to gamble and take it now. He unrolled it from its foil wrapping and popped it into his mouth. An hour and a half later he knew that it would be death that would claim him rather than nativehood.

He was dying, his whole body told him that he was dying, all of his senses. The sun went down into the sea like a sun going to its death, blood red and with a score of scabby clouds following in its wake. Mulligan was convinced that he would never see it rise again. The sky became darker and more and more like a lid that was shutting down on him. The fever continued to beat against his body. He was aware of a dissolution in his coordination, an inexorable weakness that swept through his nervous system and musculature almost like a release. He could no longer lift his head from the sand. His breath became a labored and monotonous wheezing, the pellets of phlegm rattling like the wooden balls in a whistle. The sand fleas began devouring his flesh, chewing away at his neck and palms and knuckles. They were in on the play. They knew he was already helpless, as good as a carcass. If some vultures showed up he supposed he'd have to put up with their nonsense, too.

Only by that time he figured he'd probably be beyond it all. The acid was objectifying his death drama for him. The acid was helping him to dissolve bit by bit, spreading his awareness over the beach thinner and thinner, as thin as a liquid film.

The beach, thought Mulligan in his stoned delirium, funny that his death should happen on the beach like so much of his childhood.

Night settled down like a burial shroud and each star was a candle lit in preparation for his wake. A broad, white moon slice hung high over the water. Mulligan could just see it out of the corner of his eye. It was an unmerciful moon, a cold steel ingot that paled the sand and cast silent gray mourner shadows with flickering capes that ran shifting up and down the beach and in and out of the trees and brush. Each time these shadows swept by him, Mulligan's body shook with the shiver of a sudden chill that had momentarily banished his fever. It occurred to him that they might be demons come to claim his soul, but it didn't really matter. With the first rush of the night he had ridden the acid high into the freedom of indifference. Now he understood that in all of his short life he had been incomplete—there was the part of himself that he had unwittingly brought to this beach of his death, and there was the other part of himself, the part racing in over the ocean, a giant and misty carrier bird searching out his fleshy shell.

He could hear it whistling as it cleaved through the boundaries of death, slicing the still black-shrouded air, wheeling past the cold moon, skimming in over the low waves, raising a hail of muddy sand clots as it skidded onto the beach, upon him. He could feel it now, enveloping him in the damp and milky embrace of its wings of feathered fog.

And then it had passed through the pores of his heaving chest and become a part of him and he was complete before death.

In its completion, Mulligan's consciousness, if it could still be called that, extended beyond the threshold of indifference. It was not only that he no longer cared, but that he could no longer comprehend the process of caring. He was a sentient stone, he was no-thinking, he was pure sense. His body stopped fighting the infection. His fever dropped away and the disease took over and ravaged at will, carrying him nearer and nearer to death. He could feel it closing the switches that shut down the power in the various segments of his body. His legs and hands were already numb. A tingling had taken possession of his forearms and buttocks. The pain was gone from his stomach and chest. But this self-awareness, this Mulligan-awareness, was only a minute fraction of his total sensory input. At the same time he was aware of and *as much a part of* the unique audio intricacies of each individual wave as it collapsed upon the beach, the multitudinous cawings and scratchings and nibblings and rustlings of the tropical forest behind him, the perfect clockwork movement of the stars slowly revolving overhead. He was not yet dead, nor was he waiting for death, no more than a stone waits for someone to throw it. His identity had already rejoined the eternal flow and death had become as inconsequential to him as the ticking of the stars.

Now the moon was no longer white. Further down the beach someone had set up a projector and they were using its blank face as a screen. Intense jewel colors danced across the *Mare Nubium* and the Sea of Tranquility. It wasn't a bad light show, particularly for out of doors on a Mexican beach and with the moon as a screen, but it could claim no greater part of "Mulligan's" attention than the million and one other things that were happening throughout the universe. If he'd thought of it he could have called out to the projectionist for help, but he knew that he was already beyond help and besides, stones don't call.

It must have been around midnight that Death began pulling off his boots. Mulligan sat up. Not because he was curious. Death was of no interest to him. It was only a physical reaction caused by the tugging on his pant legs. If he'd still cared about anything at the time, sitting up would have been worthwhile because he got to see what Death looked like.

Death was a barefoot, walnut-brown old man in gray-white rags. His teeth, hair and eyes were the same color as his clothes. When Mulligan moved he must have startled him, because Death yelped loudly, "Aaiieaah!" dropped the boot he had been tugging on and pranced back away from Mulligan and toward the water with several quick hops. As Mulligan plopped back to his prone position, land, sea and Death fell downward spinning rapidly out of sight to be replaced once again by the speckled night sky. Mulligan had never realized before that Death would be so afraid of life. Now that he thought about, it made sense.

There followed several seconds of silence except for the interminable waves. Whoever had been running the projector at the opposite end of the beach had abandoned it, probably frightened off by Death's scream. The forest was also suddenly and remarkably still.

"Aracamar! Sitioca! Quecotalz!" Death was shouting imprecations in an Indian dialect Mulligan couldn't understand. "Buoymir! Tapeana!"

Mulligan tried to answer in Spanish, but he found it as impossible to speak as it was to move. All his throat could manage was a scarcely audible bubbling. The wooden balls had coagulated to cement.

After the cursing ceased, he heard Death's bare feet come shuffling toward him in the sand and the next moment Death was leaning over him, spreading his palms and grinning apologetically, as if to say: "Sorry, pardon me, I thought you were already gone. You're a particularly hardy one, aren't you? Most are already cold by this time. I figured if I didn't get here soon you might be washed out by the tide and I'd have to dredge the bay for you, a sticky job and I'd only get bits and pieces back anyway." In spite of this apology, Mulligan soon discovered that Death's behavior was erratic at best.

All of a sudden he grabbed Mulligan's pack, which was lying nearby, turned it upside down, and dancing back and forth began to shake it with all of his strength. Mulligan's loosely-packed spare belongings fell in a lumpy cascade onto the sand. Death picked up his harmonica to blow a few scratchy off-key notes and chuckle to himself. He wasn't much of a musician. He took Mulligan's pocketknife and opened it. The blade flashed several times in the moonlight and Mulligan thought for sure that Death had decided to finish him off right then instead of waiting any longer for the disease to take its toll. Although the acid was wearing off, Mulligan still felt removed from what was happening. The dramatic irony of having his throat slit with his own knife almost appealed to him, but Death shut the blade and tossed it back onto the ground. He finally settled on a box of matches, after which he gathered some brush and loose branches together and started a modest fire to combat the cool night air.

From Mulligan's perspective, the fire changed the beach radically. In fact, the beach disappeared. He was now enclosed with Death in the pulsing heat of a liquid yellow-orange pool. He could still make out the stars, fainter overhead. Other than that, all beyond the reach of the fire's illumination was blackness.

Death sat at a respectable distance from him, close by the fire, warming his bare feet and hands. Mulligan concluded that his job must be a lonesome one, because Death started talking a mile a minute. Mulligan couldn't understand a word of it, and even if he had he was incapable of answering, but that didn't seem to bother Death any. Not a bit. He prattled on and on, his tongue clucking like that of a garrulous old gossip. Periodically, he stopped to pepper this meaningless one-way conversation with a few disconnected and equally meaningless toots upon the harmonica.

After a time, Death produced—Mulligan couldn't figure from where—a bottle of wine. Anyway, that's what the label said, Gallo Tawny Port. Mulligan's vision was dimming, he was going now, but he could just make it out in the light from the fire. Judging from the worn condition of the label and the swirling murkiness that filled the bottle, it seemed reasonable to assume that its original contents had been either altered or replaced.

In any case, Death turned out to be something of a sadist.

He took a few swallows from the bottle himself and then moved away from the fire to tilt it over Mulligan's slack jaw. He seemed to take immense delight in pouring long streams of the liquid down Mulligan's throat and watching it gurgle around his esophagus as his lungs gasped for oxygen. It was the first and last time Mulligan ever tasted anything that was gritty, tepid and explosive at the same time. If it wasn't wine it was at least alcoholic. After several swallows the wrinkles in Death's leathery face seemed beautiful and the fire on the beach had turned the color of a ripe persimmon. Also, the fire that it started in his parched mouth made the other seem inconsequential. It flowed like a congestion of lava erupting through his chest and once it hit his stomach, it was no less than a supernova. The pain obliterated his indifference. The foul mixture was trying to eat a hole in his backbone so that it could empty itself and return to the bowels of the earth from which it had no doubt sprung. But Mulligan's hide proved too tough for it. It finally had to come up the other way. He started vomiting again. Vomiting until he thought he would be turned inside out. It was a hell of a way to go and a rotten trick on Death's part after they'd spent the night together. Vomiting, vomiting, vomiting into oblivion.

He came to nearly buried in the sand. Death was gone and the only fire was the one high in the sky. His harmonica, his boots and his matches were gone, too, and the sediment that filled his mouth and clogged his taste buds could have competed with the Mississippi Basin. Yet he was still complete. He had become a native, not an Aztec or a Navaho, but a real native, a citizen of the natural and relative universe.

Somehow, one foot after another, he made it back through the trees to the highway and got his thumb out. After that the rides came along as if they'd been scheduled for him—up to the Mexican border and past it, into and out of the smog of greater Los Angeles, through the dusty hot-rod towns of Bakersfield and Fresno, and finally back to the haven called Berkeley. Life had become an ocean and he was the fastest fish in the water.

18

"MULLIGAN is dressed in the robes of a Zen monk. He is doing a soft shoe with his hair in bright frizzles like red yarn. Every time he stops dancing, he begins to float away." *—David Jacobi*

"Mulligan stands by an open window, playing chess by moonlight, moving both the white pieces and the black. Despite the chill of the night, his shirt hangs open. His hairless belly shines with the solidity of polished stone." *—Christine Leslie*

"Mulligan with a brown suit and black dress shoes. He sits in a low-ceilinged tract living room selling an inferior set of encyclopedias to an undernourished family that can't read." *—Michael Shawtry*

19

MULLIGAN blew into New York with the force of a tropical storm, or that stained glass rain that Jacobi and Christine had been praying for, bouncing along with three bennies bouncing in his belly beneath pale blue dacron dress shirt, maroon knit tie, sixteen carat gold tack, dark gray sports coat, tight black corduroy levis, dirty blue tennis shoes, periwinkle eyes shinning behind gold granny glasses like bright beads in his rosy face, a scarred bare conga hoisted over one shoulder and held by a rainbow cloth strap into which he had hooked a chubby thumb, the other thumb helping to tote a briefcase stuffed to the hinges with contraband cosmic consciousness, and flying at half mast from a back pocket like an erect tail the technicolor flag of a Marvel comic book, *The Incredible Hulk.*

Michael and Jacobi met him at the airport, having waited an hour because the flight was late, skulking around endless racks of paperbacks and candy bars, staring and being stared at by the stereotypical middle and upper class denizens of Twentieth Century America, Michael still spiraling down from the acid he'd taken earlier with Jacobi asking him, "Why do people in airports always look so ugly?" and Michael saying, "Try bus stations if you think this is bad, besides the masses en masse are always ugly," Jacobi distracted from the answer eying a passing stewardess plastic off-duty-on but still sexy in her own plastic way, watching her air flotation butt twitch her ra-ta-tat heels click across the airport floor, sending a theoretical space probe up the cinching nylon as Mulligan's plane grew brighter in the dark sky, a silver bird blinking white lights and red.

Mulligan had left Berkeley after an invasion of occultists had laid their beachhead in his apartment house. They plastered the hallways with the map-like calligraphy of their colored pencil astrology charts, planted Tarot cards like live mines in his mailbox— usually "The Hanging Man" or "The Fool"—had long-drawn strategy sessions with knocking tables and sepulchral apocryphal spirits at three four even five in the morning. It was too much for even a seasoned Berkeley perennial like Mulligan. He had to get away. He packed his dope, changed his clothes, sent a telegram to Jacobi and split. Six hours later he bobbed down the exit ramp from the plane between two businessmen, one rushing ahead of him and the other holding back a few steps, as if Mulligan were a cutpurse or the harbinger of a crashed market. Once clear of the ramp he spotted Jacobi and took off in a short sprint, his thick legs pumping across the asphalt until he slid to a stop on the buffed airport cement next to Michael.

Jacobi took one look at him. "Who needs a plane the way you're flying?" he said.

"Aw, just a few bennies," Mulligan answered, cupping a hand to his mouth and delivering the last word in a thick whisper, his eyes circling the landing strip in search of imagined narcs. "But it was that flight that really wired me, not even a dead soul to talk to." Chortling. "Even the stewardi went mute as soon as we got past Chicago, bought off by the Mafia no doubt, the county's going down the tubes even faster than I thought."

Jacobi introduced him to Michael, who was standing slightly open-mouthed. "You can laugh at him," he said, "but don't trust him. At least not in this state."

Mulligan put down his briefcase and shot his left hand forward, grabbing Michael's extended right hand wrong way around. He pumped it as if her were priming desert water, his hand beating the rhythm of his words. "Good to meet you, glad to meet you, you look like a saint but I suppose you've been told that before, I mean it as a compliment, yes, a rare thing in this secular land of ours...get out before you're crucified...go to

India, smoke some *gangha*, talk to the holy men in person." Mulligan grinned and pulled his hand back to pick up the briefcase, leaving Michael still shaking and vibrating to the shoulder. He pivoted to face Jacobi. "Hurry, man, let's get a taxi, I've only got a week and I want to see this town, then I'm back in school again to stay out of the draft and the old man has upped my stipend to three bills a month, I won't even have to deal unless I'm in the mood."

Jacobi took the briefcase from him and the three of them tore through the bustle of the airport, Mulligan's short legs taking two steps for every one of Jacobi's —Michael skipping every three or four steps to keep up—but Mulligan always inching ahead of them both, leading the way and jabbering ever faster: stories, jokes ("coffee, tea, or me"), wisecracks, anecdotes, thumbnail editorials, grinning stoned at the people they passed, skipping around to walk backward and in front of Jacobi and Michael for several steps to deliver a punch line or irrelevant example visually as well as verbally, doubling with laughter at his own insanity as the conga bounced up and down on his back.

Outside the airport Jacobi hailed a taxi and they all piled into the rear seat. Michael wound up with the conga between his legs. Mulligan pulled out a pack of cigarettes and passed them around and they lit up. He sat between Jacobi and Michael. As they moved stop and go through the heavy traffic, he peered out the side windows at the drab environs of Queens, then leaned forward, out the front window, where the towers of Manhattan loomed in the distance. The briefcase rested across his knees as if he were about to deal a poker hand on it. He held the cigarette with his thumb and first two fingers, hidden in the cup of his hand Lorre-like, and smoked in short rapid puffs.

Michael toyed with the conga, gentle taps that only he could hear over the racket of the traffic all around them.

"Give me the travelogue, Davy," Mulligan said to Jacobi. He had the habit of addressing his friends with some diminutive form of their names, whether to reduce their stature or confirm their closeness Jacobi had never decided. In any case, he gave it back to Mulligan, usually calling him "Denny." Jacobi had discovered that if he were exposed enough to certain people, in addition to being influenced by their ideas, he would unconsciously pick up on their speech patterns, their expressions and gestures, even the way in which they walked. When he became conscious of such imitations in himself, he would complete the trend by turning them into a parody. Thus Mulligan received his requested travelogue in the form of a take-off on his own speed talk.

"Ah, you're going to love this city, Denny, my boy, cause nearly *everyone* is on a speed trip—speed, speed speed, and you sleep with the lights on and one eyelid cracked to catch the roaches and I don't mean the kind you smoke, damn it, but you're going to love this city." Mulligan attempted to break in on this monologue—"We shall see, Davy,"—but Jacobi once going and gaining momentum kept right on rolling over the interruptions just as Mulligan would have himself. Mulligan gave up, laughing and beating on his briefcase so the lengthening ash of his cigarette flew off to join Michael's tapping and crash exploding soundlessly on the surface of the conga. After that, the individual particles of ash, until they toppled over the edge, danced to Michael's rhythms.

"On your right you have a lamppost," Jacobi continued, "one of 63,412 similar posts scattered symmetrically throughout the city, on your immediate left a subway entrance, the fastest and most degrading method of mass transit as yet discovered in the Western Hemisphere, on your right again a sewer entrance, rubber hip boots are required, that's hip not "hip," and watch out for the albino alligators, straight ahead is the East River which empties four hundred and eighteen rubber tires into the Atlantic Ocean each day of the week, every week of the year, Easter Sunday excepted..."

"The subway, the subway," Mulligan boomed suddenly in delayed reaction, "let's take the subway!"

"You'll be sorry," Jacobi warned.

"We'll all be sorry," Michael added.

Mulligan told the driver to pull over. They clambered out and from a wallet as comfortably plump as its owner, Mulligan plucked a couple of bills and paid for the taxi. Then he was hopping down the stairs to the subway with Michael and Jacobi in pursuit. The way Mulligan walked, Michael kept expecting him to topple over any second and then bounce back again, like the toy balloon figures with oversized cardboard feet he used to play with as a child. Once underground, Mulligan sniffed the air experimentally. He wrinkled his nose and the freckles scrunched together. "Sure we didn't catch the sewer entrance by mistake," he asked hopefully.

"Are you kidding," Michael told him, "the sewers aren't this bad. Not as many people."

Jacobi came up with the necessary tokens and then they were through the turnstile. It was a typical subway station—piss-yellow tile, dirty concrete, battered vending machines, and all the metal in sight painted khaki. When it was hot enough to fry an egg on the sidewalk, you could roast a ham down here. Mulligan felt sure he'd be brown on both sides in ten minutes. In their immediate vicinity there were two subterranean denizens awaiting the train—a dour woman with a pitted cottage cheese complexion that looked as if it hadn't seen the sun for years, and a sagging middle-aged man in a gray suit, a gray identical to the subway cement only cleaner. The woman tapped her foot incessantly, but the man was totally immobile. This immobility, plus the shade of his suit and the tired look on his face, gave one the impression that he had grown up right out of the cement and had been standing here waiting for the wrong train ever since the station was built. Being typical New Yorkers, the man and woman took no notice of each other or the newcomers.

Mulligan collapsed onto a khaki bench, mopping sweat from his neck and cheeks with a handkerchief. "As long as it's hot as Haiti, we might as well complete the atmosphere," he stated. Retrieving the conga from Michael and handing him the briefcase, he began thumping out a beat that echoed off the subway walls. His short body moved to the tempo of his drum strokes. The cottage cheese woman stopped tapping her foot, perhaps thinking it might be a tacit sign of consent to whatever was going on behind her.

After a few minutes, from the shadows further down the track, a Puerto Rican youth approached the trio. The kid was about seventeen. He was slickly dressed, but his hair grew over his collar and his eyes were wild like he was gone on coke or reds or speed or some personal combination of all three. Mulligan looked up from his drumming to grin, and whatever the kid was on, Mulligan had discovered his wavelength. The kid grinned back and started jerking his body to the beat. Then he was sitting next to Mulligan and Mulligan spun him the conga and he took off on his own, drumming and singing.

As he played he transformed the heat in the subway station from oppressive to electric. His fingers danced lightly over the drum skin, hardly seeming to touch the surface, yet it sounded as if there were two drums going instead of one. His voice was high and feminine and jazzy, dipping off key in all the right spots. He drummed with eyes closed and his body hopping to the music. Jacobi, Mulligan and Michael stood around him in a semicircle, heads nodding and their bodies beginning to move. The woman, along with the man in the gray suit, shied away toward the opposite end of the platform. They knew something was happening or about to happen that didn't directly concern them. Consequently, they wanted no part of it.

Mulligan could hear the subway train rumbling in the distance. He began snapping the heels of his palms together, a sharp base beat for the kid's drumming. As the train approached, louder, he increased the tempo. The kid went into a frenzy of movement. It looked as if he might explode any second. His racing fingers blurred to copper feathers fluttering over the conga's surface. The sweat sparkled in his dark hair and on his forehead and began to run in shiny beads from his long saber sideburns. His voice rose in volume, piercing, shrieking, louder and louder, trying in vain to outsing the clicking roar of the subway train as it rushed upon them windows flashing and Jacobi was grabbing Mulligan by the shoulder and telling him in sign language that this was their train and the kid was still wailing voice and drum beats lost except to himself in the noise-filled station as Mulligan bent sideways yelling to peer into his face, the eyes still closed, features twisted in ecstasy, in religious fervor, in the mad mindless joy of a spaced-out kid letting everything happen, letting it all flow out through his hands his throat his body, as the people were running off the cars and Mulligan was grabbing the conga by its colored cloth strap and popping it from between the kid's legs like a stopper, pulled out so the kid's legs clapped together and still he didn't miss a beat but just kept going right on his kneecaps as Mulligan-Jacobi-Michael leaped racing aboard the closest car and the doors pushing air swooshed shut behind them and the kid disappeared from their vision amid the moving people and khaki poles and the blackness of the tunnel as they roared out of the station.

Jacobi and Michael plopped down on one side of the car and Mulligan on the other. Jacobi and Mulligan stared each other down solemnly and straight-faced for several seconds before breaking into laughter.

Then Mulligan tried to say something. The black hole of his mouth gyrated unintelligibly through several sentences before he realized that his lungs were useless in this tumult. Next to him stood a fat little boy holding onto the purse strap of his even fatter mother. The mother's eyes ran back and forth, back and forth, back and forth. She was rooted like an old oak in the solid soil of her *Reader's Digest.* The little boy stared absently at the posters that lined the car. Mulligan leaned forward to peer at him and the boy started back. Then, putting his finger alongside his nose and giving a slow wink, Mulligan drew the Marvel

Comic from his back pocket and handed it to him. The little boy took the comic book and staring at Mulligan his eyes grew bigger and bigger, as big as saucers, as big as watermelons, as big as the Twin Lakes and he was waiting for Mulligan to jump in.

20

IT was a week of nonstop living with Mulligan as the impresario in all of their heads. Sleep went out of style. They all became affected by and infected with his everyday abandon. His drugs, his talk and his actions stripped away their layers of conditioning like a thicket of dry husks through which they had misviewed the world for years. In each of them his impact was unique, he struck different chords and the symphony that resulted was far from a classical composition.

From the minute he arrived to the minute he left, and even afterwards, Christine couldn't figure him out. He was too far removed from her realm of experience. For Jacobi, nearly everything Mulligan did made sense. It was summing and reconciling the individual actions into a coherent whole that eluded him. Jacobi often thought that if Mulligan made less sense, he might be able to understand him better. To Michael, of course, it was all imminently clear, top to bottom and in the middle.

For Mulligan, himself, that week in New York City was nothing special. He was used to operating in the midst of a self-made whirlwind. Mostly he remained in the center, in the calm at the eye of the storm. Sometimes he'd let himself be snatched up by the wind, but he'd always settle back in one piece, perhaps with a loose farmhouse between his teeth to be torn apart board by board.

21

WAKE up, wake up, it's coming, it's on the way, but easy now, easy, ride with the rush, the flash, don't fight the take-off, it's like five hundred cee-cees between your legs, like three hundred pounds of polished metal up against the light, don't let it flip from beneath you, gun the throttle and feel the purity of its power, keep the legs high and the butt low, drive the brain meth fast and bright through the rapids and over the waterfalls of consciousness, it's the song that rises like pleasure through the senses, a snowflake melting in its moment of microscopic illumination, the moment before sleep when history sprouts dorsal fins and time accelerates and you are pressed back upon your pallet with the force of three-six-eight temporal gravities, when objects whirl in the tempest and life cycles condense to crystal droplets, when the pressure upon the eye forces the cornea through Einsteinian contractions and connections are soldered that light the room, a white room with schematics in blue pencil on the walls, numbers and letters and symbols of the aboriginal past, it's the clarity of the razor's edge, the precision of the perfectly executed drum roll, the fall of Usher's house, it's swimming underwater with the eyes lidless, it's a rocket beneath your belly and you are stretching consciousness through the limits of space with the stars for stanchions, wake up, wake up, wake up!

It was the second night that Mulligan opened his briefcase and woke them all up, but first...

22

JACOBI'S presence had affected Christine's apartment, but still managed to find union within it. The objects of his maleness—his cigarette roller, the scattered books of matches, his clothes thrown loosely over a chair, his shoes lying on their side beneath the coffee table—were like a roughshod coating that overlaid the lines of her room without altering its basic order.

Michael's extensions of energy beyond himself were so few and far between that he seldom interacted with the surroundings of any environment. He remained Michael, untouched and untouching, and Christine's room remained itself.

Mulligan, as soon as he entered the apartment and even before he had time to look around, was pure anomaly, purple on orange, a succulent cactus atop a long-stemmed vase, a bit of raw beef discovered in the crab cocktail. Everything about him spelled chaos, from his slightly crooked glasses, always pitched this way or that as they slipped down the slope of his nose and he thumbed them back up, to the threadbare cuffs of his levis curled around the tops of his tennis shoes. One expected that he might turn too quickly and a lamp would topple, or he would pull a volume from the bookshelf and a dozen would come tumbling after it. His appearance created an unmistakable shift in the lighting or architecture of Christine's apartment that one could sense, but not specifically discern. Still, that first evening, Mulligan was for the most part amazingly un-Mulligan-like: reticent, polite, talking quietly, sitting upright in a straight back chair while he balanced a cup of coffee on one rounded knee with unerring precision, asking Christine about her poetry. "I'd like to read the book sometime." Later he did. He seemed nearly cultured. It was so out of character that Jacobi would have been surprised if he hadn't discovered in their short acquaintance that there was no behavior that was really out of character for Botticelli.

In truth, Mulligan was slightly awed by Christine, by the fact that Jacobi had come up with such a full-blown, beautiful woman. There was no doubt she was a woman and not a girl, Mulligan thought, a bit thin and sparkly, nearly carbonated, for his tastes, but a woman all the same. Perhaps he'd underestimated Jacobi. From the airport he had become aware of the changes in him since their last encounter two months earlier in California. Jacobi seemed more relaxed, the features of his face fluid and expressive. To Jacobi, Mulligan looked smaller, redder and rounder, no longer larger than life as he had loomed in memory, almost boyish (although he was older than Jacobi).

Their separation coupled with the changes Jacobi had been going through in his lavish affair with Christine had allowed him to escape from the net of enchantment that Mulligan threw around so many people. But already he could feel the force of Mulligan's presence and the magnitude of his boundless exuberance beginning to weave their spell around him again.

That first night they talked about cities: San Francisco versus New York, New York versus Los Angeles. Christine said, "I've never been West so I can't really make the comparison. I'd like to go, but first I have to fit in another trip to Europe. European cities do have more flavor." Her hands, stretched in front of her, performed a simultaneous flourish, as if to present the flavor. "Even the gray cities like London seem colorful, more cosmopolitan."

Mulligan took a sip of coffee. "Well, cities are all right," he said, "but they're still cities. As for myself, once I finish school and get some money together, I'm going to get myself a place in the country."

"Ah, the old conflict," Christine replied nodding, "civilization versus the return to nature. That's part of what my book is about."

"And you've decided the city is better?" Mulligan, master of intimidation, asked.

"Well...for now," Christine answered, somewhat guiltily.

"Nature is the only route," Mulligan assured them all, eyes unblinking and outwardly dead serious, "a small cabin, land that you till yourself, trees, the open sky, the stars at night, Cassiopeia, The Pleiades, fresh air." Mulligan pulled deeply on his cigarette and a long curl of smoke uncoiled as it shot toward the ceiling.

"Come off it, Denny," was Jacobi's response. He had heard Mulligan hypothesize numerous other futures for himself with equal sincerity. Once he'd even said that he wanted to be a politician, probably the bummest trip of all. Another time it was a highway patrolman—"Eight hours a day on the open road and nobody fucks with you…that's the life!"—or something equally absurd.

Botticelli turned slightly away from Jacobi and centered his attention on Christine. "What I'd really like to do," he said, leaning forward confidentially, "is buy a ranch in Nevada and start a commune. We could fence off thirty acres of desert. Everything would be communally owned and there would be no rules. Everyone could do just as he pleased."

A frown of puzzlement stitched Christine's eyebrows. "But how would you get by?" she asked.

Mulligan paused, leaning back in his chair and scratching the unshaven peach fuzz that lined his upper cheeks. "Isn't this America?" he posed rhetorically. "We could sell admission to the tourists and then there would always be the hot dog and soft drink concessions?" As Christine, slow to catch on, stared at him uncomprehendingly, Mulligan tapped the ash from his cigarette into the middle of his coffee cup. At stage left, Jacobi muffled a laugh at Christine's expense.

Later that night, after Michael (who had retreated into one of his morose silences throughout the evening) had gone home, and Mulligan was passed out on the couch, Jacobi asked Christine, "What do you think of him?"

"Well, he's awfully funny looking," she answered hesitantly, "but he's entertaining…and kind of cute at the same time."

Jacobi felt the jealousy before he could stop it. Then he realized how foolish it was and he thought, we make the same mistakes over and over again even when we know what they are. And finally, after he had considered Christine's response, he decided that she was right.

23

MULLIGAN'S brief stay in New York altered Jacobi and Christine's relationship considerably. In some way it was like a parenthesis in the path of their development that both changed its course and prolonged their involvement with one another. In other ways it marked an end to the naivete of their earlier interactions.

Botticelli's presence in the apartment also cut down on their sex. That first night they tried to make love noiselessly while he slept on the couch, low snores bubbling from his parted lips. Once inside Christine, Jacobi started fucking to the rhythm of Mulligan's snores. When she realized what he was doing she started laughing with her hand over her mouth and her body involuntarily curled up pulling away from him.

"I can't help it," she whispered. "It's just too ridiculous."

24

WHAT Mulligan lacked in continuity he made up for with pyrotechnics. If nothing else, he was intense, always for confrontation, for talking about where you stood, where it was at. Jacobi had never known anyone who could break down personal barriers faster and broach the standard taboo subjects earlier in a relationship. With an audience of one or a stoned enough audience, Mulligan became less the instigator-clown and more the self-appointed guru. Once he got you alone, man or woman, he turned on his seduction process. He could charge forward with both barrels open, pumping you incessantly, or lean back and draw you out gradually. Whatever was right at the time.

He was never at a lost for words, yet sometimes he could be silent, damnably silent. He'd give you enough of a shove to start you rolling downhill, to get you talking about something you needed or wanted to talk about, and then he'd turn mute on you, as mum and self-contained as a stone Buddha. You'd keep talking and talking and there would be no question that he was listening, nodding with eyebrows arched, eyes empathetic, ever so attentive that his ears seemed to be pricking up—he'd stop smoking cigarettes, even if he had an itch you were convinced he wouldn't take the time to scratch it—and you'd be waiting for his opinion, for him to answer, comment, judge, respond, say something, anything, but all he'd do was ask you another question, and that would keep you talking all the more until your words kept adding up and soon you were spilling everything out—lies, truths, deceits, fantasies, forgotten traumas, failures, successes, conquests, defeats, molars, eye teeth, chairs, sofas, tables, picture frames, carpet tacks, rooftops, floorboards, nails, bricks, mortar, right down to your bare colorless intestines.

Then when you'd said everything there was to say and said it again and the walls of your defenses had toppled like Jericho, leveled to the foundations, he'd hit you square between the eyes and a little high—at the fount of the mythical third eye?— with one of his typical Mulligan-I-Ching comments. A sentence pregnant with the stamp of whatever meaning you chose to impose upon it.

25

THEY awoke to the alarm of clanging pots, to the static of sizzling grease. It was eight a.m. Mulligan was off the couch, leaving a crumpled quilt, and into the kitchen fixing breakfast.

Jacobi sat up in bed, leaning forward so he could see into the kitchen. "Hey, what are you doing?" he called out. "You're not still stoned on that speed, are you?"

"What do you mean speed?" Mulligan called back. "I'm running on my fat, carbohydrates converted to energy." He came to stand in the doorway to the kitchen, holding a spatula in one hand. He had pushed the bead curtain to one side and tied it in place, a tangled lumpy vine winding up the door jamb. He was barefoot and bare to the waist. His body looked more solid than one might expect. In clothes, the roundness of his face gave him the appearance of being fatter than he really was. One of Christine's aprons was tied over his black levis. It barely made the turn around his wide hips and in back was knotted awkwardly and slung low across his butt. "Don't get up, young lovers," he announced, "just tell me how you like your eggs." With the spatula-less hand he scratched the side of his neck, already bright with sweat in the early morning heat.

Christine, still waking up, stared at Mulligan, appalled that this half-naked stranger should be roaming the domain of her kitchen, but too taken aback and still too much abed to voice any protest.

"Over easy," Jacobi told him, "with plenty of butter."

"Sunny side up, " Christine mumbled, looking something less than sunny. Jacobi kissed her shoulder and rubbed against her body. Mulligan disappeared back into the kitchen. Pots clanged, grease sizzled, water bubbled, dishes rattled and cups clinked, odors began to waft and permeate the apartment—the coffee would be strong—Jacobi's hand moved across Christine's breasts, his teeth closed gently on her collarbone, the refrigerator door clicked open and was slammed shut—once, twice, thrice—Christine sat up in bed away from Jacobi's nibbling, trying to lean forward to see into the kitchen, holding the covers up about her shoulders, genuinely alarmed. "David, what's he doing in there!"

Several sounds of dubious origin followed. Crash, clatter, bang—the noise level mounted.

"David!" Christine cried in helpless desperation.

"Coming right up," Mulligan answered over the din.

Jacobi hopped out of bed to the kitchen door. The coffee was perking and the bacon draining. Mulligan was cracking the third of three eggs into the frying pan, one-handed just like Christine except that he left a slight trail of white running across the stove before he got the empty shell into the garbage pail.

"No nudity allowed in the pantry," he railed at Jacobi, raising the spatula in a threatening gesture.

Jacobi hopped back to the bed. "He's just trying to get three breakfasts ready at once," he shrugged at Christine, who drew her lips back in a flat frown, unsatisfied with the report. But a moment later Mulligan swept into the room with a tray balanced in each hand. Christine shuddered, snapped her eyes shut and prepared for the crash as one of Mulligan's bare feet momentarily caught on the edge of the oriental rug and the trays tottered. But Mulligan recovered with acrobatic grace to move with their falling momentum and Christine opened her eyes to discover breakfast, complete and neatly deposited upon her lap—coffee, eggs, bacon, a toasted English muffin and half a grapefruit already segmented and dusted with powdered sugar. She looked up at Mulligan in a new light as he hurried back to the kitchen to get his own tray.

He finished eating before either of them, licking a bit of yolk from his lower lip, and then was up again to give seconds on the coffee. Standing by the window he lit a cigarette as his eyes devoured the limited view, censored by billboards and taller buildings, which the apartment permitted. He turned back to Christine and Jacobi, still in bed, his face alive with the untempered excitement of a twelve-year-old. "I'd sure like to see this city today. Over the ground, not underneath. Too bad we don't have a car."

"I have a car," Christine said.

"What?" Jacobi responded, his face slack with astonishment, "This is the first I've heard about it."

Christine's cheeks colored and she gave a small embarrassed smile, but at the same time, as she spoke, she seemed proud of herself for having kept this secret from him. "It's uptown, at a garage. I just never bother to drive it around Manhattan because the traffic and parking are so impossible."

"I'll drive," Mulligan, the driver, told them.

"What other surprises have you got up your sleeve," Jacobi asked her. For answer, Christine extended her sleeveless arm in front of his face, the bare, light flesh, the rays of fine hair, and Jacobi felt his desire, unsatisfied from the night before and earlier that morning, rising again beneath the sheets.

"More coffee, anyone?" Mulligan asked.

So that day they took Mulligan around the city—or rather he took them around, doing most of the driving, hugging the wheel of Christine's red VW and rambling on in his usual *non sequitur* fashion. Jacobi had been right about Mulligan and New York City. The environment fit him like a tailored suit, no further adjustments were necessary. In spite of the fact that he was unfamiliar with the streets, he could handle the car in city traffic better than either Christine or Jacobi. He could bluff taxis, dodge around buses while lighting a cigarette or telling them about the marketplaces in Guatemala, and invariably find a parking place whenever one was needed. But it wasn't often they needed to park that day. Mulligan kept them on the move. It wasn't sightseeing he was interested in, but touring, covering the grid of Manhattan line by line as if to consume and assimilate the multiplicity of its flavors in one sustained draught. Later, he would retrace much of the same ground on foot, walking alone or with Michael, immersed in and rubbing shoulders with the realities of the sidewalk. Then also, it would not be the "sights" that drew his attention, but the curious shop or individual or happening. Yet for now he was studying the pattern rather than its particular manifestations. He was like a cat exploring the forms and limits of a new territory. He took them down streets they had never seen before—Jacobi almost felt that they were the visitors rather than Mulligan. He drove them uptown and downtown and around town, and with the strength of his bravura even teased the corners and edges of black jungle Harlem, where he said, "Man, what a hellhole, one of these times when it blows it's going to take the whole damn island with it."

In a bar on Fifth Avenue, Mulligan got involved with a pinball machine. They were already stoned on grass, the super-grass that Jacobi had broken out to show Mulligan, who had in turn given his stamp of approval—a happy dilated wink. They stopped in the bar because Christine had gotten an irrepressible craving for a Brandy Alexander.

"I have an irrepressible craving for a Brandy Alexander," she announced, scratching a glossy knee.

"I wish *I* were one," answered Botticelli, who was sitting next to her driving. He suddenly gunned the car backward into a parking spot which seemed to have materialized from nowhere. "Would you prefer a single or a double?"

It was the middle of the afternoon, hot and crowded on the streets, but the interior of the bar was dark, cool and nearly deserted. They sat in a cracked leather booth with tarnished brass buttons holding the leather to the wood. Jacobi decided to try a Brandy Alexander, too, but Mulligan ordered a coke. He seldom drank. When he did it was usually red wine and it brought out the maudlin side of his Irish nature. He would misrecite Yeats or Joyce, thick-tongued and with a patriotic slightly watery expression in his eyes, as if he were swathed in visions of the Emerald Isle. Eventually and inevitably, he would pass out in the middle of the floor or securely wedged and blocking a doorway. Even dead drunk he had to be a center of attention.

While Jacobi and Christine rubbed legs under the table, Mulligan walked to the rear of the bar, clinked his coke glass down on the class cover of the pinball machine and started playing. The bells and the rolling of the steel balls echoed lowly throughout the room.

Anyone could see the game was rigged. At the rate Mulligan's score accumulated it would take twenty balls to get a replay rather than the allotted five. Mulligan kept knocking the heel of his palm against the machine's side in an attempt to balance the odds. The game would flash "TILT," whir momentarily, and then click to a halt, taking the rest of his turn with it. He would have to deposit another dime to renew the contest. Yet Mulligan just kept plugging money in, shaking his head and humming to himself.

After they had finished their drinks, Jacobi managed to drag him away. But first Mulligan unplugged the machine from the wall and with a deft and surreptitious stroke of his razor-sharp pocket knife neatly severed its cord.

Jacobi thought about that, turned it around in his head for awhile before he forgot it.

26

MULLIGAN had cultivated an erotic sense in conversation, facial expression, gesture. He had transcended identification with his exterior appearance and created a sexual image for himself. It wasn't long after meeting him that you heard about his prowess and his various conquests: either he told you outright, when he was in one of his expansive moods, or you wound up asking him because of the tantalizing hints he dropped. The missing element in his amorous career was a long-term relationship faithful to one woman. He claimed that this involved a kind of illusion that he had already outgrown, both psychologically and in terms of appetite, just like his appetite for people in general, for food, for drugs and for movement.

Because of the image he projected, in any situation involving Botticelli one became aware of the sexuality inherent in the situation, waiting with anticipation for that sexuality to blossom or with anxiety for it to explode, all depending on your point of view.

Christine didn't have to be told about Botticelli's sexual dynamic. Most women didn't. She sensed it, hanging like a hormonal presence in the humid air, every time he looked at her. He'd make a joke—"My grandfather was a judge…a judge of horses and women."—to get her laughing, vulnerable, and then in the midst of her laughter she'd catch his eyes upon her, laughing too but appraising and covetous, as if he were carrying on the family tradition and she, Christine Leslie, were a bit of horse flesh he had judged worthy. She found it insulting and annoying. Was he David's friend or wasn't he? She found it complimentary and at times, even exciting.

27

"MY friends, I have brought with me a rare collection of herbs, spices and potions to titillate the already jaded cerebral palate of Manhattan." With a simultaneous jabbing of his fat thumbs, Mulligan flipped the briefcase open. Jacobi, Christine and Michael, standing in a semicircle behind him, leaned forward to see what was inside. (When they'd returned from their touring Michael had been waiting for them, like a stray dog making its increasingly regular mid-evening appearance on Christine's doorstep.) Pill bottles, tin foil and brown paper packages, dark brown leaves of grass showing through their plastic bags, disposable needles and syringes. Jacobi gave a low whistle. Christine blinked and stepped back, as if from the heat of too hot a fire. Michael, outwardly impassive, inwardly began to anticipate the chance to try something new, a different flavor. Could this fat man be bringing him a trip that would carry him beyond even acid?

"Eanie, meanie, minie..." sighed Mulligan, "that grass was nice, Davy, but now I'm feeling down and sleepy. Would you people be against a little speed to keep us going." No one said anything, so Mulligan removed one of the tinfoil packages and began to unwrap it.

"What kind of speed is that?" Michael asked.

"Crystal meth," Mulligan said, "the best kind," holding up the opened foil so Michael could inspect the small mound of white powder within.

"You can get addicted to that shit," Michael told him.

"I know," Mulligan answered, smiling. "I already have been. Now I know how often to take it and when to lay off. But believe me, that's the hard way to find out."

Michael shut up.

"As for myself," Mulligan continued, "I'm going to shoot. The more wary," he glanced first at Michael, who had crossed to the window, back turned, suddenly absorbed with the view, then directly at Christine, "are welcome to sniff some powder or..." he paused, digging awkwardly, one-handed, in the briefcase to extract a nearly empty pill bottle. "I've even got a few bennies left."

Christine met the challenge in Mulligan's eyes head on without blinking. It was a child's game—"Bet you're scared!"—and an adult's game too—"I'm more worldly and sophisticated than you are."—and being a bit of both she fell for it. "I'll try shooting," she said.

It was Jacobi's turn to blink. He'd always been shy of needles and had refused Mulligan's invitation in the past. There were still too many negative associations in his head. He was waiting for them to empty out so that he felt comfortable with the idea before he tried shooting up. But now that Christine was playing the game, within the context of the game there was little he could do but follow suit. "Me too, Denny," he said, nodding and shrugging his shoulders, "why not?"

"Why not!" Michael said loudly, turning from the window. He looked toward Christine and Jacobi. "You're both crazy! Do you think the veins of the human body were made to stick needles into." He pointed at Mulligan who was removing the syringes from the briefcase. "How can you even be sure he knows how to use those things?"

"Sure I do," Mulligan grinned a bit maniacally, "I have an uncle who's a doctor."

"And my grandfather was a blacksmith," Michael answered, nearly stuttering, "but that doesn't mean I can shoe horses!"

"Cool it," Jacobi told him. "If you don't dig what's happening, man, you can just split."

Michael spun toward him, rigid, suddenly bristling with hostility.

Mulligan stepped between them to put his hand on Michael's shoulder. "Hey, relax," he said. His voice was slow and easy, nearly a drawl. "Just listen to me for a second. I don't want anyone to get hurt either. I've taken a lot of speed and I do know what I'm doing. I'm not telling anyone to shoot up, I'm just giving you the alternative. Sure speed is addictive, whether you swallow it, sniff it, or shoot it. Still, you can take it without getting hooked and it does something to some people that makes them think it's worth taking. Just like anything else, there's good things about it and bad things.

Everybody has to decide for themselves. Everybody has to go on their own trip, not yours."

Christine watched fascinated as Michael stared hard into Mulligan's eyes for several seconds and Mulligan met his gaze openly. Meanwhile Jacobi managed to extend the line of the argument one step further. Here stood Mulligan, he thought, living proof that one could overcome the addiction to speed and not be destroyed by it. What Jacobi wondered was whether Mulligan had been so remarkably alive before his addiction, or only after the addiction had been endured and overcome.

"Okay, man," Michael finally said, glancing down, "Everybody on their own trip, but I'll stick to the bennies."

And so Mulligan shot them up: Christine with eyes closed, Jacobi with eyes open but riveted to the mantle, and himself, taking a larger dose to compensate for his tolerance and body weight and watching the spike pierce his flesh, the blood back up the needle. Michael took two benzedrine and sniffed some of the powder that was left. And they woke up.

...that's the clarity of the razor's edge, the precision of the perfectly executed drum roll, the fall of Usher's house, that's swimming underwater with the eyes lidless...

Jacobi, flashing, the rush of energy, he'd taken speed before but this was speed to the Nth degree, this room was a different room than he'd been in a moment before, each object simpler, clearer and yet more distant, each person revealed as a representative example of their total selves that could be dealt with accordingly, each moment clearly within its category, the multiplicity of the categories clearly without end.

Christine, flashing, overwhelmed by the sheer power and force of the flash, the sleepiness and hunger of the grass comedown banished to the realm of another existence, happy and strangely alert, eyes so open, nearly ecstatic without knowing why, very forward, almost too sure of herself, as if a host of complexes and insecurities had been severed with one fell stroke—in a sense this was Christine realized, but only one aspect of Christine, it was a partial fulfillment and a kind of perversion.

Michael, already a little high on what he had sniffed, observing the others and waiting for the benzedrine to take the slow path through his digestive tract, into the bloodstream and on to the brain, almost wishing he'd tried the needle, too, but still contained, always self-contained.

Mulligan, flashing, a flash no longer new by any means, but always nice, even nicer since he'd been on top of it, he took his glasses off and momentarily his vision went stroboscopic, he looked around the room gone slightly blurry, Jacobi, Christine, Michael, with their outlines fuzzy they had become less individuals and more types, the young Ulysses chasing his tail, the glamorous, neurotic American divorcee, the misanthropic would-be artist, he put his glasses back on, he liked them all, even Michael, he titled his glasses back and forth and the room, the people, the objects distorted at his will, he worked his imagination around them, he worked them into his imagination to see what could happen, he projected, he turned on the microphone in his ear and the camera behind his eyes and he kept them running, he recorded, he played and he learned.

THE METHAMPHETAMINE WALTZ

(three-quarter time, presto to largo)

Overture

The sun goes down and the speed comes on. It is an all-night trip stretching into the exhaustion of morning. The lights in Christine's apartment die only with the light of morning. The pace is fast as it must be on speed. They move from the apartment and into the street and back again and back onto the dark streets for the sake of movement and yo-yoing again to the apartment because there is no place else to go in the dead morning city. Their dialogue speaks for itself. Their backdrop is city, beyond that immaterial. The path of their journeying is irrelevant; the intermechanics everything. The four of them become closely knit, double-stitched, an instant family in the space of hours, intertwined by shared realization, confession, and revelation, by the symbol and form of a common experience. Their talk is typical speed talk, intense, sincere and demanding, yet so transient that much of the content is forgotten afterwards. Their speed encounter is atypical because of its chief hypnotist and seed-sower.

One

Expectancy has invaded the room which is a new room for all of them. In a way they are more alive; they are also different. No one has really spoken yet, but an avalanche of words is building in each. Expectancy is an axe hanging over their heads, a rug about to be pulled from beneath their feet. Mulligan is on the couch, Christine on the edge of the bed, Michael sitting on the floor near the bookcase with his back against the wall, Jacobi standing and already anxious for movement.

CHRISTINE

(*Leaning forward, knees together, elbows on her knees and hands interlocked, watching the others with a laughter and energy formerly absent from her eyes, she suddenly seems to be one particular secret up on all of them, or at least to think herself so...finally her gaze settles on Mulligan.*) It's different than I expected, but it's nice. I could see someone getting addicted, but I'm not sure I can see them kicking it once they were.

MULLIGAN

(*Basking in the warmth of her gaze while Jacobi looks on.*) Addiction is just like anything else. (*"It's just like everything else"—a favorite Mulliganism. If you listened to him long enough Mulligan would try to convince you that everything was like everything else, that for all of the questions there was but one answer.*) To beat addiction you have to understand it. If you can understand something, not in so many words but really understand it, then you can never be at its mercy again.

MICHAEL

(*Always the combatant when confronted by a proctor of any sort.*) And just how can you understand something like that if it's on top of you and eating away at you and you're already at its mercy?

MULLIGAN

(*Sidestepping.*) I got hooked right after I first quit school. The whole thing happened in a space of a couple months. Of course, if you're on much longer than that you don't have many brain cells left even if you do get off. (*Mulligan pauses. As Michael, Jacobi and Christine watch, the slightly comic cast of his features becomes serious. His awareness seems to turn inward. The story of Mulligan's addiction, after a successful run in the West, is about to open to an audience of three in lower Manhattan. Jacobi has heard the story more than once, but it usually varies enough each time to hold his interest. He pulls on his mustache and waits for someone to push Mulligan into the spotlight, just as Mulligan himself is waiting.*)

CHRISTINE

(*Leaning further forward, twining her legs about one another so that one ankle is curled behind the other.*) Go on, Denny!

MULLIGAN

(*Lighting a cigarette and shaking out the match with a flourish before beginning, taking a couple of puffs and staring across the room, as if he were getting everything straight in his mind...then, in the course of the story, looking from one listener to another, but concentrating on Christine.*) I was living in San Francisco, mainly in the Mission District. I was dealing and I moved around a lot that summer, every time my paranoia caught up with me. I was taking a lot of stuff, too much stuff. Mostly it was meth and acid. I'd take them separately and I'd take them together. Sometimes when I took them together they seemed to complement one another. The acid would get me up there, and the speed would help me understand the high and bring a little of that understanding back. At times I was so aware I felt like I was devouring reality by the barrel, that I could do anything and be anyone, that I could recreate the entire world from any given instant. (*He pauses and takes a quick pull on his cigarette.*) In each situation I became involved in I felt at least one up on everybody else. I felt I could perceive layer after layer of meaning in even the simplest statements and expressions, in every action—double entendres, triple entendres and more, meanings operating at levels far beneath the conscious minds of any of the participants except myself. (*Pausing again, for dramatic effect, looking at Christine and then down, inward, and then up at her again, his expression so frank and disarming that whether it is true or not she suddenly feels herself revealed at all levels, levels beyond her own understanding.*) But at other times when I mixed speed and acid, nothing made any sense. It seemed like they were at war with each other, in complete contradiction, almost like a Marxist dialectic. (*Smiling.*) Thesis. Antithesis. But there was no synthesis, never any resolution. There was just going up and getting more enlightened or more confused and then crashing and then shooting up again. I was dependent on the speed before I knew it, but it didn't seem to make much difference there was so much of the shit around. I just stayed stoned and on the move and I was making money hand over fist from all the dealing I was doing. Even now, I still have some of that money left.

MICHAEL

(*Interrupting.*) But how did you quit then? And if it was so great, why?

MULLIGAN

(*Speaking directly to Michael, momentarily, then back to Christine.*) It wasn't all great. About a month after I got hooked, speed suddenly became scarce and I went through my first withdrawal ...involuntarily. Jesus, I thought I was going to die. It was pure, unadulterated hell. The only good thing about it was that life became simple. Everything was reduced to a single quantity, one equation: How to get more shit. From that time on I promised myself that I would quit, just like all speed freaks, quit at some indefinite time in the future when I'd gotten my head straightened out, when there wasn't so much pressure in my life. Only on speed you don't have much of a future. Six months? (*He shrugs.*) Maybe a year if you're lucky? By then you're so careless you get busted, or so fucked up in your head you just plain freak out and get yourself committed. The only thing that saved me was the acid. I kept taking it along with the speed and the contradiction between the two finally came to a head. I'd been living in the same house on Dolores Street for about a month, the longest I'd stayed in any one place that summer. The crew I was living with seemed pretty rough. Actually, they were just confused and in the process of fucking themselves over in one way or another, or trying to recover because they already had. They could have been a road company for Ginsberg's *Howl.* (*This is a new addition to the story for the benefit of Michael and Christine. Clearly, by the way Mulligan says it, it is not meant to be funny, and no one laughs.*) They weren't what was keeping me there, but a girl among them was. I'd been together with her for about a month too, almost from the first night I moved into the place. In that kind of scene the cat with the most bread and dope, the biggest dealer—and that was me—usually gets the woman he wants. Her nickname was Curly because of her hair. Her real name doesn't make any difference. I'm not sure I ever knew it, and if I did I've forgotten. She was cute and bright and we could talk to each other and clicked together from the start like it sometimes happens. I'd been with other women that summer, but she was the first that meant anything to me. Even though we'd been together only a month, it was a month of such heavy doping, such intensity, both high and low, that it seemed that in a lot of ways we knew each other completely. (*Jacobi looks toward Christine and she returns his gaze through the smoke of Mulligan's cigarette.*) The day I decided to quit speed—not some time in the future, but right then—was the same day I left her. I remember that I'd scored big just a few days before. We already had a supply of shit, and now there was enough so that we could take it like candy. The entire house was flying in the longest party I can remember. I don't think anyone went to sleep for days. (*Mulligan stops and looks around. Everyone is staring at him with rapt attention, including Jacobi, who knows the rest of the story by heart. Mulligan stubs out his cigarette.*) I'm getting awfully thirsty. Could I please have a glass of water.

(*Christine, who has been industriously chewing one thumbnail for the last several minutes, is up immediately, speed-powered. She makes a dash to the kitchen and comes back with a glass of water. As she hands it to Mulligan, he smiles up at her. He takes several swallows and passes the glass to Jacobi. It completes a circle of the room as Mulligan continues speaking.*)

MULLIGAN

(*Licking his lips with satisfaction.*) It was the longest party I can remember. On the third morning I took some acid, but I was so wired already that it didn't seem to do much...not at first. I tried to get Curly to take some too, but when it came to dope she was a purist. She didn't like to mix her highs and didn't care much for acid anyway. Later that day, with our last shot about to wear off, we decided to go upstairs to bed. Curly was dragging her feet on the way up and I knew she was about to crash. We got into bed and got our clothes off, but before we could make love, she fell asleep on me. (*Jacobi looks at Christine again, but she is watching Mulligan.*) I should have been crashing, too, but I wasn't. I was horny, ready to fuck for hours it seemed...and there was my woman, unconscious, burnt out from too much meth. It wasn't funny, but it struck me as funny at the time and I started laughing. I started laughing and I couldn't stop. Long after it no longer seemed funny I couldn't stop. I was rolling on the bed with laughter, then on the floor, with Curly unconscious through it all. I was hysterical, crying and laughing at the same time until it had all emptied out of me and I was dry. I remember I sat there awhile on the floor, naked and numb, and then I put my pants on and walked over to the window before it hit me. I was stoned again...stoned on the acid! It didn't make any sense at all. I'd taken the acid hours before. I should only be getting the tail end of it now, if anything at all. But it was either hitting me in delayed reaction or I was totally insane. All of my perceptions were acid perceptions. The walls were gently undulating and beginning to fill with moving patterns. As I walked about the room I became increasingly aware of my body and all my senses. When I looked at things up close they had that purity and clarity that you can get only on acid. (*Mulligan is speaking more rapidly. Although Jacobi, Christine and Michael are still listening, he no longer seems to be telling the story to them. He is now reliving it through the substance of his memory.*) Outside it was broad daylight. The sun was shining and the sky perfectly cloudless. I had to shut my eyes from the brightness. It wasn't that the sun was brighter than I'd ever seen it before, but that it imparted more brightness to the street below, the windowsill, to the room, than ever before. I opened my eyes and looked back into the room. Curly was naked on the bed, uncovered. She was so thin her bones protruded. Her arms and legs were like sticks. I could see her collarbone, her ribs, her pelvis pushing through the fleshless skin. Her skin was pale, but it wasn't white. It was gray. It struck me that she was young, barely twenty, that her youth should still be blossoming, that she shouldn't look like this. I looked down at my own body. I had been losing weight, too, so fast that my pants were hanging on me and in places my flesh sagged. My own skin was gray and lifeless. It was physically clear, with a clarity magnified by the acid, that both of us were starving to death. We had not only dropped out of the system, we were in the process of dropping out of life itself. We were saying no to existence.

All this time the sun was still glaring through the window like fifty thousand watts and I was going up and up on the acid. My perceptions seemed more revelatory to me with each moment that passed. There was something metallic on the table, sparkling the sunlight around the room. It was our needle and syringe, set up and ready for another hit. I picked it up and the urge came upon me immediately, not the urge to shoot up, but to plunge the needle directly into my chest. The acid had eliminated the metaphor of addiction for me. Suddenly I understood that if I wanted to kick speed, it wasn't the drug that I'd have to grapple with, but the death wish itself. My hand actually wavered for several seconds, then I dropped the needle like it was on fire and the glass in the syringe broke as it rolled off the table. (*Mulligan looks up at Christine.*) Have you ever experienced fear? Have you ever been really frightened?

CHRISTINE

(*Readily.*) Yes, when I first left my husband and... (*Faltering because she is thinking of her abortion and she feels queasy and unconsciously presses her hand against her stomach, but something...the speed, Mulligan, the atmosphere of confession his story has engendered, prompts her to go ahead and say it.*)...and when I had an abortion. (*Jacobi stares at her sharply. This is another new one on him.*)

MULLIGAN

(*Turning toward Michael.*) And what about you? Have you ever really been afraid?

MICHAEL

(*Wary, noncommittal.*) I'm not sure what you mean.

MULLIGAN

I mean fear so great that it becomes a physical thing, so great that it pervades your entire consciousness, your whole environment. That's what happened to me after I dropped the needle. I sat down on the bed. I was trembling and I'd broken out in a cold sweat. I had just realized that the death wish was something that could beat me, that in a moment of weakness I could give myself over to it completely, that in one moment of weakness after another I had been giving myself to it gradually. I was weak with fear. I was afraid of the broken glass on the floor, of the table, even afraid of the very bed I was sitting on. It was a delusion of the acid, but it was all real enough. I got up and out of that room and I went down the hall toward the bathroom to wash my face, but I only got to the doorway. I was frightened of the water dripping from the tap, afraid I might have to confront the reflection of my dying self in the mirror. I went back to the room and Curly lying on the bed. I leaned across it and touched her gray skin and it was repulsive to me. If I was to survive I knew I had to get out of that house and away from those people, and I knew I couldn't take Curly with me. She hadn't had any revelation about speed and the death wish. Even if I could convince her to kick the shit and come with me, we wouldn't stand a chance of making it together because we didn't care about each other enough, not as much as we cared about the shit. I already knew what withdrawal was like. One of us would pull the other back or wind up betraying them. I was so anxious to leave, so frightened that I panicked, but it was that panic that saved me, that gave me the decisiveness that actually got me out of the place. I didn't want any of the things I had there, particularly the drugs, I just wanted out. I put on my shoes and a shirt. All of the cash I had was already in my wallet. I threw a jacket over my shoulder and without looking back I was out of the room and headed downstairs. I walked as quickly as I could but quietly, afraid that if someone said something and stopped me momentarily they would kill my momentum. Downstairs the party was still going in the main room of the house. I could hear the music and voices. I went by that room without looking into it, like my neck was in a brace. Then I closed the front door behind me and just kept moving. I remember it was so sunny outside and the streets were so warm that I walked all the way to the East Bay Depot. Then I was exhausted and fell asleep on the bus and the driver had to wake me up when we got to Berkeley.

(*There is a moment of silence. The story is apparently over.*)

CHRISTINE

(*Asking as if she were afraid to ask.*) And whatever happened to the girl, Curly?

MULLIGAN

I don't know. (*Sighing.*) I never went back to the house and I've never heard anything about her since.

(*The silence lengthens and thickens. Christine is swinging one leg nervously. Michael is cracking his knuckles. Jacobi, still standing, is shifting his weight from one foot to another, shaking his arms as if he is loosening up to run a dash. The confined energy of the speed has taken possession of each of them. So far it is only Mulligan who has found expression and released that energy.*)

MULLIGAN

(*Looking around the room, crinkling up one side of his face in a comic grimace to break the mood he has created.*) What say we all get out of here before we detonate?

Walking

A frame of the Village streets, circa August, 1965, fading. Blow up the lower right hand corner. The image of three men and a woman abreast on the sidewalk, trapped in time. No, three youths and a woman, for although her face is smiling and unlined it is not stamped with the freshness of theirs. On the far left, nearly edged off the sidewalk and into the street, a dark youth with a mustache walks next to the woman. Their bare arms touch momentarily as he shifts his balance to stay on the curb. To their right, half a step behind, a short and stocky youth scrutinizes the woman's profile as she pivots her head slightly to the left. He is the only member of the foursome who is not smiling. To his right, on the far right, walking a great enough distance apart so that one is not sure whether he is a member of the group or not, a frail blond youth stares straight ahead, into, through and past our lens, with features as finely cast and delicate as those of the woman.

A chemical fabrication, a common denominator, a fifth column of lightness has invaded the space behind the eyes of each.

Move two frames ahead and they are gone.

Two

Washington Square. Jacobi and Michael are sitting on a bench and Mulligan is standing in front of them, talking. They have been walking so fast they are all a bit out of breath. Christine, saying she wants to be alone for awhile, an unusual request for her, is taking a stroll around the Square. There are many voices in the park, but Jacobi is listening to Mulligan's. Michael is avoiding talking, staying the avalanche of words by trying to whistle, a task complicated by the amphetamine dryness of his mouth. He is twenty years old and he has never learned how to whistle. In more ways than one he is ill-equipped for adult life.

MULLIGAN

(Hands on his hips, looking after Christine's retreating figure.) What's she like, Davy? I bet she can be quite a woman when she lets herself go.

JACOBI

(Smiling up at him, loose and easy now that the physical exertion of walking has released his nervousness, he is riding the speed like an unreined pony in full gallop.) I'm not talking, man. You'll have to find out for yourself.

MULLIGAN

(*Ignoring the implication.*) You've been going through changes, Davy. What are you doing? Where are you at?

JACOBI

(*Knowing that Mulligan, the psychic mole, is once again after him.*) I'm right here, man. Can't you see me?

MULLIGAN

No, I mean with respect to the fair Christine. (*Nodding into the dark.*) If you're playing a game with that one you're liable to wake up and find out that it's real as Heaven or Hell. I think she's been good for you, Davy, but in case you didn't know, school starts in another week and a half. What are you doing? Are you going to stay here in New York and feed your body or are you going to return to the West and pursue…the…true… torch…of…knowledge. Tell me, what part of you wants her, anyway? (*He goes into an exaggerated pantomime, pointing to his head, his heart, his crotch, and finally in a burst of laughing inspiration he pulls out his wallet and points to that.*) Tell me, Davy (*leaning over Jacobi and letting his voice hum down to a confidential base*), do…you…love…her?

JACOBI

(*Suspecting the question is facetious, but still knowing that Mulligan is asking it for a reason, even if the reason is only the amusement of Mulligan.*) Are you serious, man?

MULLIGAN

(*The prosecutor.*) I'm always serious, dead-straight serious. Really. Plain and simple. Do you love her?

JACOBI

(*The psychic mole has hit pay dirt. Despite his resistance, Mulligan has now involved him in the conversation. Jacobi knows this is exactly the question Christine would be asking him morning, noon and night if she hadn't thought it would put him off. This was the question she was asking implicitly with her repeated "I love you"s, although again and again his only answer was silence or a momentary embrace.*) I don't know what that means, Denny. I can tell you the things we do together. How much we talk to each other and about what. I could give you the details of our sex life. I could tell you what I like about her and what I don't like about her. But as far as love goes, it's your word (*And Tina's, too, he thinks.*), so you figure it out.

MULLIGAN

Ah...love! (*Spreading his arms as if he is about to burst into an aria.*) The man needs a definition...so I'll give him one. This is what I mean. Do you want to consume her inch by careful inch? Do you want to reach out and make her a part of yourself? Do you want to become a part of her at the same time? Do you think about her when you're with her and when you're not with her? Do you wish she were sitting by your side right now instead of Michael? (*Pointing into the dark.*) Are you following her around the park with an invisible tether? (*Pointing back to Jacobi.*) When you walk down the street together do you compare her with all the women you pass and each time, invariably, your eyes come back to her. Does she make you feel lucky when she touches you? Is it different than the touch of anyone else? If she's ten minutes late do you hold your breath and envision her in a hundred calamities, a thousand surreptitious affairs? And finally...finally...when all is said and done (*Pausing and gathering his breath and stabbing a finger at Jacobi once again.*)—Is she your reality?

JACOBI

(*Silent for a moment, thinking about everything Mulligan has said, letting it all run through his head and a little bowled over trying to sort it all out, knowing that it's a summer night, that the moon is passing overhead, knowing that Christine is walking just a few hundred yards away and admitting to himself that even after a few minutes he wishes she were back, feeling the conclusion coming upon him like a slow dawn until its warmth spreads from head to foot, admitting the inevitable, but still having its vocalization not feel quite right, the words catching in his throat, saying it reluctantly and realizing in the process how strange it is that he should be saying it for the first time to Mulligan rather than Christine.*) Well, if that's what you mean, I guess the answer is yes. I guess I do love her.

MULLIGAN

(*Reaching out to grab Jacobi's hand and shake it.*) Well, congratulations, Davy! (*Yet it is impossible to decipher the expression on his face.*)

MICHAEL

(*Cynic and spoiler, chirping belatedly between two abortive whistles.*) That's not love...that's infatuation.

Pristine

She has surrendered a score of acquired postures and is perceiving with a kind of A-B-C simplicity. She is young again. Surrounded by her entourage of three young men she is very young indeed, perhaps even a virgin again. She is listening to the click of her heels, watching her steps, the polished toes of her pumps. She doesn't know who to thank for this new and novel certainty in her limbs, for the litheness and sense of purpose. Should she thank the trees, the benches, the shrubs, the speed? Mulligan, Jacobi, Michael? She'd thank them all if she knew how.

Her entourage of three young men. Her entourage of three young studs. All attractive in one way or another, she thinks, even if two of them are a bit odd looking. Almost an entire male spectrum at her fingertips. For the moment she enjoyed watching Mulligan most because he was someone new, interesting, animated, just right for the speed. She'd have to start dressing younger, she thinks. With more color. And her skirts should be shorter to show off her legs?

A block outside the Square, in a small boutique, she finds a floppy broad-brimmed hat the color of apricots! She tries it on, strikes a Garboesque pose before the mirror, and without thinking twice, she buys it. Certainty. Clarity. Purpose.

Back in the park she smiles at the men she passes, even though it is mostly too dark to see their faces or for them to see hers. She smiles at her mirror reflection, still bright before her eyes. In a certain sense, the speed has made her feel asexual. She is crossing a calm and temperate plateau above the vicissitudes of sex and desire. She feels invulnerable, untouchable beyond her choice of touch, and yet she wants to embrace the entire world.

Ah, sweet youth! What a glorious thing!

Three

Still the Square, with Christine returning. They all notice the hat immediately; it is impossible to miss. Jacobi smiles. Michael stops whistling and stares. Mulligan yells out, "Très chic! Très chic!," then charges toward Christine and by her, with a sweep of his arm snatching the hat from her head. Christine squeals in protest, but just as she is turning to pursue Mulligan he runs back past her in the other direction and she is forced to turn full circle before spotting him again, this time with the hat upon his own head. After that it makes the complete round. Mulligan hands it to Jacobi who places it carefully upon his dark mop, and finally to Michael who grins goofily as the hat slides over his ears and succeeds in breaking them all up. By this time it has become more than a hat. It has become part of another unifying experience, like the glass of water passed from hand to hand in the midst of Mulligan's story.

Mulligan plucks the hat from Michael's head and brushing off imaginary dust, bowing, hands it back to Christine. Just as she gets it on he encircles her waist with one arm, begins talking to her and walking her away from the bench. After about fifteen feet, he spins her around and brings her back past the bench, then fifteen feet in the other direction before pivoting again. This back and forth motion goes on for some time as they talk. Michael and Jacobi remain seated, their heads moving from left to right, right to left, watching this pendulum dance as if it were a slow-motion tennis match, straining their ears to catch the conversation at each apogee of its swing.

MULLIGAN

(*As he first takes her by the waist.*) In your absence, we've been having a very revealing philosophical discussion about the definition of...love. (*Proceeding to alter his inflection every time he says the word, as if it were a consecration or a blasphemy.*) What do you think...love...is?

CHRISTINE

(*Feeling elated enough to play along with Mulligan's nonsense.*) Well...in point of fact, there is no comprehensive literal definition, but...

MULLIGAN

(*Interrupting.*) Not even Webster's twenty-four part one?

CHRISTINE

(*Smiling.*) Not even Webster's, but if you'll...

MULLIGAN

(*Interrupting again as they turn in their walk.*) You mean that...love...is nonverbal?

CHRISTINE

(*Insistent, her voice rising.*) No! Wait! Let me finish. There's no literal definition, but if you'll take the trouble to read the poem on page forty-three of my book, you'll find a perfect metaphorical one. (*Nodding smartly.*)

MULLIGAN

(*After a second's hesitation, slowly, breaking the banter of their talk.*) But that's no kind of definition at all. Metaphors can mean whatever you want them to mean.

(*They pace in silence for a few turns, with Mulligan's head bowed and his faced screwed up in thought. As they pass the bench, with Christine on the outside, she leans back to look over Mulligan's bent head at Jacobi, shrugs her shoulders and cocks her own head to one side. Jacobi responds likewise.*)

MULLIGAN

Tell me, Tina, have you been with many men?

CHRISTINE

(*Somewhat defensively because this is a blow at her illusion of youth, but ready with the right answer because she has been asked this question before by men who had no apparent right to ask it.*) Enough.

MULLIGAN

(*Clapping one hand against his thigh in applause and laughing.*) Bravo! The perfect response. Coy and aggressive at the same time. Would you care to enumerate?

CHRISTINE

(*Counting on her fingers.*) Well, let's see. There was Fred and Pete and Sebastian and Carmichael and Luigi and…

MULLIGAN

Luigi Pirandello?

CHRISTINE

(*With a pained expression.*) Please! I'll admit to a few years on you, but I'm not quite that old.

MULLIGAN

(*Pointedly returning to his original topic.*) And how many of these men did you…love?

CHRISTINE

(*Seeking the safety of repetition.*) Enough.

MULLIGAN

(*Turning her around again and this time, in the process, executing a waltz step.*) But that's impossible. How can one love enough?

CHRISTINE

(*Removing Mulligan's arm from her waist and leaving his last question unanswered.*) Denny, if you don't mind, I think I've been walking long enough. I'd like to sit down for awhile. (*She crosses to the bench and sits next to Jacobi, who slips his arm around her shoulders.*)

(*Mulligan's eyes follow her as he bends to tie the laces on one of his tennis shoes. He stands to resume his pacing alone, now with a shorter arc and his hands in his pockets.*)

MULLIGAN

And what about this one? (*He is still talking to Christine, but nodding toward Jacobi.*) How does he stack up with the rest? What do you think of him?

CHRISTINE

(*Reaching out her hand, placing it alongside of Jacobi's chin and raising his head a little, appraising the result.*) I think he's pretty.

JACOBI

(*Taking her hand away, but leaving it in his own.*) It's only the soft light.

MULLIGAN

(*Stopping in front of them and with one sentence stripping the veneer of jest off their conversation.*) And do you...love...him?

CHRISTINE

(*Telling Jacobi, not Mulligan, and serious now.*) Yes, of course I do. (*And then to Mulligan, the veneer back on.*) Why else would I put up with his friends?

MULLIGAN

(*Speculatively chewing on his lower lip.*) What about you, Davy? (*Leaning forward conspiratorially, with one foot up on the bench between Michael and Jacobi.*) What do you think of her? I bet she can be quite a woman when she lets herself go?

(*Jacobi doesn't say anything. He just glares at Mulligan menacingly.*)

MULLIGAN

(*Concealing his smile half the time and the other half letting it break through.*) You know, Davy, you're different. You've been going through changes. I think she's been good for you, but tell me, where are you at?

JACOBI

(*In a slow, measured tone as he silently damns Mulligan a hundred times.*) I'm...right...here...man. Can't...you...see...me?

MULLIGAN

No, I mean, do you...love...her?

JACOBI

(*Sensing Christine's hand tightening in his own, knowing at this point there is no alternative, but hesitating anyway until it emerges in what seems to him a very small voice.*) Yes, I guess I do. (*Then feeling relief, as if he has expelled his breath after holding it for too long, feeling Christine's hand tightening still further and her own expelled breath warm upon his cheek.*)

MULLIGAN

(*With sudden ministerial solemnity, grabbing their clasped hands and lifting them.*) Congratulations and sempiternal blessings! I now pronounce you lover and lover. (*As his thumb rubs against the flesh of Christine's wrist.*)

MICHAEL

(*Who has been watching the three of them for the last several minutes as if they were deranged.*) Hey, I'm dying of thirst. Let's go get something to drink.

Lemonade

It is supposedly a coffeehouse, but the owner, being a true American entrepreneur operating in the spirit of New York summer capitalism, has discovered he can make more money with lemonade than espresso, so that is what tops the bill of fare. It is not the best lemonade they've ever tasted, but it is far and away the most refreshing. They all have two large glasses and Jacobi and Mulligan split a third. Christine drinks hers with a straw. Jacobi gulps his so fast that it soaks his mustache and afterward runs down his chin. Mulligan crunches the ice between swallows. Michael uses two straws and masticates their tips so thoroughly they resemble withered reeds.

By the time they get back to Christine's apartment, they have to form a line at the bathroom door.

Four

Mulligan has started a joint going around to ease their come-down. The subject is acid, acid and ecstasy, an all-time Mulligan favorite. Jacobi is thinking, here we are again, stoned on dope and talking about dope, déjà vu, déjà vu. Christine is all interest, nods and questions. She has come to attention and Mulligan is the commanding officer. Michael is as uncommunicative as ever. By being the proper nonperformer, he has discovered that he can sometimes dampen the energy of an entire room.

MULLIGAN

(*Standing with his back to the window, blocking most of the view.*) To have one peak experience after another, that's what it's all about. Some cats spend fifteen years grooving on their navels in a cave in the Himalayas to get there. Now, with the right cap of acid and the right environment, a lot of people can get there in a few hours. The question is—How do you stay there? How do you keep from coming back down again? Each time you have to bring some of that ecstasy and enlightenment back with you, hold onto it and incorporate it into your existence.

CHRISTINE

But isn't there a limit to how much acid you can take? Can't too much be bad for you, just like speed?

MULLIGAN

It all depends on the person. Some people can handle it and some can't. (*Pausing to take an extended drag on the joint, which shrinks noticeably. Mulligan could suck more off a joint in one drag than anyone Jacobi had ever known, as if his body were a hollow cavity for pot smoke.*) One thing for sure, it's not addictive. I've taken a hell of a lot and I'm still in one piece. (*Patting his arms, his shoulders and chest as if to make sure.*) Usually, if something is damaging to your body, your body will let you know about it. You don't need scientific studies to figure out that alcohol and speed are physically bad for you. Both of them make you pay for your high by crashing you afterwards. With acid, pure acid, even if you have a bad trip, physically you feel okay afterwards. The main problem is the same problem that cat in the Himalayas would have if he achieved his *satori* in New York instead of Tibet. After a lot of acid, taken regularly, you lose touch…not necessarily with reality, whatever that is…but with reality as it is defined in this society. You lose the ability to function in the hive of everyday America. This country has never made any room for visionaries, for holy men, unless they were orthodox enough or could retreat into the wilderness. That kind of behavior just isn't acceptable in the land of the free, the brave and the parochial. (*Passing the joint to Christine and touching her hand in the transaction.*) The other danger is that acid is indiscriminate. It's a lot of other things besides enlightenment. It can be a purging, a soul-cleansing, every time you take it, and if you get purged too often…well..the soul kind of gets rubbed raw. (*Turning toward Michael who is sitting on the floor with his back against the wall, legs drawn up, arms crossed, a narrow frown etched on his narrow features.*) You've taken acid before, what do you think?

MICHAEL

(*Looking up and around, making sure the question is addressed to him, although he already knows that it is.*) Me? I don't know. You're the expert. I don't think anything.

MULLIGAN

(*Staring down at Michael's hunched and compact form, deciding to temporarily abandon Christine's acid education and tackle the yet-to-be-scaled Mount Shawtry there and then.*) Then why are you registering such negativity?

MICHAEL

(*He cannot deny it. It is obvious to everyone in the room and he knows it is obvious.*)

MULLIGAN

You know, it's a dubious accomplishment to stay quiet on speed.

MICHAEL

(*With an awkward grin.*) It's still an accomplishment though.

JACOBI

You're wasting your time, Denny. You've heard about water from a stone, blood from a turnip.

MULLIGAN

(*Rubbing his palms together, speaking in mock sotto voce to Jacobi.*) That's no turnip, Davy, that's a juicy apple. It just needs to be bitten. (*And then to Michael.*) Look, man, let your defenses down for awhile. That's part of what speed is all about, getting people to talk to one another. Don't fight it. Let it happen. Let it flow out of you.

MICHAEL

You're forgetting, I didn't shoot up. I didn't get as much speed as the rest of you.

MULLIGAN

You don't have to have any speed to be more open than you are.

MICHAEL

(*Raising his voice.*) I'm just being myself.

MULLIGAN

(*Raising his voice higher.*) And I'm telling you that you should try to change yourself. Give some energy to other people. Then you'll find out what it's like to get some back.

MICHAEL

(*Standing suddenly, with his hands forward as if he is about to grasp the argument bodily. The apple has been bitten and it is giving off energy, negative energy, but energy all the same.*) And how about you telling me something? Who are you to ask all the questions and make all the pronouncements? You're still functioning in this society. You're not a holy man. You're not enlightened.

MULLIGAN

(*Back in a conversational tone.*) You're right. I'm nothing special, but I'm also not greedy. You ask the questions for awhile. (*Stepping away from the window and leaning back against the wall, sliding down it to adopt the same posture Michael has just abandoned.*) It'll be worth it if it will get you to talk to us.

MICHAEL

(*Left standing in the center of the floor with all eyes upon him, but no opponent to confront. After thinking frantically for several seconds, the speed racing his thoughts, he faces Mulligan again.*) All right. Remember what you said about addiction before?

MULLIGAN

I've said a lot of things today. Refresh my memory.

MICHAEL

You said that once you really understand addiction, you could never be at its mercy again. Well...then...what about cigarettes?

MULLIGAN

(*Raising his eyebrows.*) What about them?

MICHAEL

(*Who hates the weakness of his own cigarette habit but who has never been able to resist when he is around others who are smoking, who has only been able to reach the compromise of bumming cigarettes instead of buying them.*) You seem to be just as hooked as the rest of us, that's what!

MULLIGAN

I smoke them, but I'm not addicted to them. I can quit when I want.

CHRISTINE

(*Who has long since given up any attempt to stop smoking.*) You mean just like that. (*Snapping her fingers.*)

MULLIGAN

(*Reaching out and snapping his back at her.*) Just like that.

MICHAEL

Sure you can.

MULLIGAN

What do you think, Davy?

JACOBI

(*Who has seen Mulligan go on and off cigarettes from one day to the next.*) I don't care about you. You buy your own. It's Michael I'd like to see quit.

MULLIGAN

Well, these should keep him going for awhile. (*Removing the pack of Camels from his pocket, taking one out and handing the rest to Michael.*) Just one more, then I won't touch the poisonous weed again until I go back to California.

MICHAEL

(*Taking the pack and pulling one out for himself.*) Well...good luck, man, but I don't think you'll ever make it.

Wired As One

The grass on top of the speed is like one lens atop another. If it dims their focus, it also heightens their sensuality. But the grass is premature for they are not coming down. Although the hour is late and the speed should be wearing off, they are still wired. They are still running strong on inertia and Mulligan-power, strung out on cigarettes and talk. The longer they are in the speed state the more removed they become from the reality they have left behind and move into a world of their own making. They become more of a group and less four distinct individuals. Their conversation begins to reduce itself to free association, moments of madness, real poetry. Then someone opens a windows, spilling their laughter onto the pavement where it breaks dying like the last joint, and they are drawn forth stumbling into the city streets once again. A dark and slumbering city before the light of dawn. A silent city before the black and white newspapers screaming noise.

Five

A dark stage but for the light upon their figures, a refracted light that emanates from above, light enough for recognition yet too little for fine distinction. Beyond this illumination a thickening darkness surrounds them, creating a sense of enclosure rather than space. To them, this is a secondary impression. Their group consciousness is centered upon the mechanics of their own quartet. They are ranged across the stage, left to right: Mulligan, Christine, Jacobi, Michael. They are walking four abreast upon a wide conveyor belt, facing the dead footlights. The belt is black rubber, almost invisible, and it is impossible to tell whether it is their movement that propels it, or whether they must stay in motion merely to remain in place.

MULLIGAN

(*Without cigarettes.*) Energy. It's always a question of energy, from the most complex human relationships down to the simplest animal ones, from the stars to the atoms.

MICHAEL

(*Looking up.*) Where *are* the stars?

JACOBI

(*Laughing.*) Stars in the city? What stars?

MULLIGAN

Don't worry about the stars. Just let it flow, let it happen. Do whatever seems appropriate. Direct your compulsions in the proper creative direction.

CHRISTINE

(*Of the lean ivory breasts.*) I was young then. I was only a girl.

MULLIGAN

(*Making up a fact.*) Still, it remains a fact that in most civilized nations throughout recorded history the removal of the fetus after the second month of gestation has been considered criminal.

CHRISTINE

(*With startled eyes bluer than their shadow.*) I wasn't my own woman yet. I was younger than you are now, so much younger.

MULLIGAN

(*Turning around and walking backward for several steps, eying Christine up and down, not undressing her with his eyes but dressing her differently, more to his liking.*) Being beautiful is one thing. Being unique unto oneself is something else again.

JACOBI

That's the reason I came to New York, to define an identity for myself, to become unique.

MICHAEL

(*Looking up again.*) Without stars, the brilliance of the sun is elevated to an absolute. A planetary system with one sun is simple. A system with two suns is dynamic and complex. It is also less stable, more likely to change orbits or explode unexpectedly.

MULLIGAN

No, Davy, the real reason you left Berkeley was to get away from me.

CHRISTINE

(*In a faraway voice.*) Sometimes when I write the whole panorama of my life is there before me.

(*Mulligan turns his forefinger in the air, pointing as if he is seeking a target. Michael continues to look upward at the undifferentiated light. Jacobi takes Christine's arm but she for once seems oblivious to his touch. The conveyor belt begins to squeal as if it is in need of oil. The noise rises in pitch and volume throughout the remainder of the scene.*)

JACOBI

Reality is like an onion. Tell them, Denny.

CHRISTINE

I can pick and choose as I please. I can relive both the best and the worst.

MULLIGAN

Reality is like an onion. You peel away layer after layer until there is nothing left but your self.

CHRISTINE

And your tears.

MULLIGAN

And your knife.

MICHAEL

(*Looking inward.*) The absence of the sun excludes the concept of light.

MULLIGAN

Iron tears from the cauldron of your eyes. Textile tears from the loom of your eyes.

JACOBI

Mechanical tears from the factories of your eyes that can run their engines up the brow...

MULLIGAN

...bore through the skull at pressure points, explore the brain with hook and trowel.

CHRISTINE

Silver tears from the mines of your eye that can lace the throat with light linked chain or swing from ears erotica...

MICHAEL

...or fill your teeth with shredded rain.

MULLIGAN

But none of us is as picturesque as... (*The squealing of the conveyor drowns his words.*)

JACOBI

Still, this is political economy, the kings bereft of their titles, the fat bosses munching their political potato chips.

MICHAEL

(*Waxing romantic.*) He rode across the desert sands, with sweet rose water on his hands; the sun was his stallion and the moon his consort, and the stars...

MULLIGAN

...are gone.

CHRISTINE

I can pick and choose as I please...Paris, Rome, Madrid...

MULLIGAN

...Poughkeepsie, Hackensack, Yucatan, New Zealand...

JACOBI

...Borneo, Atlantis, Patagonia...

CHRISTINE

...stop it...

MICHAEL

...Stop it!...

(*The conveyor screams intolerably. It is surely consuming itself. The footlights explode like flash cubes blinding both the audience and the actors. The conveyor grinds to a gear-wrenching halt upon a totally black stage. The absence of light excludes the concept of the sun.*)

Tired As One

The crash hits them all at once, powerfully, like a group revelation. Their heads buzz and ache. Their thoughts become distracted. The dryness in their mouths and throats is now a foul dryness that lemonade could never faze. Each cell of each of their bodies is crying for rest.

They make it back to the apartment, but once upstairs they hold out against the desire to sleep. Sleep will destroy their unity and make them separate individuals again. They listen to music. Mulligan tries to play his conga to Bach. They smoke another joint. Christine opens the curtains to welcome the first light of morning. It is an attenuated dawn due to their own attenuation. It shows each of them their own exhaustion reflected back in the exhausted faces of their companions.

Six

Everything has slowed down, Johann Sebastian on the stereo, the clocks and the rate at which the sun rises, even Dennis Patrick Mulligan. Yet he is still managing to do most of the talking. The words continue to roll out of him. He is mostly incoherent now, changing the subject in the middle of an anecdote or even the middle of a sentence, repeating himself. He is like a plane without fuel, gliding in on its altitude and the right air currents. But the words continue to roll.

MULLIGAN

(*Wedged upright against one arm of the couch, gesturing broadly with a slack hand.*) Well, the night's no longer young, but we still are. Let's keep the party going. Davy, why don't you roll us another joint?

JACOBI

(*Sitting on the edge of the bed. His head turns slowly as he looks around the room several times, trying to remember where he'd put the grass, before he gives up from lack of interest.*)

MULLIGAN

(*Laughing softly and shaking his head.*) It's just like everything else.

MICHAEL

(*Absently, sitting with his back against the wall again. He appears to be abandoning chairs as he has so many other conventions.*) What is?

MULLIGAN

Everything...like the crew I was living with at the time had a theatrical bent...

CHRISTINE

(*Leaning on a pillow propped against the headboard, her legs up on the bed and her shoes off, she is trying to listen to Mulligan but her head keeps nodding and her eyes keep sliding shut on her.*) When was that?

MULLIGAN

You know...what I was saying before, on Dwight Way...we were living just a couple of blocks off the Avenue...

CHRISTINE

(*Sleepily, lying.*) Oh...I remember.

MULLIGAN

We used to... (*Yawning.*) ...put on plays for our own amusement, variations on the masters, mixtures...of course, just like everything else they'd get crazier when we were stoned...we used to...Davy, I thought you were going to roll a joint...I remember once we had Willie Loman meet Hamlet in a hotel corridor on his way to an infidelity...not Hamlet...that is...but...(*Mulligan has fallen asleep with his chin in his hand. He looks the same as a moment before only his eyes are closed and he is breathing evenly. He looks a little bit like Boswell or Catherine the Great, but not at all like The Thinker.*)

MICHAEL

(*After several seconds of silence.*) Well...guess I'll be splitting. (*After another several, lying down on the floor with eyes closed to curl up at the edge of the rug with his thin arms for a pillow.*)

JACOBI

(*Lifting his head to look around the room, saying his friend's names one at a time, quietly and slowly.*) Tina...Denny...Michael...(*Adding his own for good measure.*)...David...(*Before he lies down next to Christine with his clothes still on, drapes an arm across her side, and gives up the ghost like the rest.*)

(*They lose the entire day. The sun shifts across the sky and the city awakens and goes about its city business. The market sags until a flurry of trading in the final hour returns it to the morning line. Airplanes land and take off and streak the sky. The shadows in the apartment flow and bend and lay their lines differently across the floor. Somewhere desire is sated and sated and blooms again. The shadows fade. The sun goes down and it grows dimmer by imperceptible degrees. Then there is no sun at all, the absence of light, and once again it is dark.*)

Dreaming As One

As it turns out, Mulligan's trip to New York is not exclusively an excursion of pleasure. Business is involved also. Concealed in the false bottom of his briefcase are two Jim Beam bottles—emptied of their original contents and filled to the brim with pure lysergic acid. Mulligan is to deliver them uptown to a certain Mr. Black.

They take the VW with Mulligan, Jacobi and Christine ranged across the front seat. All things are possible in dreams. Christine is driving with her skirt hitched up and she is leggy as a fawn. Mulligan is carrying the whisky bottles in a rumpled paper sack and each time the car turns a corner the bottles clink against one another and the back of his hand brushes her thigh. Mulligan has somehow learned of Jacobi's fiasco at Billie Raintree's and there is an air about him that says: Watch how a real dealer operates.

They arrive at the house, outwardly no different from those around it except that its entire facade has been painted black. As they are climbing out of the car, Mulligan sticks his head back in. "If we're not out in thirty minutes," he says, "come in shooting."

"Okay, boss," a voice croaks, barely intelligible since it is forcing itself to speak several registers below its normal key. Michael is in the backseat, attired in a zoot suit and slant-brimmed fedora. His head is dwarfed by the width of his lapels and the tommy gun resting across his lap.

The apartment they are seeking is on the ground floor, but they must climb several flights to reach it. Mulligan assails the door with a prearranged knock, long and complex as a telegraph message, and they are ushered in by an Oriental house boy. The house boy is wearing silk pajamas identical to a pair of Christine's. He leaves the three of them in a wide, dimly-lit room. The room is richly furnished, and Jacobi and Christine wander around, examining its objects—an abstract ebony statue, a three-inch dragonfly encased in amber, a silver and ivory inlaid box. On the mantle above the fireplace there are three photographs of three different women entrapped in gilt frames. In spite of one's dusky complexion, another's auburn hair, the third's exotic make-up, they all have high cheekbones and cool blue eyes. Jacobi pulls on his mustache as he examines the photos. Christine quickly steers him away before he can recognize her.

With dream-like inexactitude, Mr. Black is suddenly in the room with them. And he *is* black, black and bare to the waist, wearing gray dress slacks creased as sharply as folded paper. His arms and upper torso are heavily muscled, but his middle is thickening with premature fat. One can tell that he is a bit proud of this fat because it is a sign of how well he has made it. He and Mulligan, who have met before, greet one another with excessive warmth.

Although the acid is at the forefront of everyone's mind, apparently the subject is to be approached circumspectly. Mr. Black begins by leading them to the opposite end of the room to show them his stereo. It is a component system with waist-high speakers encased in mahogany. Mr. Black thumbs through his record collection, all black jazz, Miles, Mingus, Thelonius. He settles on Davis' *Sketches of Spain.* The tone of the machine is beautiful, nearly a live performance the separation is so perfect.

Opening the inlaid box, Mr. Black removes a joint rolled with black paper. They stretch out on the floor upon cushions, allowing the music to transport them. They travel to Barcelona and Madrid, track through the Basque high country, run with the bulls at Pamplona. They lose track of time. Before they know it the thirty minutes have transpired and Michael, in perfect emulation of Baby Face Nelson, comes charging through the door. He is snarling and his pendulous necktie, broken free from his collar, streams behind him. His tommy gun is blasting and spitting white lightning and he doesn't stop firing until the entire scene—the stereo, the cushions, Mr. Black, the photographs, *objets d'art,* Mulligan's paper sack, Christine's fawn legs, Jacobi's Zapata mustache, Pamplona, Madrid, Thelonius, all and sundry—is blown to dream confetti.

28

THEY weren't sure what meal it was. They might as well have turned the clocks to the walls because they were on a new schedule, a nonschedule. Dinner was breakfast and breakfast an afternoon brunch. The kitchen had never fully recovered from its encounter with Mulligan, and now Christine was trying to cook and restore order at the same time. Jacobi stood with one arm on the refrigerator, leaning against it, watching her work. Michael and Mulligan were making a run to the corner grocery to pick up cigarettes and wine to go with the meal Christine was preparing. As she rushed back and forth, her face sweating from the heat of the stove, her hair pinned up and back, she looked like the young Cape Cod housewife Jacobi had never known. This was one of their few moments alone together since Mulligan's arrival. If Jacobi had thought there was time, he would have taken her right then.

He has been watching her for the last few days, fully conscious of the new Christine who was blossoming before his eyes, a Christine that moved with confidence and grace, suddenly more aware of other men because she was more aware of herself and the impact she had upon them. Jacobi knew that Mulligan was in part responsible for these changes. He was aware of his friend's maneuvering, sometimes covert, often blatant. Mulligan had to go after her, Jacobi thought, whether it was to come to anything or not. Otherwise, he wouldn't have been Mulligan. As for Christine, Jacobi didn't mind her flirting. He felt that this was part of the woman he was helping to release. If anything, it was Christine herself who felt guilty.

"Sit down and relax for a minute," Jacobi told her. "There's a few things we need to talk about."

"I can't right now, David, there's still too much to get ready." She was bending over the open oven, her back to him, and her dress had risen enough to reveal the small quarter-moon scar on the her right thigh, as if to accentuate his sexual state. She spooned up a bit of the gravy from the just-beginning-to-sizzle chicken and blew on it heavily before taking a tentative sip. "Hmmmn, it's going to be delicious," she said, widening her eyes as she turned to hold out the spoon so Jacobi could sample it.

He licked his lips and nodded his approval.

But we still need to talk, he thought, and if she can't sit, it'll have to be standing.

"I'm not jealous of Mulligan," he said.

She'd closed the oven and was about to open one of the pots on the stove. She paused for a moment with the spoon in midair, her face serious, contemplative, perhaps injured. It was a long moment. Jacobi was glad he hadn't held his breath.

"Why should you be?" she said at last, turning toward him. "There's no reason to be. I don't want Mulligan, David, I want you." She said it in such a way as to let him know that she wanted him right then, just as he wanted her.

"Well, in any case," Jacobi smiled, "we both know he's after you, and I think you enjoy it a little."

"But if he's your friend," Christine asked, "what is he trying to do? Doesn't it bother you?"

"As to what he's trying to do, I can never be positive about Mulligan. I'm not even sure he always knows himself. I do know that he always comes on to any beautiful woman in his vicinity, just to keep up appearances if for no other reason, just to keep things lively. But that's only part of what I wanted to talk about."

"What then?" She was back to cooking, but still listening.

Jacobi was momentarily quiet, trying to think it out and put it all together, then he shrugged and just let a number of ideas that had been running through his head spill out at once.

"What I meant by saying I wasn't jealous of Mulligan was that caring about someone isn't possessing them. You're your own woman, not mine. I'm my own man, not yours. Sex doesn't always have to be something special, so damn important. It can still be good without being wrapped up in a package with commitment and love. That causes more confusion than anything. I could desire and sleep with another woman tomorrow without it having anything to do with our relationship. You could go to bed with Mulligan tonight and enjoy it...and if you love me now you'll still love me when you wake up in the morning."

"You make it sound plausible," Christine said, shaking her head dubiously.

"It is, if you can handle it," Jacobi told her, wondering at the same time if he could handle it.

"So what are you telling me to do?" She asked.

Had she missed the point completely? "Whatever you want to do," he said. "You're your own woman, not mine." After a second he added jokingly. "But if you're into charity work, Michael's the one who needs a woman, not Mulligan."

Christine scolded him. "That's not a nice thing to say about America's next Walt Whitman."

"Should we get white wine or red?"

"White to go with chicken."

"Why always drink white wine with chicken? Why not red for a change?

"Because it doesn't go as well."

"Yeah, I guess you're probably right."

"Now let's see. Chesterfields for Jacobi, Salems for Tina, and you want Camels, right?"

"No thanks, nothing for me," Mulligan answered.

"Aw, come on," Michael said, "that was dope talk. No one really expects you to stop smoking."

"That'll make it all the more surprising then."

Michael felt in his pocket. "I've got a few Camels left. You can have one before we go back. I won't mention it."

Mulligan stared at him and shook his head. "What's with you, anyway? Is your family fortune in tobacco plantations or something?

Outside the store, with the jug of wine tucked beneath his arm, Mulligan turned in the opposite direction to that of Christine's apartment. Michael took a few steps the other way before he pivoted and came back to stand next to him.

"Let's go for a walk," Mulligan said, starting across the street.

Michael followed. "How come?"

"Oh…to give the young lovers some time to themselves, to loosen our joints. Because it feels right. Whatever reason you like."

"Okay," Michael shrugged. "Where do you want to walk to?" He was in the process of opening the cigarettes they had bought for Jacobi. Michael was a choosy beggar and he found that Camels were a bit too strong for his taste.

"I think I'd like to see some water."

"How about the East River?"

"Fine."

They took Bleeker Street to The Bowery, then swung south to Houston. They walked the first several blocks rapidly and in silence, Mulligan moving with a straight and solid gait, as if walking were his profession, Michael erratic and less coordinated, bouncing up and down at Mulligan's side. They had momentarily become a part of the streets, no more distinct than any of the pedestrians tracking across them without end. A few blocks before they hit The Bowery, Mulligan broke the silence.

"So poetry is where it's at, huh?"

Michael felt strangely candid. As much as he hated to admit it, he was impressed by Mulligan. He was accustomed to walking the city by himself, particularly when he walked to the

East River, his standard pilgrimage when he was wrestling with the lines of a poem or any of the other concerns that obsessed him. With Mulligan by his side the sanctity of his isolation, his individuality, was in a sense destroyed. Yet at the same time Mulligan seemed to be offering him the chance to give that individuality further definition through expression. "Poetry can get you there," Michael began, "if you've got the talent and you're committed enough. It's the level of involvement that really counts. I can get high writing…and I can write things that can make other people high if they take the trouble to read them and understand them, and that's really where it's at, getting high." He paused briefly before going on. "Only thing is…acid has done more for me than writing ever has, taken me more places and shown me more things, gotten me higher. Maybe I don't have enough talent *or* commitment to make it with poetry." It was the first self-doubt Michael had expressed to anyone in some time.

"I'm willing to listen and try to understand," Mulligan said. "Get me high. I'll trade you a cap of acid for one of your poems."

"We're not far from my place," Michael answered. "We can stop off and I'll show you some."

"No, recite one for me…if you can. The one that will get me the highest."

"You mean right here? Now?" Their pace had slowed gradually once they had begun speaking, and now they stopped completely as Michael turned to face Mulligan with his question.

"Sure," Mulligan replied, "why not? Is there a better time or place?"

Michael looked at him. Although Mulligan must have outweighed him by fifty pounds, they were almost the same height and their eyes met evenly, as they had before the speed trip when Michael had objected to Mulligan and his needles. And just as in that confrontation, Michael could detect no duplicity in Mulligan's gaze. Although a few people had asked to see his poetry before, this was the first time anyone had asked him to read it aloud, and had offered to give him something in return. As contradictory as Michael's principles might be over a period of time, at any given moment he was doggedly faithful to them. If he were a poet, a real poet and not just playing at the game until his inheritance came through, he couldn't very well turn Mulligan down. He would recite his last complete poem from memory, one that he had finished in a burst of creative activity after the second cap of acid.

"All right," he told Mulligan uncertainly, "you've got yourself a deal, a poem in trade for a cap of acid...but let's keep walking."

As they took up their path again, Michael was suddenly nervous, more nervous than he'd ever been before the groups where he'd read. He realized, without knowing why, that he cared whether or not Mulligan liked the poem, cared far beyond the proportions of what made sense. He lit another of Jacobi's cigarettes to postpone the inevitable.

"Has it got a title?" Mulligan prompted.

"It's called 'A Thousand Faces,'" Michael answered automatically. Then Mulligan didn't say anything else, so there was nothing to do but begin.

Mulligan listened as Michael recited the poem, at first brokenly, then with growing confidence as he was caught up in his own creation. There seemed to be four stanzas, but it was impossible to be sure where one line ended and the next began. Mulligan had to strain to hear over the noise of the traffic and the street, yet Michael's thin voice managed at times to either capture the intensity of his words or be seized by it. This was Michael revealed and speaking openly, the guise of cynic and introvert stripped away, chanting a kind of lyrical blasphemy against the walls of stony ignorance and mediocrity he perceived all around him. And in the course of reciting the poem, in the incongruity of its content played against the environment of Manhattan, he was able to transform and overcome a fraction of that environment, just as the Puerto Rican kid had with

Mulligan's conga, just as Mulligan himself so often did in the worlds through which he moved.

The old man comes down from the mountains
his hair filled with brambles and
full and wind-flowing like a fine robe
and the old man comes down from the mountains
his hair filled with brambles and
full and wind-flowing like an intricate tapestry
the work of a thousand dancing needles
and the old man comes down from the mountains
his skin wrinkled and laced by concentric networks
overlaid and moving to fine filigree
and the old man comes down from the mountains
to the north where he has been meditating
with the lost tribes and feasting on lotus roots
and pine berries and the old man comes down
eyes flaming with the knowledge of bestial altars
thoughts rich with forbidden drugs and
the forgotten dances which swell the veins
spawn of Dionysus and the old man comes down
from the north with ice white teeth and
huge hands leaping from his loose sleeves
and the old man comes down from the mountains
with an intensity almost painful and he refuses
our questions and will not speak with us.

Michael paused to finish his cigarette. There were only a few drags left. He took them, stared at the burning butt curiously, then tossed it into the street. He considered looking at Mulligan, but thought better of it. Just before he started speaking again, he noticed that the two of them were now walking stride for stride.

Finally the father figure
self onto self
begin the same   no difference

like the cycles of the sun
that clock between her legs
the warm juices of her mouth   no difference
begin a soft seed breaking the rhythm of the womb
the chain is detonated   no difference
each cell embryonic in its brother
liquid and linked in geometric precision
the woman grows heavy with child   no difference
the birth trauma is completed with a metallic
tour de force as the razor slits the dancing umbilical
no difference   no difference

And the old man comes down from the mountains
disguised as a pedlar in the night
and I follow him along the shore and
ask how one knows the true self
and he gathers the mottled and ribbed shells
to string seaweed necklaces and I ask
how one knows the true self and he chants
mantras to the growling white-tipped water
and I demand how one knows the true self
and he dances in the rising tide
until the wet sand clings to his feet
in soft clotty bundles and as morning
light edges across the beach slantwise
and I fall drunken from sleeplessness
at last he whispers that one knows
the true self like a stream running.

So I follow the stream high into the hills
and higher still in the mountains and
at its fount there is a garden with a temple
and at the bottom of the garden
a cypress tree is standing
and on the walls of the temple
its green jade walls
there are a thousand faces
each of them my own.

They walked the three remaining blocks to the river in thoughtless silence. The poem had filled them with its vision and emptied them of thought. They saw the river, dirt gray and nearly motionless, like a dull steel band strapped across the girth of the planet. They were close enough to the ocean so they could smell its salt in the air. Mulligan took the wine he had been carrying out of its paper sack. It was a large bottle with a cap rather than a cork. He broke the seal and lifting the bottle with both hands he took a long drink. He offered the bottle to Michael, who swallowed deeply several times.

"I'm high," Mulligan said. "It's a beautiful poem."

"Thank you," Michael answered. The two words, generally foreign to his nature, seemed all right.

Several miles behind them Christine's dinner was waiting. Mulligan could already taste the chicken. It would be crispy and tender, just the way he liked it. He was feeling very good. On his cue, the two of them turned around and began their journey back.

29

Mulligatawny Stew

When Jacobi asked Mulligan why he wore tennis shoes so much of the time, Mulligan told him it was because he had to do a lot of running around.

The existence of Mulligan is predicated upon such a raft of fortuitous combinations that one isn't sure where to begin: sun, air, earth, water, precipitation, vegetation, amphibians, mammals, man, woman, conception, digestion, illumination…

A week spent with Mulligan on the move. A week of communion and marathon encounter. A week of drugged sensibilities. A field of dry grasses flaming to the sky.

Mulligan standing in Times Square, turning in a circle with his hands in the air as if he wants to embrace the whole city. His stoned smile transforms his face to a happy moon. "There it all is…but when does it start falling on us?"

Mulligan talking them into going to a greasy diner near Times Square because he suddenly wants a hamburger and while Jacobi is at the counter trying to order Christine putting her hands down on the speckled formica table top and then quickly lifting them off her fingers covered with salt and her face cracking with an expression of distaste and Botticelli sitting across from her shaking his head and grinning irrepressibly until she is grinning back at him.

And Jacobi coming back to the table and her face awkwardly trying to discover another expression.

And Mulligan grinning all the more at her confusion.

Mulligan munching on sunflower seeds. Mulligan downing a carrot in four giant chomps. Mulligan devouring Christine's meals, recreating her creations (tabasco on her herb omelet!). Mulligan eating, eating, eating. It was surprising he could remain even as thin as he was. But then again, he did do a lot of running around.

Mekas coming to the door, ostensibly to complain about the noise from the conga, and Mulligan meeting him, bare to the waist.

"Oh, I was looking for Miss Leslie," Mekas giggled, fixing Mulligan's smooth belly with a fishy stare.

"The mistress is currently indisposed," Mulligan purred.

"Well...someone was playing a drum up here last night, very late and very loud, and it kept me awake!" Leaning forward in an attempt to peer into the apartment.

"Drum? There's no drum here," Mulligan said.

"Well then, what was it?" Mekas insisted, voice rising in indignation.

"That," said Mulligan ingenuously, "was the pulsing of the stars, the syncopation of our souls, the eternal chatter of the cosmic pizzicato."

It didn't really matter whether the stories Mulligan told were true or merely drug-powered flights of fantasy, when Mulligan told them they seemed real enough.

One of his favorite stories involved a graduate student at the Sorbonne who had gotten some medical students to drill a small hole at the base of his skull. This was supposedly an ancient Buddhist technique that led to a state of permanent *satori.*

After the operation the student's disposition changed radically. Formerly a gloomy, withdrawn youth, he now became affable and intolerably cheerful. His appetite improved. He was reconciled with his wife, from whom he'd been separated, and moved back in with her and their three-year-old daughter. He became the perfect student, the perfect family man, attending all of his classes, studying in the library until five every day, then home to dinner and bouncing his child on his knee. There was no doubt that despite a few false starts and his earlier bizarre preoccupations with drugs and the mind, he was going to make something of his life after all.

One day he failed to come home from the library.

Three years later a postcard arrived from Tibet. No one could translate the language in which it was written.

Mulligan had an I.Q. of 136, which wasn't bad, but certainly nothing to write Dublin about.

When Jacobi asked Mulligan why he wore tennis shoes so much of the time, Mulligan told him it was because of his bunions.

Michael contributing his energy and his dope, bringing hash for them all to smoke. Mulligan trying to sliver it with a razor blade and cutting his finger. Christine wrapping a bandage around the cut and saying" "Poor Denny! Poor Denny!"

Mulligan disappearing for an afternoon to roam the streets of Manhattan alone and at large.

Botticelli returning to stand with a bottle of cough syrup in each hand, scrutinizing the list of ingredients" "Ah, dextromethorphanhydrobromide...what a mouthful. You get a little of this stuff in you, wait half an hour and blow some grass, and you'll be ready to make love to the whole world!" Looking up to give his most lecherous grin as Jacobi watches Christine watch him.

Mulligan on Grass Dynasties: "Instead of smoking your joints down to the end, you save all of the roaches and seal them in a jar. The roaches are stronger because all the other dope has filtered through them in the process of smoking. After you get enough roaches, you break them apart and roll a joint from them. This is know as a Ming One and is more potent than any of the joints used to make it up. But you don't smoke this one down all the way either. You save the roach from this and put it in another jar. After you collect enough Ming One roaches, you can then roll a Ming Two, which is stronger yet. Then you just keep on going—Ming Threes, Ming Fives, Ming Fourteens—until you've got a super joint that's the ultimate pure distillation of cannabis and you can blow your mind completely."

Mulligan telling Michael: "In the moments of ultimate tribulation, when all else has failed, with your back against the wall, you are always thrown back on your metaphysics...whatever those might happen to be."

Jacobi and Mulligan talking late into the night several nights in a row after Christine has fallen asleep, talking about anything and everything, prompting Christine to tell Jacobi, a bit jokingly and a bit jealously: "I have the feeling you two are as intense as lovers when you get alone with each other."

Mulligan reading Christine's poetry and giving her the honest criticism so hard for a writer to get. "This is a good image. This one is unclear." Getting to the poem on page forty-three of her book and saying, "That's not love, that's infatuation."

Christine trying to guess what Mulligan was majoring in at school.

"Political science."

"Nope."

"English?"

"Unh-uh."

"Economics?"

"Not a chance!"

Finally having Jacobi whisper in her ear, "Dramatic art, you ninny, what else?"

Mulligan taking a shower and emerging from the bathroom wrapped in a giant blue bath towel, still a little wet and red as a cherub, forgetting to comb his hair before it dries so that it tumbles in soft tangled ringlets onto his forehead.

When Jacobi asked Mulligan why he wore tennis shoes so much of the time, Mulligan told him that he was making a fashion statement ahead of its time.

Christine putting *Alexander Nevski* on the stereo and Mulligan beating the conga sporadically as invisible armies clashed on the ice fields of St. Petersburg. Prokofiev would have undoubtedly shuddered.

Mulligan teaching Michael how to whistle.

Mulligan attempting one of Michael's yoga postures and falling off the couch.

30

KNOWING what a stone drag it could be, Jacobi was against the idea of taking Mulligan to a poetry reading, but Christine, with feminine tenacity and her newfound self-assurance, prevailed in the end. It turned out to be worthwhile.

The scene at St. Marks hadn't changed. It was the same crowd and the same room. Jacobi wondered who kept it so spotlessly antiseptic. Christine read, or rather reread since she had written nothing new, several short poems. Jacobi watched, struck by her appearance in contrast to when he had seen her for the first time in these surroundings. The things which had attracted him to her he now saw in a different light. She seemed less sophisticated to him, but far more human and alive. Now he knew the secrets of her body beneath its clothes, and a good share of her strengths and weaknesses. Yet his familiarity had by no means bred contempt or even indifference. Her body continued to arouse him without fail. Her mind continued to intrigue him. Now he watched her to see how she would confront each new experience, how she would realize or alter his expectations.

Michael read, too. It was the same poem he had recited to Mulligan and perhaps inspired by that experience he read it from memory. For once he faced the audience, and he was the only poet of the evening to receive applause that contained a degree of legitimate enthusiasm, though admittedly it was spurred on by three particular pairs of hands.

But Mulligan, without doubt, was the one who made the show complete. After listening to several poets he walked quietly to the back of the room and to the amazement of his companions added his name to the list of readers. When he was called upon, he marched to the center of the floor and proceeded to recite a poem, apparently off the top of his head, in a voice that began as a painfully slow bass but rose in pitch, volume and speed of delivery until he was hysterically shouting. Simultaneously, with like acceleration of movement, he transformed the silence of the room from polite to stunned, by performing the following acts: he took off his glasses and put them in his coat pocket, he unbuttoned his coat, he untucked his shirt all the way around, he yanked off his tie and hung it over his arm like a waiter's napkin, he unbuttoned his shirt from top to bottom—

> Loving involves giving-sharing
> with each other one another
> worship implies the insignificance
> of the lover, to be worshiped is
> a polar game, deification, a minor
> deity of the household, father
> figure, the ionic pillars of a
> building in ruins, picture postcards
> sent from Tripoli, 1917, the family
> of twelve sitting on wine barrels,
> old man has a black mustache,
> is wearing a tweed cap and
> a Sicilian version of jodhpurs,
> other than that he is totally nude,

a statue in marble, buffed yet grainy finish,
curled locks of stone, frozen hair,
the observatory closing like an armadillo,
the china has teeth,
I heard them clicking,
the ball bearings,
the store bells,
the slate blue eyeshades,
the tinted eyes, damn oh damn it,
the mattress is burning,
my fingernails are growing together.

—he undid the top snap of his levis, took four long steps to the door, turned to nod and grimace, opened the door and took another step through it, and just before closing it behind his retreating form, his hand swung back to catch the light switch, plunging the room into the pitch blackness of the windowless enclosed vault that it was.

In the dark, thirty-four throats gasped for breath at once, while another three, without much success, tried to swallow their laughter.

Outside, Jacobi and Michael looked up and down the street in vain. Mulligan was nowhere in sight.

"He'll turn up," Jacobi said. "He's probably back at the place waiting for us already."

Christine was still smiling. "You know, he really is crazy," she said, shaking her head.

"Sure," Michael added, "like a fat fox."

They walked back to Christine's apartment, but Mulligan wasn't there either. At the top of the outside stairs, Jacobi turned to Michael.

"You know something?" he said.

"What?" Michael asked.

"No offense against your company," Jacobi told him, "but I think I'd like to spend some time alone with my woman."

Michael's reaction was delayed. Then his face crumpled in an expression of annoyance. "All right," he said, "catch you later." He turned, bouncing back down the stairs with his hands in his pockets.

On the way up, Christine said, "Poor Michael, you shouldn't have been so brusque with him."

"You want me to go bring him back" Jacobi asked, putting his hand on her waist and sliding it down over the hip, pulling her toward him.

"Not a chance," she smiled.

They got inside the apartment and they undressed. Jacobi suddenly wanted her so badly he was trembling. It had been five days since they had made love and it seemed longer. Then they were into the bed and upon one another, with Christine kissing and biting with such tenacity as if to devour him. And just this once, perhaps because he was so anxious, perhaps because he expected Mulligan to come knocking at the door any minute, Jacobi couldn't hold himself back and he came without waiting for her.

Mulligan took the subway, the Central Line south at Houston and Second Avenue, across the lower East River and into Brooklyn, to the end of the line, his destination, Coney Island.

Initially he shunned the lights and rides and carnival shows. He made a beeline straight for the beach, for Jones Beach deserted in the dark. He found himself a spot in the sand and blew a joint and then another until the world seemed very right. He rolled back and forth in the sand laughing to himself. He rolled a third joint just in case. He went down to the shore, walked along it and teased the edge of the lapping Atlantic with his tennis shoes until a wave, faster and higher than the rest, drenched his feet and pant legs. Then he found one of the rickety sets of wooden stairs that led back up to the boardwalk and the brightness. He dived into that brightness, the crowds and the noise. He became a kid again and again. He ate hot dogs, cotton candy, pistachio ice cream. He rode The Bullet, the Roundup, the roller coaster, the Milkshake. He left his stomach five hundred feet in the air and caught it next time around. He became stoned on centrifugal force and weightlessness and the loss of balance, high on the movement that transformed his vision to an abstract and ever-changing canvas.

Finally he stumbled onto the slowly turning disc of the merry-go-round. Through a gap in its central machinery, at the opposite periphery of the circle, he saw her. A dull-looking girl wearing a tight sweater and tighter capris. Her short dark hair was set in a mass of skullcap curls. As she caught Mulligan's eyes upon her, she smiled at him wanly, a reflection of her wan sexuality. Yet even at a distance, Mulligan could sense there was more. He knew immediately that he had something to tell her...something to give her.

The next instant he was off his horse and walking across the turning floor, past spinning children, through the garishly painted and bobbing menagerie, a candy cane zebra, a stunted giraffe with laughing teeth of wooden gold, a black-lacquered unicorn with a lacquered-red conical horn, and beyond the struts and poles, a slowly revolving world. The girl saw him coming straight for her, now saw his tennis shoes, his still-damp pant legs, his flapping shirttails, his wild stoned eyes, his fat. Her smile fell slack and her chin grew smaller. Her fingers tightened, grappling with the baroque pommel of her fake saddle. She was petrified, she couldn't move, was afraid to move a muscle with this rubicund maniac descending upon her.

Then the ticket taker saw him, too, and abandoned his post to run up to the side of the merry-go round, to scream uselessly since it was impossible to hear anything above the insane calliope music spilling up from some box lodged in the oil and ratchet depths of the machine.

Mulligan, without slowing his pace, grinned at him and mouthed a stream of nonsense syllables. Each time the attendant's irate face swung into view, Mulligan radiated such affability and assurance that the man paused, nearly convinced that nothing was amiss. It gave Mulligan the moment he needed. He was upon the girl and in close up she seemed cheaper and more pathetic. Glitter speckled her hair. An oversized gold crucifix glimmered in the nap of her sweater. Her cheeks were heavily powdered. The lipstick reshaping her mouth twisted in a paroxysm of fright. Yet in the liquid brown depths of her eyes, in the instant before they darted away from him, Mulligan saw that his guess had been correct. Then he was moving around her, behind her, momentarily astride the butt of the sorrel she was riding, yelling into the shiny pink shell of her ear "MADNESS IS HOLINESS!", pressing the last joint he had rolled into her trembling palm and closing her fingers upon it. And then into the other ear, now turned blushing red, to complete his message, "HOLINESS IS FOR US ALL!"

And cackling like a mad-holy man, Mulligan leaped from the merry-go-round, over a wooden guard rail with far greater alacrity than one would have credited to his bulk, and was almost instantaneously another dot lost in the crowd swirl.

31

CENTRAL Park is a joy on acid. Ask David Jacobi. Ask Christine Leslie. Ask Michael Shawtry. Ask Dennis Mulligan, but don't believe what he tells you.

After having taken so much else together, it was inevitable that they drop acid together to complete Mulligan's stay. And it was inevitable that Mulligan, their guru and con man, should decide when, where and how. The nature boy in him came out and he picked Central Park, a planned nature, but the closest they could get to the real thing without leaving the Manhattan. For the acid, he chose some sky blue caps he had brought with him. It was the same acid Jacobi had, only it was "laced with a little speed, since everyone seemed to like that so well." For time, he decided on the early morning, when the summer heat was still tolerable. For how, there was always the tribal circle.

They sat in the tribal circle, alone in a sparse grove of birches, a small tribe of four, holding hands and letting the acid come on in waves that washed tingling across their bodies, through the linked extremities of their limbs, carrying them effortlessly higher as they watched the leaves that enclosed them rippling against the sky blue sky.

Perhaps it was as early as the park that the nature of the trip began to formulate itself. Perhaps it was when Mulligan had stepped off the plane. Despite the alleged speed, their trip was physical from the very beginning—smell, sound, texture, warmth, vision, sensuality. And from the very beginning, at some level of comprehension, they all understood what was happening with them and between them and what was about to happen. At some strata of consciousness it was all clear, but so intangible and unspeakable that they kept losing it. It kept slipping into the back brain, lost in the attempt at conceptualization until it surfaced again the next time around in their tied circle of thought.

Christine lay back in the grass with her eyes closed, overcome by the transformation of the world within and without, her body beneath its crepe blouse and soft cotton skirt—shorter to show off her legs—trembling gently to the acid vibrations. And the three men with her knelt by her side, their own sensations in touch with hers, their pulses keyed to the even rise and fall of her breasts, their eyes fastened to the acid glow of her cheeks, forehead and temples, to the dark eyeliner and sky blue eye shadow iridescent upon her lids, to the smile of ecstasy upon her aquiline features, the resonant humanity of her womanhood sounding the depths of each of them. And each of them saw or projected upon her their image of woman complete and woman incarnate, the giver of life and the taker of seed, the warmth of the earth mother and the white grace of the vestal virgin. And Mulligan desired her as he desired all women. And Jacobi desired her to complete his existence. And Michael closed his eyes against her woman's softness and woman's blood and reached out with his mind beyond the colored patterns shifting through the blackness to encompass the essence of her being.

When everything ties together and makes sense there is an absence of juxtaposition, a leveling, a way to reconcile all incongruity. All that is done, all that happens, is meant to be done, is meant to happen, could just as well not happen. When the validity of the causal chain is as relative as everything else, conclusions are superannuated. When all is pattern and form and each moment of the continuum is of equal value to the rest, there is only the way it will be.

They ran across rolling grass lawns over stunted hillocks that still seemed to reach very close to the sky blue sky and the thousand and one greens of the greensward undulated and buckled before their vision. They ran along the iron fence railings that shielded them from the city traffic only a few feet away. They raced one another from one clump of trees to the next with the mindless joy of children—Jacobi's long loping stride taking him into the lead, Michael and Christine following behind and running side by side, and finally Mulligan, sweating from the exertion, his short legs pumping—until Michael cried out stumbling over the protrusion of a sprinkler cap to sprawl with his limbs flopping and loosened to butter by the sensations of the acid—and Jacobi and Christine stopped to kneel by his side to make sure he was all right, so close that Michael could see the individual hairs in his friend's mustache, smell the clean fragrance of Christine's clothes—while Mulligan just kept running to win the race all by himself.

She wanted to tell Mulligan something, but she didn't know what it was. The acid was beautiful and she so wanted something beautiful to happen. She felt a little confused when she tried to think, but not frightened, not frightened at all. She was secure in the company of her entourage—David, Denny, Michael—she felt so close to them all. Even Michael with his obstinacy and singleness of purpose, and yet the way their minds could meet on a line of poetry. David, of course, she loved, though in some ways she was more impressed with Mulligan. Only Mulligan was not the kind of man for a relationship. Once this occurred, he would cease to be Mulligan.

From a nodding and wizened street vendor, upon whom Christine hallucinated the hoary hooded figure of Father Time, they bought snocones to expel the cloying acid dryness from their tongues and throats and rehydrate their bodies. Cherry. Raspberry. Strawberry. Lime. The experience of snocones on acid was unique for each of them. The sweet cool fruity wetness inundated their senses from tongue to toes. Jacobi consumed his so rapidly that the iciness laid a sharp throbbing pain across his brow. He bent forward squinting to block it out and when he straightened again he found himself facing away from the park and staring across Fifth Avenue, his eyes inexorably following the dull buildings upward from base to summit and then the afterimages of their parallel rising windows clinging tardily to his retina, projecting their height even further to fill the sky.

Manhattan, he thought laughing out loud, what a hell of a place to drop acid.

Country, Flag, Family, Father, Mother, Good, Evil, Order, Chaos—abstractions, thinner yet, vaporous abstractions, acquired customs of the mind dispersing long before the death of more basic illusions such as the solidity of matter or the absolute nature of space and time. But does the death of old laws call for the creation and enactment of new and more clever ones, or merely for the license of disbelief, the freedom beyond morality.

Mulligan: "Are we any more real than our selves?"

Three of them sat upon a bench, but Mulligan perched, his feet up on the seat and his butt atop the backrest. They watched an uptown bus unload its cargo of New Yorkers—an elderly coiffed and braceleted woman with her coiffed and braceleted poodle, a young housewife, infant in arm, already turning drab with the tedium of motherhood, unemployed nondescript men in short sleeve shirts who would wander the park aimlessly, an aged

Hasidic Jew, profusely bearded, who would wander the park with his mind steeped in memory or Old Testament repetitions, a bored black governess attired in nurse's white with several white children in tow, a pair of gangly high school students, hand in hand, both slenderly underdeveloped in their sexuality. Through the lens of acid, one and all appeared as parading caricatures.

Christine thought of them naked, stripped of the identities their clothes and adornments provided, and they seemed still more absurd. Giggling self-consciously she asked, "My God, do we look as ridiculous as everyone else?"

"Only to the other people stoned on acid who don't know us," Mulligan assured her.

As the day progressed and the park filled with people and the traffic crossing it and swirling past its borders thickened and became hectic with honking horns and exhaust fumes, their attempted nature trip became progressively less natural, the park itself became more apparently manmade (with sudden visions of artificial flowers and styrofoam squirrels!), the sky lowered upon them (claustrophobia!) and their minds began to buzz frenetically.

Michael was suddenly possessed by the urge to retreat, not only from the park but from his companions, to retreat into the certainty of his own limitless internal vistas. This was the first time he had taken acid with other people and he found himself unwillingly drawn into a whirlwind of group dynamics that clouded over the metaphysical clarity he had cherished in his previous experiences with the drug. He kept shutting his eyes, pretending that he was alone and trying to trip out by himself, but there was always Mulligan's babbling calling him back, Jacobi's laughter calling him back, Christine, the woman, calling him back to interrelate on a level where he had always been, even in his normal state of consciousness, grossly inadequate.

With the aid of Mulligan's guidance—the unruffled calm of the experienced tripper—they made it back to Christine's apartment, but the quantity and variety of sense impressions that assaulted them on their path through the city was nearly overwhelming—noise, noise, noise, the mountainous grain of the street's asphalt, the changing geometry of the sidewalks, the bumpy iron of the manhole covers ballooning like elastic, the technicolor traffic lights, the technicolor-bright blue-suited policeman (paranoia! paranoia! he knows we're stoned! so stoned how could he not know?), the flower vendors and ice cream vendors and hot dog vendors, the hansom cabs at the south end of the park like an anomaly misplaced from the last century (lost in time!), the bustling polychromatic crowds with their mottled polychromatic faces (white, brown, black, yellow, pink, chartreuse!), the assorted cats and dogs and wet canine teeth snapping (carnivores!), the throbbing bass of the subway beneath their feet sending vibrations through their bones (no one else seems to notice!), the taxi driver speaking some extraterrestrial tongue only Mulligan could interpret, the freaky-familiar environs of the Village suddenly acid strange, and last but not least a chance speechless encounter with bug-eyed Mekas as they shot thankfully up the stairs to the relative quietus of the apartment.

Cellular history is as tangible as any text once its language is understood, but the history of the psyche is less palpable, unassailable by logic and the external senses. Its language by definition is a language of its own invention: representational, approximate, each word a likeness, each sentence a given posture, every paragraph an idiom with axioms posited and conclusions inherent before the argument entails.

Dialogue that attempts to move beyond externals is invariably a mix and confrontation of idioms, a miscommunication. Poetry is the ultimate realization of internal language in its communicative form, the recognition of the word as symbol.

One does not hold a dialogue with poem, one attempts to grasp its metaphor, the meaning beyond the meaning.

When the internal senses achieve equal credence to the external, their impact is immediate and undeniable. There is no necessity for translation, no need to drape their perceptions in language cloaks in order to understand.

When translation is accepted as such, when the word-become-flesh is severed from its flesh, touching one another begins.

Quietus, retreat, a world unto themselves—draperies drawn against sight of the city, air conditioning humming against the heat and coincidentally dampening the sounds of the city, the door doubly locked with key and chain from paranoia of the city. The four of them—together, alone, on acid—safe in a universe of their own making.

Mulligan took off his shirt and his shoes and socks, and his bare toes curled, tugging at the strands of the shag rug by the couch. Michael stared at him askance, the contradictions that were Mulligan compiling themselves in his head, thesis and antithesis but no synthesis. He was taken with Mulligan's personality, yet appalled by the excesses implicit in his fat. He was drawn to Mulligan's energy and simultaneously put off by what he saw as the useless dissipation of that energy, Mulligan's short span of attention and apparently undifferentiated interest in so many different things.

Christine stared at Mulligan's body and for her it signified the power of a squat rocket, the solidity of a snub-nosed bullet. She leaned forward to get a cigarette from her bag and her hair slid across her eyes, and looking again through the net of her hair, still through the changing liquid lens of the acid, she started back, her hands tightening to knuckle whiteness on the curved wooden arms of her chair. Mulligan's form had wavered. The opacity of his flesh disintegrated in a stream of milky vapors and became transparent. She saw his veins and arteries, the sinews of his musculature, his internal organs—heart, lungs, liver, kidneys—in all the detail of a living-breathing anatomical exposition. Her mind grappled with the impossibility of her perception as she looked down quickly to light her cigarette, and when she glanced back up Mulligan was once more comfortably ensconced in his ruddy skin.

Mulligan, oblivious to the fact that his innards had been on display, was painfully aware of that cigarette. He chewed his lower lip in steely consternation. He fished a weathered toothpick from his pocket and shoved it between his teeth.

Jacobi saw that toothpick and knew its function. He'd employed the identical sublimation himself, without luck, while trying to kick his own nicotine habit. Now he flashed on Billie Raintree, and suddenly saw Mulligan in a new light, as merely a brighter and more interesting version of Billie. Suspending that thought in midstream, he reminded himself of the ease of revelatory conclusions on acid, that nothing was that simple. All day he'd been trying to figure out whether or not he was actually jealous of Mulligan, trying to disassociate himself from what he knew of Mulligan and perceive him the way he really looked and acted, or at least the way he looked to Christine and acted toward her. After awhile, he'd decided that in his present state the question was meaningless. In the acid state he'd left behind jealousy and possessiveness as he had a score of other game emotions. He was feeling so euphoric, so grand about his very being and so positive toward his companions that he was ready for "a fuck of loving friendship with one and all" (a Mulliganism from some stoned episode in the past).

Now he watched Mulligan as he replaced his toothpick with the wooden tip of a stick of incense and struck a match to light it. Once the incense had caught, Mulligan rose and with an exaggeratedly slow step, dipping up and down, moved about the room, wafting the sweet musky smoke with its overtones of Arabian decadence to each of them, the glowing punk bobbing as the stick swung up and down in delayed reaction to his movement. Jacobi forgot about Billie Raintree and flashed on a different identity for Mulligan. He was a plump Fu Manchu. Beneath the broad rectangle of his freckled brow he was undoubtedly hatching plots to establish a new world order.

A world unto themselves, a universe of their own making. Will they rewrite the social contract or live by the laws of whatever jungle they mutually inhabit.

A new and more clever reality? Freedom? License?

Begin at the beginning, from scratch. (Don't forget pleasure! Don't forget reality!)

Begin with the unconscious, begin awake and don't fall asleep.

Begin with a declaration for the unalterable freedom of consciousness. Come forth from the salt water onto the shore trailing the primeval ooze like clouds of glory. Sprout legs to walk and hands to hold. Reenact the primal scene with open eyes. Leave the senses in the body and the hieroglyphs on the temple walls.

The sun has crossed the sky—no longer sky blue but a watered pastel—and now hastens to meet the rising horizon. It has been hours since they have taken the acid. Hours. Years. Centuries. They have accumulated more impressions in this single day than in the past hundred. At one level or another, in one way or another, they have been forced to question their every concept of reality. Individual empires have toppled to ruins. Ruins have crumbled to fragments that are beyond excavation. Cultures have gone under in the bat of an eyelash, subsumed without a whimper. Wars have been bypassed. By the time the forces were arrayed for battle, the reasons for the conflict were already forgotten.

Now they sit awaiting nightfall in the darkening apartment (Decor: mid-Twentieth Century, North American. Art: non-objective, European, 1880-1933; Books: Western, Plato to Beckett) and within the limits of Christine's record collection, Mulligan spins the platters and becomes their classical-acid-jazz disc jockey, laying one mind-blowing set on them after another. (With their heightened and accelerated associative awareness, how can he miss?)

Bach vs. Brubeck.

Ornette Coleman sandwiched between Satie and Schoenberg

The hip new trio of Beethoven, Mozart and Coltrane.

The sounds are all familiar to Christine, although on acid they have taken on further dimensions. She is aware of the individuality of each instrument, each distinct note. Yet ultimately, she cannot lose herself in the music. No matter how deft the throw or how finely polished the sphere, the spinning ball must finally succumb to gravity and fall back into the slot of a particular number on the wheel. So it is with Christine's consciousness in its tied circle of thought. She keeps returning, even more than the men around her, to the sensual current and undercurrent that has run woven through the entire fabric of the day: her sexuality, her desirability as a woman and her role as a woman.

Each of the cuts that Mulligan selects only serves to amplify a different aspect of this theme for her. The laid-back beat of the jazz drums trips her back briefly to Tony and his drumming. A somber Mozart concerto gives her the dread impression that Leonard's somber presence has swung in from the north on a high tail wind and has now settled to envelope the apartment in a gangrenous fog. Offenbach's *Orpheus* she links to the film *Black Orpheus*, and from there easily to her own black lover.

But one look around the room tells her that she is with three very different men (boys?) now, and they are demanding a different identify from her than she has ever assumed in the past. She has felt the folds of their projected mantle of womanhood closing about her. Mulligan has been relatively quiet during the day (as they all have) and unassertive (as if he has bowed to the direction of the acid), but not uncommunicative. Jacobi has looked at her in a different way, his eyes full with the same acid wonder with which they'd surveyed the grainy, swirling bark of a tree together in the park. Even shy Michael has stared at her unabashedly until he noticed that she had noticed.

Christine wonders if her silence, her passivity and lack of protest, have been taken as an acceptance of whatever expectations their projections involve.

"Look, the candle is moving to the music."

"He's right."

"That's nothing, so is the rug."

"So is the pattern in the rug!"

(pause)

"Maybe not."

"Huh?"

"Maybe the music is keeping time to the candle and the rug."

"But the music is prerecorded."

"So maybe the candle is, too."

"But the record always sounds the same."

"Yesterday you would have told me that the rug was always the same, but take a look at it now. I wish I could change that fast."

For Michael, more obsessively the poet than Christine, the music is a different experience. The music is poetry in media translation, each note a word that finds and loses itself again in the space-time of its sounding. If he had his notebook he could try to write the words down as they flip through his mind. But he realizes that it would be a pointless exercise since their beauty, like the notes they reflect, lies at the heart of their transient nature, their meaning is only relevant in the moment. And in any case, despite his attempted preoccupation with this note-word game, the music is secondary for him just as it is for Christine. He is trapped in and as much a part of the current of the trip as any of the others. Some time in the last week his sacred isolation has slipped from between his fingers. The thoughts in his head are like spokes, radiating out from and pointing back to the hub of a wheel that is their origin and their destination, and lying in the hub are his two peak experiences of the day: the first, looking down into Christine's inscrutably smiling face (a blond *Mona Lisa*!) aglow with the mystery of the woman's psyche he could never fathom, and the second, when their positions were reversed and he had fallen upon the grass and she knelt above him, her body softly desirable within the sheath of its soft fragrant clothes, the body that Jacobi handled so freely, the body that Mulligan now touched casually and with such calculation, the body that the thought of touching made Michael tremble with his long-starved wanting and the weakness of that wanting.

Evolution refuses to wait upon us. Ontogeny continues to extend itself.

Go back to the shore. Play among the breakers until your toes and fingers are webbed, until your body is the color of copper ore. Gather doves and eagles. Gather bright birds of fiery plumage and a catch of silver-green marlin. Build a tower of copper coins upon the sand and watch them spill into a row of concentric interlocking circles. Spread the coins one by one and bury them.

Find a jagged shell. Or break one upon the sea rocks until it will cut like a blade. Slice the webbing until your fingers and toes are once more free.

Jacobi, the thinker, is thinking too much and trying to stop himself from thinking, thinking the speed in the acid is taking over and that's why he is thinking too much. He is thinking about the music as much as he is listening to it, thinking that most of it, except for some of the jazz, reflects a dead world of rigid structures, hopelessly historical and slightly pompous, dated by the accelerated change of the Twentieth Century. It seems to him that the raw electric instrumentation of rock—The Airplane, the Beatles, the Stones—can come closer to both the realities of the day and the eternal energies released by the acid. He realizes, at the same time, that this structured and measured music is also a reflection of Christine's world, and indulging in a bit of acid megalomania, a part of himself recognizing it for what it is, he looks down upon her, not with love so much as paternal devotion. She is learning, he thinks, she has been forced through changes that have made her learn in the last month with me, the last week with Mulligan, today with the acid—and perhaps still more before the night is done.

"But if the candle is prerecorded and the rug is prerecorded, then so are we!"

"Sure, it's all happened before and it's all going to happen again—eternal recurrence. First time around it's a tragedy, next time around a farce, next time whatever you decide you want it to be."

"So what do we do next."

(pause)

"Better check the script?"

"Who's got the script?"

"We don't need a script. Just follow the music."

"But if you're playing the music, that makes you the director."

"No, I'm just in charge of casting."

(laughter)

"What would you like to hear next?"

"The Stones—"I Can't Get No Satisfaction."

(long pause)

"Hmmmn...I don't think we've got that on the play list today."

Mulligan is one with the music for awhile. He comes out of it to see how things are progressing around him...then back with the music. One moment he is a dulcet tone billowing from the bell of the clarinet or he is inside the base, such a tight fit that the vibrating strings tickle his belly. The next, he is talking to Michael while his eyes follow the pleasing lines of Christine's crossed legs. He is not as stoned as his comrades (tolerance has its disadvantages), but he is more relaxed and has fewer internal barriers to oppose the flow of the acid (experience has its advantages). If Mulligan is calculating, as Michael believes, it is a strange sort of happenstance calculation that has been with him so long it is an unconscious part of his nature, a calculation that perhaps he becomes aware of only in the moments of its realization. Consciously, he is without expectations, living from moment to moment by the dictates of his senses, internal and external. Consciously, he is capable of enjoying many things, but if he doesn't get them all this time around, there's always...

Due to Christine's lower body weight, she has taken a relatively stronger dose of the acid. She is amazed by the way it just keeps rolling over her. For awhile she'll think that it is wearing off and she is coming down. Then a new wave will hit and carry her to a different peak as totally unfamiliar and mind shattering as the last. She doesn't know what she'd do without Mulligan, David, and Michael by her side...but then again, in her more rational moments, she doesn't know what she is going to do with them. The apartment has succeeded in shutting off the interference of the city, but Christine now feels the need to shut off still more, to banish the three pairs of eyes that are constantly upon her, to come together with herself.

Behind a closed and locked bathroom door, she surveys herself in the mirror, trying to rediscover the proper perspective. The normal symmetry of her face seems off kilter. She is looking into the joined halves of two different women's faces at once, neither of them particularly recognizable. She is able to suspend belief in her senses momentarily and credit it to hallucination; but when the whiteness of her skin in the bright bathroom light turns to a powdery dead plaster of Paris white and begins to crumble before her eyes, she becomes frightened. Filling the sink with cold water, she splashes it over her cheeks, temples and forehead. Turning back to the mirror, she sees herself, her normal self, for a second...then the water still upon her face turns white, droplets solidified to icicles. She feels the cold as a palpable presence and becomes frightened again, so back to the sink this time with warm water, again and again, until in the midst of the water playing over her hands, in the midst of playing with the water, her vision recedes. The water itself claims her consciousness and she decides to take a shower.

The stereo is silent, but the impressions of the music still hang in the air. Michael has succeeded in assuming his normal acid posture. He is stretched lengthwise upon the couch with eyes closed. Jacobi sits cross-legged on the rug, rolling a joint from Billie's supergrass. Mulligan is crouched upon his heels next to Jacobi, his broad forearms wrapped about his pant legs. He hears the water from the shower and imagines it running over Christine's shoulders and breasts.

Hot water, steaming and cleansing water, the water of purification. Wash! Wash away the dirt and sweat of the day, the dry skin of the past. Wash away the past—Tony and Leonard and abortion and mistakes until the skin is rubbed a fresh baby red (But wait, the cells of memory are not dead cells, they continue to change and evolve with every advancing inch of the present!)

The water is a heated spray of stinging needles on her face and shoulders, a moving gown of warm streamers over her sides and down across her thighs. She laughs aloud with the returning thought of Mulligan as casting director. With the natural plasticity of his face he could play all the parts—Michael, David, herself, the snocone vendor and the cop on the corner.

After the shower, she towels herself dry vigorously. Her naked form, in the full length mirror, is beautiful and clean and roseate, not a line of excess, not a line out of place. Her flesh seems especially solid and real to her. With slight surprise, she sees and senses her own body as the body of an animal.

Break through those mirrors bending light to purpose. See that bird gliding against the sun for the tumid black cross that it is, and sun no longer sun but brightly burning ball. Let your senses have their way.

She comes forth from the bathroom wrapped in a giant blue bath towel (just as she has seen Mulligan do). The only light in the room is from several candles, the glowing incense and the flaring tip of the joint as it passes back and forth between Jacobi and Mulligan. Michael sits up on the couch. In the dimness, Christine, without shoes and stockings, without make-up, her hair still damp, uncombed and darker in its dampness, is hardly recognizable as the same person. She is plainer and at the same time more beautiful, even more the universal woman than before.

Michael stares at her. She shouldn't be doing this, he thinks, not after the park, not after today, it isn't right to bait them like this.

"Ah," Mulligan quips, "the return of the water nymph," as he reaches up to hand her the joint. Then he is back to the stereo to give them another record.

Jacobi looks up at Christine and smiles slowly. He feels them all drifting in the current of the trip: inexorably, without resistance, they are being carried out to sea.

...at some level of comprehension, they all understood...what was going to happen...it was all clear from the beginning...but they kept losing it...until it surfaced again the next time around...

Like a shot of adrenalin, the grass fills them with fresh energy. Christine realizes that she had been wrong, the acid had been wearing off, the peaks had been descending gradually, almost imperceptibly, leveling down toward the respective drabness of reality. But not now. Now, internally, she still feels more coherent than earlier, but externally, her sense impressions, although different and lacking the pure clarity of the acid, are as vivid and kaleidoscopic as they had been at the park. She watches Mulligan and at last feels that she has pegged him with a single adjective. Mulligan is *convincing*. Whether in truth he is totally honest or total pretension and guile, he is convincing, like a rain-swelled river rampaging beyond its banks is convincing, like the heat of the New York summer is convincing.

Then it happens. They are all laughing about something and in the middle of that laughter Christine's mind goes blank and she forgets what that something is. The music, which a moment before she had been oblivious to, swells up to enclose her. She has just passed the joint to David and she is standing by the bookcase looking down at the oriental rug, fixated on the rug. It is her rug, but she has never seen it before. Not really. The music is one of her records (Vivaldi? Scriabin?), but the sounds are so disparate and original that she must have never listened to it before. The rug is dancing with the music. Her senses are interweaving, playing with one another, her perceptions broken down to a dancing synesthesia, she is lost, she is a young girl again, she is a little girl before the mirror, before the bar, bending, stretching, and the steps come back to her—arabesque, glissade—she places one foot, one leg, of her newly discovered animal body forward as the rug rises up three-dimensionally to swirl around her ankles, then the other leg—jeté, pas de chat, pirouette—and the first again until she has joined with the music, until her movement has become one with the dance of her senses. (But this is not ballet or even an approximation. Her limbs are too fluid, her steps too heavy. This is the dance prelude to a bacchic ritual. It is closer to the abandon of the turning dervish than the precise orchids of the ballerina.)

Her action is so spontaneous, so out of place and character, that the men about her, Mulligan included, look on dumb with astonishment. If Michael's eyes open any wider they will become lidless. His breath catches in his throat as Christine sweeps by him, the towel somehow still around her, her damp hair flying out behind, winding across her face as she reverses direction, faster or slower, her self bound helplessly to a body obeying the tempo of the music, *andante, allegro, presto,* to the point where the only spots of light in her vertiginous world, the candles, the incense, the tip of the joint, are stretch-blurred to solid bars, to parallel seismographic lines racing to meet at infinity, at the pitch of her hysteria, while the music mounts in crescendo-conclusion, even too rapidly for her abandon to follow, and she is one step behind, two steps, three and a half, hopelessly out of step but dancing on with the blind momentum of a spent runner to collapse falling prone before her speechless audience only once the finish line has been crossed and the stereo is clicking mechanically to a halt.

...this is the way the world begins, this is the way the world begins, not with a bang but a fall, not with a bang but a leap...

The sudden silence is relieved only by the hum of the air conditioning and by Christine's heavy breathing

"Bravo," Mulligan says slowly in deadpan anticlimax.

Christine doesn't respond. The towel, rumpled and in disarray, still covers her loosely from mid-thigh to breastbone. She has fallen near the center of the room, at the height of the room's illumination where the wavering light of the candles overlaps. She lies facing the couch, at a right angle to it. Michael, looking down the foreshortened length of her body can see beneath the edge of the towel the shadowy split between her breasts that leads down to her belly.

Jacobi and Mulligan move across the floor until they are kneeling, one on each side of her. Christine's eyes are closed, her flesh rosier (more flushed?) now than when she had emerged from the shower. Her skin is damp, not a dewy fresh shower dampness, but from the sweat of her exertion. As they look down upon her, the rate and intensity of her breathing seems to increase. (She cannot give herself. She can only offer.)

Riveted to the couch, with his hands kneading tightly against the resilient pressure of the cushions, Michael watches the tableau being portrayed before him. He is afraid to keep watching, but he can't help himself. He watches as Botticelli swims ahead of the trip's current (with calculation? without calculation?) and takes the single definitive action of the day, carefully, as if he is opening a present, his own special birthday present, lifting back the halves of the towel over Christine's arms, lying close by her sides, so that except for her arms her body is exposed completely, the tight line of her thighs tapering to her hips, the sandy shadow of her pubic hair, her bare breasts, rising and falling, breathing petals, white petals tapering to the tightness of their rose dark centers. Michael's mind fumbles upon his perception of reality and catches, fumbles and catches again. What is happening? What is happening? He tells himself that with three men and a woman alone together, isolated from the world, it is natural that they should come together sexually. It is a normal tribal grouping. He tries to hang onto this thought, but it is impossible, for they are not a lone tribe. Beyond the covered windows, easily accessible, lies the rest of the city, the rest of the world. (Is he a realist after all?) Still, the bare flesh of the tableau holds his eyes. His skein of asceticism is split and rent asunder against that wall of flesh. Mulligan shirtless, Christine naked, Jacobi now shirtless, too. Mulligan's solid flesh, Christine's soft flesh, Jacobi's lean and muscled flesh. Michael finds his pent up desire for Christine, for a woman, encompassing all of that flesh and suddenly that is what he wants, not only Christine, even more than just Christine, and he is truly frightened and full with revulsion for when Michael has thought of homosexuality he has thought of those magazines in the back of subway newsstands, or the Greeks or Rimbaud or Oscar Wilde, but never of himself and his own brothers' hanging cock and balls. And no. And no. And no. It is wrong, all wrong—his homosexual desire, their adulterous grouping, the nudity, the dance, the park, the day, the acid, most of all Mulligan, Mulligan perverting the acid, Mulligan forcing this all upon them, Mulligan with his hand on the precious ivory of Christine's belly.

"Nooooooooooo!" It breaks without control from Michael's throat. (Now it is Christine's breath that catches, Christine's hands that tighten.) "Nooooooooo!" Screeching. "It...isn't...right!" He is up and moving toward them. Righteous. Enraged. Freaking. He is charging upon their startled faces. Freaking. Christine's upside down open eyes. He sees them. He sees all three of them for what they are. A glutton, his fat expanding in an attempt to consume the world. A swarthy and vicious Machiavellian prince. Freaking. Freaking. A woman's bleeding white body, a body covered with bleeding scabs. He is about to sprawl lengthwise upon that witch's poison flesh. Pivoting at the last instant he strikes the fat man. His hands grapple with the hot and solid flesh. Unable to close upon the goiterish throat. Carried by his crazed momentum, tumbling over the squat body. Footing lost and turning across the dark floor.

Michael's rolling body strikes the bookcase. The bookcase rocks and bangs against the apartment wall. The volumes tremble and the leaves of the volumes tremble (Plato to Beckett), but unlike Michael, maintain their posture. One floor below, Daniel Mekas, who has listened to all that he is able to hear—the music, the muffled padding of Christine's dance, Michael's screams and Michael's falling, the sharp thump of the bookcase against the wall—imagines a thousand different scenarios, some more, some less impossible than what is actually happening...only knowing for sure that he is a part of none of them.

Christine has lost her breath and her color, but has regained her towel, after a fashion. She is still on the floor, back against the end of the bed, her legs drawn up together. Her face registers confusion, disbelief. She isn't sure what has just happened, what is happening or about to happen.

Michael's body rests against the bookcase. He is motionless and totally withdrawn. Knees upon the floor, forearms on the floor, head on the floor. The reality of his freakout has superseded the reality of their perverse coupling, and for the moment, he is unable to face either. Eyes closed, arms over his ears, thin lips bloodlessly compressed, he has become three monkeys all at once. See no evil. Hear no evil. Speak no evil.

"God damn, he's like a statue." Jacobi is bending over him, trying to get him to sit up. He can only pull the locked body away from the bookcase, beyond that his efforts are futile.

Mulligan, like a trained physician, has already moved into action. He has his briefcase open on Christine's desk and is preparing a hypodermic. When he has finished filling the syringe, he crosses the room to Jacobi and Michael. Jacobi puts his hand out to stop him.

"Do we have to?"

Mulligan bends down to feel the rigidity of Michael's body, bends closer to reach between clenched arms and peel back an eyelid. He glances toward Christine and then back to Jacobi. "I've seen this before," he says. "More than once. It's the best thing we can do."

So Michael, who had consciously refused a needle filled with waking, now without protest, takes one full with sleep.

Brothers in fratricide...sleep by my side.

They carry Michael's limp body to the couch and their tribal circle reforms itself upon the floor, tighter now that it has been reduced by one member. Jacobi sits with his elbows on his knees, chin in his hands, face frowning in puzzlement. Christine is quiet and still, totally withdrawn with eyes downcast. Jacobi hears Mulligan sigh heavily and he looks up.

It is a rare moment. Mulligan appears totally exhausted, the flesh of his face and body sagging. He looks as if all the needles and pills and experience and running around and mile a minute conversations have finally caught up with him, as if all the freakouts he'd witnessed and all the ones he felt responsible for were weighing on his shoulders, hanging around his neck. He breathes deeply for several seconds (so deeply that it makes Jacobi think of Michael's hyperventilation) and then he is back to himself.

"Shit," Mulligan says. He is throwing a closed matchbook against the rug, picking it up and throwing it again. "Shit. Shit. Shit."

Silence. Silence. Silence.

"It could have been good, good for all of us," Jacobi says, "especially for Michael."

"No," Mulligan responds, nodding in the direction of the couch, "that one was meant for other things."

But still it has to happen. In the silent candleless dark, in the limbo where Michael's freakout has left them, with their own motivations prematurely clouded by reawakening morality long before the light of dawn.

Four hands upon her body, two mouths, the pleasure multiplied accordingly, a baby at each breast, a mouth upon her own, a mouth upon her cunt, so much touch that she stops thinking and is only feeling, so much that she can no longer tell whose hands are whose. Then there is a man on top of her and it is his body, familiar, David, his cock within her, and it is the same as it has been before with them, so good, but there are still those other hands moving upon her, making it different, making their bodies different, until she loses herself again, giving in to Jacobi's fucking, his movement, the culmination of his acid high, the last of his stoned energy expended on her, foreshadowing the death of all energy, the final flowing, the end of flow, the granite stasis of atom and molecule signaling the gestation of the last and the first holocaust that will spring from empty space, until they come together with an orgasmic simultaneity in space-time-touch that could only be pulled off by the blind genius of the mating force above and beyond either of their wills.

While upon the couch Michael sleeps the sleep of the dead, dreamless, safe within another space, nearly antediluvian he is so far removed in the distance of his antiquity.

And then there is a second man on top of her and it has to be Mulligan, just Mulligan, whoever that is, not in as deep at David, but thicker, steadier, with his feet braced against the foot board of the bed, fucking like a machine, moving her as if she were a fine machine, and now despite the dark room and her first coming, despite all of the dope, she cannot lose herself and she is more conscious of the physical act of fucking than she has ever been before, painfully conscious of her weight pinned to the bed by a greater weight, the stabbing at the apex of her being, the sweat and the tears and the cries that issue from her throat with each blow that he delivers, and she tries to find David's hand in the dark but can only find his flesh and what part of it she can't be sure, and with an inescapable cry louder than the rest she encircles Mulligan with her arms and legs, fat Mulligan, funny Mulligan, Mulligan the juggernaut, Mulligan the impresario, moving above her and with her, his mouth full upon hers and taking her breath, and she can feel her second orgasm rising from within her long before it comes, it will be slow and sustained, flaming like a pinwheel, radiating at its peak to cover the length of her body, she is almost afraid that its duration and intensity could short circuit her nerves, her consciousness, but Mulligan will compromise for no less, growing larger within her, about to come himself, the rhythms of their bodies beating against one another, in pleasure, in conflict, and there is no compromise between them, and there is to be no compromise between them, and at the last instant before the act can be consummated an involuntary muscle contraction (physical, she was sure it was only physical) causes her knees to snap upward sharply in the bed forcing Mulligan out of her so that he comes into emptiness, expelling his breath sharply from between clenched teeth with the head of his cock trailing along the inside of her thigh.

Botticelli never told Jacobi about that, but it made an interesting story to tell to others.

32

WHEN Mulligan woke them up it was already late morning. He was standing in the center of the floor, naked and bleary-eyed. "I've got to get into gear or I'm going to miss my flight," he said, stumbling over a corner of the rug that had been turned up by Christine's dancing. "Stay where you are. I don't want you to get up. Just help me find my glasses and I can get going."

"No, man, we're coming too. We've got to see you off," Jacobi insisted, and Christine chimed in, "Yes, of course, Denny!" blinking the sleep from her eyes and sitting up to stretch so that the sheet fell away from her breasts.

"Well, get some clothes on then," Mulligan told her squinting, "or you'll get us started all over again."

By this time Michael was sitting up on the couch. Despite the heat of the day, the blanket they had thrown across him was gathered about his shoulders, the pillow they had placed beneath his head was clutched across his chest. His eyes were puffy slits, obscuring his expression.

Mulligan knelt by his side. "Are you all right, man?"

"Just get away from me," Michael barked, turning his head from Mulligan's nakedness. "Leave me alone!"

Christine slipped on a robe and came to sit next to him. Jacobi, watching from the bed, couldn't hear what she was saying. Michael wouldn't look at her, and when she tried to put her arm around his shoulders, he pushed her away.

"I told you I was all right," Michael said, which he hadn't. "I told you...just...leave...me...alone!"

Jacobi and Mulligan found their clothes where they had left them, scattered about the room. Jacobi had never seen Christine's apartment in such a mess. Books, records, cigarette butts, ashes, dirty dishes. There was no time to straighten anything, no time for breakfast, so they stumbled into their clothes. Michael curled up again on the couch, ignoring them. Christine came to his side again before they left the apartment, but was careful not to touch him. "Don't go anywhere," she said. "Wait for us to get back."

"She means it, man," Jacobi added, "Wait for us."

There was no response.

They hurried downstairs, deciding to take a taxi to the airport so they wouldn't have to hassle parking, besides which nobody was in any shape to drive, not even Mulligan. Once they found a cab and got into it, a strange silence settled over the three of them. They sat crammed into the rear seat, arm to arm and thigh to thigh, with Christine in the middle, just as they had slept the night before. Her knees were higher than theirs because of the hump for the drive shaft and she hadn't even had time to put her stockings on. They watched the traffic ahead of them, bunching up at each red light and spreading out again as it turned green. Mulligan kept looking at his watch.

Jacobi, examining the silence, decided there was no reason to talk, nothing left to say: they'd already said everything there was to say together and done everything there was to do. Christine was feeling rushed, still half asleep. They had found Mulligan's glasses, but not her brush and comb. Her hair was a mess. She wished that she had at least applied some eye make-up, so if she were going to look dissipated, she could do it with style. Mulligan was just coming fully awake. His stomach was grumbling and he was speculating about what there would be for lunch on the plane. He was anticipating his first cigarette in days.

They made it to the airport several minutes before the flight was due to take off. Jacobi got them some coffee in paper cups from a snack bar. They stood drinking it in a corridor near the boarding area with streams of people rushing around and past them. All of their clothes were hopelessly wrinkled. Their faces were still red and puffy from sleep and all the dope they'd taken, and Jacobi and Mulligan were both badly in need of shaves. The coffee was too hot and Christine burnt her tongue. The steam spiraling up from the paper cup momentarily fogged over Mulligan's glasses so that you couldn't see his eyes and he couldn't see anything. They stood in their small unkempt circle, still slightly spaced and wordlessly smiling at one another, an island apart from the bustle going on around them.

Before they could finish the coffee, Mulligan's flight was being called for the second time.

Leaning forward, he put one hand around the nape of Christine's neck beneath her hair and gave her a quick kiss, falling crookedly across her mouth. Then he turned to Jacobi who thought for a moment he was about to be kissed too, but Mulligan settled on a handshake and a hug.

"Well, thanks for everything," Mulligan said, looking from one to the other, almost bashful. "Come see me in California."

Perhaps they'd expected something more, but that was all.

And then he was gone. Through the glass doors, running across the field, his briefcase in his right hand swinging to his gait like a metronome, his wrinkled unbuttoned coat flying up behind.

Christine and Jacobi, standing together, moved closer to the glass and waved. "Good-bye, Denny," Christine said, more to herself than anyone else. And then suddenly realized aloud "David, David! He forgot the conga!"

"I not surprised," Jacobi laughed. "He's always leaving something behind. It's like a calling card."

By then Mulligan was out on the field. He was listening to his tennis shoes clap against the asphalt, listening to his breath. The plane was huge and growing closer. Behind him he knew that Jacobi and Christine were growing smaller. It felt good to run, to perform the simple act of running, and for a moment he was just running, with nothing in front of him and nothing behind.

Christine and Jacobi watched through the glass as Mulligan turned, nearly to the plane, blew them a kiss and doffed an imaginary hat in a low, sweeping bow. He cupped his hands like a tunnel around his mouth and yelled something, but of course they couldn't hear him. Several other passengers near the boarding ramp spotted him for the lunatic that he was and hurried past.

Within minutes, Mulligan's plane was a great silver bird rising into the sky, blinking white lights and red.

Christine was standing with her arms tightly around Jacobi's waist. "God," she said, "I feel like I've been on a roller coaster ride for the past week."

And later that same day, after they'd returned to the apartment and discovered Michael already gone, and Jacobi had run a hot bath for the two of them and they sat washing and soaking in the warm soapy water and sliding their slippery limbs against one another, Christine added, "David, let's get off the roller coaster. Let's get out of the city," and with little-girl excitement, "Let's get a place together in the country!"

PART THREE

Sojourn in Ithaca: The Sub-Hero Speaks For Himself

"...the phallic personality needs a receptive audience or womb. Separately, both actor and audience are incomplete, castrated; but together they make up a whole: the desire and pursuit of the whole in the form of the combined object, the parents in coitus."

Norman O. Brown
Love's Body

September 2, 1965

In the stillness of Ithaca the lakes cool the night. Cayuga. Owasco. Seneca. Otisco. In the stillness of Ithaca there are trees I cannot name—white bark to black, mossy to bare paper bark, reptile skin bark. In the stillness of Ithaca the tall grasses weave an Indian autumn amidst the Indian lakes, the fresh fall of my twenty-first year, the fall into knowledge, the apple of reality eaten to the core, the seeds prepared for a new sowing and newer harvest.

In the stillness of Ithaca I am living with a girl-woman ten years older than myself and ages younger. She is my lost earth mother and downy urchin bride. She greets the morning with puerile delight yet her down turns to bristle in the sun. She is both whore and virgin, captious nun and comely courtesan. From that provocative gap in her perfect white teeth she can exhale the decadence of age.

In the stillness of Ithaca I am becoming a sensual mystic, and soon I will project all women onto every woman. Do not laugh. Ten years from now we may all be mystics dancing naked in the cold blue fires of rebirth.

In the stillness of Ithaca we are loving one another and torturing one another, turning our life games into sex and our sex into play.

You may watch our scrabbling if you allow my theatrics. You may disagree if you trust my indifference.

Sept. 4

The shutter clicks several times in rapid succession while she is moving, the exposure is multiple, catching the rapid grace of her running legs in blurred white beauty against forest green, the vulpine head with hair pulled back, the face of a model, a model's body leaping through fat picture-book Vogue magazines to keep pace with the proper fashions, it's all in the bones and how they niche the flesh, it's in the camera's angling eye, yet when the camera clicks too often bone beauty can turn bone ugly, when my mind's eyes dispatches her grace she freezes awkwardly in mannequin plaster, her traumas spill across the negative like loose teeth she has worried to devil's points.

Catharsis-cathexsis and I am the chosen father. Already my beard begins to grow.

3 a.m.

In the woods at night she moves above me, an amorphous white form shifting against the black screen of the sky, so tenuous that the pale globe of her face seems to billow with the wind. Slowly she comes down upon my cock as I rub my hands up and down her thighs. Her bones press against my hips and belly. We are fucking underwater…no, slower yet…we are trapped in a viscous pudding or bound by the gravity of Jupiter.

My chin points to the North Star, Dog. Her breasts are hard as iron harness bits. Far above us the wind is ruffling the treetops in patterns that we sense but cannot see.

Sept. 15

Two weeks spent in furious redecoration! The house has become a monument to our joint imaginations and Tina's anal artistry—she can work with the energy of a speed freak—a backdrop for spontaneous theater, a sheaf of landscape panels awaiting our comic book karmas. She is producer—the house has been paid for with Christine coinage just as I am now paid for—cue girl, and leading lady. I shall be her make-up artist and director. Our unrealized fantasies have penned the script for years beneath their carpet cloak of sublimation.

Life in the country! Life in the country! We drove up Highway 17 in Tina's candy red VW, into and through Ithaca. It felt good to be behind the wheel for a change instead of hanging my thumb in the cold highway wind.

When we had left the city behind we found the house almost immediately—though we nearly missed the cardboard "FOR RENT" sign, curled back upon itself from age and past rains—a loose board white frame cavernous in its disrepair, the backyard an overgrown swamp of uncut grasses, yellow straw weeds, graying tree stumps, their past growth graphic with rings of age. A oval rock-boundary goldfish pond murky with algae hides like a muddied opal among the grasses. By the pond, two closely set and stubby trees hold each other's arms like crying sisters.

The landlord has a nose as bowed and cavernous as the house he is renting. One can imagine cobwebs and tendrils of dust gathered in the lost darkness of its twin caves. The landlord has a fine fringe of white hair waving from the borders of his bald dome and eyes like over-fried eggs, hard yellow-brown irises with crispy brown veins in the white. I have dubbed him "Shylock." He may be Arab, Arapaho, or Croatian, but I have dubbed him "Shylock" nevertheless. One can tell he is curious about who I am. Husband? Brother? Friend? No, dear landlord, I am her son-lover and father-analyst. I am a peddler of illicit drugs from the other coast. I am an ex-track star now running for the title of holy man. You are more interested in her money than her morality anyway. You stuff the check into your dry one-way wallet and cluck your greasy tongue with chuckling hints of unimaginable obscenity.

Two weeks spent in furious redecoration. Our joint contributions— chic hip and acid hip—both clash and complement one another. We now have an ecru kitchen with forest green trim, a bronze bathroom with a tinfoil ceiling, a pagan living room with rough brick fireplace, scattered fur rugs, hanging thuribles of incense, Warhol pillows in soup can simulacrum. The bedroom is in cerulean blue with a canopied four-poster and sheets of satin. Here Tina can paste a beauty mark on her high cheekbone and become Marie Antoinette. She can don rings of moonstone. Cool pearl necklaces can ride the ridge of her collarbone. She can drink sweet amber wines, and disguised as the French Revolution, I can lick the icing from her cake and savor the aftertaste of almonds clinging to my pallet.

Back in the kitchen she can become my dimpled suburban wife, clean as a soap commercial, all coffee and curlers, nylons, gossip and tv dinners. Her fresh frozen cunt will thaw only for my wingtip cock, the one with dollar signs for balls. She will spit out blue babies for Little League and the American junk heap.

And before the living room fire her whiteness can turn to dusk and gypsy yellow. We can perform atavistic sex rites amid the fur rugs and smoldering incense.

The extra bedroom she has reserved in pristine white for her study. Yet I shall have her there, too. I shall fuck her on the hardwood floor until her similes and metaphors clank against the walls in jumbled disarray. I want orgasms bursting from the tips of her toes until the pink enamel peels and cries for a redder coating.

Destruction! That is what I am about in my own slothful way.

Tuesday, early morning

If she could discover the proper identity she might live up to it, but her roots and aspirations are too far apart. Sky above and mud below. She has been unable to kindle the spark of commitment necessary to jump the gap. Her poetry has given her the illusion that she could become something other than what she has been. Now I have arrived to give flesh, bone, blood and gristle to her illusion.

As part of that process I am, like Mulligan, learning the art of listening.

Sometimes after we fuck at night, Tina will start talking. She'll prop her pillow against the headboard and sit with legs pulled up so that her knees are tucked under her chin, smoking cigarettes and combing her love-tangled locks with her fingertips, or rubbing her palms up and down her calves and the backs of her thighs. Once she gets going she can run on into the night like a lost dog in search of its home, random sparks flying from the links of its loose leash as it trails along the sidewalk. An occasional grunt of appreciation from me is enough to satisfy her. This is the best reception she could ask for.

Last night she paraded her past relationships in front of me like some historical menagerie. "In some ways Tony was the easiest because he never made any real demands on me, whereas Leonard demanded everything. Raymond wanted me to be just the way I was, only more so."

When I interrupt such vague meanderings or press her on certain points I am "badgering" her. She tells me to be quiet the way an analyst is supposed to be—at least the way hers was. "Let me unfold" she says.

"No, Tina, let me tear you to pieces," I tell her, rolling across the bed and trying to grab a handful of flesh on her lean belly as she kicks and squirms away from me.

Afternoon

There is open country all around us, wild grass fields studded with broken ranges of trees. New York seems distant and small from this vantage. Manhattan could be an island of reeds in our stagnant fish pond. We could lean across the dull, slightly mildewed water and snip off the tallest buildings with a pruning shears.

Sept. 19

In the low peak-ceiling attic we discovered a dusty and dilapidated steamer trunk forgotten by some earlier unknown denizen of our playland. It is the kind with knobby brass buttons that scraped metallically as we hauled it across the floor. In the living room I pried it open with Tina's silver letter opener. Inside there were old dresses, empty record jackets, faded underwear, water-stained news clippings, yellow picnic snapshots with faces bleached white by a photographic image of the sun. The remnants of other lives and another era, when apple pie and bayonets were still the order of the day and Hitler a handy silver screen for the projection of our evils.

Three of the photographs, each dated June, 1943, impressed me particularly.

Photo One—Our front lawn only the grass has been trimmed and edged. A neat line of rose bushes marches around the corner of the house. Three bodies face the camera. A tall smiling soldier in baggy brown Eisenhower jacket encircles Mom and Dad with long arms. Mom and Dad are plump and shorter, the expressions on their pudgy faces lost in the pudginess. The soldier's hands, seemingly disembodied from his body, curl around his parent's shoulders gripping tightly, two pale starfish abandoned by a fast falling tide yet clinging fiercely to the sand as if it could save them.

Photo Two—The soldier stands by himself on the porch, one leg a step lower than the other, his stance slightly wooden. His cap attempts a rakish angle but only succeeds in looking awkward. He has rolled up one sleeve to display the tattoo of an American eagle on the white and hairless flesh of his inner arm. His grin is mostly grimace.

Photo Three—A distant three-quarter shot of Mom and Dad. The sun is too high and their noses throw dark shadow blips like patches of electrical tape slapped crookedly across their tiny mouths. They stare squinting to the right of the camera, as if into another sun setting on their soldier son as he marches off to war.

"Tell me, soldier boy, how many Krauts did you kill with those pale starfish hands? Did you drop an A-bomb or empty a flame thrower into a Jap cave? Are you still alive? Has your tattoo faded? Do you know that America has discovered other wars?

"If I could reach into the pictures I would straighten your crooked cap, give your grimace a cigarette, or better yet a joint. I would peel the tape from your parents' lips so they could tell you whether to go or to stay."

While I examined the photos and spoke to the soldier, Tina had been changing. She emerged from the bedroom, a green velvet vamp of the Forties with flat breasts, square shoulders, batting eyelashes and lips like a fat cherry gumdrop. Somehow from the back of the record stack I came up with a Guy Lombardo and we made love in front of the fireplace to the pudding strains of "Moonlight in Vermont."

Slow building orgasms that exploded with lazy nonchalance.

By the time we finished, our incense and the breath of our sex had mingled with the contents of the trunk. Its artifacts no longer seemed magical, but merely old. We consigned them to the fire and the soldier's head shriveled to a black death mask before it dissolved to gray white ash.

?

Last night I started fooling around with Mulligan's conga, and naturally we wound up talking about him. Tina's not the first person with whom I've tried to take apart and put together the puzzle of Mulligan to no avail. Already his appearance in New York and what happened between the three of us seems to exist in my mind as an unrelated event, a pointless *tour de force* that partially misfired without apparent cause or reason.

"It's too bad he couldn't have stayed longer," Tina said, "so that I could have gotten to know him better."

She won't believe me that Mulligan's best only in small doses, just as she won't believe me when I tell her that the acid he gave us really didn't have any speed in it.

"It must have. There's no reason he should lie to us about that, David."

All I know is that I've taken enough acid to be sure that my cap didn't have any speed. And Tina fell asleep that night before I did.

Sept. ?

If you ask me what I am doing, I'll tell you that I am living my life day by day. I know that there are seven days in the week, but I haven't gotten that far ahead of myself yet.

In the mornings I awaken twice. At first when she does. The rays of the rising sun spill through the sheer curtains like spun gold. In her still-sleepy eyes the gray flecks have submerged the blue. She stands naked and posing before the bedroom mirror, turning her body this way and that, stretching on tiptoe with her back arched, out of the pages of a men's magazine, but not *Playboy* since her cunt is bare. She has gained weight since we have come to Ithaca. Her hip bones are sinking back into flesh. Her face is rounder and regaining the lost rosiness of youth, she is more the girl in the swing and less the slinky model. She slides a bracelet up one forearm, mussing the milky hairs, and then her hand sweeps them back to patter like a straight wind through a wheat field.

"You're losing your model's figure."

"Maybe I'm pregnant."

"No, it's just country food and good loving," I tell her.

She dresses and puts on her make-up and her eyes are now fully blue and the lashes like slivers of dark chocolate above the whiteness of her cheeks.

After she leaves the room I go back to sleep, stretched out completely in the double bed with the quilts pulled to my chin. For an hour or so I fall in and out of sleep, tumbling first one way and then the other off the edge of waking. Letting my dreams percolate. The sun transcribes its rising arc across the center of our eastern window. If I lie on my side facing the window I can stare into its naked brightness until the warm tears fill the cup of my eye and spill over to track liquid furrows down my cheeks and temples, cooling as they fall. I can close and tighten my eyelids so yellow fades to red, to reddish brown tints and shades of purple. Then I can relax them again and be drenched in an endless orange sea. I can open and close my eyes until I am lost in the changing shades of the sun's illumination.

After the sun has passed the window's upper edge and the room grows darker again I sleep more deeply, finally to awaken around noon or one. If she has not gone into town I hear her moving about or typing in some other part of the house. Yet sometimes, although she is there, I hear nothing. Then I am surprised when I emerge from the bedroom to find her curled on the living room sofa totally and soundlessly absorbed in her latest bit of esoterica, *The Poetics of Charles Olson* or *Folk Tales of Medieval Spain.*

Upon awakening the second time, I survey the bedside ashtray. (I am now on a sloth trip, a giant sloth trip. I have given up cigarettes and smoke grass all day long. It mixes well with such a trip.) Among the dead and crumpled white smokestacks of Tina's Salems, I spot the shiny red plastic handle of the once-alligator-clip-used-for-electrical-connections
now-roach-clip-used-for-cosmic-connections, a step up on the reincarnation wheel no doubt. I pull it out and light the quarter inch roach remains of last night's final joint. Once I am stoned I go out for a walk, mixing the country air with the grass smoke

in my lungs for a heady combination. I walk the woods until I become a part of them. There are wild holly bushes and young eucalyptus, their leaves dressed in a silvery powder that comes off on my hands. I envision small forest animals, dabs of leaf brown fur with dark glistening raindrop eyes, who watch me from the underbrush.

Sometimes when I return, Tina has breakfast waiting for me—bacon, eggs, waffles or pancakes, steamy strong black coffee—yes, I am gaining weight, too, perhaps preface to a dumpy American middle age. If not, I scrounge through the refrigerator and kitchen cupboards for leftovers to assuage my grass-born hunger. Then, if it is sunny, I stretch myself on the front lawn shirtless and puff a joint rolled with white paper, especially for the outside. Indoors, I always use licorice paper. The "wicked weed" belongs in a black suit.

Tina comes out in her blue bikini to lie beside me, reading, and immediately I want her. Once in a while I can lure her back inside or into the woods for a quick fuck. Usually we wrestle briefly in the grass and then she laughs and rolls away from what she calls my "insatiable paws." If our summer were to become an illustrated classic, this is the picture I would choose for its frontispiece—Tina laughing in her blue bikini, white body trying for a golden tan, grass green, the length of her limbs and her waist accentuated by the bikini's smallness, her belly like that of a wiry adolescent boy, and smoky slate blue sunglasses making a mystery of her eyes.

Ah, Tina, your body! My thirst does not abate. My infatuation grows tumbling like a snowball on a downhill run. Your body is the flavor that consumes my day. You can cook broasted ostrich, pile plates hill high with smoked oysters and caviar, serve me aperitifs and chocolate cake, and still they will taste like Tina to me. Your face may grow hazy in my visualization, the finer lines indistinct, but the lines of your body remain like a photograph preserved in plastic. I have memorized its curves, crevices and secret passages. I know the turn of your calf barefoot or with heels. I know how the line of your thigh runs into your belly. I have computed the arching angle of your backbone, measured the upswing and downswing of your breasts. The positioning of your birthmarks is forged rigidly in my mind's eye and like a blindfolded aviator I fly from one to another. I kiss your birthmarks one by one. Your limbs must be lengthy for my vision never reaches their end.

A cloudy afternoon

This morning a rambling vitriolic letter from my father, Air Mail Special Delivery, no less. It's a good thing I didn't send him the phone number or we would have gone through a long-distance sparring match.

"What the hell are you doing in Ithaca?...What about your education?...You'll lose your scholarships...I hope you're not fooling around with drugs...We didn't raise you that way...How do you expect to make a living?" and so forth and so on.

It's all the cliches he has learned from television and the newspapers coupled with a few of his own. It's the American myth swallowed to the hilt and he has the bleeding ulcer to prove it.

If he could comprehend my mutant tongue, I know how I might answer him, but by now we are beyond communication. Our points of reference are rushing apart with such velocity that even the task of taking a fixed bearing approaches impossibility. Rockets teasing the speed of light cannot carry my messages to him.

Dear Father, the American myth will remain a myth.

Dear Father, my scholarships are already lost.

Dear Father, I am living in sin but I'm definitely not *fooling* around with drugs...I'm very serious about them.

Before acid I was a like a water coolie bowing my back under a wooden yoke. The existential dilemma weighting one shoulder, the threat of thermonuclear war and the draft dragging down the other. Acid, a pointblank shotgun, riddled those water buckets. The water dissolved into the earth or steamed dancing to the sun. I threw off the yoke and started screaming like a delivered banshee. I clambered out of the existential oubliette. I decided to pick and choose my own illusions.

Before acid my senses were atrophied, ruled by the language of others. Ruled by words and dying since the cradle. Experience was reduced to a geometry of sets and subsets, lockstepped in the prison rhythm of repetition-compulsion. I was grinding through the sophomoric miasma of selecting my life's vocation. Law? Medicine? Anthropology? Sociology? Econometrics? What would it be, death or the devil?

Now the categories seem like patent nonsense and I know the University offers degrees only in science and tapioca. The best-paid scientists are the ones who build the best killing machines. Tapioca slots you a notch higher on the American conveyor line. Too many have ridden that line already. It revolves in circles and nirvana is not even a whistle stop along the way. The line is a rack and in exchange for torn tendons you get tv baseball, tap beer in you own home, triple sequential tail lights and four hundred horses in the gut.

One night with Christine is worth more. Two hundred micrograms of lysergic acid are worth more. The wings of a dragonfly, seen for the first time like webbed exclamation marks, are worth more!!

Dear Father, is it not fitting that in a world of change your son should be a different man?

Sept. 23

She is everything special and there is nothing special about her whatsoever. When she bleeds upon the sheets, it is as red as any other woman.

Sept. 25 (late)

In the evenings, after one of her masterpiece meals and more dope, I clap the earphones to my head and let her stereo and records trip me out of Ithaca. Most of her music is a bit stodgy, classical recordings trapped in the stylized rigidity of black-tie performances. There are not enough driving drums and crying electric guitars to pace my racing thoughts.

Sept. 25 (later)

I can go no further without mentioning her poetry. She closes herself in her room and works at it for hours on end. One night she told me: "Sometimes when I write the whole panorama of my life is spread before me, within reach, and I can pick and choose as I please."

Still, I often wonder what all of this writing really means to her. Is it a communion with the gods of the collective unconscious, a celestial chit-chat with universal archetypes? Or is it merely an opiate for the ego, stand-in for a lost Catholicism, sublimation for the acts she is afraid to commit. I think it is all of these things rolled into one, kneaded like dough into a giant fetal ball that plops onto the page, unrolls itself, and claws its way scrambling to all four margins.

She is reluctant to show me most of her current work. If I try to glance over her shoulder while she is revising something in the living room, she'll bend the sheet forward and lean into it, holding it close to her breasts like a baby, turning her lovely face toward me with a look of irritation. "It's not part of your world," she tells me. "You won't understand it."

From what I have seen I can tell that she is now going through her "intellectual" phase. The freshness and simplicity of her earlier work has been superseded by the dry grapey constipation of Eliot imitation. There are no more "stained glass rains," only Time, Death, Eternity and Alienation draped to the gills with carefully calculated prime symbols. She is prolific, oh yes. She is erudite, my God! She grants no footnotes to unravel the riddle of her voluminous puzzles. Soon she will make *The Cantos* look like a child's bedtime story, but still, I wonder who will bother to read her gargantuan grumblings, even if she publishes them herself.

Besides her first book she has already been printed in a host of little magazines, the kind with high contrast photos of old people, children, and gaunt landscapes, the "literary" kind, which means they give you a complimentary copy of the mag instead of paying you any money. She collects her complimentary copies. They are the first thing on the bookshelf, upper left, a handy reference library from which to quote herself. Let's see, there are *The World*, the *Colorado Quarterly*, The *Pegasus Anthology*, *Occident*, and a tri-score of others.

Does she know in the end that it's all words and more words? Fat scabby crab words that inch up the inside of my pants to itch my balls. Why has she hung a sestina from my navel? Why is she trying to tie a metaphor around my cock? Can it be possible that to her the body is more a poem than it is a body?

Sept. 27

Her baths with their colored pearls of oil to refresh and rejuvenate her flesh. Her afternoon beauty naps, her creams and facials and special make-up. That a woman in her early thirties should be so conscious of her age amazes me—until I catch myself with similar thoughts.

Last night we attended a vintage movie at the University. It was *Petrified Forest* with Bogart in his gangster debut, Leslie Howard throwing effete pronouncements into a black and white desert you had to imagine was painted, and Bette Davis, young as myself, saying: "We don't accept tips. It's un-American."

The ticket taker was a rather plain-looking black girl. Her broad brown face was younger than Tina's.

Sept. 27

Tina and I share and analyze one another's dreams, our dreams feed upon one another's, often seemingly nonsense dreams, sometimes frightening dreams of infidelity and betrayal. I could compose a Freudian catalog of our dreams for inclusion in a Twentieth Century time capsule—*The Manias, Phobias, and Fascinations of the Unconscious Mind in the Early Atomic Era Preserved in Symbols Contemporary and Universal.* The prime theme would be a pervasive and recurrent paranoia. Sometimes I think we create omnipotent antagonists to make our lives more exciting and to give sentient body and bone to the amorphous fears that trail each of us.

I have dreams that flavor the day, dreams that are the axis for other dreams. Some mornings I awaken from dreams with the hunger for particular women I have known but never "known." Flying dreams and falling dream, celestial or wild animal dreams, yearning backward medieval dreams, dreams of…wet Gothic trees hung black against a fairy tale castle with the great white worm Time gnawing at their roots…veiny leaves pressed between the pages of the books on the receding shelves of eternity…the running future and running bloody inevitable revolution…dreams of a giant house crammed with knick-knacks, its corridors as convoluted as the labyrinth of Crete, a tall skinny three-story San Francisco house with cupolas, cornices, archways, ticky-tacky railings, circular leaded glass windows on each side of its peaked oaken door, wooden steps bowed by the weight of so many feet, with paint-scaly walls and hallways that smell of mothballs and menopause and old ladies' lavender sachets—this particular dream, this internal creation, seems rooted in my memory with greater clarity than any house I have inhabited in the flesh—and looking through its circular windows, staring out through its eyes of cheap distorting glass distorting my view in horizontal ripples I see Tina passing through a flux in time as she passes through the ripples, warped to science fiction grotesquerie, changing, little girl, woman, mother, little girl, woman mother, aged crone.

Tina's dreams are less surreal. They remain closer to the here and now just as she does. She exhausts the stock symbols—candles, forests, guns, buildings. Her most recurrent dream involves myself and her three children. All five of us are in bed together at her New England home. The blanket is red. A drift of snow cuts the windowpane in half. We make love while the children sleep and it is a tremendous orgasm that sends us all tumbling onto the floor in a tangle of limbs, pillows and covers. Her oldest girl wakes up. Grinning and rubbing sandy eyes with pink knuckles she says: "We knew it was you all the time, Mommy." Or sometimes she shakes her head and exclaims: "Mommy, you should have told us you were coming home!"

Then Tina awakens startled and puzzled to the darkness of our bedroom.

But I can put her back to sleep and finish the dream for her. As her daughter stops speaking there is a tremendous crash from the living room. We all rush out to find Leonard, her ex-husband, sprawled in the fireplace wearing a Santa Claus suit. A billowy sheaf of soot-stained white whiskers conceals his chinless chin. He has just crashed down the chimney with a fantastic bag of toys. He distributes them to the children and soon the room becomes a chaos of whirring electric trains, bouncing balls, screeching "ma-ma" dolls. Turning to Christine and me, he wags his finger in reproach. There will be no toys for us this year. We have been naughty.

She is cursed with a high metabolism and not enough to do. She is constantly uncovering a reason to make the trip into town, often two or three time a day. An extra light bulb, a head of lettuce, a sprig of parsley. She manufactures errands by the boxcar, clacking mundanity back into our lives like a fast freight. She crams note cards with busybody lists and tacks them over the kitchen table, crossing out each item as it is attained, an endless series of goal posts with new cards replacing the old.

With cigarettes and clocks she divides her day into tight tick-tock intervals. There are clocks in every room of the house to pace her hours. The heels of her flickering legs tap out an electric tempo, racing the sweeping second hand as it races thin air. She doesn't ask herself if she's hungry or sleepy. Instead, she asks what time it is—dinnertime, bedtime, time to take a pill, time to take a piss. I, on the other hand, have sunk into a sort of drugged timelessness here in Ithaca. My eyes avoid the number and circle running of her clocks. I ignore the whirring and ticking of her infernal array of chronological devices. I sleep when I'm sleepy, eat when I'm hungry, light a joint when I'm straight, and fuck her when my prick is up.

Her metabolism also seeks out its escape routes within the house. She sweeps the kitchen floor, vacuums the bedroom. To her anal New England upbringing dust devils are really devils. It was not enough to decorate the entire place. She has to keep making changes and improvements. It must be decor in flux. New paint here, varnish there, another tapestry to hang in the living room, a second vase for the mantel, fresh wild flowers throughout the house every other day. One gets the impression she is striving for some classical ideal even the Greeks were unaware of.

Today it was a new mirror—as if there weren't enough already— she picked up at one of the antique shops down the highway. She hauled it awkwardly from one room to the next, searching for the proper point of placement.

Thus she compensates for my physical sloth twice over and then calls me lazy—joking, yet partly serious like all joking. Lazy? Can't you see, Tina, that I am hoarding all my energy for you? Don't you realize that my mind is a buzzing beehive of honeyed possibilities, that I am the prime conspirator in a revolution to overthrow your hierarchies of order.

My drugs will distort your Newtonian universe and I'll turn you into a relativistic barbarian yet!

???

Days and nights of dope sex food sunshine sex music food dope books sex—one merging into the next. Yet it is not all candy canes and roses. We have had our differences, too.

She searches the house frantically for a misplaced notebook, tearing through one room after another, emptying drawers, shining a flashlight under the bed. She stands in the center of the living room, breathing heavily, legs spread and slightly bent, eyes flared, a tawny lioness about to pounce—only she can't decide in which direction. Then she spies me from the corner of her vision. Seldom does she meet my eyes when we fight. She looks everywhere but my eyes, as if she'd rather not recognize me but hold me in the status of an object that will receive her wrath.

"Where is it? Where is it? I left it right in the middle of my desk and it's gone. Where the hell is it, David?"

Her paranoia has reared up, thrown its rider, and is taking a wild palomino gallop through the forebrain. Obviously David Jacobi, the only other soul in the house, is hiding her notebook from her. She couldn't have mislaid it. Not her. Not the pristine Christine. The thief has tucked it within his shirt. It is warm against his belly, hot stuff. He will sneak into the bathroom and pour through her secret thoughts while he takes a crap. He will use them against her.

"Look, Tina, I don't know where it is, I haven't seen it, I don't even know what notebook you're talking about. Just because you finally lost something, don't take it out on me. Break a vase, beat your head against a door jamb, go masturbate! What would I want with your lousy notebook, anyway? I get enough of the garbage dumped from your unconscious as it is." At one level I am so removed from these sorties, yet at the same time I dive into them as if I wanted to be high scorer for the home team, racking up points each time I put her down. I dive in as if they were at the very core of our theatrics and I were bucking for an Oscar.

"The hell you do," she taunts back. "You resent anything I keep from you. You'd like to be able to read me like a book." She stabs a rigid forefinger roughly in my direction, her proxy penis. "Besides, you're the only other person in the house."

I knew it, I knew it, now it's in the open.

"All right, Christine, you've finally seen through my plans. I confess. I'm out to get you. But this is only the beginning. Tomorrow, I'm going to hide your shoes so you can't go out. The next day...tranquilizers in your coffee." I lower my eyebrows and add an ounce of gravel to my voice. "I'll bring in a bogus doctor, our dear landlord in disguise. He's part of the conspiracy, too. We'll fill the basement with test tubes, create new diseases to afflict you with." She is just coming to a boil. "I'll trick you into signing over your bank accounts." I crouch on the sofa, arms spread and fingers dangling. "And then, and then..."

"Oooaaahhh!" she yells as I leap upon her, catching her waist and carrying her to the floor. "Get off of me, you bastard, get off, get off!" She pounds her fists against my back furiously. I roll off her laughing and she stalks from the room, stifling an exasperated scream.

The notebook finally turns up made in among the bed covers.

Another time she starts in on our age difference. Maybe that day her mirrors have revealed an extra crease in her right eyelid or a gray hair next to her temple. Sometimes I wonder how many ways she can turn in front of those mirrors before she grows weary of her own reflection.

I am sprawled on the couch, stoned as usual. She is reading in the easy chair, legs without stockings, crossed tightly and drawn up to her body so there is a small triangle of space between the top of one thigh and the bottom of the other, her skirt riding up nearly to her waist so that the triangle of space reveals the pale blue triangular crotch of her panties. I imagine that it is warm and slightly moist and envision another triangle beneath, the dark irregular one of her pubic hair. Typically stoned thought progression. Triangles *ad infinitum* if I let myself go.

I am sprawled on the couch, rambling on about vague, fantasy plans concerning our future. We will go to Europe next summer, the complete tour, sunbathe nude on white French beaches, guzzle chianti at Tivoli Gardens, see the Beatles in person at the London Palladium. Tina looks up from her book and strikes out unexpectedly, the blue of her eyes flashing blue vitriol.

"Sure, that's great for this year or next. But what's going to happen to us, to me, ten years from now! I'll be over forty and you'll still be a young man. What about then?"

"I guess I'll have to trade you in on a newer model."

She hurls her book to the floor. "You think it's funny, don't you? You think it's so damn funny." Shouting now and for once meeting my eyes head on with the old hardness rampant again in hers.

What can I tell her? That I'll be long gone in ten years from now; that I'll never leave her, even when her flesh puckers on her bones and her tits are wrinkled and black as rotten walnuts; that I'll discover a fountain of youth that will keep her meat killing floor fresh; that everything will probably be hot ash in ten years anyway.

"Look, you can't live for ten years from now. Ten years ago you were a prim and proper Cape Cod housewife getting ready to manufacture babies. Now you're living in sin, fucking and supporting a former dope dealer. Speaking of dope, where did I put that joint?"

"Oh, go to hell with your stinking joints!" Dashing from the room and a crash of springs as she catapults herself crying onto the bed.

After such arguments the night descends like the black cape of a villain and silence reigns supreme on the stage of our domicile. Of course we come back to each other through sex. We go to sleep edged to our own separate sides of the bed. Then awaken to daylight holding one another, my morning erection already nudging open the door of her cunt.

Or sometimes she comes back to me through her poetry. Her bare white arm reaching over my shoulder from behind and pointing toward the window. A multitude of dead leaves have fallen to the earth with the first rain of fall and the trees have suddenly become bare, black-boughed and shivering in the wind and water. "Look, the trees of October do a different dance."

And once, while she awaits me in bed, I find a poem she has "accidentally" left upon the couch, penned perfectly in the parallel calligraphy of her printing:

I have slept with you as different men.
In acid-high fixations you are a compendium
of all men, our bodies making orgasm
like sacred music in an empty cathedral,
like the flame from a wick of growing brightness.

Blow the flame softly, love,
and it will flicker without dying
and throw our patterns dancing on the walls.

I can't, Tina. My breath blows stronger with each new truth I uncover beyond the level of language. I want to explode inside you in all directions, bring down the church, the organ pipes, the musty tapestries all around us. Then we can walk out from the debris of the past like a gutted building and make love together in the street.

October 1, 1965

There will be no more days in the sun. Fall is upon us almost before we know it, an early fall, quick and colorless, the leaves covering the ground like a brown khaki army in corporal array. Now the morning woods are filled with a heavy mist that dampens my clothes and soaks through my thick hair to the scalp.

If she will take me into her depths like a dark autumnal river muddied by the rain-washed soil, I will fuck her until she comes like fire and snow, like all the joy of Christmas morning.

Oct. 6

Last week Tina found a tomcat, his face and head scarred from past battles, stalking imagined prey in our backyard. His coat was a hybrid of brown, orange and white, the fur of his face a patchwork quilt that further concealed his already inscrutable cat glances beneath the pattern of the quilting. He greeted us with scratchy meows and unblinking yellow eyes. Tina fed him milk from a bone china saucer. As she knelt down next to him she seemed equally as feline. He rubbed in winding circles about her legs and purred like a well-oiled engine.

Today he returned, crying at our back door. We lured him into the kitchen with a can of tuna. While he was eating, I began to shower the room with bubbles from a ten-cent bubble blower I had picked up at the local five and dime, about to go out of business, the last of a dying American phenomenon even in this rustic outpost. At first the cat ignored the bubbles, but once his hunger was sated he began to bat at and puzzle over the falling crystal spheres. An occasional bubble popped near his nose, threw a speck of soap up his pink nostrils and set him to sneezing. As I increased the intensity of the game his batting became frenzied. The bubbles fell all around him, breaking on his back, tickling his ears. He was surrounded. He was facing a parachute jump of the Red Chinese Infantry: for every bubble he chopped down three more loomed out of the sky. With a final despairing yelp, he leaped out the kitchen window.

Tina compressed her lips and shook her head at me as if I were a truant and trouble-bound adolescent.

?

When her eyes have demanded humiliation I have given her humiliation. When she has asked for control with the vulnerable and wanton weakness of her open limbs, I have not denied her wish.

I strip her clothes off quickly on the living room floor, stretch her on her back, naked on the rug before the fire. I pin her arms crossed at the wrists above her head and tie them with the sash from her robe. My hands move up and down her body at will. I pinch and bite her nipples until they are tight, tangle my hand in her pubic hair, pry her legs apart and push my finger into her cunt. She is dry with nervous anticipation. I pivot her body closer to and facing the fire, so the crackling waves of heat beast against her bare flesh. I tie her slender ankles, binding them to her wrists. She lies on her side with body bowed, her back forcibly arched, the fire pulsing reds over the muscle taut and bare curve terrain of her flesh, a snowy nightscape illumined by a blood coral moon. The heat starts her sweating, glistening sweat that shines on her breasts, stomach and thighs. Yet she endures like a rapt and stoic martyr, closing her eyes from the brightness of the fire's glare, neck and face flushed from the heat, teeth clenched and a vein throbbing in her temple.

Now I roll her back and moistening my hand with her sweating force it within her, two fingers, three, plunging it in and out, masturbating her roughly. She digs her heels into the rug, lifting and arching her back of her own accord, squirming, wriggling her butt, short pleasure-pain-love cries escaping huskily from her throat. My teeth sink into her tender unshielded flesh. I tease and bite her clitoris until she begs for my body, then silence her cries with tonguing kisses that hold her head to the floor.

She comes once, shaking uncontrollably, sobbing.

I do not let up. I bring her to another peak, then freeing her arms I pull her forward with my hand clasped tightly around her neck and force her face between my thighs. She laps at my cock hungrily, she can't get enough, licking, kissing, sucking like a mad woman while my nails rake across her back or my hands reach underneath to grab and pinch her freely hanging breasts.

Finally I press her to the floor again and enter her, my full weight upon her body, my forearms like a harness against the rising ridge of her collarbone. Or sometimes I spin her around and take her dog style so the penetration will be deeper. She rocks back and forth fiercely and her hands clutch at the fur of the rug. I fuck her until she comes again and again, coming until exhaustion and still again. And it ends with my coming, sitting on the couch with Tina kneeling on the floor in front of me, sucking me until we are both sated, her hands sliding over my belly, hips and thighs as if my body were some kind of salvation.

Perhaps after such a scene she feels sufficiently atoned for her imagined culpability and I have succeeded in loping a limb from her towering statue of guilt. Perhaps now she will stop torturing herself with too many cigarettes. Perhaps she will read and talk of her poetry without the noxious specter of self-deprecation haunting each of her words.

Oct. ?

We trade roles in our play.

Her nails, sharper than mine, leave more lasting marks on the flesh of my body. Her thighs scissor my head, a soft yet inescapable vice, blotting out sound, my mouth and tongue buried in the hot bowl of her cunt, mixing my saliva with her juices and sweat until my jaws are aching and the taste of her fills me completely. Then she pulls me up by the hair and laughing like a beautiful evil witch, she bites my neck and demands still more.

We trade roles in our play. Yet at the same time we never trade. For as each teases and tortures the other, each projects upon the other until we are irretrievably bound.

Now if we could become true polysensuals, transform ourselves into hermaphrodites like the blind Tiresias, if we could metamorphose to slender Arab urchins with butts firm as ripe peaches, white-sock-falling nymphets downed like peaches, sweating black-thewed African drummers, Sausalito gays with prick-cinching levis, saffron-skinned geishas tutored in the flesh and pleasure dens of Hong Kong, if we could snare fetishes like rabbits hopping through our unconscious, if we could compile our members and apertures in geometric progressions—then we might complete the round of our perversions and drive out each of our demons one by one. We might just uncover our true sexual identities.

Oct. 12—Friday

Today a crazy letter from Michael, brilliant and unintelligible, landed like a bombshell, reminding me in a roundabout way to keep asking myself what the hell I'm doing here. He's been taking a lot of acid and going through changes, but just like the last time I saw him in New York, there is not a word about

Mulligan and what happened between all of us, as if the whole thing had never been.

Eleven sheets of paper altogether. The first four are rumpled and stationery-sized, two lined and two unlined, each a different white of the innumerable shades of white that paper can take. On the unlined sheets the writing bobs up and down in an irregular and nearly illegible topography. The train of thought seems noncontiguous. The letters are cramped. In places the ink changes colors as if the writing had occurred at different times, and the overall impression is one of false starts and random thoughts. The last seven pages, in contrast, are eight and a half by eleven and contain a neatly typed story, different than anything I've seen from him before.

When I showed the letter to Tina she said it sounded like the "pretentious ravings of an adolescent holy man." Who knows? That may be further along than the rest of us. Besides, who is she to talk about pretensions.

NYC — Oct. 11

Jacobi —

I have been trying to send my thoughts to you a hundred miles away. If the reception has been cloudy and fringed with static, here are the words. I do not know whether or not you will understand but still you will understand.

The synthetic has superseded the organic. Our old bugaboo, technology and all that rides shotgun with it, has brought us back full circle to the mystic vision of the East, dehumanization leading to supra-humanization. After three thousand years of "progress" the West has proven victorious both physically and spiritually, the best food for the body and the mind. All that went between can now be labeled a material parenthesis to forge the bedrock for the first mystical utopia. The tools of the Devil have at last completed construction on the Tower of Babel, in perfect miniature in a gelatin capsule. Its heights lead the way back into the microcosmic.

For all of our questions there is but one answer, the one running in our blood. The only truth is subjective truth.

Whether a state of reality is evoked or chosen—self-evoked or externally evoked—is the key. All externally imposed environments are states of perversion, i.e., the condition of man. Each individual must fashion his own reality as he extends beyond the self, thus the need for fantasy and also an explanation of the individual and temporal discrepancies in perception. Conflict is always the confrontation of opposing environments, personal fantasy facing the reality of the existence of other fantasies.

I am writing with unbending intent. I am writing with a kind of manic clarity that now overcomes me in snatches throughout each day, like the clarity of vision on acid. I know the price of such vision yet still I cannot deny it. The ten caps you gave me are gone, one consumed each Sunday like the blood and body of the Savior. Fasting and meditation could never do anything like this. I can see you laughing with your slinky poetess cat-curled by your side.

The language of metaphor, for language *is* metaphor, continues to propagate its metaphor. I understand the false dichotomies, the falseness of dichotomy.

I have reread my notebooks and they are no longer mine. They are delusion, a clue here or there, but mostly delusion. When I was (past tense) a poet I wrote with labor to expel a chant from my head and chest. I thought I could uncover my personal metaphor and interpret the world through it. Now I know that every event in the world is the perfect metaphor for what is going on in my head, every event explains the ultimate order of things. Thus all metaphors have become mine and not mine, all equally valid or invalid as the case may be. Some are more complex, richer than others, yet they are all still words, symbols, man-made and mind-made. Water is reality—depth and fluidity—and words are like oil poured upon its surface. A flaming match stick thrown by a child can burn the oil off and leave the water untouched.

And there I am again, trapped into the language of a poet, the leftover habits of a former self. But you can see that it doesn't make any difference, for now like Rimbaud I can leave my poems behind and tramp the desert with money belts of gold wrapped round my belly, or like Gurdjieff I can tramp to the East and join some dark totemic brotherhood. To the Devil with recriminations. Each object that I touch or see extends to all others. Each second is the gap and spark and connection between two others, hiatus and content, space and shelter, void and voided (by content). Each of our acts, no matter how minor, is divorced from its intentions and channeled into a prism. There, all of its facets emerge scattered in diverse directions, throwing out unintended ripples in the fabric of our existence. You light a joint in Ithaca and two weeks later I inhale a mote of your exhaled smoke while standing on the corner of Broadway and Forty-Seventh and the traffic lights momentarily glow with an extra red for me.

Yet it is not important to understand the random repercussions of our acts, or to ferret out their symbolic connotations. Rather, we must break through the cocoon of our calluses. We must live out our compulsions in reality rather than in symbol.

—Michael Shawtry

P.S. Enclosed, one final creation, a painted parable fashioned in my own particular prison cell.

BREAK

This cell is small for two men. The prison bars are parallel, yet the sun passing through casts closed octagons of light on the worn cement floor. Parquay lies sleeping in a bunk just a few feet away, his face a study in pores and stubble, while in the exercise yard the marching men pack the baked tan earth ever tighter. No insects escape their heavy tread. No shadows survive the unmerciful eye of the sun.

Night clicks down like a shutter when the sun drops below our prison wall. For the next hour the bare electric bulbs in their protective wire mesh cages will be our only illumination – then blackness. Parquay is awake, sitting hunched on the edge of his bunk, rubbing his rough strangler's hands against one another to restore their circulation to life, blinking the sleep from his dark vicious eyes with their red-rimmed pouches. He stretches and yawns like a well-muscled tom, and the stretching of his thick torso pulls the shirttails from his pants. Now he will begin his pacing, back and forth unceasingly, shaking his head with its coarsely cropped red mane from side to side and mumbling to himself. He has instinctively measured his stride to cross the length of our narrow cell in exactly four steps, his toes curling up against the wall at one end, edging between the bars on the other, as if he were testing the strength of these boundaries. Some nights I try to read through the noise of his pacing, but tonight, this special night, I do not read. I lie back breathing evenly, my eyes tracing and retracing the widening cracks of the plaster ceiling.

Although we share the same cell this is a different prison for each of us. Tonight, we shall leave it together. Tonight we make the break for freedom and as a team we complement each other well. Parquay needs my mind to remember the corridors we must cross, my skill to have fashioned the key notch by hasty notch in the machine shop, my thin hands and tapering artist's fingers to reach through the bars curving back to insert the key in its slot.

And I need Parquay. I need his strength and spontaneity, his animal cunning and blind bravado.

It will not be the first time an escape has been attempted.

Before they have always gone over the wall and tried the run across the desert. Two or three days later they are brought back crying with their lips cracked and their tongues swollen and they are locked in the pen hanging above the yard. We must listen to their cries and smell their dying bodies until they are silent. I have chosen a different route. My reading has served me well. We will run inward instead of outward, lower and lower, down into the abandoned cell blocks, through subterranean passages that have been long-forgotten among these modern heights of construction, down into the underground river that flows to freedom.

I am convinced that herein lies the only way.

The lights suddenly fade, sooner than I expected, catching my breath in my throat and throwing our cell into darkness. Parquay stops his pacing. On other nights this is the time when he would come to my bunk with his sweat and his heavy breathing and take me against my will and reason. He has told me that what he really needs is a woman. Yet he has told me that I am passive and that my body is soft like that of a woman

I could have resisted his advances on those nights, but there was little to keep the brute from strangling me with his hairy paws. Besides, I still need him until I am free of this wretched place. Then, once he has served his usefulness, I can reassume the cloaks of my disguises and pass along the city streets unnoticed. Then he will be a hindrance. There is no way to hide his hulking frame and heavy bullet head and flaming thatch of hair.

Tonight, when he stops his pacing, he does not come to my bunk. He squats on his heels with the base of his back resting against the cell wall, his eyes gleaming and faintly luminescent. There is a soft filtered light permeating our cell, and I can't be sure if its source is the pallid half-moon trisected by the prison bars or whether it springs directly from those hard glowering eyes, from the unshielded fires that burn within him. I know that my eyes do not shine like that. Instead, they are opaque milkiness or dim gray slits.

After several minutes or hours have passed timelessly and the sounds of regular breathing rise from the cells around us, I feel Parquay's hand upon my shoulder. He has moved across the cell more soundlessly than I would have imagined possible. He hands me the key, the key that I have fashioned but he has held, and with the bastard breathing down my neck I reach through the bars and turn it in the lock. There is a mind-staggering moment as it catches, but then the tumblers fall and we are quickly into the corridor. Parquay leads the way, gliding forward on the balls of his feet. Ahead we can see the light where the hall turns into the guard station. We pause, before the turn, then suddenly rush around it as we had planned.

There are two guards — one playing solitaire at a table, the other watching over his shoulder. Before their slow prison wits can respond, Parquay moves into action like a killing machine. Seconds later both guards lie senseless, one slumped across the table, the other stretched on the concrete floor, a pool of blood spreading from his broken skull.

But the noise has raised an alarm. We hear a cry from further down the corridor. I point Parquay toward the door we are to take and crying out he charges straight into it, leaving only a rain of dry splinters showering the room. I dive after him, into the blackness beyond.

The passage drops away quickly and I nearly pitch forward with the speed of my running. Parquay is moving too fast for me to keep pace. The fool will lose our way, the way I have planned, but there is little for me to do now but follow.

We race down and down, deep into the endless pits below the prison. The air is at first dry and musty, rasping hot upon my heaving lungs. Then the walls and the floors become slimy with moss and moisture and the air is cool and damp. I hear a crash ahead and a muttered oath as Parquay collides with something. Sliding on the slippery floor I pitch over one of his outstretched limbs.

I pull a box of wooden matches from my pocket and light one. We have come deep, perhaps too deep. I do not know this tunnel. The walls around us are cave walls, rough with jagged stone and rounded overhead, natural rather than man-made. Parquay has run directly into one and his nose is bleeding and there is a jagged cut swelling across his forehead. There are two passages branching from our tunnel in opposite directions. I lead the way to the left, lighting one match after another. Now it is Parquay who follows, moving slowly, mopping his bloodied face with his sleeve.

They have let the hounds loose and we can hear the sounds of their baying, distorted and warped as it echoes down the catacombs, piercing our hearts like the cries from the mastiffs of Hell. The noise starts Parquay off again. The bastard pushes by me with his fear and his madness for freedom, knocking the match from my hand. Once more we are plunging wildly into the blackness below, falling and tumbling, colliding with one another, our racing feet knocking rocks or perhaps the forgotten bones of other subterranean runners clattering against the tunnel walls.

But then at last we hear the river, the crashing song of the blessed river, the way out, louder and louder, drowning out the dogs behind...there is a cry before me, almost inaudible against the static of the roaring water, and the floor drops away and I am falling through space lost in a moment of sickening weightlessness, deafened by the thundering water, then deep into its icy currents that chop my muscles and tendons with cramps and surfacing somehow with my numb hands grasping Parquay's drenched collar as he tries to shake me off and tries to swim but even his strength is useless against the river as we are buffeted back and forth, our bodies cracking against one another again and again like two berserk wrestlers hell bent on the destruction of each other, the destruction of the self, the water filling our throats, robbing our voices, carrying us rushing into the blackness of the unconscious.

I awaken on a fog-shrouded beach. It is morning. In the east the sun is rising like a heavy yolk through the liquid mist. Over the sea, unseen birds shriek a chorus in the salty air as if to herald its coming. Parquay is nowhere in sight.

I move inland, walking over a low range of dunes, stripping off the wet prison garments until I am completely naked. My body seems filled with a new heaviness, stronger and surer.

Gradually, the sand is replaced by vegetation and I am soon in a wood filled with waving knee-high grasses, wild birches, giant sunflowers nodding on their stalks. It is the lost country of my boyhood and I have thrown off my prison stoop and am walking through it swiftly and with an animal grace that has always been foreign to my limbs.

My throat is still parched from the salt of the sea. In a clearing I find a small stream trickling into a wide pool. The mist is gone now. The sun burns brightly overhead and as I lean forward toward the pool I see my reflection rising up to meet me -- the hair now tinged with red, my once pale face blended into that of another, the thickened features, the burning eyes, the jagged cut slicing across the forehead. I dig my rough strangler's hands with their tapering artist's fingers into the turf, plunge my head into the pool, and drink until my thirst is quenched.

Ithaca
Oct. 14

Dear Michael,

Immediate thoughts in response to your letter:

If fasting and meditation never took you as far as the ten caps, what now, that the acid is gone. Fasting and meditation may keep you there longer, you may go up in snatches of manic clarity, but they are going to be fewer and farther between. Eventually you'll be coming down. I was flying as high as you when I left Berkeley. By the time I hitched across the country and spent a little time in New York it was a memory. Ecstasy in America is not only against the Protestant Ethic and The Law, the very atmosphere of the country militates against it. Each cubic foot of air contains 500 to 800 milligrams of bring-me-down, and the rate is higher in the cities. Mulligan was right. There's no room for "holy men" in America. If you try to sit by the river and smoke dope you get busted.

And there is still another possibility. What if the acid vision, after all, only leads us back into our own particular brands of insanity? Sometimes when I take it I get the feeling that I'm trying to psychoanalyze myself with a sledgehammer. What if each of our enlightenments is different and we wind up even further apart, contemplating our own unique navels in the great voids of our individual padded cells.

Some parts of your letter ring with notes of truth for me, yet on the whole, if I am moving toward mysticism, it is a less didactic and more sensual variety that I'm after.

As for myself, I have been trying to live with my senses immersed in the everyday objects I find around me. Here in the country I have become a happy and lazy drugged provincial. My mustache has stretched into a beard. My "slinky poetess" continues to excite and fascinate me, her body and her mind. She treats me like a prince—love, food, money—and I intend to enjoy it while I can. In the spring I'm supposed to start school at Cornell.

Next week we are dropping acid together. It will be Tina's second trip and our first alone together. I'll know more then, or at least I think I will.

—David

P.S.—You've come a long way from Park Avenue, even if you still are in the city. Yes, yes, yes on the story. Two from me and one from parsimonious Tina.

Oct. 18

Our acid trip together as fast as I can remember it and write it down—returning like a canister of movie film spliced and put back together with temporal and spatial sequences awry—two or three cameras shooting at once—inside and outside the self—with and without the self—all we could have asked for and more—mother, father, sons, daughters, lovers—all we could have dreaded—all that we knew without explicit realization—all that a part of us perceived and another part refused to accept—up early blinking the sand from our eyes like children—the acid downed on empty stomachs with hot black coffee steaming to heighten the rush of the take off—a day at the lake and in the woods—a cloudless sky and the shadows are sharp—my feet walking the soil of another nation—not Amerika—a non-nation rooted in earth trees and water—so many greens just like Tilden with Mulligan—just like Central Park with Mulligan—every leaf making its individual imprint on my retina—the veins of every leaf—in the dead tree stumps miniature forests of gray-green moss repeating the forest around us—the wind rising and shaking the limbs of the trees with their burden of leaves and the shadows flickering as if the sun were about to go out—the shift of sun and shadow suddenly reduced to a two-dimensional abstract—the forest of thought unfolding in our brains—the mind shows—wearing green jewels by the bluegreen lake—her bejeweled nakedness—her face stripped clean of accouterments—her face searching for a bare patch of sky or the solid background of a leafy tree to strike a profile against—so stoned that it won't focus for me as a whole—a different detail each time I look—soft hair at her temples—black dots of her nostrils—line of a cheek—pale eyelashes—the wrinkled dome of a small brown mole on her neck—bits and pieces of her physiognomy—all we really know of each other—even what I know of her one moment I am forgetting the next—clearer and clearer—the multiple implications of every act, word or gesture—clear how the future balanced on the edge of each moment about to topple this way or that—trapped in passivity and waiting for the other side to push—entangled in history—our own and others—history coming down like a hammer on the neck bone—discovering our addresses as something less than neighbors—the end of one age and the beginning of another—she is linear and I am a child of the atom—if I am half-McLuhan she is all Gutenberg—while she is recounting the bars of Meursalt's prison cage I am sprouting mutant limbs from the seeds of bop and beat—sprouting like the living forest all around us while she is rock bound—like Sisyphus—tortured and self-torturing—and what about Michael—alone in the city with six million others—sitting in their boxes awaiting even a false dawn with hosannas of welcome—binding their wounds with ticker tape—at times their hopelessness so inevitable that one must stop feeling for them—and what about Mulligan—he doesn't count, not really—Mulligan is an aberration—a nonverbal experience like acid—an experience that we had the fortune or misfortune to undergo depending on your viewpoint—and what about us—still and all products of America and American sexuality—trapped in the ancestral recreations of power and bluff—let me into you and you can come into me—no, yes—yes, no—her body only a body—her eyes with their shadings of blue atop one another—her shields collapsing and her openness blooming until I really try to look—her freakout blowing the beautiful soft glide of the acid come down for both of us—her freakout screaming for the identities we left behind on the grass in stoneless graves—with sudden shock telling me: "My parents are gone forever. I can't ever speak to my parents,"—her face crumpling like a white bakery sack as the acid unwinds the stuff of her head like cotton batting—sitting with bare knees together, hunched and shaking—internally crashing through the mind shows of chaos fear despair—the goose bumps on her thighs—hairs standing, her legs amid the reeds—flesh puckered in fear with the intensity of her confusion—the day turned stale like the morning's uneaten toast left upon our plates—the weather joining the conspiracy against us—the sun shut off by a tight rind of clouds—flocking gray sheep-clouds between us and the sun wherever we go—while she is trapped circling within her head—withdrawn in paranoia rampant as her thoughts can manage—first afraid of me, then clinging to me as if I were the lone buoy in an open sea—leaning into and against my body walking—feeling better but then worse again—afraid again—feeling sick and dizzy and her throat too dry and her clothes rubbing roughly against her tender flesh—waiting for it to be over—wanting it to be over—"It's too long, David, too damn long!"—and sobbing "I've seen it all already...I don't want to see anymore...I don't want to think anymore."—sobbing out of control—until I get her back to the house and the couch—to the somnolent sanity of a tranquilizer—and the tears end and before sleep comes her soft face stares up into mine with the sponginess of a water-soaked flower—is there an ensnaring strength in the sum of her weaknesses?—is that what I want to possess—is Ithaca a stage or an arena?—does the sun go out in the sea?—will language ever say what it means?—who is Botticelli?—who does Botticelli think he is?

Midnight

There were just as many greens, yet they were the same greens. Just as I grew accustomed to smoking grass, I am now growing accustomed to the backdrop of the magic theater of LSD-25. But just for that reason I am all the more able to assimilate the content of whatever plays are performed for my benefit. Now I can see that a major part of the learning process, real learning, is no more than a process of disillusionment. The mind creates illusions through projection, and experience serves to either alter or obliterate that projection, that expectation. Now I can see that all things have the reality we choose to impose upon them—ideas, objects, experiences, and our very own lovers.

Still, in this age of self-consciousness, I have to keep asking myself how to avoid approaching everything as an intellectual exercise. Yet now the answer begins to emerge—to be true to the self that I alone hold, beyond the superstructure, beyond the demands of intellect or the demands of any other, to be true to the self that is my loneness.

At least I'm *sounding* more like a mystic.

Oct. 24?

We've just been through a week of nightmares that she refused to talk about. Just like the acid. Her confessions have also stopped. She's become more withdrawn than ever. About the acid trip, she only says: "It gave me enough to think about for a year."

"You won't be taking very much acid at that rate," I tell her.

"Maybe I'll never take it again," she says. Then she gives soft sad smile and adds like an excuse, "Oh, who knows? I probably will."

Oct. 26

At night, already abed, listening to the rustle and zipper of her undressing before her cool limbs find me warm beneath the covers. A candle makes the canopy above our heads a flickering burnished and pyrite sky. We hear the frogs in the backyard pond croaking bass and behind them the faint soprano whistling of distant trains. Quietly the barefoot hours step away, punctuated by our orgasms, talk and low laughter.

That's the way it was last night, as good as the beginning and better. Yet some nights we have to start all over again. Her blue blood begins to reassert itself. She offers me only a counterfeit of her self. No, a double counterfeit, the after image of a image. Her imagination jams at the bedroom portal and she drops it with distaste like a soiled pair of panties. Her sex sinks hiding to the marrow of her model's bones. The bare flesh of her body is left bare of eroticism, corpse cold beneath my fingers. And my fingers are as cold to her as the prying steel tongs of a meat hook.

She is forever trapped in the Catholic yin-yang of crime and punishment. She has no mustache but a beard of penitence sprouts from her flawless chin. Perhaps if I could don the white and purple robes of a bishop she would recite the sins that besiege her and sneak beneath my surplice with hot Catholic kisses for my sacred cock.

I grow tired of playing guru to her orgasms

Some nights I scream silently to the tinfoil ceiling: "Enough of frigid Ithaca! My balls for a corpuscle of California bloodshine!" The foil shines back with the monolithic silence of an American god, Alcoa Aluminum, Inc.

The end of October

Fragments from the biography I have garnered from her and imagined for her: an American fairy tale gone awry.

She was their first and last child. As their tried and true family doctor pulled her from the womb, it collapsed behind her. They could not improve on this creation, so they decided to make her perfect, to spoil her to perfection.

Imagine this—as a little girl she went swimming in the cold blue waters of Cape Cod Bay. She picked berries bluer than her veins in the woods of her grandmother's estate (as a little boy my lungs toughened trying to pick some oxygen out of the L.A. smog). Menageries of stuffed toys overflowed her bed. Velvets and satins and laces filled her closet. Other children, surrogate siblings in bright gingham, danced across the pink wallpaper walls of her little-girl room. Shepherds tended flocks of cotton-candy sheep. Paper rivers crammed with paper boats ran unquestioningly around the corners and over the ceiling. The moon went down smiling like an idiot and came up underneath a cow.

The gave her piano lessons and violin lessons. They hand-picked her friends. They forced the bitter pill of Catholicism down her throat. Sex was finally to bring it up but by that time it was partially dissolved and like a cumulative poison had left its traces in the blood.

Short of turning her into a nun, her mother chose the virginal white ruffles of a prima ballerina. Her dancing master was the first man she could remember touching her body. He was German, with an accent like old iron. His hands were firm and insistent, but "Chrissy" was an awkward, ill-proportioned child. Her gangly limbs could only miss the bar or collapse upon it like wilting stalks. "She is impossible," he stated after three years of instruction. The columns of muscle in his neck did a jerky *pas de deux.* "I can make nothing of her."

Little did they know that her limbs would pace their growing to proportion, that her flesh would find the perfect shade of pale and she would begin to glide from room to room with feline grace. At the age of twelve, in the space of one year, she claimed beauty all at once. The scabs fell from her knees. Her freckles, all but a few, disappeared. Her blue eyes turned wide and serious. She refused to wear braces and despite ongoing forecasts of orthodontic calamity, her teeth straightened themselves. They were perfect, except for that tiny gap between her upper incisors. To complete her transformation, her mother dispatched her to an all-girl Catholic finishing school and she was almost finished in that world of sacrament and lesbos.

Imagine this—the fall of her fifteenth year. She is tall and leggy and her summer tan has just begun to fade. One of the nuns catches her with two other girls in the lavatory, sharing a cigarette, giggling as they pass it back and forth underneath the stalls just like a joint (yes, Tina, shades of your future falling across your past). Further investigation leads to the discovery of a pack of cigarettes hidden in her locker. Along with the other girls, Tina is brought to the Mother Superior's office. The three girls stand in a row in front of the bare oak desk where the Mother Superior sits. One is softly crying. Tina's hands are behind her back and she is digging her nails into her palms. She is still a Catholic. She is sorry for her transgression and is awaiting the grace of expiation and forgiveness.

The Sister who caught the girls stands behind them and to one side. Her manner is solicitous, as if she were presenting a gift and is unsure of its acceptance. Outside the window the sun shines pale as a grapefruit. In the distance, Tina can see her classmates doing calisthenics on the prickly brown autumn grass.

Mother Superior sits huddled in the folds of her robe against the chill that inhabits the ancient stone building. Her face is old, but her eyes are bright and avid. Her thin lips barely part as she spits the words at them. She lectures on the evils of tobacco and where it can lead. She warns of the dangers of sin.

She quotes the scriptures and misquotes the scriptures. One hand emerges from the loose dark cloth of her sleeve, and in it she is turning a stub of chalk.

The other girls are given a penance and dismissed. Tina is left alone with the two women. She can feel the cold of the room, yet she is trying not to shiver because she doesn't want them to think she is afraid. Mother Superior continues to talk, repeating herself, on and on with the chalk bouncing in one hand, angrier now that she has the perpetrator of the crime alone. Tina is no longer listening. The words roll over her. Her legs are aching from standing so long in one place. She is watching the chalk, the wrinkled palm covered with chalk dust.

And Mother Superior is suddenly shouting for her to come closer, and closer still, and Tina can see that the old woman's gums are nearly toothless as she steps forward until her plaid schoolgirl's skirt is touching the edge of the desk. And Mother Superior is telling her to bend over, and the hand having dropped the chalk comes forth with a wooden ruler and Tina is thinking, I'm fourteen, almost a lady, they can't punish me like this. And Mother Superior's hand moves close by Tina's bowed head, passing the ruler to the Sister who now stands behind her and is lifting her skirt and pulling down her pants. And Mother Superior's eyes are fogged over like a damp glass as the stick begins to fall against Tina's bare flesh, an unbending strap that forces her to cry out and pitches her across the desk. And Mother Superior is rocking in her chair, the folds of her black gown shaking as Tina tries to stand. And Mother Superior is up and moving around the desk, holding Tina down, as the ruler falls again and again, a dancing brand that won't leave her backside until she is crying uncontrollably and the tears are streaming down her cheeks. And Mother Superior's palm descends, cold, rough and chalky amidst the fire, caressing Tina's burning flesh.

And fourteen-year-old Tina, at last aware of what is happening to her, is turning and screaming in blind rage against the undulating black cloth wall around her, "You dirty bitches, stop it, you dirty, filthy bitches!" and pushing past their astonished faces, running from the room yelling, "You dirty old bitches! Filthy dirty bitches!" all the way down the hall and into the yard across the prickly brown autumn grass.

Once the other Sister has left, Mother Superior bends slowly and picks the pair of panties up off the floor. They are worn and slightly soiled. She folds them carefully and places them in the bottom right hand drawer of her desk.

Nov. ?

At times I want her so badly I can't think of anything else. Her limbs look new to me, the virgin flesh of the King's first daughter, the royal flesh of the Queen herself.

This morning I awoke and smoked a joint as usual. The house was still and when I got out of bed I discovered that she had gone somewhere. All at once the desire for her, intensified by the grass, came upon me so strongly I thought I might explode. I paced from room to room, filled with fantasies of her body. I tried to read. I tried to write a letter to Mulligan. Everything paled next to my visions of Tina's whiteness.

I lay down on the couch and was about to masturbate to expel her from my mind when I heard the VW come putting up the driveway, and then her shoes clicking on the walk. Kneeling on the couch I watched her through the curtains, my erection still in hand. She came toward me as if she were on camera in her breakthrough cameo role—stockings and heels, short blue skirt, bunchy knit cream colored cardigan, a long blue woolen scarf twined once about her neck and flowing freely like her hair. I realized there was no longer any diffidence in her gait, no fault, each step certain and identical to the one before. Her face seemed expressionless and so shockingly beautiful in its perfect symmetry and blankness that it was hardly recognizable as an individual face. It is at moments like this that I perceive her sexuality as inviolate, when I understand that no matter how many times she is taken, and by how many, she will remain untouched.

Once she was inside the hallway I began pulling her clothes off before she knew what was happening. At first she protested and tried to push me away, but with my hands moving over her body she was soon as anxious as I was. I took her right there on the hallway floor, the front door still hanging open a fraction of an inch. Of course there wasn't a soul around for miles, but I knew this touch of exhibitionism would add to her excitement. Oh what a scene if our dear landlord had shown up with his eggy eyes and pushed the door open with a knock to discover my bare buttocks bobbing like twin buoys.

It was over almost as soon as it began. I drove within her so hard and fast that I thought her belly would split open. Her fingers were grasping my hair and digging into my neck and her short high-pitched screams built rapidly toward climax. We came nearly simultaneously in a rapid flailing of movement, a chorus of cries. I carried her into the living room and we curled up before the fireplace with a quilt wrapped around us.

An hour later I was awakened by a susurrus of rain and wind rattling the windowpanes. Tina was still sleeping, her face so close to mine that I could make out the fine wrinkles at the corners of her closed eyelids. Underneath the quilt my hands were around her thighs. Her stockings were still on and one of my hands was touching bare flesh and the other, nylon.

Sometimes I love her.

Nov. 7

There wasn't much happening in American colleges in the Fifties besides the round of learning. Yet after the years of Catholic incarceration, Radcliffe came as a release for her. Once on her own, Tina soon found her way beyond those ivy walls…south to

Greenwich Village and the Beat culture of the day, to ideas that outraged one generation and claimed "the best minds" of the next. She was prime for rebellion, and given her background, given the flavors of the day, what better rebellion than an affair with a black man?

Raymond was not only black, he was older and more experienced. Under his tutelage her dress became less restrained and more provocative, more like that of a woman. She affected a black beat in her walk and talk. Back in Cambridge, before the privacy of her mirrors, her thin lips practiced a sullen pout. Still, I wonder how many nights he spent sweating uselessly over her cold youthful flesh, trying to thaw the chill she had picked up from those icy blue Cape waters, wondering if, despite hints of something else, the chill were bone deep after all.

Imagine this—she has just turned twenty and she goes with Raymond to a party in Harlem. Their evening together is perfect. They eat and drink and laugh until they are bursting with laughter and food. All of his friends eye Tina enviously, and she behaves exactly like the snow queen he wants her to be. Afterwards, he takes her to one of the numerous hotels he has taught her to inhabit. The novelty of his world has not yet paled for her and Tina remains thrilled with the tawdriness of it all. The room is barren and drab: a bed, an empty bureau, a scarred nightstand, a mirror mounted pitching forward so you have to crouch to look into it. It is the same kind of room he'd go to with a whore.

They turn off all the lights and undress on opposite sides of the bed. It is silent in the dark, startlingly silent for the city, until they begin to fuck. Then the bed rocks with their movement and its springs creak like a machine with metal parts in disagreement.

He fucks her, God how he fucks her. Long and hard and with every trick he can muster, and still she won't come. On the nights when he really tries and can't do it, he believes that she has in some way escaped him.

Finally he comes and rolls off her, exhausted and with his groin aching. Now that he has stopped moving, the sweat that covers his body turns cold. Tina is still close beside him and she snuggles closer. Her tongue begins to lick the sweat from his shoulder and neck. She whispers wetly into his ear. He feels her hand sliding down his chest, over his belly and around his cock. Even in the darkness he can tell the hand is white and he is growing in it again.

?

She is capable of seeing the absurdity in things, but not the humor in that absurdity. The one thing she really wants from me is one of the most impossible. She wants me to take her seriously.

Tina, I have to stop laughing at myself first!

?

The days are mostly gray days with a sky the color of the gray satin lining her silver fox coat. The dark wooded hills on the horizon are the ragged pieces of fur curling within and clumping from too much wear. I usually don't get out of bed until afternoon, sometimes nearly sundown. At times it seems that the outside world has ground to a halt and we have created our own special time zone her on the outskirts of Ithaca. I wonder if the energy I have expended on drugs…on sex…on love…is finally catching up with me.

Nov. 16

A black lover is one thing, but a black baby is something else again. Even at twenty, she knew that much. She chose an abortion and in return for her speedy wisdom she got a trip to Europe as part of the bargain.

For Tina, the culture of Europe became a cock culture—the Greeks, the Italians, the Spaniards. (She had already discovered how well darkness sets her off. Even to this day she follows her pattern.) Soon she was to be back under her mother's control. In what respite there was, she behaved as wildly as the healthy young animal she was, rooting through the bed-bogs of Europe. She ran up an impressive total for less than three months on the Continent. Or it may have been just because of the way she drew them. In any case, the Italians were "the prettiest," but she liked the Spaniards best. Their long guitar fingernails traced the most licentious rhythms up and down her spine.

After Europe she returned to her mother and then to seven years internment on The Cape with Leonard, a hand-picked husband fifteen years older than herself. She bore him three children, not as wife and mother, but as a baby machine (that black baby unborn in Switzerland was her only real baby, her "love" child). The chill of The Cape reclaimed her flesh past bone and to the marrow. Days conspired to become months, months drifted into years. Her life became a facsimile of Betty across the street and Ruth next door, with even less meaning since she'd had a taste of something more. When its reality became too much for her, she would retreat to her spacious colonial bedroom and devour books in place of life.

Imagine this—she is twenty-seven and Leonard is on the down side of forty. They have been married five years, nearly a fifth of her life. She has spent the evening in her bedroom, reading Flaubert, and now the lights are out and she is close to sleep, dreaming, more Madame Bovary than she is herself. She is immersed in a world of subterfuge and desire that her half-conscious mind has colored like a sepia print. Leonard opens the door without knocking to devastate her illusion. He pauses, his body in its quilted robe blocking the light from the hallway and throwing a blunt shadow across the bed. Each time he wants her, he comes to her room. For him, sex is a woman's domain he need only enter when the need arises. After he has finished, he will return to his own room to sleep.

Once inside he folds his robe across a chair and sits on the edge of the bed. Christine undoes the sash of her nightgown so the front of her body is bare. Her blue veins remain hidden in the darkness. Leonard briefly fondles her breasts and goes so far as to take one nipple between his lips and play his tongue against it. Then he climbs on top of her. His cock is a soft worm curled in the doorway of her cunt. His balls are a pair of small hairy plums. They are between her thighs and they have become hers. She plays with them until his erection is moving within her. She lies with legs spread, arms at her sides, eyes closed. (She doesn't even pretend to enjoy it. Once again she is cast in the role of whore.)

Leonard grasps her shoulders, his manicured nails digging into her back. His breath becomes labored as he empties the seed of their third child within her.

Nov. ?

It wasn't long after her third child that she got herself together enough to split. It was money that allowed her to do it, money plus her own determination for something besides a slow death by mental and emotional gangrene. Without Leonard's money and the changing series of nannies—which he hired and she fired—she would have been the one to have taken care of the kids. They would have become her life above and beyond Leonard and they would have held her to him and a married existence. Without her own money, her inheritance, she would have had to fight for the financial independence that was already hers. And without her determination, she could have gone down unquestioningly, holding Sylvia's hand on the right and Ruth's on the left (glub-glub!)

So she kissed her children good-bye, one, two, three—"Mommy's going away for a little while now."—and came back to the Village to rediscover and nourish the child in herself. After that there were a number of false starts, her poetry, and Tony. But Tony doesn't really count. He was a child with less sense and nourishment than herself, a shield against something more real—like me.

And there we have *The Capsule Biography of Tina Leslie.* I've swallowed worse capsules, and no doubt some nourishment has occurred along the way. But wait—let's give her another chance, let's reverse cause and effect—run the film backwards in the projector—winter into fall, fall into summer, summer into spring...birds take off with their tails into the sky, the cue ball punches the stick back in your hands, explosions implode, politicians run from office, babies rediscover their umbilicals and retreat up their mother's wombs—grant her one of her fondest wishes, make her younger rather than older— at the right juncture begin again and rewrite her history, obliterate her unwanted pregnancy, return her to the black lover she still talks about so much and so often, see how long and well it lasts between them, see if she still finds her way to me through the rush of changing years...see if I still want her.

Nov. 28

The seasons have changed on us again, driving us totally indoors. Winter in the country consists mainly of being trapped in a box in the snow in the country. The only time I go out is when we go into town, or to gather wood for the fireplace. The copse to the south of the house is so thick that the trees have intertwined and snuffed out their weaker brothers. There are plenty of dead branches, but we have to let them dry before we can burn them.

Although Tina and I are thrown together more often, I feel that we are further apart than ever. A new rigidity has set in with the snow. Part of it is that due to our constant proximity we are running out of things to say to each other. Still, we repeat our oft-laid plans to give one another the assurance of security. In the spring I will attend Cornell to stay out of the draft. Tina will publish her second book of poems and start working on a novel. Next summer we will travel in Europe together. At times it smacks too much of a play we've seen before and over again and twice too often.

Also due to our inescapable proximity, we begin to get on one another's nerves. Perhaps we are even doing things consciously to irritate one another. Her latest gimmick, in an effort to create a summer tan, is a blinding sun lamp that drives me from whatever room she has decided is her spa. Of course, she has legitimate complaints, too. When I crack my knuckles she shivers and nearly jumps out of her skin, but still I continue to do it. And she is after me for smoking too much grass. It's going to dull my mind, or some such rot. Maybe she's right, but at least I know *how* to smoke it. Cigarettes, she smokes like a man, but grass she smokes delicately, as if the roach were a real bug that was going to bite her. And of all the ways of getting stoned, she gets hung up on the most bothersome: trying to remember and reiterate what led us on a particular train of thought, craving unattainable foods, hot fudge sundaes at two in the morning when it's twenty-seven degrees outside and the bitterest of winds is searching out every crack in the house.

When we meet sexually now it is often like hammer and anvil, physically and emotionally. At times there is no doubt that our bed is a battlefield. First we became lovers, then friends, and now we are enemies, too. After enough years together I could see our relationship boiling down to a one-on-one internecine existence, an undeclared trench war of attrition in which neither side could gain the upper hand for long.

Nov. 29

I have a frightening vision of her as our National Poet Laureate—given her mind set how could she deny such official recognition?

They give her an anonymous cubicle in an anonymous room in an anonymous office building in Washington, D.C. She composes lyrical sonnets by the bucket to whitewash and commemorate our atrocities at home and abroad.

December

On these chill winter nights my thoughts return again and again to that mad week in New York when the sun was still shining and Mulligan was with us and how Tina give her body to him. She insists: "He wasn't very good. He's just not that attractive," which may be the case, but still I wonder what key he turned in her smooth belly that made her so free that she was ready to climb into bed with both of us...and no doubt Michael, too, if he'd been able to handle it.

Mulligan's conga is still sitting in the corner of the living room. It's become another antique. I never play it anymore—it would seem too muffled by the snow—and it would be gathering dust if Tina weren't such an immaculate housekeeper.

Earlier tonight we started talking about and around him again. It was Tina who brought him up this time. There is no doubt that he is the type of person who leads to endless speculation, but that's what it remains—speculation. The farther Tina gets from the experience of Mulligan, the farther she seems to get from any semblance of the truth. Her latest theory is that "his drugs have deranged his mind and he actually is crazy, but crazy in such a way that he can still function."

My question is: Does too much dope make you crazy, or merely aware of your insanities? And what is insanity anyway?

Much of what is considered sane, even admirable, in this society, seems far crazier to me than any of Mulligan's antics.

Dec. 8

The Freudian dream image of her body like a mountain. I scale it with block and tackle to reach the summit of orgasm. Over knees, thighs, belly, breasts and shoulders. The summit is snow-capped. Beneath the snow there is a shelf of weathered shale.

Dec. ??

Now that the days are shorter the sun doesn't come up early enough for when she wants to awaken. She has gotten into the habit of setting the clock radio. Each morning I am called from sleep to face a rundown of the world news in the semi-darkness, destroying my illusion of retreat and isolation.

—The war continues to grow. Two-hundred-and-forty Americans dead this week.

—The United States rejects the pleas of thirty-two nations in the U.N. for an unconditional atomic test ban.

—Mobutu seizes power in the Congo and cancels elections.

—Pope Paul reaffirms The Church's stand on birth control. (I pray for Christine's immortal soul.)

—Twenty-five thousand march around the White House to protest the war.

—India complains of a Chinese build-up at its border.

—President Johnson predicts a record year for the American economy.

As I try to convince myself that all of this must be happening on some other planet, I see Tina's shadow moving across the room and hear the rustle and zipper of her dressing mixed with an occasional stifled yawn. She has taken to wearing boots and earmuffs when she goes outside. She has taken to wearing pants instead of dresses as an additional protection against the cold. Stylish pants, but pants all the same.

Dec. 17

Christmas is soon upon us and she will be visiting her children on the Cape. She will leave me for the holidays, alone in frigid Ithaca with snow blocking the doorway and the tinkle of ghostly sleigh bells bouncing around the attic. Each year since her divorce, she has made this trek north to fulfill her maternal duties, to level a patriotic blow for the expired spirit of the American family, rent deader than the spirit of '76 by far, succumbed to divorce, alcohol, college, dope, politics, and change change change so fast and encompassing that the world of each generation takes on the aspects of an alien planet to the next.

We fuck throughout the afternoon on the living room floor, filling the room with the smells of our sweat and sex, animal smells that impart a cloying thickness to the air. It is to be our last sex for awhile because tonight I am driving her to the station, but it turns out to be nothing special. Somewhere along the way our minds wander back to their own personal preoccupations and it becomes just another series in a long string of orgasms, good but far short of ecstasy, satisfying but not transcendent.

Tina lies back on the rug, still naked, smoking a cigarette and rubbing her hand up and down her belly. She begins to talk, the first time she has really opened up since the acid—childhood remembrances, sex fantasies, dreams, Europe and other lovers. We've been over most of this ground before, reruns that she plays back a little differently each time so that even the subplots and minor characters get their turn at frame center. How many of these memories are real? How many the way she imagines it to have been? How many complete fantasies? I'm sure she doesn't know and neither do I.

She talks and talks, yet despite all of her confessions there are territories we never cross—nameless fears of which she cannot speak. She talks and talks yet there is still so much she holds within her own secret realms. Her goal is not giving, not what I mean by giving, but rather a half-giving, a wavering compromise between my demands and the demands of individuality.

Why then is she holding back?

She cannot figure out who is doing whom a favor, who is getting hustled. She cannot decide whether the money she gives me is my fuck fee, my analyst's fee, or even a fee at all. She doesn't know if she loves me or merely tolerates me as a necessary adjunct to her woman's world. In spite of all her linguistics and poetics she is still groping lost through nonexistent categories, still trying to define segments of reality and consign them to their relative cubicles like overnight guests.

Let me compose a chant, a special rosary for you my Catholic Christina to send you speeding on your way. It will grease and set your bearings, tune up your engine, charge your battery, set your weary plugs sparking fresh fire. Get your beads ready and do not let me surprise you. Each of us has the capacity for petty meanness.

Christina, I have known you as whore, child, mother, coquette, virago, wench, lady and teasing bitch.

Christina, I have turned your cold butt red with spanking. I have fucked you bound spread-eagle to our bed until your eyes have begged for mercy and still your voice would not admit the limits of your masochism. I have forced your head unwilling between my thighs.

("Can you hear me?" "Yes, I can hear you.")

Christina, it does no good to fuck you, fuck, you, fuck you. The impression I make is as transitory as a card house. It is like pouring semen into a sieve. You piss it out, sweat it back at me. Your attrition outruns my accumulation.

Christina, stop feeling your legs, stop handling your body. Your body was made for the hands of lovers. Give it to them completely, without reservation, and you will no longer need to rub your limbs for warmth.

Christina, you are oh so clean!

Christina, you are soft plastic. You are polystyrene. You are inflatable and unbreakable.

Christina, sometimes you are more than clean! Yes, you are even antiseptic. You reek of the mouthwash and deodorant manufactured from the bodies of America's victims. Some night I expect to reach between your thighs and pull out a square paper slip reading: "INSPECTED BY NO. 5. STERILE."

("Do you want more?" "Yes, more, still more.")

Christina, the flavor of America is catsup and carcinogens, apple pie and anesthetics.

Christina, you are devoid of politics. You are a lady in so many unwanted ways. Unknowingly your coupon-clipping scissors are the ones that slit open the bomb bay doors. You are not a war baby, but an American Madonna. Hail Christina, full of grace, beneath your mouthwash and deodorant the inimitable flavor of catsup and carcinogens, of golden delicious indifference.

Christina, stop throwing your shadow in front of yourself and you will see the shape of the future better. Look from far enough and close enough at the same time. Become telescope and microscope and you will see the shape of the emerging pattern far less tenuous than you imagined.

Christina, the market is closed today so why don't they stop the killing?

Christina, do you think clamped thighs can hide your bleeding cunt?

("Are you still there?" "Yes, I'm here, still here.")

Christina, you have unleashed hidden cornucopias of lust. You are the virgin spring for a fountain of wet dreams. You are Juicy Fruit. You are Shiva. You are the pause that refreshes. Little boys masturbate to your technicolor image, adolescent pricks pumping heat into the cold seclusion of their bedrooms. You think young and you dress like an heiress. You are the cover of *Cosmopolitan.* You *are* cosmopolitan. You are a figment in the moneyed imagination of Madison Avenue, a bit of undigested bone or gristle.

Christina, you remain inevitably yourself and alive for yourself. Each one of us is alive for ourselves, yet not so much as you. You dodge the beam of my projections even at its high power setting. You shed my labels like a spring-time dog giving up its coat of winter hair. Your natural coat is deception—summer, fall, winter and spring.

Christina, you are a fine thoroughbred, but not the first and not by far the last. Your mold has not been broken. You have become an increasingly available ideal. Soon there will be Tinas by the dozen, by the thousand. The market will be flooded and your price will plummet. Tinas will cover the country like storm troopers, marching through the streets in their spike heels, a thousand sparkling shins and calves swinging in baton-like unison. RA-TA-TAT-CLICK! I've had enough. RA-TA-TAT-CLACK! Take back your arms and thighs. RA-TA-TAT-CLICK! Take back your servo-mechanisms. RA-TA-TAT-CLACK! Take back your hydraulic lifters. RA-TA-TAT-CLICK! I don't believe you. RA-TA-TAT-CLACK! I don't believe you. RA-TA-TAT-CLICK! I don't believe in you! RA-TA-TAT-CLAAACCCKKKK!!!!

Dec. 18

The house is quiet, crypt-quiet, a hollow sarcophagus sunk in the snow. The land about the house is silent. The bare black branches of the willows hang limply against the sky, nearly as still as a Japanese pen sketch. All day the sun has been struggling to break through—turning the clouds lighter in its path—but without success. It remains a gray day. Finally in setting it manages to show itself just above the horizon. But the sunset is colorless, a flat white disc dropping behind a jagged black wall.

Her departure last night was something of an abortion. She was packed ahead of time, so there was nothing to do but leave early. In the car she fidgeted, filled with the tension of her return home. Like so many times before she could not open up to me. Her conversation remained trivial—water the plants, don't forget to pay the phone bill, etc., etc. It's all on the list she's tacked to the kitchen wall.

To top it off her train was late. She repeated herself with long awkward pauses in between. Time dragged. Time became a crippled snail, a net from which we were trying to free ourselves. Still her eyes wouldn't slow down long enough to meet mine with any meaning, even in the moments before and after we kissed good-bye.

It may be that I have wandered long enough over the landscape of her body and through the labyrinth of her psyche in search of some nonexistent lodestone. Perhaps after all she is no more than what she seems to be, an aging and neurotic American divorcee obsessed with the errors of her past and afraid of her future because the years ahead are years of aging. Perhaps I have been lost among the multiplicity of my projections while running from her reality—no, *our* projections and *our* reality.

I have spent the day reading and rereading her notebooks. If she didn't want me to see them she should have written more illegibly or taken them with her. I felt like a kid opening my

Christmas' presents early and finding a few things I didn't expect and even more I didn't like. Some of it is all so clear to me, almost too clear, while other passages remain enigmas no matter how many times I read them. There is not a mention of acid anywhere, and hardly a mention of me. It is mostly notes for her planned novel. The past. The past. The past. Her childhood and her adolescence and her black man. How can I know so much of her and still understand so little. The depth that she exhibits often seems like a mere thickening of the surface rather than any extension beyond it. At times she becomes like one of her many mirrors, that one can look into but not reach into...and viewed sideways is no more than a wafer-thin sliver of flickering silver.

All in all I begin to see that she could never hunger for experience like me, but would have to be backed into it (or tricked into it like Mulligan tricked her), a cornered animal ready to bolt at the slightest sign of an opening that could lead to sanctuary.

To hell with such endless speculation. I'm going to get myself some dinner. In this cold, wet season I need more for sustenance than the dry thoughts of her dry brain.

Very late.

Canned food in a dark kitchen, in a silent house.

Afterward I rolled three fat joints with the last of our grass and with them secure in my shirt pocket I took her car out for a destination-less night ride through the winterland. I found a rise higher than the rest, which gave me a view of the spectral countryside and the lights of Ithaca clumped like a star cluster in the distance. I shut the engine down just off the road and felt the night's cold creeping into its still metal hulk and closing around my body. I smoked the joints one after another in rapid succession, with the fierce and frantic zeal of a condemned man, and in my stoned lucidity the cold became a presence sitting beside me, the astral body of my Snow Queen. And as she wrapped her arms of ice around me and her breath like frost came close upon my mouth, sexuality and all that follows from it dropped away from me. My stoned lucidity became a strange neutered lucidity, the same that I had often experienced immediately after climax when I perceived her flesh as plain sweating human flesh no different than my own.

And in my sexless objectivity, I understood that in trying to expand on the varieties of sex we had discovered that our sex was a different idealization for each of us. The realization of our fantasies was never a fulfillment, always short of the fantasies themselves. I saw that when my desire for her confronted the reality of her, as a person rather than as an object of pleasure, that desire faded.

I have just returned from that ride and I am back in our house stretched before a roaring fire, but still I am shivering.

Dec. 19

If I wanted her now, if I needed her this very minute, my want and need would of necessity lie fallow. There is no way for me to reach her. She has left me without an address, without a phone number to call. She has moved back into that world of her past. She has become a different Christine, beyond my touch and the need for my touch.

Dec. 20

I have reread my notebook, too—this notebook. In its pages a Tina lives for me, far more real than the one I took to the airport just three days ago.

Dec. 21

In the back of my head I have always been sure that I would leave her...but when, where, how? As our joined past accumulates the question grows more immediate.

In that past, our acid trip together looms like the wrong word written with indelible ink, ineradicable just like the rest of her history. Just like her culture that I have devoured in my leisure at a fantastic rate. Her books, her music, her art, her food—I have consumed them all. But now, like an amnesiac who had been reeducated with respect to his past, I am ready for the present and the future.

Dec. 23

Tina, you'd be surprised how rapidly our domicile disintegrates when lacking the expertise of your direction. The order of the house collapses all around me. Dirty dishes pile up in the sink. A river of unjacketed records, of books and clothes, winds it way across the floor. Formerly forbidden dust particles gather to hold silent caucuses on the mantle and the top of your stereo. The flowers you have bought wither and die. (I know you won't believe me, but they're just as beautiful that way. Have you ever really looked at a dead flower?)

You'd also be surprised how quickly my domesticity disappears. The itch of time is upon me again. I am hungering for other things besides your return and the continuation of our life together. One can go for only so many walks in the woods. One can read only so many books (print remains print) and listen to the same tired records grown scratchy from overplay so many times. One can fuck the same woman for only so many hours without finding repetition in her limbs. I need more lives than this to follow all my possible paths, play all the games that it is possible for me to play, love all my possible loves. I don't want to sample different realities like a wine taster who learns the subtleties of each flavor but never the rush of intoxication. I want to swallow each one whole, chew it up, and spit out the rind.

The day before Christmas

Damn it! With the grass gone, I'm back on cigarettes again. I've got to get out of this lonely hellhole and go back to the city for awhile.

PART FOUR

"...that the truth is the appearance of things, that their secret is their form, and that what is deepest in man is his skin."

Andre Gide
The Counterfeiters

33

THE beginning of a long winter. New York City under two feet of snow. Central Park a dim and shrouded winterland amidst the city lights. The artificial lakes frozen cloudy as milk-water. The iron spikes of the fence railings like sharp upside down icicles. Tree boughs bending from their load of white weight. Crack! Crack!

Look! A man-boy runs naked through the snow. His sparse beard is hoary with new frost. Dodging and leaping, he runs. The snow is white. The colorless flesh of his body is patterned with strange hieroglyphs, veins and tendons become letters but letters rendered unreadable by the speed of his movement. He runs, skirting the circle pools of yellow lamplight as if they would melt his colorless flesh by giving it color. He runs, the skin of his ribcage taut, corrugated, showing bars of light-shadow in the luminescence of a sinking half moon. He runs with scrotum skin tight from the cold, his cock bouncing in miniature and belated contradiction to his leaping, down as he goes up, up as he comes down, a frozen flailing erection. He runs, dancing like a graceless child. He runs with awkward limbs to stumble and fall, his foot glancing off the protrusion of a sprinkler cap, head over heels to land sitting, a spherical mass of snow atop his head like a thick skullcap.

His mind still races over a white desert with three shadow forms racing by his side. He yanks it back like a wayward camel to feel his body sinking into the sand, into the melting snow, no difference, no difference. The desert night is cold and his breath puffs smoky plumes into the chill air, clouding the pinpoint stars, so few stars, there should be more stars in the desert. He cries out. He cries and cries again. He feels a dull throbbing in his right foot, climbing up the calf. Clutched tightly in the warm pocket of one hand throughout his running, a small box of wooden matches, yes, ice and fire, fire and ice, some say in fire, some say in ice, no difference, no difference. He takes a match from the box, plows a narrow furrow in the sand-snow as he tries to strike it. A second match he strikes on the box's side, and once it is lit holds the light over his foot. The toes are splotched a dark running red, the big nail sharply askance. Drops of blood still dripping have stained the snow in a growing circle. Cherry snocones, raspberry snocones, strawberry, no difference. He scoops up the reddened snow, slips several lumps into his dry mouth, rubs the rest over his beard, his neck and shoulders, yes, communion with the blood of the Savior. He watches the moving flame yellow descend the match stick, gripped firmly between thumb and forefinger. He sees the flame orange curl and lap around his numb fingers, blacken his nails, then sputter out for lack of the fuel his fingers still conceal. He drops the match and there is a split-second sizzle as it hits the snow. Water in the desert, he thinks, the riches of a secret well. He starts digging but there is only sand, no difference, no difference.

He crawls to the base of a nearby tree and leans back against the trunk. Strange to find a tree in the middle of the desert. Still it is so cold, so cold in the desert. He should have stayed where there was warmth, he should have stayed in Paris. The boat to France, an open boat drifting toward sleep, toward drunkenness and dreaming and a numb death. He is once again walking the streets of Verdun, letting his hair grow over his shoulders, smoking his pipe upside down. He is in England. He is back in Paris with Verlaine. He is about to shoot Verlaine with a cowboy pistol. He pulls the trigger—one, two, three, the chamber empties. The explosions reach his ears like thunder from across a valley or the concussion of distant artillery shells. The bullets spin from the barrel revolving in slowed motion, visible to the naked eye. Verlaine, like a preening jay bird, puffs his chest to meet them and they carom off the buttons of his vest. Two lodge in the mattress, one clicks a clean circle in the window glass, another shatters the shaving mirror. And suddenly Verlaine has grown in stature, thrown off his perpetual poet's stoop, sprouted broad shoulders, a dark Zapata mustache and glowering Svengali eyes.

Snapping to cold wakefulness, his hands clutch the sand-snow. There is a stellated night-blooming desert flower in the periphery of his vision, its turning crimson center, at first all red, spewing out the color petals of the rainbow. A desert mirage but still so beautiful, he thinks, so beautiful.

Then the flashlight beam hits him full in the face and he is momentarily blinded.

34

AFTER Michael Shawtry was once again left alone in New York City—Mulligan gone, Jacobi and Christine gone—he began to fall back on acid as his sole recreation. Day by day, night after night, as the world of fall descended upon Manhattan, Michael moved increasingly into what would eventually become known as the world of the acid freak, altered and enhanced by his own personal touches. The acid did not succeed in making Michael less of an anchorite. He was not prompted to seek out new friends and companions to replace those who had departed. Rather, the drug allowed his own natural inclinations to run full blast. Now he became totally removed, totally the omniscient observer. He saw no one on a personal level. He spoke to no one personally. He achieved a degree of anonymity only possible in the isolation of a mountaintop or a desert island, or in the undifferentiated mass isolation of a metropolis. For all practical purposes he had joined the ranks of missing persons.

But Michael was not missing to himself.

He felt more together with himself than ever before. He felt as if he were passing through the most intense days of his existence, a journey as magnificent and peril-wrought as ever undertaken. From his waking breath every morning to his last conscious thought at night before the coverlet-shroud of sleep enclosed him, each of his solitary experiences now washed across his perceptions with overwhelming clarity. He began to spend time away from his room, more time out of doors. His pale skin tanned slightly in what light the paling autumn sun had left to offer. He dropped acid beneath that sun, beneath the cloud cover that increasingly obscured it, while walking in the cleansing fall of rain, and his acid highs spread increasingly beyond the chemical borders of the trip itself and continued their rain of knowledge down upon him in sudden, momentary and momentous flashback highs in the times between one capsule and the next. Jacobi had been wrong, Michael thought, Michael knew, the effects of the acid need not lessen due to tolerance, but with the proper set and conditions the effects could be cumulative. The inchoate and intangible visions of his earlier trips were crystallizing, form and substance coming with growth, the details of each vision enhancing its richness, confirming its consistency. He was approaching a grand canvas. He was surrounded by the three-dimensional canvas of life. He could sense and nearly understand the artifice operative in its creation. From distance, it gave the appearance of an immense landscape, something like a Breughel, but as the successive doses of acid progressively altered the chemistry of his consciousness and allowed him a closer examination, Michael saw that it was more intricately detailed and more densely and strangely populated, at least a Bosch, and probably beyond that some fantastical, undreamt-of creation that would dwarf even Bosch's strange genius.

Michael Shawtry was not blindly accepting all he experienced. He was not without questions. But just as it had from the beginning, the acid kept blowing his mind by answering questions he had yet to pose. When he took the time in reflection to once again consciously examine the laws, the everyday reality, of the society around him, he discovered that he had become a veritable alien. For him and his exploding vision, few of society's pillars remained uncracked and most had already toppled outright. He saw beyond the foibles and insanities of the societal structure that had spawned him. He saw that it was a structure geared to endless production and homage to the gods of death. The production of objects. The production of waste. The death of the mind. The death of the senses. The death of the body. He understood more completely than ever that it was only his singularity, his discipline, his anonymity and his vision, which could protect and save him from this world.

Michael also questioned the realization of his homosexual urges experienced on the group trip with Jacobi, Mulligan and Christine. This was another truth the acid had presented to him before he'd asked, long before he'd been prepared to accept the answer. Yet now, with the acid still pushing him forward, he forced himself to look at that answer, to test its soundness and explore its consequences.

Sexual invention was long foreign to his nature. In that realm his imagination was next to atrophied. It was only after prolonged effort, after disregarding the stock epithets—queer, faggot, homo—that Michael managed to picture himself in the particulars of the act of physical love with other men, men chosen from the street, or ideal men created internally—mouth upon cock, cock within mouth, breastless bodies moving against one another's. He retreated to corresponding images involving women to make a comparison, masturbatory dreams he had willfully shunned since early adolescence, and then it was not a chance face from the street or some fanciful creation that danced before his mind's eye, but again and again it was the white face and body of Christine Leslie. Ultimately, Michael admitted not to homosexuality, but to bisexuality—and that was where he stopped. He had read the textbooks when he'd still been in school, the psychoanalytic case studies. He knew that homosexuality often had something to do with a dominant mother and an absent father—that fit, Michael thought—but he didn't care to understand the causal particulars of his case. He wasn't interested in an explanation or "a cure," since he didn't intend to pursue sexuality in either direction, male or female. He had been epicene for too long to try to foster a sexual identity now. Besides, just as before his discovery, his true interests lay elsewhere. The acid was showing him the paths that he could follow and must follow. No longer need he ferret out portents for the future. They were spread before him and all about him, bountifully, like a spray of glorious blossoms. He would discover them in the chance opening of a book, a newspaper headline, a fragment of conversation eavesdropped upon in a coffeehouse. It was clear that enlightenment was his destiny, and for now it was clear that the pathway led thoroughly into his lone self, more deeply into the acid. Michael was aware that at some point the path could branch and carry him in Mulligan's direction. He could use his perceptions to become a master at playing at the game of life, but he would avoid that at all costs. For him, that meant a false enlightenment, as tied to the circle of *samsara* as the living pieces—the "Jacobi"s, the "Christine"s, and yes, even the "Michael"s—that Mulligan gamed with. The new Michael believed that once the game was mastered, one must rise from one's chair, sweep the pieces and the board aside crashing to the floor like so many ten pins, and carefully examine the grainy surface of the table wood beneath.

Physically, Michael began to establish limits for himself extreme enough to parallel his extended perceptions and subdue any weakness he discovered in his flesh. He performed the routine of his yoga postures three or four times per day. He repeated his breathing exercises to the point where he could feel the flows of energy they released taking command of his being, to the point where the identity of Michael Shawtry *became* those energy flows. On the bare boards of his room, with back rigidly arched, he sat in the full lotus, trance-like, tripping endlessly on the pantoscopic internal vistas stretching out before him—forests, mountains, rivers, villages, all vivid as jewels—like the countryside of some fabled kingdom. He sat withdrawn until his legs were senseless, dumb with sleep, and he couldn't stand until the circulation returned inch by inch from the knees downward in tingling needles and jets of pain.

Michael had already demonstrated to his own satisfaction that he could exist in New York City with practically no money; coming from wealth as he did this satisfied a necessity to prove himself beyond that wealth. Now it was to be without food and warmth, too. He embarked on a program that reduced his already ascetic diet to nothing less than calculated starvation. His fasts became longer and when he did eat it was only what he considered the "pure" foods—organic fruits and vegetables, cereals, nuts, brown rice. He was purging his body of the poisons accumulated in past lapses from his diet. Although the mercury was steadily dropping he kept the radiator in his apartment on low, and when he went out it was in the same spare outfit he had worn through the summer, his no-longer-so-white trousers and his black sweater, with a thin dirty t-shirt beneath. In his more exhilarated moments, Michael had begun to suspect that his body could regenerate itself spontaneously without normal sustenance, that sunlight, water, acid and the strength of his convictions were all he needed. He knew that Indian fakirs had already proven that the body could exist for extended periods of time with very little oxygen, let alone food, water or external stimulation.

If Michael's course were virulent—and there were times when he realized this—it was also sustained and totally enthralling. And the portents, the positive signs, kept coming to him. In the midst of his fourth trip, Michael realized that he hadn't had a cigarette for nearly three weeks, that he had forgotten about them and stopped wanting them, and now even the thought of smoking made him feel slightly nauseous.

And what of Michael the literati, Michael Shawtry, Poet and Poetaster?

Always a voracious reader in his hours of solitude, except when he was writing voraciously, Michael now read very little, only sporadically in short fits and starts. Books were either totally meaningless to him or he could pick the key to the ones that did mean something after only a few sentences. His own self, revealed through the acid, became his favorite volume, his best source of knowledge.

It was natural that his heightened perspective should change his writing, too. If he was a different man, he must become a different creator. He felt now that his work should become a mode of expression solely at the service of the eternal forces that he touched, that it must become a channel exclusively for the demiurge. No longer could the themes of his poetry be minor or even secondary. No longer could he redo exercises or distill or improve upon expressions that had been made clear in the past. Now he wrote only when he felt himself tapping the central fount of creation. He wrote poems once, first draft, and he didn't look at them again. The kind of poems that had been the exception for him previously, inspired poems, now became the unalterable rule. And with the change in content and inspiration, an alteration in form followed. His lines began running the width of the page, moving past the standard boundaries of poetry. He was fashioning prose poems and verbal collages. Somewhere between his third and fourth trips he completed the transition to prose. One major poem—begun during and as an adjunct to his reflections on his homosexual urges—evolved into a story, only three thousand words, yet the longest single work he had completed to date. In the middle of writing it he understood that for him it was obsolete. He had already sewn up that aspect of his life and left it behind. But he decided to finish the piece anyway. It became another act of discipline to add to his list of accomplishments...like when he'd realized school was obsolete for him but had to post a semester of straight A's before he could quit, before he could condemn the system without the taint of self-doubt mitigating the force of that condemnation.

The fifth acid trip, the midway point in his ten-leg chemical odyssey, was the one that liberated his writing. It allowed him to see his typewriter for what it had now become—a mechanical hindrance that was keeping him removed, preventing him from getting closer to the pages he was filling. It was a product of the machine age, an unnatural device that made part of the process of writing, part of the sacred act of creation...mechanical. Michael had written most of his poetry on the machine and he was attached to it, but now was a time of change, a time for doing away with old attachments. At each year's end the stag must shed its antlers, the snake its skin, for new growth to occur. Michael would return the typewriter to its point of origin in his life, the same pawn shop where he had found it, and thus reverse the past. And if any further obstacles emerged he would overcome or eliminate those also. He had come too far to allow anything to allay his progress now.

He awoke early and clear-headed, as he always did after the acid. He opened his eyes to grayness, the soiled grayness of his bed sheets (there were other sheets in the closet, clean sheets, but he wouldn't-couldn't use them because they were ones his mother had given him and they were marred by the pale washed-out rust stains of her menstrual blood.) It was gray outside, too. The spotty cloud cover of the previous night had coalesced to a tight lid reaching from horizon to horizon that made the sky seem closer and promised rain before evening. His newly discovered nemesis, the typewriter, still stood upon the table with the blind, dead, solidity of an unwanted object.

Shivering in the dawn chill, Michael pulled his t-shirt and sweater on over his bare torso. He had slept with his pants on. In the bathroom, the faucet offered him a blast of icy water that he splashed across his face to wash the particles of sleep from his eyes. His overgrown hair was twisted and awry from the night, standing up wildly in all directions. With his still-damp hands he brushed it back from his forehead and temples, watching himself in the mirror. He was beginning to like his own face more and more, particularly the eyes. Leaning forward, he sucked in his hollowing cheeks even further to complete the examination.

Back in his room he went through his morning ritual of exercises and in the kitchen prepared a meager breakfast, weak green tea and wheat bread with honey. When he turned on the overhead kitchen bulb a host of shiny brown forms scurried rapidly for cover—back into the cupboards that were ajar, under the refrigerator and the stove. He wasn't really alone, Michael thought wryly. As was the case in most of the East Village, he shared his abode unwillingly with hundreds of other beings.

Standing by the desk, Michael consumed the food with complete concentration, chewing each mouthful to extract the sum of its flavor and then washing the thoroughly masticated pieces down with a slow swallow of tea. Most probably, he wouldn't eat again until nightfall.

The meal completed, Michael turned his attention to the dark imposing bulk of the typewriter. The winds of change that were blowing through his life had not carried it away for him. It was still there, solid and inanimate as ever. He would have to realize his plans of the previous day and dispose of it himself. There was no case for the machine and the cardboard box in which Michael had brought it home over two years ago was long gone, so he set about creating something with which to carry it. From the morass of the closet, he came forth with one of his "clean" sheets. He ripped off a large rough square from one of its unspotted corners and wadding up the remainder he tossed it back into the closet. He placed the square on the floor, hefted the typewriter off the desk and slantwise upon it. Then he pulled up the corners of the cloth, two by two, until they were taut, knotting them at the top. Now he had a sling with which to carry the machine and that was what he did, hoisting it over his shoulder and against his back like a laundry sack. Out the door, down the three flights of stairs to street level and two blocks uptown in the direction of the pawn shop, before he was forced by the weight aching his arms and digging against the soft uncallused flesh of his palms to pause and rest.

Sitting upon a curb ledge with Manhattan's morning rush, traffic and pedestrians, shifting rapidly all around and past him without a glance, Michael realized that something was amiss. When he'd first lifted the typewriter, it had seemed far heavier than he'd remembered it, and increasingly heavy as he walked. For a moment he thought that the extent of his recent fasting had weakened him. Then it occurred to him that the typewriter seemed to weigh more now because when he'd carried it home for ten bucks it had been a blessing, whereas now it was a burden, figuratively as well as literally. Yes, that must be it, he concluded.

As he tried to lift it again, just as he strainingly got it across his shoulder, a section of the sheet ripped so that part of the machine's black carriage protruded awkwardly. He lowered it onto the sidewalk once more, and resumed his position on the curb. There was a portent here, he knew it, if only he could understand what it was. He relaxed and emptied out his mind. He breathed in deeply, counting, holding it, centering his consciousness and blocking out the noise around him, then exhaling through his nostrils, then in again, holding. It came to him. It had been there all the time. Only how could he have forgotten? The pawnshop where he'd purchased the machine was no longer in existence. Was his preoccupation with the spiritual destroying his ability to function practically? That was a danger he would have to guard against. But for now, what was he to do with the typewriter? He could take it to another pawnshop, he'd already passed one on the way...but that didn't seem right. He could just get up and walk away, leave the machine perched upon the curb. But then someone might run after him to tell him what he had forgotten and he'd have to talk with them. Or worse yet, what if it were a policeman. Then there could be explanations to be made, complications...trouble. He could take the typewriter back home and dismantle it, dispose of it furtively, piece by piece scattered throughout the city. But that would take time and it meant hauling the machine back up the stairs.

Finally, Michael saw his error. He was treating the typewriter as if it were only an object, when in fact it was something more than that. In the time he'd possessed it, it had taken on a portion of his identity. That was a major element in its present hindrance. But in consequence, it deserved a decent burial. He would take the it to the East River and let it be "carried out to sea as all things inevitably must"—a line from a poem he had written upon it.

Now, he raised it off the sidewalk gingerly, aware of its identity, hoping the rent in the sheet would grow no larger. It was lighter for him now, easier to carry, as he made his way east toward the river. At the corner of Houston and First he picked up a route he had traversed many times alone and had once walked with Mulligan. As he retraced his steps he tried to remember where the game had begun and the levers had been pulled that had emptied him like a split cask, that had led to the fiasco at Christine's apartment.

It didn't matter, Michael concluded, all of that was history, ancient history. It was a far different Michael who now toted this bundle wrapped like a stork's delivery, yet headed for its death rather than its birth. Who was he at the moment anyway? Sisyphus with his pernicious boulder? Jason with the bleeding head of Medusa? Why not? Hadn't the typewriter been turning his words to stone. Wasn't the actuality of the present fodder for the myths of the future?

The extensions of his analogy caused him to laugh, soundlessly, mirthlessly. The rock of Sisyphus a typewriter. Jason as a blossoming acid addict.

When he reached the river, it seemed even dirtier than usual, churning sluggishly against its banks, awaiting the rain. It appeared to Michael as truly a passage for the city's debris. He would add his share—over the guard rail, a quick splash, going down without a bubble as the sheet filling with water billowed about it. He crossed himself twice, once with solemnity, once in stylized mockery, and now he laughed aloud though he wasn't sure why.

And as he turned to face the city looming at his back, one of his acid flashbacks struck him in all of its indescribably beauty. He penetrated more deeply than ever before into the grand canvas. He saw through the landscape. It was not a Bosch or even some supra-Bosch. That had been a deception, a clever fake painted over the original master work. Beneath there was an abstract of connecting line and pattern, a many-colored web fading in and out, in and out before his eyes like the mysterious canals of Mars, a constantly changing plexus that delineated the ultimate interdependence of all things.

That afternoon he shifted his desk and chair closer to the window and facing away from it so the light fell across his shoulders. He sat writing, bare to the waist, so that when the cloud-filtered daylight entered the room, his own naked shadow fell across the pages that he covered.

"The secret is to become mad," Michael wrote, "not the sham madness of a Mulligan, but the divine madness of total commitment, awareness, spontaneity, the madness of Blake or Van Gogh or Nijinsky. The secret is to see angels in the British Museum and alligators in your teapot, to dance the *Rite of Spring* with leaps that say "NO! to gravity. The secret is to burn in a conflagration of madness."

35

Poses for the Play to Insanity

He stands stock still in the dead center of the floor, slouching, arms crossed and wrapped around his body, hugging himself, eyes fastened to the raindrops beating and off-beating against the room's sole window. His body has the angularity of a wire frame beneath the loose draperies of its clothing; his face, the pinched-pulled look of a portrait by El Greco. His sweater, weighted by its own accumulation of dirt, has stretched still further out of shape. The pants, dun gray with soil, are damp and muddied about the ankles. He has been doing his yoga postures outdoors in the wet turf of Washington Square.

Each trip continues to carry him further and leave him further out. He has acquired a new sense that gives full reign to his megalomania, the associative sense, a power of the mind operating as automatically and naturally for him as his perceptions of vision or touch.

Now he is not only a poet, he is an artist, too, a painter of kaleidoscopes. The rain-splattered, quick-silver-beaded window that he watches with such attention has become his canvas, a play of light and shadow intricate and ever changing upon which he can project for his mind's eye a thousand and one fantastical worlds that shame Dali, Picasso, Leonardo, Van Gogh…

It is evening without stars.

It is midnight and the clocks, slightly off time, chime in syncopation from one building to the next.

It is early morning, still dark.

He rises quickly from the bed, where his supine stillness might have led one to believe he had been sleeping, and begins to move about with frantic enthusiasm. He doesn't need to turn on the light. He knows the fixtures and limits of this room as well as a blind man knows his room. The desk, the bureau, the closet—delving into each he hauls out notebooks and sheaves of paper, pushing them together into a jumbled pile in the middle of the floor.

Freed from the typewriter, his writing has been going through new transformations again in the last week. He has begun working with colored felt pens, shaping his letters and words. He has become an engraver of illuminations. On the papers taken from the desk, his script turns and dovetails across the page interwoven with detailed designs, chosen fragments reproduced from the perceived plexus of association. But just as the typewriter had proven a mechanical limitation, the physical limitations imposed by the rectangle of the page are holding him back. His words spill off the edges; his shapes, like living organisms, crave further space to occupy, further forms to devour.

Now—the cause behind his present haste in the dark morning—he has just realized why he'd never been able to complete a major epic poem: because the true epic poem of the Sixties, of the now of changing America and the changing world, had to be a poem in flux, a poem of movable and replaceable parts. He would begin from scratch. He would build a poem around the walls of his room, always incomplete and changing, completed and reborn again in each instant of creation. The walls would provide the freedom of space necessary. He need no longer be an artist of miniature portraiture and precise delineations. It was time to throw craft out the window, time to use the axe rather than the scalpel. Henceforth, his creation would be one of broad brushstrokes—broad and telling. And then, once the walls were overflowing, he would be ready to turn inward and explore the freedom of real space, the limitless topography of his own personal awareness where he could build poems without words. His images would be clearer than ever before. His metaphors would be ultimately correct, but there would no longer be a need to commit them to writing. They would be private metaphors only Michael Shawtry could decipher and he would be truly the artist creating himself for himself, for the sheer joy of creation.

Michael looks down upon the hillock of paper he has spread before him, nearly three years of work, exercises to prepare him for the present, ties to hold him to a past he now views as inconsequential. He has crumpled up individual pages around the edges of the mound so the blaze will catch. He strikes a wooden kitchen match along the floor and lights the pile in several places. Soon the room is no longer dark, no longer cold. Michael's face, etched by the firelight, becomes graven, flushed and moist. His pulsing shadow is thrown across the wall and ceiling, gargantuan and misshapen. The cone of flame spits higher. Michael sees it—a radiant rough-hewn obelisk he might embrace if it weren't for the heat driving him back. The dancing cone splits to many tongues, the voices of his poems, twisting streamers that call upon him to join in their funeral dance.

The room fills with smoke, acrid, burning his throat and nostrils, watering his eyes, and he has to throw the window open to breathe. The paint of the ceiling begins to blister and crackle from the fire beneath. It may be that Michael has underestimated the worth of three year's work. Perhaps its death will consume the whole building, the entire block. But as that thought occurs to him, tempting in its magnificence, in its vision of himself as incendiary, the fire is already folding back upon itself, steadying and tamed by the fuel of several thick notebooks in the center of the pyre. Within minutes there are only embers showing on the charred floor, concealing unburnt papers bunched too thickly for the flames to feed. Michael has to prod and relight the smoking mass several times in order to complete his task of incineration.

Hours later, the morning sun, rising clearly for a few moments beneath the level of the cloud cover, finds him kneeling in the dead ashes, ashes that smudge his pant legs and, soft as velvet, collapse between his fingers. He carries a handful to the wall and with saliva-dampened fingertips begins, ever so faintly, to sketch in the base lines for his mural.

He has left Manhattan for the first time in months and traveled south, by subway, to Brooklyn and the New York Aquarium. He is moving through time. He is recreating an episode from the life of eight-year-old Michael Shawtry. Just when he thought he'd left his past behind it has come crowding back upon him, not as a set of shackles, but as a further section of his abstract completed. His monism has reached a new height. With the addition of time, the pattern has become four-dimensional. The total plexus, temporal and spatial, is now within his reach. He can extrapolate the entire universe from any single datum of information.

Episode: His mother dragging him by the hand from tank to tank. His eight-year-old self, goggle-eyed, holding back, wanting to examine and commune with each of these strange varieties of life in detail, feeling a greater kinship to the walled-in fish with their bizarre natural colorings than his washed-out mother with her bizarre artificial colorings, wishing his own self could shed its shell and slip between those beautiful scales to float weightlessly, effortlessly. And in the midst of this childish wonder, his earliest inexpressible metaphysical yearnings... wondering how all the wonder came about.

Now walking the same path with perhaps some of the same fish staring back at him, the memory returns as accurately as if it had been preserved on film. Why not, Michael thinks, the information is there, one need only tap it, initiate the proper chemical reaction for total recall to occur.

This time, without the hand of parental authority, he walks slowly, at his own pace, zombie-like from one glass to the next.

He is swimming through the liquid himself. He has become a traveler, not only into the past of his present identity, but into his cellular past, into the past of other lives and his own primeval origins. In millennia before the first acid he had already swept through that soundless world. He had eaten with razor teeth and moved with limbs like spotted lace. He had known life and fear, food and death, where water was air and the naked sun only a distant god, a blurred legend of the future.

He consumes the entire day immersed once again in that underwater world, circling wordlessly from one cubicle to the next. His absorption becomes so complete that at closing time a gray-uniformed guard, appalled by Michael's dirt and emaciation, must tap him upon the shoulder and pointedly direct him to one of the building's exits.

He is in his room, naked, kneeling upon the floor. Three capless snub-nosed felt pens lie drying nearby. His body has become a perfect slate, a white slate laced with lines: black, blue, green, red.

As if a drunken tattoo artist has had a field day, his flesh is covered with words and symbols, illumined with the thoughts and images of his own mind. He is a self-made illustrated man, who, with head thrown back, watches the walls and ceiling, where he sees his own personal and private Sistine Chapel. He sees words, designs, pictures, symbols, patterns, blending naturally with the pealing paint and dirt and water stains.

In the glare of the hanging bulb his upturned face glows translucently. His skin is like a layer of plastic molded in perfect precision to the neural and skeletal structure beneath. The lines of his face and body carry a sureness, a force that is both frightening and beautiful. Only there is a certain repulsiveness in the strength of his piety. It is an unnatural, egotistical piety with which he has explained the world to his own satisfaction and continues to do so. He is worshiping an extension of himself that he is reaching out to capture. He is playing tag with his own projected image. He is masturbating.

Having swallowed the last cap of acid and returned to the beginning, he lies motionless upon the bed with arms crossed over the sunken shell of his chest. Now there will be no more poems, no more words. The energy that found expression through his poetry has been internalized, funneled back upon the self. He has grown in stature. Rather than reaching out into the world, he has taken the world within. The astronomical universe is flowing through his body. His internal organs have atrophied, shrunken to insignificance, a spot or two of dead fungus clinging to the lower sacrum. The Earth revolves slowly, clouds, oceans, continents, in the space once occupied by his heart. Mars with its attendants, Deimos and Phobos, Mars with its elusive canals, now clearly delineated, is a rumbling war god in the vacuum of his belly. Saturn and its spinning rings throbs in the pulse of his left wrist. A comet races up the lean tendon of one leg. Luna parades through its period in the cosmic basin of his recently formed uterus. And lodged securely in the cavity of his skull is Sol, molten and incandescent, so brilliant that when he looks into his eyes he is unable to see himself.

36

DAMN him, Michael thought, damn him, damn him!

He had been three weeks without the acid, only three weeks, and already Jacobi's prognostications were being fulfilled. Michael had penned his letter to Jacobi in the days following his comedown from the last cap, and mailed it along with the by-then-dated story, which had somehow escaped the burning. He had written down to Jacobi, translating into words the aspects of his vision that were translatable. The reply had come back quickly, knowingly, telling him that without the acid he would lose his vision—and he was losing it, minute by minute, helplessly in the moments of his sleeping, just as helplessly in the moments of his waking when he let his guard down and his concentration wavered. It seemed to Michael that Jacobi saying it, writing it down on paper, had somehow helped to bring it about.

"Damn him to hell!" Michael exclaimed aloud, his words reverberating in the hollow cave of his room.

The acid had become a way of life for him in those ten short weeks. The decline from the clarity it had produced was a trip in itself, a bad trip. Unfamiliar thoughts of confusion, questions and doubts, began to blunt his purpose. The teleology of the universe was no longer clear, the precise canals of Mars suddenly blanketed by the amorphous cloud cover of Venus. He was forgetting because he had no words with which to remember. But words would have killed it anyway, he reminded himself, words would have killed it anyway.

Michael wandered the streets, his eyes violet and violated in the sewer twilight of city winter. He felt like a cripple, as if a part of his perceptions had been decapitated. He felt like a bird beating its wings against the leaves to free itself from the net of a tree. But the leaves only bunched more tightly together as his sensibilities withered. He strained his eyes but he couldn't get the lids open wide enough. His vision remained incomplete, as if he were looking through a greasy windowpane. Where once he'd heard the music of existence, there was now, once again, only the unpatterned racket of the city. At the summit of his vision, turning in all directions, he had perceived Manhattan as insubstantial, a random blip in the infinitude of time, a matchstick structure—and if one man, any man, could pull the proper pin, the whole frail construct would come toppling into its moat. Now the solidity, the returning unalterable reality of the city, began to weigh heavily upon him once again. Disease, greed, ugliness, lust. Where before he had seen only perfection, now he noticed so much without apparent redemption in the plan of creation.

He withdrew to his apartment, to despair and ennui, and worst of all to periods of blankness when he would stare blindly at the wall for hours on end, possessed by a kind of deadening trance. He tried going back to his poetry, but that was dead for him too, as dead as the pile of ashes carelessly swept to one corner of the room.

In addition to his loss of awareness, there was something new at the edge of his consciousness, crossing back and forth over its borders, distracting him. He didn't like it and he didn't understand it. It was an old specter, a wraith of his sexual urges come back to haunt him. Hadn't he already wrestled that demon and brought it to its knees? No. That wasn't the way it had been. There had been no confrontation, only avoidance. He had resolved the problem by repressing and ignoring it. But with the first soft falling of winter's snow, he could suddenly ignore it no longer. Alone, with the cold all about him, that blanket of whiteness, perfect in its first falling before it was soiled by the city, tripped him back to the whiteness of Christine's bare body as he had seen it on the group acid trip. The cold, in juxtaposition, recalled the easy deceptive warmth of their group camaraderie during the week of Mulligan's visit, and set him worrying about *its* plexus of entangled motives and relationships. He knew that their oneness had been an illusion. He knew that Christine's body wasn't whiteness like that, not really. There were hairs on her arms and legs and all over her body. There were layers of skin and sweat glands, hair follicles, sebaceous glands, fatty tissue. Inside her body there was the raw pinkness of internal tissue. There were intestines filled with waste like his own. There was that aperture with its cycles of menstrual bleeding. And he knew that her soul wasn't white either. She had betrayed herself with Mulligan, with an abortion. How many other times? In how many other ways? She was human; she wasn't an ideal. She was flesh. Was that what he had wanted— her flesh and Jacobi's and Mulligan's? Was that the way it had been? Could he remember just how it had happened? Could he recapture the past, the goddamn past?

Reincarnating the dead tip of a felt pen with his own saliva, Michael wrote upon the wall, illegibly: "Each of us outlives the anima in a different way, each of us buries her within the self."

A winter morning, just past dawn. The exterior of the city, dun and white, was nearly deserted. Its inhabitants were lodged like drones in the comb-like structures of their heated cells. Plows had pushed the snow into melting piles, smudged and speckled by the dirt of the streets. The buildings, with their flat facades and rectilinear windows, row on row, rose up on all sides of him as he walked. He reached his destination and ducked down the narrow passage between two buildings. The bottom rung of the fire escape was beyond his reach.

With bare hands against the cold galvanized aluminum of the garbage can, he tilted it slightly and wheeled it crunching through the fresh snow. He moved ever so slowly. From distance he was a still shot...a minute hand.

The lid of the can buckled under his weight when he climbed atop, but did not collapse. His hands closed on the bottom rung and he began hoisting himself up. A sharp lancet of pain cut through his stretched abdomen and his feet fell back noisily against the lid. He doubled up, breathing heavily, hands clutching his belly. The pains had been coming on and off now for several days. Several weeks? He wasn't sure just when they had begun. He must have eaten something bad, though he'd been so careful.

On his second try he succeeded in pulling himself up again and he began climbing, one rung after another. A cat bandit, a human insect, that's what he had become. He stopped short of the roof on the third landing and removed a butter knife from his pocket. Its blade and handle were sticky with dried honey. He could see that stickiness, but his hands were too numb with cold to feel it— one sense betraying another. Slipping the blade between the wood of the sill and that of the window frame, Michael unhooked the simple latch. He knew that latch and had known the knife would work. The window swung outward on its hinges, finding its natural center of gravity, hanging freely a few inches from the sill. Michael lifted it a few inches further, enough for his slender form to ease between, through the slit in the drawn curtains and onto the floor of the apartment within.

It was emptier, the stereo and records were gone and most of the books, but it was the same room: scene of friendship and freak out. As he walked about, his damp shoes left their imprints on the rugs. He was searching for something, but he didn't know what. He ran his fingers up and down the clothes remaining in the closet, her clothes, over the underwear, blacks and reds and cool pastels, left behind in the nearly empty bureau drawers. Without the acid was he a fetishist rather than a mystic? Was that to be his calling?

In the kitchen he examined the photo of her children. This was the first time he had really looked at it. Here was Christine sullied once more, he thought.

He went into the full lotus on the floor, just where she had lain naked. He relived the group trip, telescoped down to the space of a few minutes, sifting through the memories without resolution. They returned as schizophrenic as the experience itself. Finally giving up, he lay down at the foot of the bed, on his side with legs drawn up, running his hand over the short nap of the rug. A longing welled up in him, abstract and incalculable. His mind, without purpose, without energy, without portents of any kind, began to wander. His undernourished body slipped thankfully into the escape of sleep.

He awoke to darkness, choking, garroted by the fright of an already-forgotten nightmare. The unfamiliar surroundings multiplied his fear until his hands, clawing at the fibers of the rug, brought back to him the events of the morning. As his heart beat and breathing slowed to an approximation of normality, Michael recognized the apartment and the dim, still silhouettes of the furniture.

These rooms were dead. There was no sustenance for him here. Michael realized there was only one thing left for him to do.

Hurriedly, he left the building, by the door of the apartment and down the inside stairwell. He left, forgetting to relock the window by which he had entered, so that when Christine returned, as she eventually did, she discovered it banging in the wind, and the curtains hopelessly water stained. Only she couldn't understand why nothing was missing.

Michael paused outside the door to Billie Raintree's basement. The windows were dark and not a sound issued from within. Michael feared momentarily that the dealer had finally been busted, but when he knocked, disturbing the tomb-like silence, it was Billie himself who answered the door, a deflated Billie, toothpickless, wrapped shawl-like in a blanket, and stoned out of his head. He had been busted all right, but not by the cops. He had been ripped off in grand style by his own cohorts and hangers on.

"Imagine me getting cleaned out. Me!" he raved to Michael. "It was a fucking conspiracy, a mutiny. A revolution. It was that bitch, Curly! No, it was all of them but she was behind it. She was the one who turned them against me."

"Curly?" The name meant something to Michael, somewhere he had heard it before, but he couldn't make the connection.

"Yeah, Curly. Louise. My woman! Some woman, huh, after what I tried to do for her. She was the only one who knew where the spare key to the trunk was. She must have been planning it for weeks, the bitch, with the others too, behind my back. I should never have trusted a speed freak. Some thanks from all of them! They left me one lousy lid of grass, and Connie and I have finished off most of that since yesterday." Billie sniffled and wiped his nose on the blanket. "You want some?"

"No," Michael answered. He was looking toward the couch. On the table before it, two burning candle stubs stood upright, embedded in their own wax. By their light he could make out another figure huddled in a blanket. It leaned forward into the oval thrown by the flames, lifting its head so the long dirty blondish hair fell back from the face.

"Hello, lover." It was the fortune-telling girl. Her face was thinner. Another tooth was missing from her smile, which seemed just as crazy as before.

Billie picked up a nearly empty plastic bag from the table. "Shit," he said, laughing, "We've been smoking it like cigarettes and we can't even feel it anymore." He stopped a moment, holding the bag in midair, as if his thoughts had been suspended. Then he dropped it and started ranting again. "On top of it all the fuckin' landlord won't give me enough heat!" He crossed the room. "That bastard's running an ice house, not an apartment house." A booted leg emerged from the blanket and dealt the radiator a vicious kick. "Four years of paying rent and every fuckin' winter I have to fight for a little heat."

Michael watched the performance impassively. "Have you got any of Jacobi's acid left?" he asked.

"What?"

"The acid you bought."

Billie shrugged and shook his head. "Nah, gone with the rest. Though I'll take some if you're selling. That stuff wasn't bad. I tried some myself, not bad at all." He flopped down on the couch, close by the girl. "It'll have to be on credit right now, but you know I'm good for it."

"If I had any, I wouldn't sell it," Michael said.

"Oh yeah! Well, each to his own, that's what I always say."

"Have you got any other acid?"

Spreading the blanket, Billie displayed his empty palms. "Look man, I told you, I'm clean…stripped bare…but wait a minute…there might be something." He was up again and headed for his room. "I never let anyone leave without satisfaction if I can help it. Don't go away. I'll be right back."

Michael was left alone with the girl. He looked down at her, still grinning up at him. It seemed necessary to say something. He felt a kind of kinship with her, the kinship of freaks, of village idiots, of pariahs and hunchbacks. But his mind failed to release the proper words and whatever it was remained unsaid.

Billie was back, holding a discolored purple capsule up to the candlelight. "The last one of its kind, a real bomber," he proclaimed. "They put a little of everything in this."

"What's a little of everything?" Michael asked.

"Oh…acid, speed…belladonna, mescaline," Billie laughed again. "Who knows? Come back next Tuesday and I'll give you a chemical analysis. Some people like it and some people don't, but I guarantee it'll shake your head around. Only five bucks! You'll get your money's worth and more out of it in colors alone."

"No," Michael answered, "I've taken it with speed before and it's not the same. It has to be pure acid."

Billie spoke to the girl, Connie, ignoring Michael. "Well, you can't say I didn't try, baby, but this one's just too hard to please."

Michael turned and headed slowly for the door.

"Hey, wait a minute," Billie called out.

Michael faced back.

"Here, catch! I've got no use for it."

Billie tossed the capsule across the room. It struck Michael on the chest, then fell to the floor to roll in a short quarter circle before it was still. Michael bent to pick it up. Billie had given it to him. It was now his. The portent was clear.

37

IF it is madness that you crave it is always in the offing—only you cannot pick and choose the kind. Swallow that lump of gorge that rises to your throat amidst the subway roar and stench, and look! These underground cars filled with cloying, heated air, the putrefying effluvium of humanity's breathing pores, bodies trapped too thickly to move, as on the shuttered trains trundling their meat to Auschwitz. Still the trembling of your limbs! You are not a Jew, not that blessing and curse, but only an outcast. You have deserted the truths of your fathers and are now defined solely by your differences. Apostate! Sinner! If you crave madness it is always at your elbow. Look! That stout woman with the tan handbag and lambent eyes is watching you. She is an indirect emissary of your mother. And what of that spectacled man who pretends to read *The Times* with such devotion? Your mother has related your aberrations to your father who has informed the proper authorities. All these months while you thought you were alone your every action has been taped, filmed, monitored. That tan handbag is an intricate and devilish contraption stuffed with sophisticated tracking equipment. These people are trained. They have photographically infallible memories. They have cataloged and summed each of your outrageous acts and on the blank side of the equation have placed the balancing factor: criminal insanity. You are a homosexual, a pervert, and consequently should be registered with the local authorities. You are guilty of breaking and entering, a misdemeanor; possession of marijuana, a felony; possession of hashish, a felony; possession of an unregistered drug, lysergic acid diethylamide, a misdemeanor. They are only waiting for the proper moment to make an arrest. They are compiling further evidence, and you, compulsive and insane, are no longer capable of preventing your transgressions. It may be that this car is already carrying you to your prison. The heavy steel doors will clang shut behind you and you will be swallowed up, lost to the world and the sun forever. In a dark cubicle you will be humiliated to a plea of guilty rather than facing an even more humiliating trial. They will place a cage of hungry rats around your head until you cough up a confession with your own blood. They will flay your skin with a hail of barbed whips until you perform rituals of atonement. Yes, you can feel it now, the madness, the criminal insanity, the concatenations of fear bristling along your neck and down the spine. You are quivering taut as a bowstring with it. But wait! You are not the only one who has been watched, not the only criminal. What of the others like yourself, your friends? Friends?

They have fled, fled to the West, to the country. You would not share their flesh. You would not give of your own. They have formed their coventry safe in the wilderness without you. You would not commit their crime, only conceive of it. Wait! Wait! You have flesh to give, morsels of flesh, pounds of flesh, flesh quivering in concatenations of madness. Flee the belly of this racing subterranean snake with its mephitic human stench. Flee the trapped masses. Dodge the trackers and the spies. Your powers have waned, but you have not been defeated yet. You have found them out and there is still time. You have flesh to give. Run. Run! Out! Out! Out!

The cold. The snowy earth. The moon. The air. The sky. The wheeling stars. Free! You are running free! These car horns that honk, these breaks that squeal with your passage, they are insubstantial. Their bumpers and shining fenders are gaseous. You can move through the space between their atoms. Running free! To the park. To the spectral trees. The wilderness. Running to your friends on the winged heels of Mercury. Running from the clinging tendrils of paranoia into the cancellous web of a belladonna nightmare.

A mottled purple capsule, a vitreous indigo world, jets of blood ink released through the ocean of air, poison for the lungs and the belly, a stitch running in your side, pain in your belly, your shrunken stomach digesting itself, the worm endlessly gnawing at its tail, swallowing its own jellied spine, the running snow and sky seen as if through a poisonous mist, you blink and the mist shatters to racing fragments on a black spaceless ground, irreparable shards of disconnected content, broken puzzle pieces. This is the end. No! The universe is collapsing molecule by molecule. No! You have flesh to give! The earth is still upon its axis and the winds are blowing with hurricane force. The maelstrom of madness has begun. Atoms, dumb as the scientists who watch them, have forgotten the secret of their binding force. Nuclei explode and disintegrate. No, you must find your friends! Electrons careen off their tracks like lunatic trolleys. The chain reaction marking the end of creation has begun. No! Wait! Force order from chaos! Use your powers! Find pattern. Bring the falling shards together for one last act, a final spectacle. You have flesh to offer! Fuse sky, trees, snow and earth. Listen to the wolves howling their hunger in the wilds. On the plains, hyenas anticipate your bones. The guests have gathered round the banquet table. You have flesh to give, painted flesh, cups of burning flesh. You have blood. You have cock and balls. You are not impotent, not impotent, not impotent!

Look! A man-boy runs naked through the snow...

The two officers wrapped him in one of their policeman's coats, oversized, flapping around his ankles but concealing his nakedness. They half-walked, half-carried him to the patrol car with its turning light and drove him to the station, where other faceless officers photographed his torpid face and fingerprinted his numb hands, more ink on his inked-in flesh, and booked him: a "John Doe" charged with indecent exposure. They couldn't get a name, they couldn't get anything from this mute, mad boy, this blubbering village idiot. His clothes were still lying miles behind, scattered in the snow like late-falling leaves. Even if they'd recovered them, they wouldn't have found any identification in the pockets. Michael had abandoned that convention even before the advent of acid in his life. Perhaps if they'd known he was possessed by spirits, if they'd had a shaman who could mumble the proper incantations or some old hag of a witch who could mix an emetic potion to exorcise his soul. But this was 1965. This was Manhattan, New York City, New York, The United States of America. Magic was no more, no less, than a stale stage trick, and these guardians of law and order couldn't even stare into his unblinking eyes long enough to find any verdict other than that of "freak."

This was a real jail, not a painted allegory. The prison bars were parallel and the sun passing through cast parallel bars of light on the worn cement floor. But before they put him in a cell, a cell crowded and smelly, they ran him through the stock humiliations required for entrance to a city prison. He was propelled and prodded up and down corridors, in and out of numbered doors, by rough anonymous hands, heavy emotionless voices. In a dank stall-less shower room scalding jets of water scourged all but a faint shadow of the writing from his flesh—they hadn't even bothered to read it, they had seen this trick before. A doctor of sorts gave him a cursory physical, shining a pencil flashlight into his several orifices, balking at the severe dilation of his pupils. Disinfectant sprays obliterated his bodily germs, clung to his pores and seeped their poisons through his system. Finally, they dressed him in gray ill-fitting garments of coarse cloth, prison attire that had disgraced hundreds of bodies before his own, and deposited him in a detention cell with others of his ilk. Once again he was entrapped amidst the smell of the masses, this time the manly masses—alcohol, tobacco, halitosis, and sweat, all finely frosted with the stink of germicide.

All of this was a ritual held in common for incoming inmates at the city jail. To mad Michael, wedged tightly in the cradle of his egocentricity, it was taken as a personal affront, a torturous game designed to debilitate him further. The other dwellers in his cell had been planted there, he was sure of it. They would attempt to reduce his defenses in subtle ways, through the guise of friendship. His true friends were far away, unaware of the fate that had befallen him. He wouldn't speak to these fake prisoners who pretended to share his misfortune. He would give in to neither the hard sell nor the soft sell of the American penal institution.

After several hours they removed him for interrogation, a further attempt to establish his identity. First, an amiable sergeant tried to cajole him. Then a sadistic sergeant, venting his own frustrations, convinced himself that Michael's voicelessness and blank gaping were an act, and backhanded him across the face bloodying his mouth and nose trying to get him to speak. It was pointless. Despite the present reality of bars, walls and blows,

Michael was for the most part functioning in a different realm. Billie's purple capsule had left his mind full with the aftertaste of madness, a brand of madness in itself. His thoughts could focus only partially and momentarily on the dull, beefy, animalistic faces that ordered him about, screamed at him, and offered him poisoned food that he would not touch. He escaped this prison world by retreating inward, to the equally confusing, though less terrifying, jumble of his thoughts. When he did try to center his attention on the present, he was not incarcerated here because of his naked run through the snow, he had already forgotten that, but because of his other crimes, real and fictitious, because his mother had betrayed him and his father had reported him.

The reason for Michael's refusal to give his name was that he knew it could be used against him, not on a police report, but because there was magic and power in the possession of name. It could become an object of spells, curses and summons, and that was why they tried to force and trick it from him. But he would not yield. He had read Ian Fleming when he was younger and knew what diabolical tricks he might expect. His enemies had robbed him of his powers, yet his will was still his own and as indomitable as ever. He would play the role of mute until they were fooled into relaxing the walls of their defenses. And then he would escape by the course he alone knew. He would run inward rather than outward, lower and lower, through subterranean passages long forgotten in these modern heights of construction...but wait, hadn't he tried that already?

By morning, his virulent course had realized a further step in its consummation. His inadequate diet and his recent exposure combined to overcome him in a way in which his enemies had failed. He fell sick. The delirium of the purple capsule was superseded by the alternating delirium of fever and chills. His muteness disappeared. Now he spoke although he was not being spoken to, he howled and he raved, he spoke in tongues. A river of fiery mucus invaded and rampaged through the channels of his body. Large tear-shaped droplets of sweat fled his decontaminated pores to dampen and darken the coarse fibers of his gray suit of shame. His five cell mates—two blacks, two Puerto Ricans, and one other white man, a grizzled inveterate wino thankful to be out of the elements within this cozy prison sanctuary—watched him suffering, this waspish boy who had been misplaced in their midst. They shut their ears to his babbling. They didn't want to hear hints of the madness that might be raging beneath their own conscious thoughts. They watched as the fever burned him up. It wouldn't take much to finish off this leaf of a boy. And finally they called the guards, not because they cared about saving him, but because whatever malady he had, they didn't want to be stricken with it, too.

Michael was lifted from his bunk and laid upon a stretcher. His turbid mind and tabescent body were transported to a hospital, a prison hospital. Around his thin wrist they clipped a cloudy plastic band with a typed paper insert—"John Doe, 37415GB." He had become another piece of meat hooked onto a conveyor chain. They placed him in a bed in an overpopulated ward. Its yellowed walls echoed round the clock with the dolorous moans of pain, imprisonment and hopeless desperation. 37415GB added its own unintelligible cries to the infernal din.

After a time the diagnosis came: malnutrition, anemia, bronchitis, acute congestion of the superior lungs. The tortures continued. Attention to his condition was methodic and impersonal. Nurses hit him with the needle again and again, penicillin to fight off the infection, a transfusion to raise his blood count, tranquilizers to still this chattering bag of bones. His mouth would seldom open for food and when it did his shrunken stomach couldn't seem to hold it down. They tunneled out a choice vein on the inside of his left forearm and embedded a needle taped to his flesh, attached to a hanging bottle of glucose solution so that he could absorb sustenance intravenously. Michael pulled the needle out, making a mess of his arm.

They bandaged him up, strapped him to the bed, and reinserted it.

Finally, his bemused and sedated brain concluded that this was no horror show performed expressly for his benefit. This was Hell, plain and simple, and he had already been consigned to eternal damnation. He gave up resistance and allowed the sea of misery to engulf him.

38

THIS hospital wasn't like the other one. This wasn't even a hospital, it was a clinic, a small, select clinic buried split-level in suburban tree-lined Scarsdale. And if it was whiteness he wanted, he had it now. The white-walled solitude of a private room, the white curtains, the white bed rails, the lily white nurses, the white sheets, the white hospital gown rubbing against his calves when he tried to get up and walk. And through the immaculate window, the powdery snowflake whiteness of an American Xmas landscape.

Five days after his arrest, on the fourth day of his hellish hospitalization, 37415GB's fixation on maternal betrayal had been realized in fact. He had been identified for the authorities, his enemies, by his very own mother, as Michael Shawtry, age twenty, second son of Mr. and Mrs. Gerald Shawtry of Manhattan.

Up until the time of his acid mania, Michael had made regular visits to his parents' uptown apartment. They were his sole concession to his mother's demands on him, these biweekly confrontations where she would ply him with money and gifts, and talk *at* him, of his brother's accomplishments—only seven years older than Michael and already a successful lawyer in New Hampshire— of his father's preoccupation with business, of her own trials and tribulations and how much she missed him. Michael would assume the role of the laconic, brooding artist to the hilt, nodding and mumbling noncommittally as only he could. When his annoyance with one of these visits rose to an intolerable peak, as it generally did, he would leave curtly and abruptly, as if he had suddenly been offended.

Beyond these meetings, Michael had painstakingly preserved his separation from his parents. They didn't know where he lived and there was no way for them to find out. He had no telephone. He received his mail at a post office box. He paid his rent by money order under the pseudonym of "Ambrose Bierce." His father didn't really care. He had given up any hopes of communicating with the boy and abandoned him emotionally some time ago. There was nothing Michael's mother could do, short of having him followed by a detective after one of his visits. Although she wasn't beyond this, she knew her son was too clever to fall for it.

Thus she had to content herself with unleashing her tirades of smothering affection and piteous recrimination during the few hours she saw him each month. After the abrupt termination of Michael's intense interlude with Jacobi, Mulligan and Christine, his obsession with acid absorbed him without a trace, and he had rejected even the concession of these brief visits.

Naturally, the mother in her panicked. Days passed without word and her imagination aggravated her panic to the point of hysteria. Her son had left the country without telling her. He was lying sick without friends and no way to call for help. He had been kidnaped! He was dead!

Now detectives *were* hired, but to no real purpose. She couldn't possibly describe her son to them for the freak he had been, let alone the freak he had become. She couldn't tell them that he wore the same clothes day after day, that his hair was uncut and usually a matted, uncombed mess, that he had sprouted an adolescent pseudo-beard on his soft German cheeks where no beard could yet grow. She could only give them his high school graduation picture for purposes of identification, a clean-cut Michael, suited and tied, forcing a closed-lip smile like a cincture demarcating his inadequacies. She could only pray and make their retainer a handsome one. But Manhattan was an extensive wilderness in which to pinpoint a lone, poorly defined prey, and Michael had already traveled a long irretraceable path since high school graduation.

It was only after his arrest that the Bureau of Missing Persons finally made the connection in its weekly check on police reports. Mrs. Gerald Shawtry was requested to come forth to either confirm or deny the identification of her offspring.

She trailed the slouching, bullish attendant down the center of the long yellow ward, her heels tapping diffidently on the spotted parquet as she navigated a course of careful equidistance between the rows of beds with their diseased, criminal inhabitants.

Could this be her son!?

This debilitated boy strapped upon a prison bed, this aged youth with the lax jaws and toneless flesh and purblind eyes. But no, those eyes were not sightless. They watched her as she watched him and they asked who this woman was? Could this be his mother, the betrayer, who stared down at him with such horror!? This garish, platinumed dowager with the flaccid and powdered winter flesh. Or was this merely a mockup fashioned in demonic workshops and meant to torment him further?

Could his very own mother, with her marching band of virtues, have plummeted to this eighth circle of Hell? Or was this manifestation among the damned merely the ultimate extension of her well-wrought earthly martyrdoms?

She had come closer to the bed now, along its side, closer to him, leaning over him, and she was speaking in a hoarse, tautly wired whisper, afraid to make a scene in public, even before the private institutionalized public of these expiring outcasts. What was she saying now? More castigations? More recriminations? "...shame...a disgrace...how could you...I knew something like this...should have never...never...always...gave...everything...every advantage...I gave...everything...never...I should have known..."

His own shield of words had been washed from his flesh. *Her* words now settled into his unprotected body like barbed plumb lines. She had not given them up, she would pull them back to take with her when she left, to be used again and again, just as she always had in the past. Their lines tangled in his flesh, lay leaden in his empty stomach blocking his unused digestive tract, pressed about the bronchi of his mucused lungs, caught like thorny anchors in the systoles of his pounding heart. Their removal would once again be an ordeal of excruciation. She was stringing him like a puppet with her words. She would, if she had her way, fashion a dancing-doll marionette with invisible tethers deeply embedded in its petrifying wooden soul. This was no mockup that stood before him, no counterfeit! This *was* the betrayer, the mother, the lover, the devouring womb. Michael summoned the shreds of his disjunctive and febrile consciousness for a final outburst—guttural, wordless, howling—straining forward eagerly against the binding straps.

Her brittle whisper froze and cracked with fright in the face of his unadulterated madness.

The slouching attendant snapped into action with another needle of sleep.

There was no time in this undifferentiated whiteness, no night and day. Their were schedules, rounds, meals, sleeping and waking and routines of exercises. There were visiting hours. There were progress reports and thermometers and blood pressure gauges. White had no right to be this white, this perfect, this pure, rigid, suffocating and timeless. Even the food, which he now ate without resistance, seemed coated with a uniform chalky tastelessness. It was only that singular odor which permanently infected the air, drowning out the lesser smells of starchy nurses and freshly cut flowers, that escaped. It was not white, only sterile.

His mother, ineffectual in the vacuum of her shock, had transferred the entire matter to Michael's father. His father had made the necessary arrangements for Michael's transfer and had taken care of all the expenses. The authorities understood that such cases involving persons of wealth and influence were delicate. A scandal would be beneficial to no one. Such cases could best be handled by the individuals involved, providing they were sufficiently perceptive and understanding, as persons of influence naturally were. And even if they weren't, they nevertheless remained persons of influence. Consequently, Michael had been released to the custody of his parents. He had been moved on a gurney by a quiet gleaming, gliding ambulance without his will and against his will. They were ever so nice to him now—the solicitous attendants, the polite drivers. He had become a different sort of anomaly to them than a homeless, nameless, penniless freak. He was now a wealthy freak, a different breed of animal, a completely different species altogether.

The room to which they delivered him in the clinic was private and large, larger than his own deserted living quarters in the East Village. There was a television set suspended against the whiteness. There was a window with a white winterland scene that he pretended to turn upside down like a glass Christmas ball so the snow could settle to the dome of the sky and prepare to fall again. There was a dresser, empty until his mother sent clothes for when he would be better, up and around. There was his own personal buzzer to call a nurse for personal attention. All in all, for Michael, this was as much of a prison as the prison ward from which he had been dispatched with such haste as soon as his identity was established. Once again, he had become powerless within the all-encompassing power of his family's wealth.

His span of attention was lengthening and he could concentrate now for brief periods. His thought processes were settling down, wavering for the most part back and forth within the accepted standard deviation known as normality. There were still gaps, jump-circuits in the continuity of his consciousness, but those could be attributed to his general listlessness and the quantity of drugs they kept pumping into him. Mostly downers, yet he had never dreamed that he could have remained so indifferent to so much free dope—not the old Michael anyway. Physically, he remained weak. He slept a great deal, or rather half-slept, drifting in a mindless, emotionless crepuscular zone, a stationary sea without a wavelet of misery or a ripple of joy. When he attempted to stand and navigate the room he experienced lightheadedness and vertigo, and his knees went rubbery beneath the hospital gown. Each of his continuing violent reactions, now partly feigned, to the successive appearances of his mother, left him utterly exhausted. However, they succeeded in convincing Dr. Benson to advise against future visits until such time as the patient demonstrated a course of steady improvement.

Dr. Benson was his friend. Dr. Benson wanted to help.

"I want to help you," Dr. Benson told him. "I'm your friend. With you, not against you." He doubled his hand to a friendly fist and raised it by his side as he spoke, as if the entire problem were a question of school spirit. "I not only want you to feel better, but to understand yourself better. I want you to become a satisfied and functioning member of society. We can do it if we work together. It's the trying that counts."

Dr. Benson was the select staff psychiatrist of this very select clinic. He was young, stuffed to the gills above his white smock with self-assurance and a kit bag of the most advanced theories. The journals in his office, progressive journals, exhibited dog-eared testimonial to the thoroughness of his professional dedication. He unloaded a well-recompensed sampling of his talent and craft at Michael's bedside each weekday afternoon. Intensive personal therapy, he called it.

"Well, where shall we begin today...with your mother," Dr. Benson began. He yawned with one hand over his mouth. His lunch was still percolating through the channels of his belly, drawing off blood from his cranial machinations to the mundane matter of digestion. "Excuse me!" he apologized, with extravagant concern for his patient's sensibilities.

Michael eyed him with restrained but unveiled hostility. Dr. Benson was smiling openly at him, seemingly as guileless as a puppy, but his eyes gave him away. Every time, his eyes gave him away. He was watching Michael, trying to catch him in something, hanging on any oddity the patient might exhibit. Sometimes that watching was only a few inches behind Benson's eyes, sometimes a mile, but this patient wasn't being fooled, he could perceive it. Michael was always tempted to make a game out of these sessions, to fake an irregular twitch in his cheek or pretend to play with himself beneath the covers. The old Michael would have, the pre-acid and pre-freakout Michael, the mischievous Michael. Only he never felt that light or trivial anymore. Always more solemn. Perhaps his youth was a thing of the past. He would be twenty-one soon. Did that mean he was now a man...a crazy man?

"You know, your mother wants to help you as much as I do," Dr. Benson poked.

Unconsciously, Michael began to toy with the sore on his thumb. He had burnt the thumb on the matches in the park, and it had never really healed. Each time a new layer of skin began to form, he would pick away at it until the flesh was raw and bleeding. The action annoyed Dr. Benson and he shivered slightly. He always tried to identify with his cases, particularly the brighter ones, and for a moment it seemed to him that his own thumb that was undergoing self-mutilation. Nevertheless, he felt that he knew the significance of the act, so he fastened his attack upon it.

"There you go again. Why are you doing that?" He nodded toward the thumb. "It's minor, but another example of your continued urge toward self-destruction, aggressive instincts turned back upon the self. I know you're no ordinary individual, Mr. Shawtry." Respect for the patient, professionalism always. "I know you're different. You records show us that. You're creative, intelligent. But you must learn to use your abilities constructively, to channel your aggressive instincts in a positive direction. If only you can do that, there's no telling what you might accomplish. Not only a normal and satisfying life, but an exceptional one."

Michael did not pause in his skin peeling. "You're wrong, Doctor. I'm only doing this to feel something," he said.

Benson, ever the voice of reason, answered with perfect equanimity. "Feel? Is it pain that you want to feel? Can't you see how unnatural that is?"

Michael cast his glance around the corners of the room, indistinct to him in the solidity of their unrelieved whiteness. "Although you may not know it, Doctor, pain is better than some things...better than a lot of things."

And so their daily sessions went. The metaphor that came to Michael's mind was that of an ape fencing with a brick wall. Only it wasn't funny.

It wasn't anything.

And so the days went, stacked atop one another like colorless checkers, unchanging and tasteless as the meals, tedious as Benson's journals. Mentally, Michael's "recovery" continued. He could order his thoughts more clearly. He began to read haphazardly, nothing heavy—popular fiction, mysteries, best sellers. They served as a minor escape from his hospital doldrums. It felt strange to be moving through the experience of reading a novel again after so long, holding the book in his hands, turning the pages, being drawn into a world of paper and print illusion. Some of what he read even piqued his interest and started his intellectual curiosity wheeling into motion once again. He began to reflect upon what had happened, what he had done and what had been done to him. Obviously, he had made a mistake in dropping Billie's bastard psychedelic. He had been coming down from the cumulative high of the ten caps of acid, but his consciousness was still too rarefied to handle the horrors that Billie's cap had generated. It had flipped him over the edge. He had stripped off his clothes. He had run naked through the snow, exposed his body. He had inflicted harm upon no one other than himself. In turn, he had been seized by the supposed guardians of his freedom. He had been jailed, bullied, scalded, deloused, poked, yelled at, insulted, beaten and humiliated. There was "no room for holy men in America"—Jacobi again, Mulligan again. The injustice of it all was baldly apparent, but Michael could only deal with that injustice as a philosophical observation. He could not feel outraged, not yet. That would have been a moral response, an emotional response, and the rate of his emotional convalescence did not parallel his mental. It lagged, nearly static, nearly lobotomized, as if the feeling portions of his being had been decapitated. He had experienced such intense feelings with the acid, that perhaps now there was nothing left for him to feel. He remained drifting in a crepuscular zone where the sand was the same color as the sea, with no telling as to whether the half light he experienced was that of morning or evening, whether it predicated a coming day or merely the descending umbra of eternal night.

Physically, his condition wavered. He was eating enough to maintain himself, but not enough to make any progress. His overall weakness and spells of dizziness persisted. He had no will to recover. There was nothing he wanted to do, no place to go except maybe back into the past. But he was no longer capable of that, he had lost the ability to time travel along with his other heightened perceptions.

Coupled to his general weakness, he still experienced fever and chills, but his worst affliction was the congestion. When he awoke each morning his throat and nostrils were inundated with a treacly no-color phlegm that he would expel into a bedside enamel pan, coughing and wheezing. The river of mucus had settled to a swampy lake within the environs of his body. It churned turbidly in his lung cavities, inhibiting his breathing, sapping his oxygen intake and thus his energy. Michael didn't think much about it. It was just another undifferentiated element in his undifferentiated world.

Then came word of the operation.

One day, Dr. Benson strolled into the room for their regular afternoon session with something new lurking behind the translucent shields of his eyes. He began smartly, without preamble, without hesitation. "Well, good afternoon, Mr. Shawtry, I've been asked to inform you that the medical staff has decided that a minor operation can best alleviate your physical condition."

Michael's pinched scrutiny of Benson narrowed further, darkened. Was there a certain satisfaction in the doctor's voice that his uncooperative charge would soon be going under the knife? "What kind of operation?" Michael asked.

"Oh, nothing serious, just a draining and scraping of the interior lungs so that they can be restored to a healthy state in which they can eliminate fluids of their own accord."

"No," said Michael flatly. "Nothing doing. Not a chance." The reality and consequences of Benson's announcement were beginning to sink in—an operation, his flesh severed and bleeding, strange hands and metal instruments within his body. He was suddenly feeling something. He was feeling fear, actually feeling it.

"Come now!" Benson answered, buoyant and outwardly as benign as ever. "If you're going to get well you must allow us to treat you. Of course the body isn't my province, but let me say that you should consider yourself very fortunate. You've met the men on our staff—Brown, Mealy, Atkinson. You can trust them. They're among the finest physicians in the state, even in the country. You're very lucky, Mr. Shawtry, not everyone can afford such care."

"No," Michael repeated adamantly, staring in front of himself, speaking more to the whole oppressive, impersonal white world that was enveloping him than to Benson. "I don't want an operation. No, I won't have it."

"Well, I'd hoped you might be more receptive to the idea," Benson bumbled on with a sigh, "but, in any case, the decision ultimately rests with your parents."

Michael swallowed the bile thickening in his throat and looked unbelievingly at Dr. Benson, who wanted to be his friend, who wanted to help him. His parents. His parents! After all his declarations of freedom, after all his carefully planned anonymity, after all of his preternatural visions, his fate had fallen back into their dumb hands once more. The absurdity of it was truly, physically, horrifying.

"Well, where shall we begin today...with your run through the snow," Dr. Benson began ritually. He popped a cough drop into his mouth, working it back and forth with his tongue so that it clicked against his teeth.

The operation, it loomed before him like a black-faced cave alive with unknown beasts, blood-letting beasts, white-masked beasts with claws of slicing steel. After all he had suffered and endured, the forces arrayed against him couldn't let him be in his blankness. They had to chase and prick at him still further. His resurgent mental alertness now had a problem with which to deal—avoidance of the operation. Yet his new emotion of fear rose to play havoc with his reason and send his thoughts spiraling on frightful flights of imagination. His old paranoia came creeping back into his bed like a cat in the middle of the night.

If his parents were to be the arbiters of his destiny he should ask to speak with them, only he knew his father wouldn't come. Given his previous performances, Benson might not be prepared to let him speak with his mother. He had to convince Benson that he was sane enough, rational enough. But what good would it do? His mother would side with the doctors. She was too much of a fool to see that the operation was probably just another way to get money out of them. He didn't need an operation. He was breathing, there was no severe pain. And even if their claims were justified, still he didn't want an operation. All he needed was time to get well, a little more time. How much time did he have anyway? Had they already talked to his parents and the decision been made? Could Benson's declaration have been *post facto*, merely a test to see whether he would go under the knife voluntarily or if they would have to trick him, knock him out with a shot first?

They might come to take him in the morning. What could he possibly do to stop them?

The more fiercely Michael attacked the problem, the more anxious and confused he became. His eyeballs ached. His head buzzed, and spells of shaking and dizziness came over him although he was not even attempting to stand.

Suppose Benson were even more mendacious than he seemed, Michael thought. What if they actually planned to operate on his brain rather than his body, lobotomize him as a physical fact to complement his psychological condition? Was the twilight he experienced really only a prelude to the end? Yet with the news of the impending operation hadn't his world already begun to lighten. He was feeling emotions again, or at least the single overriding emotion of fear. His senses were coming back to him, grasping frantically at the few life-like impressions the dull hospital world had to offer. Nurse William's small careful hands as she brought him his dinner tray, the short dark hairs on the backs of her wrists, the odors of the food, the steam from the dishes rising against his cheeks, the wool of the blanket furry like an animal pelt beneath his fingertips, the sweet decaying smell of wilting flowers inhaled in brief snatches like a hint of thyme upon the disinfected air. All of it was suddenly so vivid, so valuable and irreplaceable. Even the view through the window, static but for the falling snow, at last impressed him as real. There was a world out there with millions of sense impressions to be drunk in just as he now drank these, as if they might be his last and he must prepare to cherish and relive them *ad infinitum* in some sense-less purgatorial eternity.

When they brought him his evening sedative, Michael only pretended to swallow it. Instead, he concealed the tablet beneath his tongue and held his face rigid as waves of bitterness beat against his taste buds. He couldn't allow himself to sleep. He still needed time, time to think, to decide what he must do. But time and thought brought no answers, just further combinations and permutations of his fear, and finally a nightmarish sleeping in which he was pursued by strange shapes and unintelligible voices—up stairs, down fire escapes, across icy lakes, into the roughhewn cave of a surreal subway where bodiless all-knowing eyes flickered and flashed and watched him careen through the darkness.

The heavy door of the hospital room clicking shut brought him partially awake, his mind muddled with the reality of his dream. It was still dark and there was someone else in the room. He could make out a silhouette against the white wall, just discernible in the scattered luminescence of the night light. It moved toward the bed without speaking. Michael could sense its approach and he was of a sudden benumbed, motionless with terror, dream terror and real terror.

Had they come to take him already?

Then the silhouette pulled up one of the visitor's chairs ever so noiselessly and sat down close by the bedside, within the pale patch of illumination thrown by the night light. Its shadow form took on detail. Sitting up, Michael could make it out now. It was a small walnut-brown old man attired in the gray garb of a janitor. His deeply colored facial skin was finely wrinkled and tight upon his skull. His eyes and hair were the same colorless color as his clothes. At one side of the man's belt there was an enormous ring filled with keys uncountable, glinting a dull gun-metal in the dimness.

"Good evening. How are you doing tonight?"

The voice was cultured, British, nearly Oxfordian, an uncommon voice for a janitor. Michael's throat, still clogged with phlegm from the prone posture of sleep, managed only a garbled response.

"I would have dropped by for a chat sooner," the old man continued. "I like to get to know all of the patients, only I've been busy lately, so very busy. Tell me, have you been sick long?"

"No...just a few weeks," Michael answered. He noticed that this man's eyes were not in the least like Benson's. There were no shields there, no attempt to hide the content of their depths. There was a demand for something in those eyes. Michael didn't know for what, but it was something other than simple conversation.

"Good. Good." The old man spoke in a slow steady tone. "A long illness can mean a great deal of suffering. I've seen a lot of them here. Their money doesn't help them much. Some make it and some don't. After enough misery some just give up trying. It's easier that way."

"I'm getting better," Michael assured him uneasily.

"Good. Good." Nodding slowly. "If left to its own devices nature will take its course. Life, disease, death. Doctors are supposed to help, but much of the time they just make things worse. I'd call them stupid, but 'stupid doctors' is a bit of a redundancy, isn't it now?"

After a well-timed pause, the old man gave a soft chuckle at his own joke, and Michael found himself joining in. The comment reminded him of his own dry wit. Perhaps this fellow wasn't such a bad sort after all, he thought, a bit strange, but he seemed more genuine and open than the rest of the hospital staff combined.

Crossing his legs, the immense nest of keys clicking softly, the old man pulled a small flat box from his shirt pocket. Flipping it open with his thumb and holding it out toward Michael, he inquired politely, "Would you care for a smoke, young man?"

Michael eyed the box dubiously. The "smokes" were Balkan Sobranies, one of the best and most expensive of cigarettes, one hundred percent Turkish tobacco. Michael had tasted and relished a few in his time, but had never allowed himself to purchase such a luxury. How long had it been since he'd had a cigarette of any kind? Two months? Closer to three? It might aggravate his condition, but could it really make any difference if they were going to slice him up on the morrow anyway?

Nodding his consent, Michael extracted one of the tightly packed white cylinders, sniffing the sweet fragrance of the dark tobacco, another sense impression to savor. The old man took a cigarette for himself and struck a wooden match along the length of one slim white leg of his chair. As he held the flame cupped, Michael noticed that the skin of his hands was worn and cracked as ancient leather.

The cigarette was delicious, but Michael's nervous system was no longer accustomed to nicotine and after a few puffs his head began to spin. He slowed the pace of his own smoking and watched the janitor vicariously. The man inhaled each drag with measured satisfaction, a lupine smile spreading across his tight countenance. He inhaled the French way, letting the smoke rise out of his mouth and then drawing it back in through his nose.

"They think I'm crazy," Michael suddenly found himself confessing. Perhaps he had found an ally.

The old man shrugged his gray shoulders. "Who are they to say? Who are they to judge?" he stated from behind a billowing cloud of smoke that now blanketed his expression.

"Who is anyone to say?" Michael was quick to agree.

Then the smoke began to clear, dissipating to the limits of the room, and Michael found himself looking into the depths of the old man's eyes. They held his gaze steadily through the wisping trailers of smoke. Michael felt his reticence beginning to return as an element of traction against the vacuum of their pull. What were those eyes demanding? A gesture of friendship in return for the cigarette? An homage? A sacrifice? Michael was not sure how long those eyes held his own, but before he could put his questions into words, before he could share the threat of his impending operation, the cigarettes were finished and the old man was up and already heading for the door, departing as unexpectedly as he arrived. There was only time for one final query of the multitude that were filling Michael's head with regard to these strange janitor.

"What's your name?" he blurted out at random.

The old man was almost to the door, once more only an indefinable shadow in the still-dark, now-smoky room

"I'll be back." The door opened. "Don't worry." His silhouette bobbed and rippled in the light branching from the hall. "I'll be coming back soon."

Michael's questions did not cease with the departure of their cause. His curiosity about the old man continued to plague him, pushing even thoughts of the operation momentarily aside. The visit, coming like an apparition at the end of his dream and passing so quickly, seemed like an extension of the dream itself. Only the visitor's chair still stood next to the bed where the janitor had shifted it. And atop the nightstand, in the formerly spotless enamel tray, two cigarette butts lay side by side in their own ashes.

Balkan Sobranies? What was a janitor, presumably living on a janitor's salary, doing with imported cigarettes at well over a dollar a box?

What was a janitor doing with a cultured British accent?

Where had he learned to French inhale?

And hadn't Michael seen a gold Phi Beta Kappa key, just like his own father's, buried in the nest of that giant ring?

The realization came upon Michael gradually in the hospital night, in contradiction to his vague liking of the man and the way in which he felt drawn to him. It came wordlessly, by degrees, accompanied by the returning chill of his terror. There had been no portents for some time, but this one, once the pieces fell into place, was as clear as the gray depths of those invidious eyes. The news of the operation, the appearance of a "janitor" when there had been no janitor before, the promise to return. The old man would be back all right, now that he had surveyed and staked his claim. After the operation he would return to take his prize. Or during the operation he might appear in the midst of the white-robed surgeons, invisible in his colorless garb, and with one scabrous hand he would nudge the wrist of the scalpel-wielder to induce a fatal incision. It was plain that his demand was not for conversation or friendship. It was a demand for Michael, himself, body sealed and soul delivered.

Michael did not pause to name the old man. He was no longer *thinking* about how to get out of the operation. In the face of his fear, he was suddenly moving without thought or reservation, taking the only course left open to him—that of flight, from the hospital, from Benson, from this counterfeit janitor, from the certain demise that awaited him if he remained. Almost before he knew it, his bony legs were out from under the covers and he was on his feet in the dead hospital night. His dizziness was still a burden but no longer an insurmountable obstacle. He had subdued the weaknesses of his flesh before, and although they had resurfaced to conspire in his downfall, he would subdue them again now. He stripped off the hospital gown and stood naked, almost expecting the forces of decency, the forces of oppression, to come pouncing out of the white woodwork and down upon him again for his audacity.

In the bureau he found the clothes his mother had brought— neatly folded button-down shirts and pressed cotton pants, apparel for the university student and lawyer-doctor-teacher to be who still lived, booked it, and made good in a steel and glass college dormitory somewhere in the west end of her head. He put the clothes on. They were too large, his mother overestimating him again, giving his small angular frame the look of a listing scarecrow as he tottered about the room on his unsure footing. For shoes there were only the loose hospital slippers that would slap noisily against his heels and give him away. He discarded these and donned several pairs of socks one atop the other to protect his feet from the forthcoming cold. He was now a clubfooted scarecrow.

In the next instant he was into the hall without hesitation, stagger-blinking in the fluorescent brightness. The ceiling lights were placed with such frequency and intensity that the corridor held not a speck of shadow. Michael broke into a loping run, a shadowless refugee in stumbling fright from the consequences of his past and blindly shaping the consequences of his future. He stopped. He tried to stop the swimming in his head, to remember the layout of the building from when he had been wheeled in. His heart beat plangently, a telltale heart resonating down the spotless corridors to raise the alarm against him. But no, not his heart, those were footsteps coming from around a bend in the hall, coming after him. He ducked into a room. A room dark but occupied. A man on the bed, breathing thickly, encased in the filmy plastic of an oxygen tent, a picture relayed to him from his own possible future. Then he was into the closet of the room as the steps in the hall grew closer. Clinging to the heavy cloth of an overcoat in the blackness so as not to lose his clubfooted balance, to find a still point, a solid and motionless ground zero from which to coordinate his whirling thoughts. He inhaled the musty cloth, his open mouth dampened and tasted the tasteless cloth, his body weight hung suspended through the coat to the bending wire frame of its hanger. The coat slid from its hold and he tumbled against the closet wall and onto the floor, still grasping it. The wire hanger followed, clattering. He untangled himself and wrapped the coat about his shoulders. Standing, Michael slipped his arms through the sleeve holes. The coat was oversized, heavy material, the proper ballast to offset his lightheadedness.

The footsteps were gone now.

He was out through dark of the room and into the brightness of the hall again.

Operating from instinct, moving with steeled unconsciousness toward the back of the hospital. To the left. To the right. This brightness is killing me, he thought. To the left. Literally killing me, it's not just a metaphor. Retracing the course of his entrance. White-killing, bright-killing. To the emergency exit where he had been wheeled in. Its sliding glass doors. Its platform, a concrete loading dock splotched with melting snow. Its dead untended ambulance, gleaming silently, awaiting the next victim.

Michael Shawtry walked out from the hard cold whiteness of the hospital into the soft cold whiteness of the snow.

39

JACOBI drove into New York City, coaxing Tina's VW through traffic jams and drifts of snow. Manhattan seemed just the same except for the snow, a dirty snow that lined the streets, muffled the sounds of the city to a low roar, and turned the city's inhabitants into scurrying hulks wrapped in dark swaddling clothes against the cold. The only parking spot he could find was three blocks from Michael's. He had to leave the car and walk shivering, with his limbs locked against his body and his hands shoved deeply into his pockets.

He climbed the dingy stairs, involuntarily flashing on all of the changes he'd been through since his first ascent of those stairs half a year earlier. He was no longer the middle-class college kid, no longer the would-be dealer. He had begun to acquire a past with a more individual identity, only he wasn't sure whether he liked it any better or not.

When he knocked, the only response was a feeble, unintelligible yell from within the apartment. He opened the door to find Michael sick in bed, the sheet like a gray-white chrysalis twined about his body, his body tucked upon itself in fetal mimicry, curled like a shrimp, his pale skin nearly shrimp pink with the flush of fever. The room was dirtier and in complete disorder. Assorted junk from the closet was scattered about. A pile of ashes lay in one corner and there was a charred spot near the center of the floor. Michael had covered the wall over the bed with illegible doodles; it looked like one of his notebook covers. Despite the accumulated debris and the marks on the wall, the room seemed emptier. It took Jacobi several minutes to pin down the cause. The missing typewriter.

Between coughs, Michael told Jacobi the story of what had happened to him, or at least what he could remember, adding poetic embellishments of his own for style. The thing that seemed to have impressed him most was how white everything had been in the hospital, how its all pervasive whiteness had made everyone's flesh seem dark. "All of us, even the doctors and nurses, where like niggers oppressed by that whiteness, under its control."

When Michael had finished, Jacobi shook his head. "Jesus," he said, "why did you have to do all that?"

Michael blinked watery eyes. "It seemed appropriate at the time."

"How do feel about it now?"

"It seemed appropriate at the time," Michael repeated momentarily.

"Do you always do want seems appropriate at the time?"

"What else is there to do?"

Jacobi thought for a moment, but his only response was a shrug.

"Are you and Tina still together?" Michael asked.

Jacobi tugged at his beard. "In some ways."

"Where's she at?"

"Old Cape Cod. She went home to visit the kiddies."

"I thought *you* were her only baby."

Jacobi smiled crookedly. "I thought *you* were supposed to be sick."

Over the next few days, Jacobi nursed his friend back to a semblance of health with a plethora of patent medicines. Michael would have preferred a cap of acid—he said that would get him back in shape faster than anything else. The acid was in Ithaca, but even if he'd brought it along, Jacobi wouldn't have come across with any. Judging from Michael's story and the way he looked and talked, he'd already been over the brink of insanity once. Acid could blow him into the air again and no telling where he might come down.

There was to be a party at Linda's that weekend, a belated New Year's party since the New Year would already be past. Michael had received an invitation by mail and for some obscure reason was determined to go. He mumbled something about death and rebirth, but at the time Jacobi wasn't up to deciphering it. Yet they did talk. There was little else to do. They became entangled in long wandering dialogues that stretched out through the night like clotheslines worming their way over the tenement roofs.

Jacobi was amazed and frightened and left wondering how much acid was responsible for the freak that Michael had become. His pointed yet meaningless nods, the measured slowness of his movements, the eyes that watched the world as if through a supernal veil, his impermeable "logic"—Jacobi couldn't sort it all out, he couldn't decide whether these affectations were conscious theatrics or not. The apparent clues to Michael's state of being and mind, rather than converging to a pattern, fell apart to leave him toying with fragments in a patternless wasteland. Michael seemed to have cultured the ability to take the conversation on a bend that only he could follow. When the road ran straight ahead, he would jump the ditch, charge through bracken and underbrush, and end up overlooking a sheer drop into a bottomless ravine. Some of their discussions reminded Jacobi of a cartoon he'd seen in *The New Yorker* where two characters passed through complex, different, nearly impenetrable mazes to confront one another on different levels, one staring at the other's kneecaps and the second not even conscious of the first's existence.

When he would plead with his friend, "Jesus, man, tell it to me straight," Michael would shrug and shake his head as if he didn't really care how much Jacobi understood. Once he answered, "If I ramble, it's because the world rambles. Don't you see? Each one of us can only be whole when the world is no longer in bits and pieces."

Thus Michael persisted in remaining an exasperating puzzle even after hours of talk...and hours of talk there were. The poet was sick, but by no means was he silent. His taciturnity had become a thing of the past and he was now more didactic than ever. Most of the time Jacobi couldn't shut him up. His opinions were endless and he would speak with positive assurance concerning things for which he had little or no evidence. When Jacobi called him on such points, Michael would stare directly into his eyes and simply say, "Believe me, I know."

It wasn't so much that all of the acid he had taken had changed Michael's views. He still insisted that sex was "a superstructure built upon the reproductive urge." Yet now, he not only thought this way, but had created a hundred extensions, examples and analogies derived from this belief that both reinforced it and resulted in his own personal superstructure of complex dogmas. Such a system, linked with Michael's native intransigence, made communication with him both frustrating and explosive. He seemed the most lucid to Jacobi when he wasn't rapping away on acid or metaphysics or himself, but his discussions inevitably dovetailed into one of these subjects or a conglomerate of all three. Even when their talk held to other topics, the two of them found little about which they could still agree. Of course the subject of Mulligan came up.

"A clown?" shouted Michael, "sure he's a clown, an evil clown, a sick clown!"

"No," Jacobi argued, "it's just that he makes things happen, maybe faster than they should sometimes, but the seeds are already there. He's just an expert at making the seeds sprout. It's like having a green thumb with people."

"Green thumb, bullshit! Tell me something? He fucked your woman for you, didn't he?"

"What if he did?"

"What if he did?" Michael repeated incredulously. "He's got you so sucked in on his trip you can't see up and down anymore. And you know what that trip is? Mulligan's hung up on playing the god game. It's as simple as that. He digs and pulls people apart and then uses the pieces to manipulate them. It's sort of like psychic blackmail. No, not really, nothing that specific, but after you've been around him awhile you start to feel his power dragging you down like a magnet onto his level. Sure, he's magnetic. That's how he can do it. He gets you so you're dependent on reflecting his light, so you need his approval and look up to him. And it's all calculated. Calculated and malicious. A malicious clown, that's a good label for him."

Jacobi didn't need any labels for Mulligan. He already had enough to populate a small town. He gave up, shrugging. "What does Mulligan matter anyway? He's three thousand miles away."

"Not really," Michael answered with one of his enigmatic nods.

"Well, let's not talk about him, anyway."

"Why not?"

"Because I'm sick of talking about Mulligan."

Jacobi turned away and looked out the window. Michael started in again, but he didn't listen. Outside, the bundled pedestrians and the tracks they laid upon the snow were barely visible in the glaucous twilight that now descended upon the winter city each evening before nightfall. They looked like black bugs, like a multitude of Gregors who were unaware of their own metamorphoses. They made Jacobi wonder if mankind were not an insect species already . If it weren't for the window glass it seemed one might reach down a thumb and squash them one by one.

It was toward the end of the second day of his stay that Jacobi found Michael's checkbook. He was cleaning the apartment. The filth of the place disgusted him and in the process made him realize that a bit of Christine compulsive cleanliness had rubbed off on him. The checkbook was buried beneath a dusty pile of debris near the closet, lying open so that the numbers, although they were written in Michael's pinched script, jumped out at him. Fourteen hundred dollars. Fourteen hundred dollars.

Fourteen hundred dollars!

Jacobi read it three times but the figure didn't change. He leafed back through the check stubs until he got close to the date when he had first arrived in New York. The total at that time had been nearly nineteen hundred. Jacobi walked over to the bed where Michael was dozing, after having talked all through the night. He slapped the checkbook down on his chest.

"You bastard," he announced.

Michael blinked and sat up. The checkbook slid onto his stomach and then into his open palm. He stared at it several seconds without comprehension before his eyes cleared.

"You bastard," Jacobi repeated, "you could have paid me for that acid anytime you wanted to."

Without looking up, Michael pressed his lips together frowning and began to play with the sore on his thumb. Then his jaw twisted askew, trembling. For a moment Jacobi thought he was going to freak, but by the time the trembling had ceased, Michael's face had become a taut but emotionless mask.

"I'm sick," he said, clipping his words. "Leave me alone. Don't hassle me with money now."

"No hassle," Jacobi told him. He took a pen off the desk and tossed it down next to the checkbook. "Just pay me what you owe me. If you're well enough to go to that party, you can manage to write a check."

Michael turned on his side in the bed and wrote hurriedly. He ripped the check from the book and handed it to Jacobi. "If you want to know, all I was trying to do was see how cheaply I could live. I would have paid you for your acid. Here, see how much I care about money."

The check was for fourteen hundred dollars.

"Damn you, Shawtry," Jacobi shouted, "I can't even cash a check this big." He ripped it in half.

Michael's eyes widened. "How big a one can you cash?"

"Forty dollars!" Jacobi was vehement. "Ten caps of acid for forty dollars!"

Michael wrote another check and gave it to him. "Your friend Mulligan would have taken a lot more than that."

"Sure," Jacobi answered, "so would my Uncle Max."

40

LINDA Bernstein, painter and sculptor, had a large cellar apartment just off Atlantic Street in Brooklyn Heights. It served as both her abode and studio, lair and workshop. Linda was a highly neurotic creature, yet a talented creature of overflowing and unbridled energy. By day she would tear about her studio, working in bits and pieces, moving from one partially finished creation to another. Her strong dark hands would knead the clay and slake it with water to begin the shaping of one image or the obliteration of another. In the space of hours, hunched friars became lithely toiling boatmen, busts of Attic beauty could develop surreal pustules and grotesquely haggard brows. Linda's broad olive moon face with its crag of a nose would set in leaden concentration as she examined a canvas prior to adding a dash of burnt umber or a wilting slash of vermilion, which would temporarily complete each ever-motile composition. This hopscotch manner of production greatly reduced her total output. Most of her works died unfinished, like the fruit of stunted trees. Yet Linda *was* an artist. The works she did complete were good enough to hang in galleries, good enough to sell, an accomplishment difficult to scoff at in the over-supplied world of modern art.

At night, Linda would scrub the paint and clay from her hands to apply a less artful and more static kind of paint upon her face. She would doff her loose painter's smock for a clinging dress that emphasized her ample figure, and atop this, if the weather demanded, a mothy brown rabbit fur coat that lent her a campy Thirties look. She would then sally forth to sundry parts of the city of her birth to draw inspiration for her further creations, which consequently ranged from rectilinear Mondrian-like abstracts, the cityscape, to interpretive portraits of pure and deadly naturalism, like her painting of Michael.

Many of her evenings out were spent in Village cafes where Linda was already notorious among various minor constellations of writers, painters, actors, dancers, talkers and would-bes. The cafes were where she had come upon most of the men in her life, or rather boys, since she preferred them young, agile and guileless. Linda would sit erect amid the smoke and laughter, a cigarette, usually unlit, slanting downward from her full mouth, long nails tucked in the balls of her fists, legs crossed and swinging, amber eyes bristling with mock innocence. Or sometimes she would draw a small ivory comb from her pocket and run it again and again through her thick brown hair as she talked. No doubt there was a certain demanding sensuality in her dark fleshiness that she had learned to play to advantage over the years, and which accounted for the quantity of her conquests. Still, she never had affairs so much as encounters, lasting only a few days or weeks, which she referred to with both affection and affectation as her "petite trysts." For her, men were first and foremost sources of energy to be funneled back into her work. She was like a battery whose voltage runs down without constant recharging, but if the connection were more than brief the plates could become hopelessly buckled. Her stormy three-month affair with Jacobi had been one of her few involvements, a rare mistake when she had become unwittingly enamored in the process of enamoring.

In bed, Linda liked to take charge. There was no humor in her sex, no play, and she expected the same earnest endeavor from her partners. One of her recurrent "trysts" had once remarked that sleeping with her was equivalent to climbing Everest twice in one night. The remark had later been related to Linda, who had received it with blithe nonchalance. But that particular climber had no further attempts at the ascent, even of the lower slopes.

Running a close third in Linda's psyche to her roles as artist and gadabout was that of hostess. Her parties were rapidly becoming as notorious as she was—stumbling orgiastic potpourris that could degenerate into brawls or more often potted seances at which Linda would prancingly officiate. Although he seldom attended, Michael invariably received an invitation to these affairs. He was a touch too thin even for Linda's tastes, and certainly not agile, yet she had been after him for some time. His sanctity, his unavailability, seemed the principal drawing cards. Michael's celibacy was something of a puzzle to amateur Village sexologists. My God, Linda thought, he might even be a virgin. She was willing to admit, at least to herself, that she found this possibility exciting.

Her attempts at seducing Michael had become most intense during the period when she had done his portrait. In fact, seduction had been instrumental in prompting the undertaking of the project. One day she had turned up at his apartment with easel, paints and canvas, insisting that he pose for her. Michael's ego was flattered enough so that her request had been granted, but of course her sexual aggressiveness only served to frighten him off. Once, after one of their sessions when they had gotten stoned together, she managed to corner him for a few unrequited embraces. This incident prompted Michael to get a photographer friend to take a photo so that Linda might complete the painting *in absentia.*

Jacobi and Michael got underway late for Linda's party. Michael held them up, dressing slowly with exaggerated invalid precaution, as if the wrong movement might send him collapsing back to his sick bed. He felt somewhat lost without his perennial black and white apparel. In place, he chose a pair of blue jeans, still dark and stiff with the newness of too few wearings and washings, and a brilliant red flannel shirt that accentuated his paleness, his pink lips and flushed cheeks. And atop these, the overcoat he had stolen at the hospital.

By the time they reached the party it was already going full tilt. They heard its booming nearly a block before they reached it. When they opened the door to Linda's cellar they were struck by a solid sheet of noise and heat that immediately enveloped them and yanked them onward into the murky, jam-packed swirling of the place. The atmosphere was so hot, so liquid, so dark, that Jacobi expected to see a thatch of hair springing up around the doorway.

On the stereo The Beatles were blasting it out, lungs about to burst in ecstatic falsetto. *Help* had opened in New York that summer and no one could get enough of their unabashed love and laughter.

To make room for the dancing, Linda's works in progress, the damp paintings and the mounds of clay on their swiveling wooden bases, had been clumped to one corner of the room and draped with a translucent plastic tarp. They now seemed to watch on with diligent though powerless disapproval as a disjointed array of arms, legs, and bodies twisted and shook in the space of their former domain. There was nothing they could do. On this night their mistress had deserted them. Even the oil and turpentine stink with which they normally ruled the air had been overcome by the musky incense Linda had peppered all about the apartment, glowing in dull orange dots on ceilings and walls like the spaced out stars of an expiring universe.

Somehow Linda, hostess *extraordinaire*, managed to spot the newcomers and made her way toward them through the crush.

"Michael!" she shouted. "David!"

She landed upon Jacobi with a liquid sisterly kiss and an embrace, jostling him against the bodies behind. "It's good to see you! I didn't even known you were in town. I like the beard! And Michael, how have you been, it's been too long." Wine had been flowing freely for several hours and she was well bombed in her own stalely way. "Come into the bedroom. Let me take your coats."

They followed her, tracking through the human maze toward the lighted bedroom door.

To Jacobi, after the snow outside, after Michael's chill company and the chill of his last month in Ithaca, the heat of the place seemed luxurious. As they made their inching progress toward the bedroom, patches of bare female flesh flashed at him, eyes drew his own. Possibilities abounded, and a dark eroticism suddenly kindled his awareness like an intoxication to match the fire of the room. At the same time, for Michael, the room seemed suffocating, a choking claustrophobic swirl. He drew in his limbs to avoid contact with the bodies around him, but the press merely flowed into the empty spaces and against him like water.

What was he doing here anyway, Michael asked himself. Why had he come? He knew what Linda's parties were. How could he mix and mingle with these mostly unknown and uniformly unknowing people? He couldn't dance. His consciousness couldn't blend with the abandon of that raucous music nor did he want it to. In his reemergence and rebirth was he still the same Michael, with the same sad inadequacies as in his past life?

Once within the relative freedom of the lighted bedroom, he began to relax and breathe more freely. The party had spilled over here and several groups had congregated, talkers more like himself, yet there was still space to move around.

Linda took their coats and added them to the hillock already on the bed. Jacobi watched her, thinking that she hadn't changed very much. She was still overweight, still full with a sexual overripeness. She turned toward him, smiling, aglow with the wine. "Well, how's the track star?" she asked.

"He's still running, I guess," Jacobi answered evasively. "Still jumping hurdles." He glanced around the room. It was a nice apartment and well furnished. "Daddy's been doing all right by you," he said, feeling old hostilities rising up in him again.

Linda laughed. "What do you mean 'Daddy'? Haven't you heard, David? I'm a success. I paid for this entire place all by myself."

Let's not start all over again with a lie, Jacobi almost said, before he realized that he didn't want to start anything over again, before he thought that maybe it wasn't a lie.

Just then the mound of coats upon the bed began to shift and topple. Linda moved quickly to catch the slide, simultaneously crying out. "Damn you, Ory!"

A thin male arm and a tousled mass of sandy hair emerged from beneath the covers near the top of the bed. Momentarily, as Linda hoisted the pile of coats upright, a naked freckled boy followed, blinking his eyes. He couldn't have been over seventeen.

"Michael Shawtry, David Jacobi," Linda said, "meet Ory Wadell. He followed me home last night and this morning I couldn't get rid of him," she added with chagrin. "We were both pretty stoned and he says he can't remember were he put his clothes."

Jacobi knew what "followed me home" meant. Yeah, he thought, tied to her apron strings.

Ory complied with the introduction by standing and offering his hand. "Glad to meet you," he mumbled. Michael took it first and then Jacobi. It was the first time Jacobi had ever shaken hands with someone who didn't have any clothes on. The act seemed completely out of place.

As their hands parted Ory glanced down. Jacobi followed the youth's eyes across his bare, hairless chest and belly. Ory's cock was nodding upward in a lazy erection.

"Excuse me," Ory said. "I have to take a piss." He stumbled past them toward the bathroom. Linda shook her head in exasperation. At the same time she couldn't help but stare at Ory's retreating figure speculatively. Jacobi laughed out loud. Same old Linda, he thought again.

"Don't!" Linda told him. "Whatever you're thinking, David, just don't say it."

If the aspiration of such a party is abandonment, if the goal is pandemonium, then Linda's party was an unqualified success. Jacobi gravitated toward the dark and the dancing, at first with Linda, until he managed to lose her among the pack in the time between the changing of records, and then with whatever women he found available, most of whom were both younger and prettier than Linda. It had been so long since he had really danced that it felt wonderful to just let his body move to the hard beat of the music and the rhythms of another body. He sensed the fire of the place catching within him, melting off the final traces of Ithaca's frost. He drank the wine. Linda might have been "making it" with money to burn, but her taste hadn't improved any on that count. Although she had poured it into nicer bottles, unlabeled decanters, it was still cheap red burgundy. Of course, after a few glasses it began to taste passable, and once one had consumed enough, it seemed downright delicious. It didn't take Jacobi long to elevate its flavor to an acceptable standard. Wine, women, and song, he thought. If he had come to Manhattan to betray Tina, to find a different woman, than tonight seemed the likely time. A number of newly-formed couplings had already retreated out the front door while further guests were still arriving.

It wouldn't really be a betrayal, Jacobi told himself. There had never been any explicit oaths of fidelity to one another, and in any case, Tina had already slept with Mulligan. Viewing the whole thing with a sportsman's sense, she was one up on him. And who knew what she might not be doing at the Cape that very moment? Yet the idea of sleeping with another woman still held the taint of a kind of betrayal for him. In spite of his rational expositions of free love and manners for a new age, he had yet to dispel the mores of his own.

As the wine took over his being, Jacobi began thinking less and acting more, going after one woman after another. Yet in his lessening moments of reflection, during the spots of surfacing sobriety in his half-drunkenness, he couldn't help but compare this party with the last party he and Michael had attended, the party where he had met Christine. That first party had established and preserved a middle ground of jostling repartee and appearance, a bohemian salon where wit was the sole cutting edge and nothing intense could really transpire. The atmosphere of this party was wilder, less stylized and more potent. This party was for dropping appearances and being whatever one felt like being that particular night, for losing oneself in the music, the wine, and one another.

To Michael, left behind with the talkers in the bedroom, the contrast was less striking. He was doing the same thing he had done at that other party, or at least attempting to do it. He was moving from group to group, eavesdropping on one conversation after another, searching for the proper jibes to put down each speaker and elevate himself. Only it wasn't the same as it had once been. He wasn't in good form for this sort of play. He was feeling the kind of clear-headed emptiness, the kind of distance from reality, that can only be arrived at through a long illness overcome. His comments were slow in forming within his mind, and even once he did summon an appropriately acid putdown, it didn't seem worth the trouble to deliver. The conversations ranged from politics to religion, from dope, of which there seemed to be a shortage, to just plain gossip. Michael listened and felt a despair for his fellow man budding within him. The puerility of the forces at play actually made him feel a bit venerable. He had lost so much since his peaks with the acid, but even now, in his present relatively benighted state, he felt supraconscious and aware compared to the most of these people. If he were Mulligan, he could have waded into the bullshit and out talked and out magnetized one and all. But whether, in truth, he was more aware or less aware than Mulligan, the fact remained that Michael Shawtry was not Dennis Mulligan.

Taking a deep breath, Michael plunged back into the other room, into the noisy crowd.

"Hello!" shouted a female voice close by his ear.

Michael started back. His eyes, still adjusting to the darkness, could only make out a dim white oval for her face, the slender white stalks of her bare arms.

"Do I know you?" Michael asked hesitantly, his words swallowed up by the music. The girl gave a drunken laugh and spun away from him.

He started looking for Jacobi but he was nowhere in sight. Someone headed for the door deposited a half-empty glass of wine in his hand and Michael began drinking. He felt a fine film of sweat break out all over his body, partly from the heat, partly from the psychological weight and pressure of the human wall milling about on all sides of him. He had to stay in motion or he felt himself forcibly moved by its movement. Then one of the dancers jostled him, splashing the wine down the front of his shirt and pants.

Well, here he was. He had reentered society, or at least a segment of it. But who was he? No longer the solipsist, no longer the megalomaniac, that was for sure. The societal structure had come down upon him hard enough and real enough to shatter those illusions for ever, and now it rankled deeply each time he recalled the impersonal injustice with which he had been manipulated. No longer the recluse, not completely, here he was at a party in the center of a crowd. No longer the proud celibate, he now felt human enough to admit that he had human needs, even those that he was inept at fulfilling. Michael felt different and yet the same, changed but not yet reborn. Back in the bedroom he could still have played the gadfly, railing at one group of speakers after another, pricking at the bubble of each structure he encountered. He could have done it, but it wasn't what he wanted to do. More than that he wanted to see a world made whole, unsegmented by the false structures and rules of society, a world where each person could be reborn free.

Suddenly Jacobi found him, a vinous dionysian Jacobi, hair awry, eyes enkindled, sweat-drenched face, a decanter of wine in one hand and his arm around a small large-breasted girl.

"Hey, man, where have you been?" Jacobi asked, refilling Michael's glass. "What have you been doing? Great party, huh?" Without waiting for a reply he pulled the girl forward and close by his side. Her nose was retroussé above slight bucked teeth. A dark complexion belied the blondness of her hair. "Michael...meet Beverly. She's Linda's cousin," Jacobi laughed, "but fortunately without family resemblance."

"Hello," Michael said.

Beverly smiled and nodded vaguely in his direction. Her eyes were elsewhere, watching the room.

Jacobi leaned forward, peering at Michael. "Hey, man, you're sober. What's the matter with you, anyway? You don't seem to be having much of a time. You're the one that was so hot to come to this party?"

"Things aren't quite the way I expected them to be," Michael answered.

"That's because you're straight," Jacobi told him. "Look at this place." He let go of Beverly and swept his open palm outward to present the room and its occupants. Michael noticed that at this stage of the proceedings several couples, taking advantage of the heat and darkness, had stripped bare to the waist. "Everybody except you is stoned and trying to get totally bashed," Jacobi went on. "I'd be bored too if I wasn't drunk. Here! Drink. Drink!" He filled Michael's glass still further, spilling a good deal of wine in the process.

"Maybe you're right," Michael gave in easily, out of character, taking a large swallow of the burgundy and crinkling up his nose in displeasure at the sour aftertaste.

The music started again and the floor exploded in chain reaction as one couple after another took up the dancing. It was

The Stones with "Satisfaction." Jacobi leaned closer, to shout thickly in Michael's ear and shove the sloshing wine bottle into his free hand. "Get drunk. Get yourself laid. That's what I'm going to do and I suggest you do the same. Forget about tomorrow, that's what parties are for...this party, anyway!" Then he turned away so as not to lose Beverly, who was already moving her full, short body jerkily to the demanding beat.

Michael resumed the train of thought that Jacobi had interrupted. Structures, he thought, the world was full of structures, artificial constructs limiting one's actions. This party had its structure, too. Jacobi was already a helpless pawn charging forward within it. Get drunk. Get laid. Wake up on the morrow with a splitting head, a jumbled remembrance and an excuse for whatever had transpired. That wasn't for Michael. If he was to have sex it would have to be cleaner, clearer, more individual than the gross undifferentiated coition the party offered. That meant a woman or a man—yes, a man—with whom he could relate on other than a drunken and physical level. If he were to get stoned it would be to heighten his awareness rather than to deaden it. That meant grass or acid, not alcohol.

Michael skirted the edge of the dancing, making his way toward the table that held the wine and food so he could get rid of the decanter. One of his hands brushed against a bare sweating back and he felt a short, sweet thrill with the unfamiliar sensation of the contact. Sweat was beading his own body beneath the thick red flannel shirt. It was hard to believe that with the mercury well below freezing outside that this Hades-like atmosphere could persist within. Michael was tempted to shed his shirt, to join and revel in the general abandon. He remembered that he had flesh to give, never-given flesh, unfulfilled flesh. But he also understood that urge was the force of the party bending him to its structure, trying to induce him to run its maze like the other human mice. He refused. The integrity of his individuality was the one thing he still had, and regardless of the price or the reward, it was one thing he would never relinquish.

By the time he deposited the wine on the table his old claustrophobia was clambering up within him again, a fear-mad monkey grasping and pulling at the pinions of his reason. With the sleeve of his red shirt Michael wiped the sweat from his cheeks and forehead. If he'd had a handkerchief he would have mopped his neck and collarbone, but as it was, he had to tolerate the itching moisture gathered there. He looked back toward the lighted bedroom door. From where he stood it seemed to lie at an irretrievable distance. Leaning his weight back against a bare patch of wall, Michael closed his eyes. He breathed deeply and evenly, trying to center his consciousness within himself and shut off the sounds of the room. He still had his yoga. He was out of practice, but that could be remedied. It would be remedied, he told himself.

The heat continued to beat against him, following him in his retreat, now become a generalized heat disassociated from the party. He recalled the last time he had felt such warmth, that night ages past when he had destroyed a part of the old Michael, when he had built and lit the pyre that had consumed his poetry. He recalled the tempting vision of himself as incendiary and his present being soared up like the poem-fire to seize and embrace that vision. Was this the nature of the rebirth he sought?

His offhand words to Jacobi now returned to him with the literal and pragmatic impact of their meaning. *Each one of us can only be whole when the world is no longer in bits and pieces.* Michael now saw that his own wholeness, his rebirth, hung on the death and rebirth of a world of which he was inseparably a part. He had attempted to deny that inseparability and the end had been disaster. Until the world became one, unfragmented by the structures that man had built against himself to dam the beauty, the power and the hazard of his natural self, Michael could never be complete. Until then his rebirth could only be—must be!—a bandit rebirth, as an incendiary, an apostate, standing outside of structures and destroying them one by one. Not through force, he alone couldn't accomplish that, but by means of his intellect and his will, by finding and pulling the proper pin. Every structure had its weaknesses, its key points of vulnerability that could be used to bring it toppling down. The acid had shown him that.

With eyes remaining closed, his consciousness successfully oblivious to his surroundings, Michael allowed this glimpse of his projected identity to settle and combine with the unchanged ingredients of his self. Michael Shawtry, incendiary. Michael Shawtry, iconoclast. Michael Shawtry, poet. He savored the mix and it seemed apropos. He wouldn't be the first to try to take on the world singlehandedly. If historical precedent indicated the task was impossible, it also showed the calling to be a worthy one. And wasn't he already an outlaw, a wanted man? He had never faced the charges against him for his run through the park, and there was also the question of the coat stolen from the hospital. Even such minor crimes perpetrated against the structures of a world he had now declared war upon him seemed to fill him with satisfaction. For the first time since childhood he thought covetously of his family's wealth, of his someday inheritance. If he survived long enough, he could really start some fires then. He might even finance an army of incendiaries. But until then...

Michael brought himself out of his withdrawal He opened his eyes and stood away from the wall, supporting his own weight. His body seemed filled with a new heaviness, stronger and surer, an alien grace that had always been foreign to his limbs. The party was rolling and roiling on all about him. The structure of the party lay spread before him. It was as good a time and place as any to begin living with purpose once again.

The proper pin, he thought, the proper pin...

Back on the dance floor, Jacobi's state of consciousness was less exalted than Michael's. Somewhere along the line he had lost Beverly, about the same time he had lost his shirt and shoes. That shouldn't have bothered him because he had found Marilyn...or was it Marilee? Only Marilyn/Marilee was tall and thin and a real blonde, and naturally reminded him of Christine.

Oh, Tina, he moaned inwardly, how can I betray you with a facsimile?

Jacobi was royally drunk, sickeningly drunk, drunker than he had been in years, ever since the advent of grass in his life, and yes, drunk on the very worst possible: cheap red wine. The dancing was beginning to get to him. The records were repeating themselves, although still bombarding the room with the energy that kept things going. An empty wine bottle was rolling and being knocked around the dance floor, and though people kept stubbing their toes on it, Jacobi twice, nobody bothered to pick it up. He was feeling exhausted and there was an on-and-off stitch dancing in his right side. Marilyn/Marilee must have come late to the party or been strung out on amphetamines because she just kept rocking away like a bop machine. On top of it all, Jacobi thought, she was a prim bitch, a cold bitch just like Tina could be. She had on a long-sleeved dress and she hadn't even shed her shoes and stockings in the face of the heat. In the lapses of music between cuts she let Jacobi embrace her, but her lips remained dry, tight as a miser's purse. Seduction seemed far off and pointless, but his drunken lust kept driving him on.

One moment he would be full with that lust, the next moment disgusted with himself, and the next feeling maudlin or chuckling unexplainably. Here he was, former track star, and he couldn't even keep up with a wired overgrown teeny bopper. It was funny and pathetic and absurd. But damn it all to hell anyway, he thought, if he didn't pass out first he still wanted to get laid, be it with Cousin Beverly, Marilyn/Marilee or another. At this stage of the game, taste was a bygone consideration. Even Linda would have fit the bill.

It was already past midnight. The fervor of the party had abated somewhat, but the place was just as crowded. In the darkness of the main room the dancers continued to reign. The few available chairs had been seized upon early in the evening and most of their occupants remained firmly entrenched. For those standing it was only possible to position oneself momentarily, drink in one hand and cigarette in the other, before being forced to move by an elbow in the kidneys or a foot tromping upon one's own, except for those already anesthetized enough by the booze to ignore such discomforts.

In the bedroom the conversations had deadlocked. They had been repeating themselves for longer than the records. The chief participants had all talked too long and too much, but they were so wound up and keyed on talk that they couldn't stop now. The pile of coats had again toppled onto the floor, this time without rescue. Beneath the covers, Ory Wadell had cornered his own bottle of wine, and curled upon his side was letting the liquid seep slowly and steadily into his open mouth. Except for the fact that Linda, his two-day paramour and current keeper, had ignored him for several hours, he was feeling very mellow in his nakedness.

Linda was in the living room, well pleased with the continuing raucous success of the evening. She had been afraid that the dope shortage might dampen things, but the wine and the music and the volume of people had proved sufficient. Her art was a success and her party was a success and several men had been pursuing her throughout the evening. There wasn't much else she could ask for, except maybe a wee joint to cut all the wine she had been drinking. Due to the dancing the wine seemed to be oozing out of her pores as quickly as she consumed it. Her damp dress clung to her body, revealing her braless figure completely. She was temporarily exhausted, waiting for a second wind. By sheer force and weight she had managed to wedge her butt onto the couch between too relatively straight-looking men whom she hadn't invited to the party and didn't recognize. The fit was too tight to lean back and the two men kept carrying on a conversation behind her head concerning the relative physical merits of the various women on the dance floor. She found their vicarious satisfactions boring and a bit pathetic. Her own attention was centered on her former lover, David Jacobi, who was trying to keep up with her friend, Marilyn. That she found funny, because she knew he was wasting his time. Marilyn was a first-class tease and mostly a lesbian to boot. Linda had her own plans for Jacobi before the night was over.

Suddenly, as Linda watched, one of the stereo speakers mounted high on the wall began spitting loud blasts of static over the music. Then the speaker shorted out...completely dead. The dancers in that area of the floor began to slow their movement, several couples stopping altogether. Linda started to stand up but a dancer stepping backward knocked her into a bony lap and one of the vicarious males became actual as his paws closed about her breasts. Near the center of the floor, midway between the speakers, Jacobi shook his head, drunk enough to be thinking that the hearing in his right ear was going out on him. Marilyn bopped on. Ory, insulated and oblivious, beneath a sheet, two blankets and a quilt, sipped his wine. Michael Shawtry, slender as a shadow, invisible as a shadow in the dark, glided from cut speaker wire to uncut, a short wooden-handled kitchen knife held so the flash of its blade was shielded between his sleeve and the body of his shirt.

The second speaker followed its mate, static and sudden death. The dancing broke up and the room milled, voices rising in confusion. "Where's the music...whatsa matter...someone put another record on...there is a record, but there's no sound." All at once a number of people headed for the turntable to uncover the reason for the trouble. Linda, who had managed to disentangle herself with a solid elbow blow, was foremost among them. The press around the table holding the amplifier and turntable thickened. The table rocked against the wall as people pushed forward bumping into it. "...ouch!...stop shoving!...well, he shoved me...damn it, somebody give me some room to move..." To Jacobi the room seemed darker without the music, which made perfect sense to him at the moment. Marilyn disappeared as he was buffeted forward by the crowd. He stretched his arms out to maintain his balance and moved on, trapped in a wobbly self-parody of his own dancing.

As the throng about the table pulsed inward the crush became intolerable for a few. They tried to force their way free, charging outward at the expense of whomever or whatever they encountered. Curses exploded in the dank air. A fist flew wildly. Another connected. The pulse reversed itself. Panic. Stampede. Arms and legs tangling in awkward haste. A woman's hoarse cry set off a crescendo of hysterical shrieking. A lamp toppled. A plaster bust toppled and crashed. Jacobi toppled backwards onto the floor by the couch, curling onto his side to protect his vital organs from a choppy torrent of spiked heels and heavy boots. A girl's bare calf brushed against his cheek. Someone kicked the empty wine bottle against his shinbone, a solid blow but it didn't even seem to hurt. Linda, who had made it to the stereo, stood beating her fists against her damp thighs and screaming, "Stop it! Stop it! Everybody stop!"

Then some genius-idiot turned on the overhead lights, which halted the stampede and silenced the shrieking, but oh God, a total of ten thousand blinding fluorescent watts that Linda had installed so that even on the grayest of days her studio could be daylight bright for painting. Beneath their glare the entire assemblage stood frozen, shoulder to shoulder, mute, fixed in stillness by the shock of the sudden flash. A few thought momentarily that the end had come for sure, World War Last, that the Bomb had finally been dropped and the wave of light would be followed by intense heat and the building crashing down around them. Every inch of bare flesh, each pore, each hair, each mole, each grain of caked make-up or eyeshadow, every wrinkle, stood out painfully visible in untempered, uncompromising reality. Scattered about on the floor lay crushed cigarette butts, chips of plaster, pieces of cheese, crumpled paper cups, spilt wine, broken potato chips and chunks of French bread. A few of the topless women regained enough propriety to cover their bare nipples with their bare arms. The stereo spun on soundlessly. Linda, as dumbstruck as the rest, groaned out loud. Within a month she would complete a painting of the scene from memory and sell it for eight hundred dollars. Jacobi, still upon the floor, with stone drunk clarity and the help of ten thousand watts was counting the air bubbles in a piece of French bread. The bread was at least two feet away from him, but he could make out each of the bubbles perfectly. Then he recognized Marilyn/Marilee's svelte stockinged legs standing close by. He ceased his counting and began inching his way toward them across the floor. The silence of the place was deafening.

The back door of the apartment, slamming shut sharply as the culprit made good his escape, broke that silence. Fifty heads snapped in unison at the sound. The spell was broken, too. People began moving again, with eyes averted from one another. Linda was lifting the needle off the record.

"Turn off those damn lights," someone pleaded.

Then the laughter began, peeling out at them, curling about them, crazy high-pitched laughter, hyena laughter. Standing in the bedroom doorway, more naked than any, but unabashedly, was Ory Wadell, drunk as a loon, legs spread and cock nodding, freckled arm outstretched and finger pointing at one and all as his body shook with wave after wave of convulsive laughter.

Linda started through the crowd after him, infuriated, pulling and pushing people out of her way. Ory laughed on. Jacobi inched on. Outside the building, Michael found the metal box containing the electrical switches. As Linda closed in upon Ory, as Jacobi attained his goal and his teeth closed upon Marilyn's ankle, the lights throughout the entire apartment went out.

The party was over, dissolving in bits and pieces. People found their coats by candlelight until Linda braved the cold in her rabbit coat and turned the electricity back on. Singly, in pairs and in groups, the participants returned to their respective homes, each a bit sobered and disoriented by the way the evening had ended. Only Jacobi remained to spend the night and get laid. A dry lugubrious fuck punctuated by Linda's heavy moaning.

41

Jacobi awoke to face the crapulous dawn, his mouth cloth dry and head hangover heavy. The apartment was still in a mess from the party. If anything, it looked worse by daylight.

Linda was standing nude and painting. Her body hadn't changed any more than she had, Jacobi thought, nor her penchant for flaunting it. When they'd been together before, Jacobi's eyes had often tried to avoid the faults in her nakedness so they wouldn't turn him off—the swell of fat at her hips, the lines on the backs of her thighs, the sagging weight of her breasts, the thorny oblong veldt of her pubic hair, thick as a rain forest, already oversized and giving the impression it might continue to advance, racing up her belly and down her thighs until she was hairy as an ape. At other times, those very faults had turned him on, imperfections defining her individuality and making her humanly desirable. It all depended on where you were sitting, Jacobi thought, on what set of lenses your current reality had clapped upon your head. Linda could appear as a plump and spreading Jewish mother, or she could be the Earth Mother incarnate, fleshy, dark and sensual. Now, at this dot in time, he could only compare the squat solidity of her nudeness to Christine's winsome and weightless grace. In his head danced Tina, sprite and water nymph. Before him stood Linda, the corn meal squaw. He shut his eyes and opened them again.

"Why don't you put some clothes on," Jacobi told her.

She pivoted toward him, breasts swinging heavily. "I'm freer this way."

"You're an Amazon, that's what you are." He sat up on the edge of the couch—where he had retreated to sleep after their abbreviated encounter of the night before—and groaned deeply. Some one was dragging a dull rake around the inside of his skull.

"Amazon women have one of their breasts cut off so they can shoot a bow and arrow better," Linda recited from some book she'd read.

"You'd still have enough left." They were twice the size of Tina's, he thought.

Linda, back to dabbing at her canvas, laughed acridly. "Thanks, baby, but just because you had too much to drink last night, don't take it out on my hide."

Jacobi dressed and managed to negotiate the kitchen, carefully, so as not to set off the rake again. Coffee, toast, a cigarette. The stimulant-depressant effects of caffeine and nicotine fell like a loose slipcover across the motley raiment of his hangover. He was staring mindlessly at the crystalline structure of the snow built up against the basement window when he heard Linda enter the kitchen and come up behind him. She put her arms around his waist and her hands delved beneath his untucked shirt and upwards, warm hands rubbing his chest and belly. Her head nudged against his backbone, burrowing. His unwanted erection rose automatically, a willful divining rod on the track of water.

No, Jacobi argued with himself, not again. I'm not even drunk this time. No excuses.

"Davy?"

"Hmn," Jacobi grunted.

"Will you do something for me?"

"Hmmmn." Softer…slipping.

Her voice fell to an undertone. "Ory's still here. Would you get him to leave? I don't care how, but just get rid of him for me, Davy, please!" Her heads were kneading his flesh, her fingers grazing his nipples.

Jacobi extricated himself and turned to face her, holding her wrists. "Why, so I can take his place?"

She pulled back and out of his grip. "Look, David, nobody asked you to stay here last night." Ever so righteous.

"Nobody helped me to leave, either."

"What is that supposed to mean?"

"Nothing, Linda…nothing. It was a swell party, only as soon as I finish my coffee I'm heading back to Michael's. I'm not bucking for the job of handyman about the house, so don't ask me to perform any odd jobs. If you can castrate, you can expel."

"And what is *that* supposed to mean?" she shouted into his face.

"Just what I said…castrate." His head was throbbing. "Ory is where he's at because that's what you are, a castrator."

"No, David, no! That's your trip!" She was raging, the maenad in her unleashed. "If you felt castrated when we were together, it was your own doing, not mine. Who do you think you are, anyway? Supermale or something? No one's asking you to stay? I've had better lays from sixteen-year-old kids!"

"Yeah, horses and dogs, too, I bet," Jacobi countered jokingly in the face of her anger.

Linda swung wildly, catching him on the side of the head with the heel of her open palm. His vision blurred out momentarily as the rake became a full-sized thresher. He recovered in time to stop a second blow, to grab her wrists once more, spinning her body around until he had them pinned behind her back.

"You bastard, bastard! Let go of me, you dirty shit!" she screeched as he propelled her forcibly back into the living room. "You son of a bitch! Let me go! Let go!"

Ory appeared in the bedroom doorway, bug-eyed.

"Beat it," Jacobi barked at him.

He dropped like a gopher back into his hole.

"Let go...you...shit." Her voice had broken. "David, let me go..." She was crying now, passive, her body limp and stumbling. Jacobi released her and she turned to fall against his chest, sobbing convulsively. There was nothing he could do but put his arms around her. Her bare flesh seemed very large beneath his hands. Although he hated to admit it, very...impressive.

This was a drama they had played before, with different words and actions but always the same denouement. The love-making, the bitter honest joking, the argument, the fight, the physical violence, the tears and then, once more, to bed. Only this time, when Jacobi felt Linda's hand moving between his legs, he broke the cycle. Pushing her away, gently and wordlessly, he kissed her wet cheeks, grabbed his coat up off the floor, and without finishing his coffee or tucking in his shirt, he beat a hasty and final retreat out the door.

After several seconds, Ory came out of the bedroom again. With the debris of the party scattered all about them, he and Linda stood staring at one another's nakedness.

"I have to find another place to live. This building's coming down in a few months. It's been condemned."

Jacobi was getting together the few belongings he'd brought with him and loosely repacking them in the bottom of the duffel bag. He was going back to Ithaca, back to Christine. "What are you going to do?" he asked Michael.

Michael thought for a moment. "Well, I guess I'll fix myself some dinner and then go for a walk in the snow."

"Shit," Jacobi mumbled, half under his breath. "If you want to talk about it, talk. Otherwise, forget it."

Michael eyed Jacobi as he slipped on a thick fur-lined coat, a coat that Christine had no doubt paid for. "I'm not sure what I'm going to do," Michael said. "I've been thinking I might go out to sunny California for a change of climate. I'm getting awfully sick of the clouds day after day." The view from the window gave testimony to his complaint.

"You could look up Mulligan," Jacobi suggested. "He'd be glad to put you up for awhile until you could find a place."

"Great, just what I need, someone who can really fuck my head around."

Jacobi shrugged it off. "Hey, I've been meaning to ask you. What have you been doing about the draft since you dropped out of school?"

"The draft?" Michael mouthed the word questioningly, as if he were tasting an unfamiliar fruit.

"Yeah, the draft. You know...Uncle Sam, the army? In case you haven't heard, everyone's expected to do his part. There's a war going on in Southeast Asia and the government is calling on able-bodied young fodder like you and me to travel across the ocean and try to slaughter some gooks for them."

"I don't think they'll call on me," Michael said. "I never registered for the draft."

Jacobi looked at him sharply, but he could no longer even summon the register of disbelief regarding anything Michael might come up with. He finished buttoning his coat.

"Well, guess I'll be shoving off."

Michael ran his forefinger gingerly over the sore on his thumb. "I don't suppose you've changed your mind about giving me some acid," he asked.

Jacobi wouldn't look at him. "No," he answered, shaking his head vigorously so that his long hair rode up slantwise, bending against the collar of his coat.

"Hmmn," Michael nodded slowly. "I didn't think so." Then after a pause. "Wait a minute. Let me get my coat on and I'll come down and see you off."

Outside, the cold was waiting for both of them. They walked the several blocks to the car rapidly, in silence, step for step like soldiers on parade. Jacobi awkwardly manhandled the duffel bag over the front seats and into the back, then climbed into the driver's side. Michael was bent leaning forward to see into the car, his weight resting on one arm against the open curbside door. He was breathing heavily from the exertion of their walk. One could hear the congestion in his lungs. Jacobi looked at him, hesitated, and then spoke. "Look man, why don't you come to Ithaca for awhile and get your head straightened out? Get out of this fuckin' town. Come right now!"

Michael glanced up and down the nearly deserted street.

"Well..." With one hand he squeezed his coat tightly together around his neck and shoulders. "Let's see what it feels like." He climbed in next to Jacobi and pulled the door shut.

After several attempts the VW putted into action. Jacobi allowed it to warm up and then edged out onto the icy street.

"It'll be good for you," he began, building enthusiasm as he went on. "You know how Tina can cook. Her food will put some weight back on you. You'll get some new sense impressions out there, get out of these same old streets. It'll probably start you writing again. I've been writing myself and I'd like to see what you think of it. Look, we can all take acid together...with nobody around for miles to bother us. You'll see, it's different in the country..."

Michael listened. He thought of himself in Ithaca. He thought of Christine, of the three of them, of himself in bed with Jacobi and Christine. Given the past and more dope that was probably how it would end up. He thought of sweating endeavors to please one another carnally, of the emptiness after orgasm, of the ultimate tawdriness of it all. No, he concluded, it didn't feel right, it wasn't right, not at all. There were other things for him to do, far better things to do than that.

"No," he broke into Jacobi's monologue. "Me coming back with you isn't any kind of answer for either one of us. Let me off at the next corner by the newsstand. I want to buy some cigarettes."

Jacobi arched his brows, but said nothing—until he had stopped the car and Michael climbed out.

"Well...so long man, take it easy. Write and let me know how things are."

"Yeah, so long, you too."

As Jacobi drove off, Michael didn't go into the newsstand immediately. He stood in the snow watching the retreating car. Jacobi was able to make him out in the rearview mirror for several blocks before the buildings and the traffic closed about him.

42

JACOBI drove out of the wilderness of Manhattan and back into the wilderness of upstate New York, pushing the car to its limit, more than a mile a minute. Once he began thinking about where he was going and what he was doing, what he had been doing, his thoughts were moving a long sight faster than that. Within his mind he was way ahead of himself.

When he got back they would have it out once and for all, he thought, not with acid or grass, not with simile and metaphor and coyly whispered "I love you"s, not within the boundaries of the bed, but with talk and more talk until they both understood what they wanted for themselves, what they wanted from each other, and what they were willing to give. Then they could either make a real commitment or dash what little commitment they had to the ground.

He thought back sadly on their last sex together, a pale reflection of the beginning, its intensity funneled and strained through a hundred different mirrors of the self and other self, weakened and split by rays refracted purposely and senselessly away from one another. They had been apart for three weeks now. Time and space had given him a new perspective on their interactions. Her absence had renewed the intensity of his feelings. He had just been with another woman. So what? It wasn't another woman he'd wanted, but proof of his freedom, his independence. Now he had that proof only to discover that freedom wasn't what he wanted either, only to discover that now he missed her more than he'd thought possible. Christine was ten years older than him. She had been with more men than he'd been with women. She had more money. More money? Hell, admit it, by his standards she was filthy rich. She was not a doper. Acid scared her more than it intrigued her. She wasn't ready to lay herself that bare and maybe she never would be. So what? He couldn't deny any of it. But he could try accepting it. He could try seeing her for what she was, loving her for what she was, rather than what he thought he could make of her. He could change himself as well as asking her to change.

Even with the pedal jammed to the floor the car didn't eat the miles fast enough for him. The volume of his thoughts proved insufficient to fill the hours of the drive. He backtracked, repeated himself, with the absence of an outlet for his new resolutions he became more and more keyed. Sexual images of the scene that would follow their rapprochement began piling up at the borders of his awareness. He refused to admit them. Sex had too often been another obstacle, another mirror, keeping him from the real Christine. By the time he barreled through Ithaca and past and reached their house, the car had become a prison and he felt as if he were about to explode from nervous energy.

He burst free from that prison and headed for the porch at a running gait through the snow, but he slowed and stopped dead in his tracks before he reached the front steps. Somehow he sensed the emptiness of the place even before it proved itself as a reality. When he turned his key in the lock and entered the hall, only silence greeted him. He found his own note still propped on the telephone table where he had left it. His slightly mocking tone of two weeks earlier now mocked him.

> Dec. 24
>
> My Dear and Dearest Tina,
>
> Without the gift of you august presence, Ithaca has become a trial rather than a sport. I am spoiling in the juices of my own solitude.
>
> I've decided to go back to Manhattan for awhile. I'll be at Michael's place.
>
> Be good. See you next year.
>
> Love, —D.

The rooms were cold with the emptiness of a house long without the warmth of human habitation. Still, he searched frantically from room to room, not really fooling himself, but hoping for a sign that she had been there and left, had run to Manhattan to find him or was merely out shopping. There was no sign. The flowers on the mantle were the same dead flowers with their heads drooping on their stalks, touching the mirror. They looked like a vase full of unwashed paintbrushes dried beyond repair. In the kitchen, mold had formed on the unwashed dishes he'd left in the sink. The food in the refrigerator was rotting: moldy cheese, mildewed pudding, brown lettuce and carrots of wilting rubber. As if in revenge for its lengthy exile, dust had begun collecting everywhere throughout the house, on the records, the bookshelves, the table tops, clinging to the vertical faces of the mirrors where it muted his features and softened the edges of his frantic image as he moved about. There was even a cobweb firmly rooted and assiduously hanging tendrils in one corner of the bedroom ceiling.

Jacobi found his usual easy chair in the living room and sat down, head in hands, to collect himself. This wasn't exactly the homecoming he had envisioned. He had hoped to find a woman who had been alone for nearly a week, each day expecting his return with increasing anticipation, a woman who had perhaps had time to reflect and search out some of the same conclusions he had during their separation. Instead, there was no woman, no one at all, only the chill unanswering walls with which to hold parley.

If she had been delayed at The Cape or in Boston she would have called to let him know, he thought, called again and again without answer because he had been absent, away in Manhattan playing nurse and profligate, courting his phantom freedom. He pictured her at the other end of the line as the phone rang on ominously in the empty house, a look of irritation and worry crinkling her features, the receiver raised close by her cheek, her slender throat, her thin downed forearm, the bell of the ear piece hidden within the straight falling locks of her hair. But what would she have done next: a telegram perhaps? Oh, what a fool he had been not to have demanded her address and phone number at the Cape before she'd left; only then, his dissatisfaction and the river of differences widening between them had stayed his tongue.

He was up from the chair and out the front door, still hanging open in the cold, striding along the snow-capped stones of the front walk to the edge of the highway. Their mail box stood like a lone sentinel by the roadside, overlooking the cracked pavement. Its metal hinges creaked painfully as he pulled it open. The box was stuffed full, the mail piled in reverse order from how it had been delivered, but what he sought lay at the very top. It had arrived that morning, beating him back to Ithaca by a few hours. A letter, not a telegram. He recognized her hand and the envelope of her pale blue stationery even before he picked it up. A thick letter, a veritable portmanteau full with dread and promise. He hurriedly scooped the rest of the mail into his hand and headed back up the walk.

Within the house, in his chair again, he flipped the pile over upon his knee and began going through it in chronological order, saving Christine's letter to the very last, attempting to suspend thought and anxiety—was he torturing himself or merely demonstrating his composure for the sake of his ego and the empty dust-filled rooms? Sandwiched here and there between the bills and junk mail, there were four other missives of significance, all addressed to him.

His letter of acceptance from Cornell University. He could register February 16th for the spring semester. Orientation activities would begin the following week.

A one page questionnaire from his Draft Board in Pasadena, which had been forwarded through his old Berkeley address. He had expected it sooner. They had finally figured out that he wasn't in school anymore and in essence were asking him what the hell he was doing.

A glossy picture postcard from Tina, dated December 25, Christmas day. The full import of the fact that she had left him alone on Christmas, without presents, without company or cheer, struck home for the first time. On one side of the card, a typical Keane portrait of three children, two girls and a boy, chosen in simulation of her own brood no doubt (only he had seen photographs of her children and he knew they were rich and pampered and lacking the sad desolation eyes of Keane's creations), and on the other side, in the even flowering of her practiced script, its style cramped a bit by the meager dimensions of the card:

Merry Christmas, David,

The way the children are sprouting up is truly amazing, particularly Leonard, Jr. It makes me feel like an old mother hen. They're so excited about Christmas, I can almost believe in it again myself. Melissa, the oldest, says that she wants to come visit with me in Ithaca. (Can you imagine that one, David!) You know,
I think they really do miss me.

Love, Tina

And last but not least, a message from the far-flung West, from the Golden State, postmarked Berkeley and bearing the single-word return address "Botticelli." Jacobi had sent two letters to Mulligan without response since his friend had returned to California. It was no surprise that Mulligan wasn't much of a letter writer—his concerns were always more immediate—and this wasn't a letter either, but a newspaper article raggedly torn from page three of the December 2nd issue of the *San Francisco Chronicle.* Across the back of the clipping Mulligan had scrawled: "I'm going down in history, Davy! Down, down, down!"

Drug Bust on Gate Span

Due to the astute eyes of a toll guard and the daring of a San Francisco police officer, two men and a woman were apprehended for marijuana possession yesterday in the middle of the Golden Gate Bridge.

Toll Officer John Pursey spotted the trio when they began walking across the bridge. "I knew something

> was wrong right away," said Pursey. "They were acting funny, laughing too much. Then I saw that they were all smoking something and passing it from hand to hand."
>
> Pursey quickly relayed his observations to San Francisco Police who dispatched a patrol car to the scene.
>
> According to Officer Richard Kilamore: "Just as we pulled up, I noticed that each of the men was dropping something over the railing. I also noticed that the wind was coming from the Bay side, going against them. When I looked over the railing I spotted what appeared to be one of the objects, blown back against the bridge and caught on a cross bar."
>
> Officer Kilamore proceeded to climb down more than twenty feet to retrieve the evidence, which turned out to be a plastic bag containing several ounces of marijuana.
>
> The suspects, booked at City Jail, were Steven Randolph Healy, 27, unemployed, Ann Louise Crosby, 22, and Dennis Patrick Mulligan, 23. Miss Crosby and Mr. Mulligan are both students at the University of California, Berkeley.

After reading the clipping, Jacobi sat steeped in silence, the silence and the cold of the building seemed to be thickening around him. First Michael and now Mulligan, he thought, the shit was really coming down. He wondered if he would be next. He idly wondered who the people were that Mulligan had been busted with.

The pile of mail was nearly depleted, the white envelopes, opened and unopened, strewn on the floor all about his chair in spotty imitation of the snow outside. Only Christine's pale blue envelope remained, lying against his thigh. He lifted it, pressing his fingers around its edges, further creasing its already sharp folds. He raised it to his nostrils, but it was odorless; she was too cool, too modern, to affect the dated feminine touch of a fragrance. It had been mailed from the Cape, postmarked "Provincetown." He tuned it in his hand, weighing it, and it seemed to forebode more dread than promise in the close stillness of the empty house. There was nothing left to do except open it.

Friday, January 4

Dear David,

As you may have guessed by now, I am not returning to Ithaca. This is not the first time in my life I have plunged blindly, irrevocably, and I doubt it will be the last. I did so when you and I came together, and now I am doing the same to break us apart. Often in the past I suppose I have chosen wrong, or at least regretted my choice, but then again one never really knows how it would have been the other way.

My oldest, Melissa, wants to come live with me. She feels the same way about her father as I once did. And if I don't take her with me I'm afraid she will flee on her own, just as I did. I cannot deny her, David, and I do not want to. I've decided to stop being a surrogate mother (that's meant as a blow at me, more than you) and go back to being the real thing. I've decided to admit that my ultimate fulfillment doesn't lie in being an artist, that writing can be my avocation, but hardly my life's goal. You've said it yourself, David —I'm still entrapped in the limitations of my conservative New England upbringing.

In a few weeks, Melissa and I plan to return together to my apartment in Manhattan. Then we'll have to start looking for something larger. After all, a girl of fourteen needs a room of her own.

And what about you and me, David. You're such a tender egotist and I so don't want to hurt you, but I'm going to be as honest as I can. So please try to understand.

In spite of what you may be thinking, I've never stopped loving you. I've loved you from the beginning and I still love you now. (That's part of the reason I've chosen a letter for what I have to say rather than trying to face you.) But you must see just as I do that our time together is already overdue. I've often felt that it was overdue from the beginning for me, that you were the man I should have known and loved as a girl rather than as a woman worn by the travails of too many other misplaced affections.

You must see that we have too often become no more than decorative pastimes for each other rather than lovers and what lovers should be and mean to one another. (You will accuse me of stealing that last from my own poetry, but it is true nonetheless.) You must see that it is better to make a clean break now with our good memories intact and unmarred, rather than trying to draw things on into unhappiness for both of us.

You might follow me back to Manhattan, David, but please don't. Between myself and my daughter there will be no room for you there. If you came to stay with us, I fear that with your sexual appetite you might soon want to devour us both. Melissa's closer to your age than I am, and she's already beautiful. Maybe I'm Victorian, maybe just a prude (maybe just full of self-accusation as you always say), but I'm not ready for that, not with my own daughter. And if you stayed with Michael or somewhere else, what then? After living together as intimately as you and I have, we cannot return to an occasional liaison.

What would be the point? It could only be shallow compared to the fullness of our past together.

I cannot uncover the reasons for the things I always felt were lacking in our togetherness. One never can. Often, I'm not even sure what those things are. Perhaps if we had brought a less soiled innocence to Ithaca, if we had come before our encounter with Mulligan. Perhaps if we'd just been able to really care for one another. It may be as simple as that, David—that it takes two people to make a relationship work, two people who really care about each other and are sure they just want to be with one another. I don't know, David, I just don't know.

I do know that showing through all of your actions was the bald fact that your caring for me, your commitment to me, was always a transitory one, always a stopping off point before other (and no doubt better) things to come. I know the things you think of me. I've never really had to hear your accusations and dissatisfactions, David. I didn't have to read them in your diary (though I confess to a bit of that, too.) I could always see them in your eyes, sense them in the tone of your voice. I have no defenses to offer. I'm guilty of it all. Yes, I am provincial. Yes, I am too particular. Yes, it's true, I've never been able to give myself to you completely, except perhaps at the very first.

But I have tried, David. I've tried to open my life and my soul to you, my realities and my fantasies. I've played your games, taken your drugs, seen the mobile of your mind revolve in full as you watched me, judged me (condemned me?). Our Ithaca was a beautiful fantasy, but it was only a fantasy. Our Ithaca was not on the map. It was three stops past the twilight zone and still moving. It was a high, but one can't stay high all the time or there aren't any lows to compare it to. Sometime, someday, you have to come down and pick a reality. I guess that's what I have done, and the reality I have chosen is to be a mother to my child. I guess it's taken me all these years of fleeing to realize that I wasn't running from my motherhood, but only from a bad marriage that wasn't even of my making.

Being with you, David, has given me back a part of the youth that I lost. I want to thank you for that. Now I can grow up and become a woman without any regrets—except perhaps that I couldn't have known you and loved you when I was twenty-one.

Love,
Christine

P.S.—I have checked with Cornell and you have been admitted. The rent on the house is taken care of through the end of February. There will be some movers coming in a few weeks to get my clothes and other things, and some of the furniture I want to keep. I've left enough for you if you decide to stay. Also, I have enclosed the title to the car, signed over to your name. You'll be needing it more than I will.

Please write me in Manhattan and let me know when you decide what you are going to do. I do want us to stay in touch with one another.

The creased blue sheets of letter paper hung limply in his fingers. The certificate of ownership for the VW, his VW, fluttered into his lap. There was no need to read the letter over again—it tone, its posture, each of its words was chiseled and burning within his brain. It was all the truth, every word of it, and it was all a damn lie. Somehow, in the letter and no doubt for herself, she had managed to transform her act of desertion into an act of sacrifice, her betrayal into martyrdom. In her limitless munificence she had even bestowed upon him the gift of the car, paying him in full, even in excess, for all past services rendered. Thus their arrangement was severed.

He thought of her posting the letter in Provincetown, her long willowy body encased against the cold in the long fox coat, or maybe a new coat she had bought in Boston, one of her soft suffering smiles etched upon her features, the striated brow, the tightening lips, as she walked away from the mailbox. Wordlessly, pitched into a zone without words, he cursed her ready-made suffering, her lacquered and lachrymose smile. His first impulse was to get back into the car, drive straight thought to the Cape, sit her down and try to shake some sense into her. His second thought was to telephone, so as to reach her immediately. (He knew the real reason she had written rather than phoning—because she wasn't prepared to confront any truth and explanation other than her own.) But he was stymied on both counts. For him, she had essentially vanished. He had neither telephone number nor address. She was as inaccessible to him now as she had been during their first separation, seemingly so long ago, when they had just met and she had flown north for her mother's funeral.

During the next few hours, as he paced and repaced the rooms they had ornamented together, he experienced all the trips a man losing a woman can go through—anger, remorse, disbelief, despair, confusion, and on down the tedious road to emptiness…stone-blank emptiness…

Even without an address to which to send it, he envisioned the classic letter of bitters and vitriol he could write in response to hers. Or should it be a letter of soul-baring, tender declarations, affirming his love, beseeching her to come back to him for evermore? He attempted to turn the fact that she was gone into an abstraction. He tried to ascend to a universal viewpoint and remember the lessons of acid, that ultimately it was only a game, treacherous with the pitfalls and snares of game emotions; that it had been going on for ten thousand years and more; that his individual tragedy, the lineaments of his winning and losing, was less than a ripple on the intricate and whorling grain of the life wheel. But if it were merely a game, he had become too thoroughly enmeshed in the coursing of its play to liberate himself from his game emotions at this late date. Abstraction proved elusive. His mental mysticism failed to extricate him from the two prongs of his dilemma. Nothing had changed. Just as always, just as in the beginning, he wanted her and he didn't want her and he wasn't sure whether he wanted her or not.

Confusion, anger...disbelief.

As he moved from room to room, Christine's many mirrors threw his dark glowering self back at him. He remembered her in front of those mirrors, posing, trying on clothes, putting on make-up, taking it off again, as if she were always preparing for a Judgment Day when she would be required to waltz through some cosmic beauty contest. Now, in each different room, with their different lighting and backgrounds, he was forced to confront his own reflection; and each time he looked he faced a different David Jacobi. There was no unity with his breast and there never had been. His dilemma was not double-pronged, but as multifarious and mutable as the liquid limbs of an amoeba. Spurned lover, angry lover, contrite lover, sadist, masochist, analyst, opportunist, track star, nicotine addict, wastrel, vagabond, dope dealer, college kid, prophet, thinker, doer, slothful mystic, would-be Kerouac, man-boy, boy-man, father, child. All realities, all identities, raging and vying within him simultaneously.

In the bathroom he glanced upward at the rumpled tin foil ceiling. A rumpled image of foreshortened color blotches, flesh and light blue cloth and dark blue cloth and dark brown hair, hung above his head. He leaped upward to meet it, venting an iota of his rage, long fingers raking the wrinkled foil. The splotchy reflection was split by a myriad of hanging icicle streamers. He turned toward the bathroom mirror and with a soiled towel polished the dust and dried water spots from its surface.

He leaned in more closely for a definitive examination. His beard was fully grown and beginning to turn bushy. That beard had been Christine's idea, probably to make him look older. They had both known that was the reason, though nothing had ever been said about it. Now, with scissors and razor he began to hack away at the dense growth. After several minutes of cutting, soaping and shaving, with the bathroom mirror progressively fogged over, only his former mustache remained. Splashing water across the glass to clear it of steam, he discovered that Christine's impact had carried beyond the beard. Even without it, he still looked older.

Was that how one aged, through broken affairs?

Back in the bedroom he surveyed the unmade bed, a bed that he had last slept in alone. That had been their most common ground, he thought. They had always been more at home with each other in bed than anywhere else. In spite of all their differences, they had been a mating man and woman.

He sat down on the edge of the bed.

Remorse...emptiness.

The sheets were beginning to turn gray, nothing like Michael's yet gray nonetheless.

A mating man and woman. But what had been the products of their mating, he asked himself. A series of days and nights together. Summer, fall, winter. A string of sexual couplings, mostly forgotten. His thin diary. A furnished house. Her sterile letter of farewell. A car trading hands. And now their mating was over. Up until the end they had remained primarily objects for one another, objects of pleasure, objects of dependence, objects of abuse, objects of affection. Now the object named Christine was gone from him. Dead for him. Perhaps the part of her that he had hoped to breathe his kind of life into had been dead for him from the very start. The idyll was over. Now she was alive for him only in his past, in the pages of his diary. Now she had become an episode in his history, a segment of the drama and nightmare from which he was trying to awaken, part of the etiology of the present.

He stretched out in the bed, pulling the covers over his clothed body, weary and searching for the surcease of sleep. But he'd already experienced more than enough sloth and indolence in this house on the outskirts of Ithaca. His obsession with examining and worrying the facets of his dilemma could not be shut off that easily.

—To be cuckolded not by another man, but by her belated maternal instincts, by the progeny of her marriage to another man, that was the worse ignominy.

—Should he go back to Manhattan and await her return, welcome her in her glorious motherhood?

—If the letter were a lie and in actuality there was another man, a new or old lover unearthed at the Cape, at least his presence would expose her...for whatever that was worth.

—Should he stay in Ithaca, attend Cornell to get his degree, move into an apartment in town and start courting the coeds?

If the letter were the truth, what would become of her in a few years? Would she be just another brittle society matron?

—At least they had decided something was wrong between them roughly simultaneously, at least they had figured out that much. It was their solutions that were at odds: his an attempt to work things out together, hers, an end to being together.

Sleep wouldn't come and his erratic thoughts failed to fill the apertures of his despair and emptiness. Finally, he decided that he at least might fill his growling belly. The kitchen offered up its stock of spoiling comestibles, a pitiful repast in comparison with the grandiose concoctions Tina had fashioned there. A meager lump of cheese, left after he had stripped away the moldy outer rind with his pocket knife. Rock stale French bread that he moistened in his mouth with swallows of canned tomato soup, watery because he had no milk to make it with, but boiling hot to erase some of the iciness of the house from his flesh, bones and marrow.

After eating, he uncorked a half full bottle of sauterne that he and Christine had begun together, and started drinking. The wine was turning sour and a bit bubbly, but it wasn't the taste he was after anyway, only the deadening effects of the alcohol.

It was twilight outside and the rooms of the house were dark. He walked from room to room once more, drinking straight from the bottle, turning on the lights throughout the house as he went. At last he got around to turning on the heat, too. It was an admission that he was staying there, at least for the night.

On his relatively empty stomach the wine went to work rapidly. Only instead of killing the pain of his suffering it served to make him melancholy and a bit queasy. Back in the living room chair, fingering the sheets of the letter and fastening on a line here or there, he was now the one with the lachrymose smile.

The car was the topper, he thought morosely. He'd eaten her food, let her buy him clothes, taken her money, but the car was the topper. The pay-off. The consolation prize. Her last little jibe at his dependence upon her.

Damn car. Damn car. He'd show her what he thought of it.

He downed the last of the sauterne in a gulping convulsive swallow, and with the bottle swinging in one hand like a mini-club he was up and out the front door, charging to the car to release his ready-made rage. Whack! Whack! Fenders, roof, hood. Whack! Whack! These French wine bottles were made of sturdy stuff, he thought. Whack! Whack! He managed a few impressive dents before he grew tired of the game and tossed the bottle away into the dark.

He fell against the car, pressing his face and hands onto the freezing metal of its roof, hoping the cold might anesthetize him. A light snow was drifting down, touching softly upon his bare head and the back of his neck. He sobbed several times from deep within his throat and the final swallow of wine backed up, a sour bile causing him to cough and spit into the snow.

The door of the house was still hanging open from his charge. Yellow light poured out onto the wooden porch, ocher light spilled through the windows to illuminate the falling snowflakes. Turning, Jacobi stared at the house and its glowing windows. He began walking, quickly, around the house, listening to his feet crunch in the snow drifts, feeling the frost gathering upon his neck. He was extending the limits of his former pacing, lengthening a tether that now existed only in his mind.

She's gone, she's gone, it's over, it's over—it kept repeating itself like a mantric dirge, a deadening echo, like a tied circle of film clipping through the projector, running through his head again and again. He thought of their relationship and it was like driving down the highway in the dead of night, following the white line, sixty, seventy, eighty miles per hour, with your lights brighter and brighter and your destination just about to come in sight, and then the white line disappears and the road widens to an isotropic concrete sea and you are lost weaving back and forth, back and forth, like a metronome, like the randomly pitching needle of a broken gauge, with nowhere to go to and no way to go back.

He lay set after set of tracks around the house until the path of his marching became mushy and his ankles ached from the cold, until his feet were wet with the snow-turned-water soaking through his shoes and socks.

She's gone, it's over, she's gone, it's over—the mantra ran on, the record was caught, he wrestled with it, he turned it in his head, trying to see it from this direction, trying to see it from that. He turned it until it was turning faster and faster and so fast that the words blended to nonsense and became meaningless...until his imaginary tether snapped. All at once he realized that if he had lived without her before, the obvious corollary was that he could do so again. All at once he understood that if his last jaunt to Manhattan had been a trial freedom, now he had the real thing, freedom with no one to return to or measure his actions against, with nowhere to go and no way to go back, with anywhere and everywhere to go.

He stumbled back into the house and locking the door behind him so that no one else might enter, he found sleep.

When he awoke in the morning the decision was already made within his head: he would return to California. Christine had been the only reason his stay on the East Coast had been prolonged in the first place. Now that she was gone from him there was nothing else keeping him here. Not Cornell, he wasn't ready to go back to any school right at the moment, he was learning too much outside the groves of academia. Not Michael—he felt more rapport with a number of friends in the West, including Mulligan. Not Linda Bernstein—that had been a drunken joke.

He gathered together the things he wanted to take and threw them into one of the suitcases Christine had left behind—a few books, his diary, some clothes, a series of photographs they had taken together at the lake, and last but not least a prescription bottle of Preludins that Christine had cajoled out of her New York doctor and they had planned to use for speed. He wasn't interested in sightseeing, and the pills would keep him going through to the other coast as quickly as possible.

He counted his money. There was a little more than what he'd left Berkeley with (not counting Michael's check, which he'd forgotten to cash, some wheeler and dealer he was). Only on the way out there had been no need to buy gas. Well, he'd just have to see what he could do.

Before leaving he stood in the snow for several minutes, staring the house down one last time. He thought and thought hard, but there was nothing else to be done or said, nothing else he could think of to be remembered or forgotten. He tossed the suitcase in back next to his duffel bag, climbed into his dented car, and drove off.

Behind him, the house sinks deeper and deeper into the snow. The players have left this play. The stage is dead and cold, the balcony dark, the lobby lies deserted. In the orchestra pit moss has begun to grow and rust dulls the cymbals. The roof, with attic boards sagging, is beginning to leak under its white burden. Somewhere a window hangs open, offering up the rooms with their objects, with their dead entrails, to the biting winter wind. Dusty carpets curl up at the edges. A river of books spilled onto the floor halts in mid-flow. It is a frozen river.

43

TUNNELING the open eye of America like a fast freight. Driving and driving and driving. We hold these truths to be self evident. That the road is a snake to be devoured and excreted. That the car is a plunging cock caught in the down-stroke of a bottomless womb. That the road is a wordy umbilical to be reread with fruition. That the road is the same both ways, but the trips up and back always different.

Driving and driving—following that winding often-broken white ribbon over grainy, cracked and oil-spotted asphalt, the four wheels beneath him bouncing upon the ruts and ridges, retracing the calligraphy of highway numbers that led back to the other coast, the path over mountains, plains, rivers, valleys and deserts;

through states, counties, cities, towns, burgs and whistle stops; past billboards, farms, hovels, shacks, gas stations and hamburger restaurants; against rain, hail, sleet and snow—nothing could stop this faithful pilgrim in the circular completion of his trek. If he could have driven without stopping he would have. He sought the roadsides in vain for hitchhikers to share his burden, the driving and the money for gas, but none were braving this cold and he remained without company in the racing steel shell of his loneness. He followed the sun, always westward, as much as the road signs. After nightfall he became a landed mariner, navigating by the stars, ancient in his own youthful way. He didn't shave; he didn't wash; he hardly took the time to take a piss. His sustenance was apple pie, cokes, coffee and diet pills, American all the way. His visions, like his life, were American through and through.

Leaving Ithaca, leaving the state of New York, swinging down into northern Pennsylvania, land of the Whiskey Rebellion, now long-sedated farm land sleeping under white winter sheets, through Mansfield, Blossburg, Williamsport, Lock Haven, running south on 15 to pick up the turnpike, the straight shoot through to Chicago. Leaving the tether, leaving the idyll, leaving the past, falling down the vertical tunnel of memory, asking the questions one must always ask, seeking the catalysts, the reagents, the products, the truths and the lies.

The turnpikes were one truth he could not deny. Pennsylvania, Ohio, Indiana. An undifferentiated no man's land. An isotropic concrete sea with no turning back except at the toll stations, with no cities except over the rise in the fenced-away distance, with no telling one state from the next except by the toll you had to pay to leave one and the toll card you had to take to register your charges in the next. Two dollars and thirty cents. Three dollars and twenty cents. Five dollars and ninety-five cents. He was paying his way out, American all the way. How else could he exorcise his nightmare and his dream?

The turnpikes with their rest stations and gas stations appearing in a chain of predictable regularity that did little to break up the gray monotony of the road. Enco, Texaco, Shell, Standard, Chevron, Phillips: kingpins of the exchange with no bowler to match them, kings of the road because there was no place else to buy the fuel to keep him rolling. Paying his way. Paying his way to the Howard Johnson sameness, one restaurant after another after another, a monopoly in thirty-one flavors where the motoring gourmet could read the menu in one state and select his meals ahead of time for the next three.

"Apple pie and coffee, please."

Smiling her frozen waitress smile. "Wouldn't you like some dinner? The pot roast is delicious."

A conspiracy. A conspiracy.

He was sure it was all a grand conspiracy at some soul-killing level, a plot to turn the open road into a road of dead security rather than free adventure, an all-out attempt to build another grinding conveyor belt with no space for vagabonds. And it was succeeding!

And it had succeeded!

There is no eye to the tunnel at either end. Our lives are finite, our memories and possibilities infinite. David Jacobi remembered. He had made this trip, crossed this country before. He had come to New York to break the pattern of his existence. He had come to New York to have women like popcorn. He had come to New York to deal dope and start the acid revolution, to deal dope and make some money, to deal dope and forge a new image for himself— strike one, strike two, strike three. He had come to New York to expand and enrich his world. He had come to New York to love one woman, ten years older than himself and ages younger with whom he had discovered a world rich in sensuality, but as sectarian as ever. In the process he had accumulated experience. He had changed, become a different person, older, more mature, that was all, nothing grander, nothing like what he had sought. His errant ramblings had brought him no closer to the possession of his particular silver chalice or any other.

Pennsylvania, Ohio, Indiana: those weren't the only states he was passing through. In spite of his realization of freedom, the specter of Christine was still haunting him, her image still tagging him as closely as the land he was crossing. *I do want us to stay in touch with one another.* In a Howard Johnson's in eastern Ohio the waitress who took his order thanked him with Tina's velvet and lace contralto. Three tables away another patron, her gray-templed husband and two tousled children in tow, watched him surreptitiously between coffee sips with Tina's wide blue eyes. When he paid the bill the cashier returned the change from his dollar with the same long, cool hands that had so often held his cock, caressed his limbs, tested the lines and dimensions of his face and tangled through his hair in the darkness of their bedroom. It was only the peroxided bouffant and dull face atop those hands that prevented him from assaulting her there and then.

Ten minutes and ten miles of turnpike later he pulled the car off the road and onto the dirt siding as a sense of loss irreparable, actions irretrievable, rose up uncontrollably in him once again. It was illegal to stop here. It was illegal to hitchhike on the turnpikes, too, but he'd done that on the way out and gotten away with it. The state highway patrol had picked him up in Pennsylvania and he had played young and innocent and they'd driven him to the next county and off the pike to get rid of him.

He climbed out of the car, stamped his feet on the frosty turf, watched the moisture in his exhalations condense on the bleak air. He had been popping the Preludins like candy and he was as wired as a fun house, a dank fun house with maze-like corridors, too much darkness, too many cul-de-sacs.

He could still go back, he told himself. He could turn the car around at the next toll station or the one after that. He could always turn around. It wasn't too late. He could meet her in Manhattan, begin afresh, rediscover that yellow brick road and seduce her all over again.

Other cars shot by him, gray bullets, colors blurred by their speed. In the tail wind of a passing diesel the VW rocked on its springs and the freezing blast of air drove him back within its steel shell. He crossed his arms upon the steering wheel and rested his head against them. He jammed his eyes tightly shut. Moments later a knocking on the window glass brought him upright. The patrol car had glided up behind him soundlessly. As he rolled down the window he could see the officer's face was unfriendly.

"Engine trouble?"

"No."

"Well, you can't stop here. There's a rest area seventeen miles ahead and plenty of motels at the next off ramp. Move on now or you're going to get a ticket."

"All right."

There was no halting the conveyor. No bandit parts allowed because they were a threat to security, or at least the sense of security. Stopping by the wayside could lead to a serious criminal offense. He might steal some of the frozen dirt, state property, or cut a hole in the chain link and escape running free across the fields and hills without paying his toll. He might even be the seditious type and tempt others to stop and do the same.

—If there is no eye to the tunnel at either end, where does the light come from?

—We are the source of the light. We are the reflection. We are the eye. We are the tunnel. We hold these truths to be self-evident, that each soul is alive and dead unto itself.

His sense of loss abated again with the passage of the miles. He didn't turn the car around at either the next toll station or the one after that. He kept barreling westward, a true pioneer, running from the rising sun and racing into its setting.

He asked himself why one's sense of direction couldn't always be as simple as a tropism.

After driving for nearly twenty hours without sleep, without any real rest or the need for it, he was becoming totally immersed in the act of driving, of stopping only to meet the demands of his belly and bowels, and the VW's gas tank belly. The inside of the car was becoming as familiar to him as any habitation he'd ever had—its tight instrument panel, the beige steering wheel, the black rubber floor mats, the gray roof liner a bare inch above his head, the droning semi-musical modulations of the engine like a running stream of consciousness explosions as he moved from one gear to the next, the different noises, the new squeaks and groans bubbling up from the structure of its insides as it was driven at it had never been driven before over roads it had never known before. And through its small squarish windows the stereopticon of America, the vast Sahara of cultural aridity, played before his wired, undrooping eyes. It was all there for him to see, to be devoured and excreted. The states, the counties, the farms, the rivers, the mountains, the valleys. The lineaments of his past and his future were bound like a root to the lineaments of the land he was crossing. He had been born into this context without choice and without question. By the time his "I" had become conscious enough to question and choose, the context had already rooted and grown within him, incorporated itself inextricably into that "I," become a major segment of that "I."

We are the tunnel and we are the eye. We are the skin and we are the snake. With a metallic *tour de force* the razor slits the dancing umbilical. Her body like a mountain, a shelf of weathered shale. The estuaries, the shoals. The city is like a swamp tonight, a mud gray swamp. Old man wearing a tweed cap and a

Sicilian version of the jodhpurs. The total plexus was within his reach. No difference. No difference. The child is father to the child.

Even an isotropic concrete sea must have its shore. When one has paid enough there comes an end to paying. At the Illinois border, David Jacobi drove off the turnpike and off the highway. His sense of direction deserted him...and suddenly he found himself wandering the venation of streets known as Chicago, the dirty, windy city, stopping-off point for the push to the West.

All he needed was gas and food, but the car fell into the city as if sucked into a pit, swallowed by the streets, and before he knew it he was lost on the Southside between gray industrial torpor and black ghetto winter, thinking it was too bad Mrs. O'Leary's cow hadn't finished off the place for good, thinking that he'd only come a third of the way back and ahead of him lay most of his journey: the Great Plains, their wheat fields empty in winter, the northern fringes of the Dust Bowl, the badlands of Wyoming, the Rockies, Great Salt Lake, the plastic and tinsel casinos of Reno, the Sierra Nevadas, and finally the descent back to sea level and the Pacific shore.

Eventually, he found a grimy two-pump corner gas station with a grimy diner next door. The dirt was actually a relief after a thousand miles of Sani-flush, saccharine, and spotless formica counter tops. The apples in the pie tasted like real apples, with no chemical aftertaste of monosodium glutamate and calcium stearate, and that was nice, too. It was only the handful of middle-aged black working men with their sullen threatening eyes, or his own paranoia, that caused him to eat hurriedly, gulp down half his coffee, and leave without even a relaxing after-dinner smoke.

On a residential side street he parked the car, locked the doors, and stretching out his rangy form as well as possible within the narrow confines of his mobile home, he attempted to take a short rest before finding the highway again and plunging onward. Moments later a knocking on the window glass brought him upright. Recurrence. Always recurrence. The short of it and the long of it. The relative and the absolute. The programmed blue-suited minions carrying out their masters' programs, the soul-killing lockstep lockstep lockstep to the prison of death. If you try to sit by the river and smoke dope you get busted.

—Yes, Officer.

—No, Officer.

—I was just catching a little sleep, Officer. Yes, I'll get a motel room next time.

—Yes, I was planning to get the car registered in California.

—Yes, I am a student.

—Yes, I'll be moving on now.

—Yes, I need a shave.

—Yes, my hair is ragged.

—Yes, my eyes are wild.

—Yes, I've read my Marx.

—Yes, I've smoked the devil weed.

—Yes, I'm up to no good.

—Yes, I need a bath.

—Yes, I want to blow the whole blessed mess up and start all over again.

—Yes, your sky is falling.

—Yes, your own wife wants me, dirty ragged hairy as I am.

—Yes, I will come while you are sleeping just as you have come to me.

Joliet, Moline, Rock Island, Davenport, Iowa City, Des Moines. Not the turnpike anymore but the open road, toll free Interstate 80. Not regulated monopoly commerce anymore, but the free enterprise of the open road, the junk road, damn the torpedoes and full speed ahead, every man for himself blossoming up on all sides with a makeshift forest of business establishments that threatened to overrun the highway. Jacobi had known that the turnpike fences had been built to keep him in, but he had forgotten what they had been built to keep out. Cultural aridity was without doubt an anathema, but Mulligan had been wrong—this wasn't cultural aridity. This was a gross-culture saturation, a mass-culture plague, a rampaging fever of consumption and despoliation.

Seldom did the land by the roadside totally escape the scars of its contamination, and then it was only for short stretches at a time. Within city limits the infection was the worst. The forest of commercial weeds often threatened to choke one another out. Here and there on a main street a deserted gas station or soaped-over plate glass window testified to the rate of attrition. But there were always two or three new growths rising up at the borders of town to replace those that had fallen and been plowed under within. Thus each town spread lengthwise along the highway with the most modern establishments at its extremities, feeding and prospering off the needs of the snake and taking physical form as well as sustenance from its host. The seeds of open market capitalism finding fertile soil and blooming with abandon along the American open road. Jacobi asked himself again and again, who could have planned this parade of signs and store fronts in a greater disarray of clashing colors and materials, with more distaste, than the infamous invisible hand of competition?

Between towns the fever abated somewhat, except for an occasional gas station or clapboard eatery looming up unexpectedly at the edges of the brown snow-speckled fields, except for the ever-present chain of billboards, as numerous as playing cards scattered across the land, wedged sideways and upright in the soil.

—How many billboards are there in America?

—How many grains of sand on the beach or drops of water in a wave? Count the points of light in a clear night sky and multiply by the largest prime.

Jacobi discovered that Christine's wraith had still not left him as he sped westward. It hung poised in the monochromatic Midwestern sky, a giant smiling face invisible except to his heart's eye, projecting its image upon the billboard screens one after another. Now she became more remote and idealized, more insubstantial to him than ever before. The different "Tina"s in his head coalesced and she became perhaps what it was always meant for her to be. With tawny thirty-foot head thrown back and her pale, vulnerable, blue-veined throat exposed and magnified to the size of her once-car, her rosy lips closed upon a bottle of America's favorite cola and called on the weary traveler to drink drink drink. With an extra fifteen pounds proportioned selectively over her slender model's figure, scantily-enticingly clad in mesh, satin and plumes, with one long leg uplifted and kicking billboard-free into the sky, she previewed the chorus line at Reno's finest hotel and casino. With eyes closed in succulent dreaming and body languorous, she advised him to take the bus next time and leave the driving to her.

—I will Tina I will in nomine Patris et Filii et Spritus Sancti if there ever is another time God forbid.

The tunnel is broad and dark and deep in either direction. Memories and possibilities are infinite. The air is thick and cloying. The air is cool and clean.

The pioneer shapes the frontier as the historian reshapes the inheritance. With the insoluble "I" of context and id, each of us strings our own dancing-doll marionettes. From our place in the cave, each of us projects the degree of focus for our own shadow plays, defines the wants of the future, the satisfactions and regrets of the past.

The tunnel is time. We are its marrow and we are its stone. We are the mephitic human stench and the all-knowing eyes that watch ourselves clattering though the darkness. Consciously or unconsciously, the catwalks that lace the depths are always of our own making.

There are no birds. There are no keepers.

"Radio 1030, Sioux Falls, South Dakota..."

"This is the late night news, final edition, from KEWK in downtown Omaha..."

"...K-B-O-P!...KAN-SAS-CITY!...THE-TOPS!!..."

He spun the radio dial like the chambers on a revolver. It was a form of American roulette, shot full with commercials. The "Top Forty" network was nearly complete from coast to coast, another victory for uniform mass culture. He could have listened to pop-rock all the way, fading out as he left one metropolitan area and booming in as he approached the next. But he already had enough speed in his head and belly. The rapid-fire disc jockeys imitating one another's puerile idiocy got on his nerves. The repetitive drill team round of commercial, song, song, commercial, rap, song, station ID, rap, commercial, song became a hammer pounding sonic spikes into his brain. Forty songs, even the top forty, just aren't enough for even one man to cross the length of a continent...so he spun the dial.

"This is KPW, the Voice of the West, in Denver..."

"KKAL in Wichita presents evening music for you listening pleasure..."

He picked up the heartbreak twang of country music stations and in the midst of the lone prairie his own heart wept along with their rhythms. He heard the story of Moses jived and bouncing up from the Bible Belt with a chorus of sotto voce hallelujahs rustling in the background like the paper reeds of the Nile. He was offered a prayer cloth for three dollars and a prayer wheel for five. He was told that there was still hope, that he could still be healed. He learned of close-out furniture specials of which, alas, he'd never be able to take advantage; of the superior fertilizers and pesticides available to nurture and defend his crops; of the renowned integrity and dependability of the largest used car wheeler-dealer in all of eastern Colorado. And always, always, in a hundred different gradations of local dialects but with the same content, direct from the wires of AP and UPI, the national and world news, a replay of a replay, the same he had always heard in Ithaca on Christine's morning radio, the same war, the same casualties multiplying, the same president double-talking, the same blind pope, the same madness, the same pain. He spun the dial to no-station and the static of the empty air waves, the eternal flux, set up mindless and random contrapuntal rhythms with the churning beat of the engine:

"…sszsszsszsszsszsszsszSSSSSSSSsszsssxssszssszsssssszsss zZZZZZZZZZZZzzzsszsszsszsszsssxssszssszssszsszssssSSZsszssxss zssz…"

When the company of the radio became intolerable, he switched it off and kept company with himself. He watched the shadow play of past, present, and future dancing in his head. The catalysts, the reagents, the truth and the lies—conglomerate and inseparable. He hummed and whistled to pass the hours. He talked aloud to the droning car, the rutted road, the passing billboards, the telephone poles breaking up the scenery like frame dividers when the film is slowed. Beyond the question of himself and Christine, behold, he discovered the question of himself and Mulligan.

Fat man, funny man, friend, hero, manipulator, fool. What about Tilden? What about Central Park? How much of what happened was you, Denny? How much the acid? How much the way it had to be? Would you tell me if I asked you, Denny? Do you even know or care or remember?

Jacobi saw that in a sense his own pilgrim's progress, all of his changes, had been from Mulligan and through Mulligan. And now here he was, headed back to Berkeley, back to Mulligan again. Had the sum of his quest been only a quest for Mulligan? Was the truth that monstrous and that simple?

Scraps of conversation swirled up at him out of the past. The many selves in his breast joined in a forensic caucus. The many faces of Mulligan joined the shifting shadow-play. Jacobi's monologue became a dialogue, a decalogue.

—Who's Botticelli?

—I'm not jealous of Mulligan.

—You came to New York to get away from me, Davy.

—Dramatic arts, you ninny.

—Too bad he couldn't have stayed longer.

—He's best in small doses.

—There wasn't any speed in that acid.

—Why would he lie to us, David?

—He fucked your woman for you, didn't he?

—What does Mulligan matter, he's three thousand miles away?

—Not really.

—He fucked your woman for you, didn't he?

—Not really.

—It's like having a green thumb with people.

—Sure he's a clown, a sick clown, an evil clown!

No, Jacobi told himself, it wasn't that simple. Mulligan had been a catalyst for him. So had Christine. Even Michael had played an influential part in the causal chain: by refusing to help him deal the acid, by kicking him out of his apartment, by leading him to Christine. And Jacobi, himself, had been a catalyst too. Mulligan would never have come to New York in the first place if he hadn't already been there. The play was always one of interaction, not of masters, strings and puppets. *Each soul is alive and dead unto itself. There are no keepers.* Mulligan was not the sum of what he had sought. Even if his friend's entire trip *were* simply a god-game, as Michael claimed, Jacobi was not ready to acclaim Mulligan's apotheosis and condemn him with that inhuman appellation. Despite his dynamic, Mulligan was as human as anyone else, not a paradigm to emulate. *There are no birds. There is no eye to fly to at either end of the tunnel.*

Bushnell, Nebraska, longitude forty-one degrees twenty minutes, latitude one-hundred-and-three degrees five minutes, population three hundred and twelve. Forty-seven miles from Cheyenne, seven miles from the Wyoming border and the climb into the Rockies. Jacobi stopped for gas and oil at a small station and was struck by what remained the clearest single image of the entire trip back, a mite of wakefulness amidst all the dreaming, a part of the nightmare that seemed very real.

It was the face of the station owner, middle-American if there was such a genetic strain: small, tight sun-worn features; narrow preachy eyes, thin lips, salt and pepper grizzle on cheeks and cleft chin, the creases running from the corners of the eyes, the band across the forehead where a cowboy hat had just been removed, the severely-cropped, gray-brown hair. It was the face of a hardy middle-aged independent proprietor of America who regarded with dire suspicion this customer with the foreign car and unkempt hair and shaggy mustache and Preludin-Christine Leslie-CocaCola-coffee-high eyes, yet pumped him gas nevertheless because business was business. It was the face of a man not rich not poor, but a man making it on his own, as solid and corn-filled as the loamy Midwestern soil. It could have been the face of Jacobi's father, or Michael's father or Christine's. With a touch more savvy and a dollop of megalomania, it could have been the face of a president.

Across the border, into the Rockies, measuring the miles now because his money was running out, measuring the cars rapacity against the rapacity of his own belly.

Running out of cigarettes, too. Crumpling up the empty pack and throwing it out the window, his contribution to the garbage of America. He wouldn't stop now, not for cigarettes, not for an addiction when he had a full tank of gas and his money was so low. He only wished he had some grass to ease the hard reality of the road, or maybe a small dose of acid, twenty-five mikes, just enough to make him glow.

"Holy shit!" he suddenly exclaimed.

The acid, his acid—in his preoccupation with the loss of Christine, with his own ego, he had totally forgotten it. It was still tucked snugly in the butter tray in the refrigerator in Ithaca. He couldn't help himself from laughing out loud, billows of laughter beating out of the car over its tin engine roar and into the empty Wyoming night. What more fitting end to his abbreviated career as a dealer than when moving from one place to another he should forget about his stash and leave it behind. The only thing that might make the irony more complete would be if Christine wound up getting busted for it.

The miles and the hours were beginning to take their toll upon him and upon the car. He had now learned the interior of that bug-like metal hulk with the same degree of authenticity with which Monte Cristo had known his prison cell, and he was beginning to anticipate his release with the same joy and anxiety. The Preludins were leaving him merely strung out now rather than wired. His external awareness seemed attenuated, dampened and filtered, something less than real. Continually, he had to fight to keep his mind from wandering from the task of driving. He had to keep reminding himself that it wasn't only an extended dream he was passing through, that at the speeds at which he was traveling a collision with a passing boulder or another car could pierce his flesh, splinter his bones, and put a premature and permanent end to all of his dreaming. If his attention wavered momentarily he might miss a turn in the road, crash the railing and hurtle over a precipice, head over heels, bumper over bumper, to explode with incandescent gas-tank glory, the perfect Hollywood movie denouement.

Luckily, there were mitigating factors besides his own self-discipline that helped bring him back to the reality of his circumstances. There were the muscles aching in his neck and shoulder blades from being so many hours in the same position, the pain in his cramped legs, the popping in his eardrums with the rising and falling altitude. There was the black mountain night spitting down intermittent blasts of icy rain against his windshield, the distant flashes of lightning, a regular thunder storm. *Ah, to be a bird flying free in that night rain, to wash the dirt and sweat and weariness from his body, to soar solo without thought from past tense, present and future!* There was the crawling bug of the car, his prison, which was beginning to fight him in senseless insect-robot resistance. New noises and complaints were grumbling up from its insides; joints, springs, rings and pistons were squealing with added protest to the way they were being pushed without rest. Ever since Omaha the brakes had been periodically pulling to the right and the gears were harder to shift. After swallowing all of this U.S. highway, the car was beginning to cough and spit America back up at him. Its German blood was in revolt, craving the Apollonian precision of a Kant or the mad Dionysian energy of a Nietzsche rather than this vast, tasteless, wasteland conceived by Howard Johnson, greed and happenstance.

A honking horn and a shutter-flash of light whipping past his side window at more than a hundred and twenty miles per hour brought his drooping head upright. In sleep-delayed reaction he jerked the steering wheel, swerving toward the shoulder of the road to avoid a collision that was no longer a possibility, knowing in the instant of movement that the action was a mistake but knowing too late to prevent it. The car bounced awkwardly on muddy gravel, spun sideways as he braked, came to a stop still upright but slightly atilt and pitched at an angle to the road.

Now fully awake, with limbs trembling, Jacobi killed the engine and the lights. He had been driving all through the night, onward and onward, more and more like an automaton, like a mechanical extension of the machine he was operating. Now, all at once, his humanity had caught up with him. In the sudden silence his ears till hummed from the sounds of the car. The wind blew out of a morning half-light, throwing a gust of rain against the windshield and across the roof. Without checking the damage from the skid, or even trying to see if he'd be able to get back on the road, Jacobi climbed over the seat, shoved his suitcase and duffel bag into the front, and curling up with the warmth of no body other than his own, he allowed exhaustion to have its way with him.

...the flower in the calyx, the seed in the cup of the petal, the cotyledon tucked within the seed, the bird within the breast, the prisoner incarcerated in his prison cell, the soul within the tunnel of memory, falling, falling, the future tacit in the past, the metaphor implicit in language, the words like brands in the flesh, the play and the playfulness inherent in the words, the symbols in the play...

...the dream that languishes within the dream:

He is crossing a different America. He has become a hobo riding the rails, hopping the fast freights. Sometimes the tracks parallel the highway, and then he sees the cars and the gas stations and the billboards and the towns all over again. But then the tracks leave the road, go shooting off in their own directions, into the wilderness to a less soiled America, green and inviting, without concrete, steel, plastic and commercials. It isn't a bad life except for the hunger and the railroad bulls who try to gang up on them in the yards, catch them singly or in pairs and beat them. When he is tired of traveling and his belly is grumbling he stops to eat and bed down at the bo camps stretched all along the tracks in the wilderness, to sit around an open fire and swap stories and smoke hand-rolled cigarettes, to pick up news on where the trains are going. California is his goal, but he can't seem to get there. News of the freight routings is always undependable and contradictory within the camps. As a result he winds up crossing much of the same country again and again without making any progress westward—and all the time the number of hoboes seems to be increasing and the camps growing larger. He plans to abandon this itinerant life once he gets to California, he plans to go back to school. There are a few others like himself, trying to get back to different states and do the same, but most of the men tell him that he is crazy, that he's too old to go to school, that he has traveled too many miles to return to anything. At one of the camp stops he discovers a dogeared booklet of train schedules in his duffel bag. He tries to make some sense out of the book, but he can't. The date on the inside of the cover is in Roman numerals, and try as he will, he can't even piece this together. He asks one of the hoboes sitting next to him at the fire to help, a tall lanky raw-boned fellow, no older than himself, but with rheumy eyes and a sallow complexion. The youth informs him that those schedules are out of date, and then produces his own more current book of train routings. The second book is in better condition, the cover cleaner and all of the pages intact, but other than that it is identical to the first book. Yet it is impossible to make the fellow understand that both books are the same. An argument breaks out between the two of them. Just as it is about to explode into curses and blows, the word is suddenly rustling through the camp that there is a freight on its way, headed straight through for California. He is running for the tracks with hundreds of other men, catching the open box cars on the fly and leaping within. The train travels all day and through the night without stopping. They pass through country that none of the men have ever seen before, more and more barren. Judging from the position of the sun, they are traveling north rather than west. It grows progressively colder. By morning light they are still moving, passing over gray tundra-like plains that stretch out from the track in both directions to the limit of vision. Nearing afternoon, the train finally begins to brake. Looking out of the open boxcar he can see a huge yard up ahead, with more trains and sidings than he knew existed. It is the biggest railroad yard of all, known in bo legend as "The Hub," the place where all tracks and all trains come together. As they approach he can make out squadrons of blue-suited yard bulls, taking the hoboes in their shabby clothes off the arriving cars and processing them, marching them in lines and clipping metal tags around their necks. He knows that he cannot let himself be taken so he leaps from the car before the train has halted. Then the bulls are chasing him among the sidings, clanking their wooden nightsticks against the tracks and the metal of the train wheels. He is searching frantically for someplace to hide. He finds a deserted box car and climbs within, yanking the door shut behind him. It is a refrigerator car and he has somehow activated the cooling mechanism. It grows colder. The door is jammed. He pounds upon it but there is no answer. It grows colder and colder. His limbs begin to stiffen. He is unable to move, unable to speak.

Upon opening his eyes his first thought, taken from the opaque whiteness of the car windows, was that the VW had been encased in a sheet of ice. It was only the effect of the low afternoon sun, pale, the yellow of it slight stretched to whiteness by the raindrops still upon the outside of the glass and the moisture from his breath condensed upon the inside.

He allowed himself to awaken slowly. Circulation creeped back into his limbs; as he moved his joints cracked, releasing their tightness. The sun had just broken through the clouds, and now its modest winter warmth began to dry the rain from the car. The dampness within condensed still further. Droplets gathered upon the film of moisture and began running down, tracking through the opacity, leaving blurred ribbon glimpses of the world outside.

Jacobi watched the water flowing, the water from his own body. He sensed his kinship with it. Water, prime life element, fount of all life. He could sense *his* life as water, see the material of his past as water flowing to his current present. He could detect the ripples of his passage from one pool to the next. He had set out from California after something vague, mystical, something he had only touched gropingly on his peaks with acid. Since then he had moved in many directions—of his own making, of others' making, of the making of chance. If he hadn't attained the spontaneity he had sought, at least his existence had been improvident. Wasn't that a kind of spontaneity? Wasn't all thought and action ultimately spontaneous if one traced it back far enough to the point of origin.

Looking through one lens he could view his entire affair with Christine as having sidetracked him from his goal. But then again, how could one be sidetracked from the business of living? There was no way, no way at all. And yes, they had lived together engaged in the business of living, played the round of *maya*, partaken of the everyday—eating, sleeping, loving, talking, moving with and against one another, sharing one another's existence. In a certain sense their relationship had been as ordinary and commonplace as possible, no different than countless other chance infatuations that had led to mismatched involvements. With their crutches of sex and insecurity and a kind of self-feeding imagistic love, they had continued to limp along together far past the cross roads where they should have parted. But no, he denied that commonness too. The flowing water could not submerge and carry away all in its flowing. The had *lived* together, touched in more than everyday ways. In total, it had not been dull, not even routine. There had been moments of ecstasy, shared and consumed together and unforgotten. Wasn't ecstasy another part of what he had sought. Spontaneity, Ecstasy. Maturity. Hadn't he come a part of the way after all. If not *the path*, perhaps he was finding and defining *his path*. If not the attainment of his goals, hadn't he at least attained their transformation.

The rest of the day could have been spent thinking about it, figuring it all out, piecing it together and tearing it down and building it up again with a new score of towers and battlements. Like archaeological sights that date back through prehistory to the dawn of man, there were as many levels to his truth as he had time to uncover. Yet there was no more time at the present. His now-clear windshield revealed a sign he could have collided with if his skid had carried him twenty yards further. It informed him that the Utah border was only another fifty-three miles. The highway called him. He would remain its prisoner until the full circle of his journey was complete.

In Salt Lake City they were waiting for him.

"We have a special today on apple pie and coffee. Only twenty-five cents."

The waitress looked Polynesian. She seemed even more out of place in this land of Joseph Smith and the tithe and the Tabernacle Choir than he did. She should have been on some coral isle, sarong-clad, swimming in brilliant waterfall pools, gathering palm leaves, offering up evening prayers to a monolithic stone statue of some native deity.

Jacobi watched her moving across the restaurant floor, her bare brown arms, her small full body still firm with youth and the absence of motherhood. For the first time in twenty-three-hundred miles he felt genuinely aroused...and his white, white poetess had nothing whatsoever to do with it.

Timple, Delle, Knolls, the Great Salt Desert, Wendover, Oasis, Wells, Elko. The appellations of the West are different than those of the East, just like the land, just like the people.

Nevada offered up its gambling to him, from nickel slots in dirty gas station johns to black jack, craps and roulette in velvet-plush casinos. Take a chance young man! You don't have to fly the straight and narrow. There are other ways to get rich in this country besides pushing a pencil or a plow. Right here, you can make your fortune overnight! Everyone has a chance, a chance, a chance.

Others, pushing the frontier westward, had taken their chances in this desert long before the construction of gas stations and gambling halls, and some had lost everything. Now, more than a hundred years later and with few frontiers left, in the year of the Christian lord, 1966, in the year of further escalation in Viet Nam, of black ghetto uprisings, of a hydrogen bomb lost off the coast of Spain, David Jacobi was taking his chances, too. As the red VW groaned on through the night, snaking headwinds threw snatches of desert up against its once-shiny chassis and added sand pitting to it other ailments. The car was consuming what little cash he had left faster and faster, using more gas and oil with every mile, robbing the nourishment from his own body. He was headed downhill now. But there was still the climb up the

Sierra Nevadas before he could reach California and begin the descent into the Sacramento Valley. If a breakdown occurred, there would be nothing for him to do but abandon the car and go back to his thumb. The likelihood of snow in the mountains did little to make him relish that prospect.

Carlin, Battle Mountain, Valmy. Every mile counted now, every inch. He made it to downtown Winnemucca before an entire wall of neon lights, burning brightly in broad daylight, lured him into a casino. His dream was not of a fortune, only enough for a square meal. It took him twenty minutes of seesawing up and down before he blew the rest of his food money, less than a dollar, on the nickel and dime slots. He had not eaten since Salt Lake and now it looked like he would maintain his fast through to Berkeley if he wanted the car to get him there. Whatever weight he had put on in Ithaca from Christine's cooking would be off him by the time this trip was over. He was even out of cigarettes again except for a nest of butts he'd salvaged from the sand of one of the casino ashtrays. All he had left to consume were the Preludins. They could offer him wakefulness, wiredness, attenuation, automation, words and more words running through his head, but not a single calorie to burn.

Donner Pass, the summit, elevation 7,089 feet. California, the final state, the end of the frontier.

He had made it, the worst was over.

After Winnemuca he had driven straight on through the rest of Nevada without stopping once. Mill City, Unionville, Lovelock, Wadsworth—he had made the ascent into the Sierra range with fingers crossed, puffing on the cigarette butts one after another until they made his empty stomach feel sick and then pitching the whole lot out the window. The car had kept chugging along without faltering. He had barreled past the marriage and divorce mills of Reno without a side glance, as if they were nonexistent. At least he and Tina hadn't made that mistake and traveled that tedious route, he thought thankfully.

He had crossed the California border with no fruits to declare—if he'd had any he would have eaten them long before that. East of Truckee the road had begun to fill up with a freshly fallen coat of powdery snow. He'd heard the announcement on the radio that chains would be required, but he hadn't given up hope until he'd seen the Highway Patrol blockade. He wasn't even sure if he had enough money left to buy the gas he needed, let alone enough to rent a set of chains. But when he checked the trunk he discovered that conscientious Christine had provided for every emergency; and although twenty-eight hundred miles absent, she had managed to provide for him once again. The tire chains were there, behind the spare, shiny and never before used.

Now he had pulled off the road and onto the siding just beyond Donner Pass to check them and see how they were holding. He moved from tire to tire, kneeling down, his cold hands fumbling with the chains as he made the necessary adjustments. As in Wyoming, it was unlikely that any cops would stop and question his presence here. This wasn't a turnpike. There were no tolls and the regulations that did exist were looser. The West was still a little wilder and freer, a little less severe in its state of malignancy than the East—not much, but a little.

This was also one of the places where the country beside the roadside was still beautiful. The tall pines, dark and straight against the sky, a few patches of hardy wild grass poking through the snow, still green even in the midst of winter. The clean air, the mountain peaks in the distance. He flashed on his dream of the hobo camps and what the land must be like once one got out of range of the road. He realized that the highway must run through some of the worst country America had to offer, that the actuality of the highway's presence and what inevitably gathered about it, helped to make it the worst. On the other side of the fences, beyond the dull rows of plowed-over fields, on the other side of the mountains, he imagined that was where the really beautiful land must be.

Here there were no fences by the roadside blocking the land off from him. If he wished, he could go hiking into the hills and never return. In another forty years the encroaching march of civilization would uncover him, a tough and stringy mountain hermit living off wild berries and grubs. He might even become another four-and-half-inch curiosity on page three of the *San Francisco Chronicle*, just like Mulligan.

Walking a little ways from the car, he climbed a rise among the trees. He was feeling very tired. The Preludins were no longer having any effect upon him. After three days of continual usage his tolerance to them was complete. He cupped a handful of snow from the ground and rubbed it over his face, hoping the shock of the cold would help revive him and keep him awake for the drive that remained. He looked out from where he stood. Directly in front of him there was nothing but the unending space of the Pacific sky. Below him, the land stretched down and away as far as he was able to see. Yes, it was all downhill from here. He'd probably be able to shut off the engine part of the time and coast. With any luck at all he'd be able to make it. There was nearly a full tank of gas from Truckee, and the two gallon can in the trunk was full. In his right hip pocket, he had seventeen cents left.

After he had spent a time with the view, the highway called him back. This was to be the final stretch. The seemingly insatiable road was about to be sated. Under the familiar touch of his hands the car chugged into action, his car, his baby now. The trip back was nearly at its end. A part of his life seemed to be coming to an end, too. In Berkeley he would search out a new beginning, choose a new direction...just as any point in time can be chosen as an end and a beginning. Now he got down to the meat of it. He tried to face each fearful fantasy of the future looming before him as if it were reality. He played different endings and different beginnings in his head. His stomach was already empty, not growling but just empty, and as he made the descent his head began to empty out, too...and the visions came to him. Visions like popcorn.

Pop!

He made it as far as the Sacramento River where he discovered that the frontier had been loped off. A giant quake along the San Andreas fault had dropped the coastal shelf of California into the sea. There was no more Berkeley and Mulligan had become truly the fastest fish in the water.

Pop!

When he reached Berkeley, he found Michael waiting for him. "The Recluse" had blown part of his fourteen-hundred-dollar bank account on a crosscountry flight and had beaten him to California by two days. Joining together under the auspices of Mulligan and with direct contact to Owsley, the three of them become the largest outlet for acid on the West Coast. In less than two years, with fire and blood, the longed-for revolution inevitably follows.

Pop! Pop!

When he reached Berkeley, he went straight to Mulligan's. There he discovered Christine and Botticelli in bed together. "Can't you understand?" Tina tried to explain, "He's the only one who can really fuck me."

Pop! Pop! Pop!

Six miles west of Vacaville, a bare thirty miles from his goal, he miscalculated a hairpin curve, rolling the VW four times and once too many for himself to survive. His mangled body, exhumed from the mangled wreckage, was flown east. He was buried at Arlington National Cemetery with full military honors, a bare thirty yards from the grave of the Unknown Soldier.

Pop!

As soon as he got to Mulligan's, the first thing he asked his friend was whether or not there had actually been any speed in the acid they'd taken together in Central Park. "Why, Davy, I thought you knew," Mulligan answered. "The speed in that acid was me."

Pop! Pop!

In Berkeley, at the western end of the University of California campus, he got out of the car and stretched every muscle in his body. He checked the campanile clock for the time, a quarter past midnight. Then he climbed back into the car, rewound the tape, and played the whole trip over again—for the empty moon, for the stars, for the amusement and flagellation of his own deflated ego.

Pop!

Two weeks after arriving in Berkeley, he received a wire from Tina in Manhattan telling him that she had changed her mind. After another week of lengthy trans-American phone calls, of talk and more talk, all was set right between them and their reconciliation made. She arrived by jet at San Francisco International, and from there the two of them continued on their way west to the East—Japan, Ceylon, Sumatra, India, the purple mountains of Tibet. They grooved on forever after in perfect felicity, hapless entrapped felicity.

Pop!

44

BY the time he rolled off the freeway and into Berkeley his head was empty. He had spent so much time thinking, he could think no more. His consciousness was clean as a picket fence washed by the rain. His values were leveled, his existence totally absorbed in the movement of his hands on the steering wheel and gear shift, his feet on the gas, brake and clutch, his weary eyes upon the road.

It was late afternoon-early evening, the end of a colorless day. The Campanile was shrouded in a low swath of dark gray clouds. Around the University the streets were mostly empty but for a few students scurrying home from the library to beat the rain. The streets were all familiar to Jacobi and it felt like home.

He parked the car in front of the apartment house where he had once lived, and Mulligan still did. When he looked at the name plates by the buzzers on the front porch, he discovered that Mulligan had changed apartments, from the back of the first floor to the front left. Before he could ring, his friend was already opening the door for him. He had seen Jacobi drive up.

Mulligan was in one of his relatively sedate moods.

"Ah, the prodigal son returns," he said, blinking slowly. "Welcome back, Davy." He was wearing a pale red terry cloth bathrobe. It was probably just another illusion, but he looked leaner and older.

He ushered Jacobi through the hallway, a hallway now thoroughly papered with the astrological charts of the houses present and bygone denizens, and into the apartment. It was warm inside and a Dylan record was playing on the stereo. A chubby blond girl sat cross-legged on the floor, sucking slowly on one of the tubes of a many-tentacled hookah. In the pipe's bowl a lump of hash smoldered slowly, explaining Mulligan's mood. The girl was wearing blue jeans and a man's blue work shirt, partially unbuttoned and too large for her in the shoulders. It was Mulligan's shirt.

Mulligan turned the stereo down a notch.

"This is Marie," he told Jacobi. "She's staying with me for awhile." He introduced Jacobi as "Davy," adding drolly, "one of my East Coast contacts."

"Hello, Davy," A soft smile.

"Hi, Marie."

Jacobi sank down next to her, crossing his own legs in the same posture. The position felt strange after so many hours sitting upright in the VW. Mulligan joined them and removed a clip from one of the pipes unmanned tentacles, offering the mouthpiece to Jacobi, who took several deep drags. Almost immediately, he could feel the drug draining the tension of the trip from his body. His empty mind began rolling on with Dylan's hollow rolling voice—"...I walked and I crawled on six crooked highways...and it's hard...and it's hard...and it's a hard rain's a goin' fall..."

"Good stuff, huh," Mulligan said. "It's Lebanese."

Jacobi flashed on a windswept field of dope plants with Lebanese peasants gathering the pollen on dark rubber sheets. What did Lebanese peasants look like, anyway?

"It's mellow," Marie added mellowly.

"Yeah," Jacobi agreed, idly fingering the clip Mulligan had removed, pressing its shiny metal against the flesh of his palm. It was real. His flesh was real, alive.

"Hemostats," Mulligan offered. "I got them from a cousin of mine who's in medical supply."

"You sure have a big family," Jacobi said.

"The whole world's my family," Mulligan beamed. "But speaking of family, what about your little nest? What happened to the beautiful Christine? Isn't that her car parked outside?"

Jacobi chuckled. He was already stoned. As always, he thought first of the Christine in his head rather than the real Christine. "What happens to all American beauty?" he posed. "She sold out to capitalism and got turned into a billboard. The car was my consolation prize."

Mulligan looked a bit puzzled, but he didn't press the point. "And what about the saintly Michael?"

"He's still in Manhattan. He said he might come out to California."

"Did you give him the address?"

"Nope."

"Well, Berkeley isn't that big a town. I guess he can find us by himself."

"Yeah," Jacobi nodded. "If he really wants to. He got busted too, you know."

"That makes sense," Mulligan answered. "They've really been cracking down lately. I can't even get any decent acid. Drugs have replaced Communism in the public eye as the chief reason for the moral decay of American youth. It looks like smoking dope has become a political position."

"It always has been," Jacobi told him. "What happened with you, anyway? Do you have to go to trial or something?"

"It's already taken care of. I got myself a five-hundred-buck lawyer, blew my savings. If you're white and clean looking and can afford a five-hundred-buck lawyer, you can always beat the first rap. That's how justice works in this country. All I got was a year's summary probation. The worst thing about it was this." Mulligan turned his head sideways and pointed to his right temple where Jacobi could make out the faded remains of a blue-yellow bruise. "I got a little too clever with the arresting officer and he let me have it."

"What's a year's summary probation?" Jacobi asked. "Do you have to go see a probation officer or something?"

Marie chimed in. "No, that just means if they nab him for anything in the next year they can nail his ass to the wall, put him away with just a hearing instead of a real trial."

"Marie knows about that stuff," Mulligan said. "She got busted for civil rights in the South, and last year in the Free Speech Movement." He added, in joking putdown, "Marie...is ...a...politico!"

"Ex-politico," Marie corrected him. "I think I've gotten my head pounded on enough for awhile. I'm going to sit back and try hedonism and wait for the revolution."

"When's the revolution?" Jacobi asked her.

"You mean the *real* revolution?" she asked back. She took a thoughtful drag on the hash pipe, then cocked her head and nodded toward Mulligan. "Oh, I don't know, maybe when there's enough lunatics around."

They all laughed at that, their bodies rocking slowly within the soft veils of the hash high.

"I'm not a lunatic," Mulligan protested after a moment. "I've just got a lot of energy." He stood up quickly to demonstrate. "Hey, Davy, I've got something I want to show you. Come on." He lifted Jacobi by the arm and led him toward the bedroom.

The room was a masterpiece, a high sultan's den. There were three double mattresses, one to a wall, and a stereo mounted on the fourth wall. The floor was piled thickly with rugs and cushions. The bedspreads were India print and so were the numerous cloth hangings. But it was the ceiling, both literally and figuratively, which was the high point. Painted a deep midnight blue in simulation of the night sky, with crowded misplaced constellations, a score of racing meteors and plume-tailed comets, and a lemon yellow moon on which Mulligan's face was depicted graphically in a dreamy stoned smile.

"Two stereos?" Jacobi questioned, thinking of the one in the living room.

"This one is Marie's" Mulligan explained. "She helped me fix the place up."

Jacobi thought of himself and Tina in Ithaca, of recurrence, of the similarities and the differences.

Mulligan went on with a sweeping gesture. "I call it my instant orgy room. There's no chairs so everybody is lying down to begin with. When you all get close to the earth it creates a feeling of intimacy. All you need is a little dope liberally distributed and then you turn up the heat," he bent to the wall heater and did so, "and blast everybody until they either have to leave or take their clothes off."

Jacobi collapsed onto one of the mattresses, rolling back and forth, chortling and watching the ceiling swing. "Man," he said, "you're fucking impossible!"

Marie was standing in the doorway. "Hey, is anybody in this place hungry besides me?"

"Ravenous," Jacobi told her, although all he could envision was apple pie.

"Why not," Mulligan agreed.

In the kitchen, Jacobi saw that the refrigerator was crammed full with food.

"You know something, Denny, you're getting spoiled with a woman around."

"It does beat jello and cokes," Mulligan admitted.

Marie cooked bacon and scrambled eggs, Mulligan served, and the three of them sat together at the kitchen table, eating the food and washing it down with ice cold beer. That was one thing Christine would never do, Jacobi thought, drink beer. Marie didn't seem to mind the stuff at all; she was already on her second bottle. But Marie wasn't a sophisticated New Yorker.

"This is great!" Jacobi said, scraping the rest of the eggs from the frying pan onto his plate.

"Thanks," Marie said, "You looked like you needed something." Their eyes met and she smiled at him openly. No, she wasn't "sophisticated" at all.

After the meal, Jacobi treated himself to the luxury of a shower. With the steaming water, he washed and soaked the dirt of the trip out of his body. He couldn't wash away Christine and the time they'd spent together. But then again, he didn't really want to. Ah, yes, the beautiful Christine.

He thought back over the return trip, of how the country had been so garishly scarred all along the highway. He remembered what he had thought at Donner Pass, that if one got far enough away from the highway there was probably beautiful country, perhaps even virgin country. Well, he was off the highway now and he didn't plan on getting back on. In the future, he would stick to the back roads in more ways than one.

When he came out of the shower wrapped in a towel, Mulligan, Marie and Dylan had all moved into the bedroom. The hookah was fired up again and the heater was blasting.

"Get under the covers," Marie said to him, "before you catch cold."

They smoked the hash for awhile. They talked and laughed and listened to the music. And then they all made love.

Marie was very satisfied that night, and the night after, and for some time to come.

45

A FEW hours after midnight the rain began and woke Mulligan up. He wasn't surprised, he'd been waking up a lot in the middle of the night lately. Sleep seemed to be becoming more and more superfluous to him.

He crawled out from beneath the covers without disturbing Jacobi and Marie. The apartment was cool, so he slipped his robe on and went looking for a cigarette. He found some in the living room and sat down by the front window to smoke.

The rain was falling in soft sheets that beat irregularly against the glass. Mulligan watched the rain. Several cars went by and their headlights cast rich colors in the dampened oil slicks of the pavement. A police car cruised by patrolling the night and

Mulligan pretended that the raindrops were bullets, or better yet, caps of acid. Then some fool came by soaking wet on a motorcycle, body hunched against the cold and the falling spray. And then it was quiet for some time.

Mulligan watched.

His cigarette began to taste foul. He'd been smoking too many lately and it was time to cut down again. He opened the window and threw the glowing butt into the rain. He felt the dampness against his flesh as the outside air entered the room. He looked down at his bare belly between the open folds of the robe.

It was hard to believe, but despite all the food in the house he was actually losing weight. The exercises Marie had shown him must have been doing some good. In any case, he was changing again. There had been a time when Mulligan suspected he was through with change, that the last block of his being had been cemented and hardened into place. Now he knew that as the world about him continued to change, so would he. He was so much into the world, into other people, that a changing world had to mean a changing Mulligan. Changing on to death, and then changing still, but without the company of his consciousness. It no longer bothered him that there would come a time when the fabric would continue to weave on without his individual thread. That seemed as natural as everything else. And meanwhile, there were still innumerable realities to be lived out. Meanwhile, he would continue to cross-track the warp as he had done in the past. It could be a dangerous business, but it was the fullest and richest path.

He felt the cold from the open window coming through the gap in his robe, curling about his body and robbing it of its warmth. He wrapped the robe more tightly and tied the sash. It certainly felt like winter, he thought, a California winter, but winter nonetheless. With the rain coming down and the house so silent and no acid and the police cars sweeping by to remind him of his probation, it seemed like a winter of the soul, a time to gather closely with one's friends and make plans for survival. The oil slicks on the wet pavement, reflecting the street lamps, were the only spot of color in the scene, glimmering like a predication of spring. And beyond that, another summer, perhaps even a summer of the soul. One could learn to flow with the changing seasons. He had known his share of joy in the past, and no doubt would again.

Mulligan shut the window and went back into the bedroom. Marie and Jacobi had rolled together in their sleep, to one side of the double bed, seeking and sharing the warmth of one another's bodies. Mulligan lay down on the bed next to Jacobi. He thought that he'd wait for his two friends to wake up, and then they could all make love together again. But after awhile, he fell asleep too.

■

About the Author

Bruce Boston has published more than seven hundred stories, poems and prose poems in a wide range of magazines and anthologies, including *The New York Times Magazine*, *Fiction*, *The Pushcart Prize Anthology*, *Year's Best Fantasy and Horror* and *Isaac Asimov's SF Magazine*. His previous books include nine collections of poetry, eight short-story collections, and the critically-acclaimed novella, *After Magic*.

Born in Chicago, of Catholic and Jewish heritage, Boston grew up primarily in suburban Los Angeles. He attended the University of California, Berkeley, at the height of the turbulent Nineteen-Sixties. A long-time resident of the San Francisco Bay Area, he has hitchhiked extensively in the United States, and lived briefly in New York, Oregon and Mexico. He has worked as a computer programmer, gardener, college professor, movie projectionist, book buyer, editor, retail clerk, ghostwriter, bibliographer, research assistant, technical writer, math tutor, furniture mover and freelance book designer.

Stained Glass Rain was designed by Lee Ballentine
with cover design by Melanie Smith and set in Baskerville and
Futura at the ProBook Electronic book production labs
in Denver

OCEAN VIEW BOOKS AND DISTRIBUTED TITLES

Fiction

All the Visions by Rudy Rucker $9.95/$40
Nantucket Slayrides by Lucius Shepard and Robert Frazier NA/$75
The New Bruce Boston Omnibus by Bruce Boston NA/$20
POLY: New Speculative Writing edited by Lee Ballentine $19.95/$40
The Secret of Life by Rudy Rucker NA/$30
Short Circuits by Bruce Boston $9.95/$20
Stained-Glass Rain by Bruce Boston $13.95/$40

Poetry

Bad News from the Stars by Steve Sneyd $9.95/$20
Co-Orbital Moons by Robert Frazier $9.95/$20
Journal of an Astronaut by G. Sutton Breiding $9.95/$40
Missing Pieces by Kathryn Rantala $9.95/$40
The New Bruce Boston Omnibus by Bruce Boston NA/$20
Nostalgia of the Infinite by Janet Hamill $9.95/$40
POLY: New Speculative Writing edited by Lee Ballentine $19.95/$40
Prayer Wheels of Bluewater by Loss Pequeño Glazier $9.95/$20
Space Baltic by Anselm Hollo $9.95/$30
Terminal Velocities edited by Andrew Joron $11.95/$50
The Umbral Anthology of Science Fiction Poetry edited by Steve Rasnic Tem $9.95/NA
The Velocities Set edited by Andrew Joron NA/$20

Art, Essay, and Rant

Book by Lee Ballentine $9.95/$40
Modern Art in Denver (1919–1960) by Elizabeth Schlosser $26.95/NA
POLY: New Speculative Writing edited by Lee Ballentine $19.95/$40
Terminal Velocities edited by Andrew Joron $11.95/$50
This World and Nearer Ones by Brian Aldiss $9.95/NA

Out of Print

Lee Ballentine—*Directional Information*; Laura Beausoleil—*At One Side of the Companion*; Bruce Boston—*Alchemical Texts, The Bruce Boston Omnibus*; Robert Frazier and Andrew Joron—*A Measure of Calm*; Jennifer MacGregor—*Attentive Listening*; Renée Ruderman—*Transition*

prices shown are paperback/hardcover

Ocean View Books / BOX 102650 / Denver CO / 80250